He took a deep breath and lifted the revolver to his right temple.

"God, this is stimulating," he said, and then pulled the trigger.

Leah jumped back, ready for blood to splatter her, but there was none. James laughed and tore off his blindfold.

"I never lose," he said, triumphant. His face was bright red, his eyes wide open and half mad. "Now let's see how your luck holds out."

He put the blindfold on her and then handed her the gun. "Do it," he ordered.

Tears streamed down Leah's cheeks. Twice before, she'd pulled the trigger. Twice, she'd been lucky. But luck always ran out.

Leah almost regained her sanity then, nearly put the gun down. But then James's hand clamped down on her shoulder.

"Come on, Leah," he said. "You know you want to do it. Live on the edge. Stare death in the face and knock it down."

Leah squeezed the trigger before she could think.

Bantam Books by Christy Cohen
Ask your bookseller for titles you may have missed

WHISPERED LIES

TWICE IN A LIFETIME

PRIVATE SCANDALS

CHRISTY COHEN

Whispered Lies

BANTAM BOOKS

New York Toronto London
Sydney Auckland

WHISPERED LIES

A Bantam Fanfare Book / September 1994

FANFARE and the portrayal of a boxed "ff" are trademarks of Bantam Books, a division of Bantam Doubleday Dell Publishing Group, Inc.

ISBN 0-553-56786-1

Published simultaneously in the United States and Canada

Bantam Books are published by Bantam Books, a division of Bantam Doubleday Dell Publishing Group, Inc. Its trademark, consisting of the words "Bantam Books" and the portrayal of a rooster, is Registered in U.S. Patent and Trademark Office and in other countries. Marca Registrada, Bantam Books, 1540 Broadway, New York, New York 10036.

PRINTED IN THE UNITED STATES OF AMERICA

OPM 0 9 8 7 6 5 4 3 2 1

DEDICATION

For my mother,
who made me believe I could do anything

1

Something was different and, to Elliot Shaperson's way of thinking, that meant something was wrong. Elliot walked up the mountainside toward his cabin and, where he usually heard birdcalls, heard music instead. It was the original version of "Peggy Sue," which shocked even the blustery blue jays into silence.

He reached the deck and stared through the open sliding glass doors. Leah, his wife, was in the kitchen with her back to him, stirring pancake batter. She had not heard him come in and was singing and dancing in her robe. Elliot felt the usual pain in his stomach, a jab just below his ribs that streaked toward his heart. He felt the same pain whenever Leah touched his hip beneath the covers at night, or smiled while she lied. He felt the pain and kept quiet, though any other kind of man would have started a fight.

After nearly thirty-eight years of marriage, he didn't know his wife at all. Who was this woman who sang and danced, who looked almost like his daughter from the back, with his daughter's agility and spirit? Could it possibly be his fifty-five-year-old wife, the same woman who moved stiffly when they walked around the block at home and made sure she never laughed too loudly at movies? This Leah, who did not know he was watching, twisted and threw her hands in the air, laughing when the pancake batter splattered on her nose.

Elliot watched her and did not say anything; he never said anything. He knew that that was the key, to ignore all contradictions, to simply stay quiet, go on as always, pretend everything was exactly the way he wanted it to be. It wasn't lies or unfaithfulness that killed relationships; it was confrontations. He'd heard of once solid marriages abruptly rupturing the instant a husband confessed he stopped for a beer every night after work, or a wife admitted she'd been spending her grocery money on facials. It didn't matter how trivial the admission; once the truth was out, there was nowhere to hide, no way to smile and pretend that you trusted each other.

Elliot could tolerate anything except the awful coming clean that nearly always led to a blowout like the ones his parents used to have. Over and over again, his father had admitted he had cheated or lied or stolen, his mother had blamed him for her life, he cussed, she shouted, he kicked the sofa, she flung her dishes at the wall, and pretty soon their love was no better than a farce. Elliot had curled up in his bed each time they fought, pleading with God to make his father stop clearing his conscience, to make his mother stop demanding to know the truth, to make them both *shut up*. They never had shut up; perhaps they'd been too far gone to be helped at that point and God had set his sights on Elliot instead, giving him all the self-control his parents had lacked. So far, Elliot had been able to take all Leah dished out. So far, he'd been able to convince himself that he still loved her, that none of the things she did were bad enough to change that. So far, he had held everything in, all his knowledge and hurt and disappointment, as if he were the ocean and all the trash Leah dumped just sank straight to the bottom.

Leah turned a little, saw him, and stopped dancing immediately. She smoothed her hands down her hips, as if that dance had been a skirt she wore and she was pushing it off. She turned off the radio, and then, very delicately, wiped the batter off her nose.

"Pancakes, dear?" she asked, as if she had been standing there calm and dignified the entire time.

Elliot nodded, not trusting his voice.

"Samantha and Dylan should be here this afternoon," she said.

She was good, as good as he at playing this game. She could slip right into her happy-wife role and a stranger walking in would think they were two of the lucky ones, with a marriage that had withstood the test of time. The pain in Elliot's stomach twinged and he grimaced.

Strangely enough, he had felt wonderful yesterday, fully relaxed during the three-hour drive from their home in Sacramento to their cabin in the Sierra Nevada mountains. But this morning, as he walked the only path he ever took through the woods, the path where he knew every rise and fall, every tree, every boulder, that relaxation had evaporated. He had kept a quick pace, trying unsuccessfully not to think about his daughter, Samantha, or the man she planned to bring with her today, just in time to spoil their annual two-week vacation.

For thirty-five years, he had held out hope that his daughter would not fall in love. Though a lot of her friends had gotten married and started families, Samantha had never had time for love. Men had tried to push their way in and she had quickly shoved them back out. She had kept herself busy with college and graduate school, then her energetic career as a political consultant, which kept her going from morning till late at night. But last night, she had called and said, "I want to bring Dylan Price to the cabin with me. He's the man I've fallen in love with." And all Elliot could think was that love had a way of breaking even the strongest hearts. One day she might find herself the way he found himself, clinging to the smiling, passionless façade of old love, spending all his energy just trying to make sure that nobody—including Leah—knew anything was wrong. She might end up with a hole in her stomach and, like him, stuff everything real and strong and uncontrollable right down through it.

"I'm going to take a shower," Elliot said now to Leah, because he couldn't talk about Samantha without feeling sad. In the last few years, he couldn't talk about his marriage without his stomach cramping, or about anything more substantial than the weather and personal grooming without feeling that he'd either disintegrate or explode.

Leah opened her mouth to say something, but when he didn't stop to ask her what it was, she just let him go.

Leah listened to the clanging of the pipes as Elliot took his shower. She poured out the batter, trying unsuccessfully to make animal pancakes. She reached for the radio dial and then changed her mind; she would not be caught out of character twice.

She flipped the pancakes and put the toast in the toaster. She put the pitchers of milk and orange juice on the table, then buttered the toast and kept the finished pancakes warm in the oven until Elliot was ready.

She walked to the east window of the living room that magnified the sun's rays and bathed her in light. She closed her eyes and felt her skin tingle from the heat.

She arched her back like a cat and smiled. She had hardly been able to sleep at all last night, and she had gotten up as soon as Elliot left for his walk this morning. She was nearly bursting with excitement and it doubled, then tripled inside of her, because she knew she couldn't let it show. She longed for a cigarette, but had no gym nearby like the one at home, where she could shower and cover herself in perfume so Elliot would not smell the tobacco. She yearned for a drink, but was certain Elliot would smell the gin in her orange juice.

Her daughter was in love. Her beautiful, successful, independent daughter had finally fallen. Leah clapped her hands and then looked around to see if Elliot had come out. She listened for the sound of the shower and still heard it. She clapped her hands again.

For years, she had been itching for Samantha to fall in love so she could fall right along with her, but Samantha had instead done the opposite: she had scorned love. She had once said to Leah, after Elliot had gone to bed, "Mom, I don't know how you stand it. You two don't even *see* each other anymore. Your eyes pass over each other's faces like you're old pieces of furniture."

Those words had been like arrows, but somehow Leah had managed to speak. "It's not always like that," she had said. "There are highs and lows, passions and plateaus."

"Well, if there are I don't see them," sixteen-year-old Samantha had said. "And frankly, I don't think you see them, either."

Samantha had been so sure of herself, but no one could outrun love forever. Last night on the phone, there had been an edge to Samantha's voice, as if she had lost partial control of her vocal cords. How wonderful that Samantha had finally lost control of something, that she would finally *feel* something. And Leah would be sucked in so closely, she would almost feel Samantha's passion as her own. This man would touch Samantha and, by God, Leah would make sure he touched her, too.

She opened her eyes when she heard the shower turn off. It would now take Elliot exactly three minutes to towel off and dress and come to the breakfast table to eat. Leah walked back to the kitchen and put the plates and silverware on the table.

What would he look like? she wondered. This man of Samantha's. Tall, no doubt, because Samantha was tall. Blond hair, blue eyes. Or dark hair, with moody brown eyes. Somewhat domineering, perhaps. Passionate . . .

Leah laughed and turned around to check for Elliot. Thankfully, she was still alone. She picked up a stack of napkins and fanned herself. This was really getting out of hand. First, there had been only one man she fantasized about, but now it was almost every man she met, even men she hadn't met like her daughter's new boyfriend. Once, when she was young and certain of her beauty, she had been so picky. This boy was too gangly, that one's eyes were slightly off center. Now, as if her graying hair and flabby middle had rendered her incapable of judgment, she found all men attractive. Fat, thin, young, old, blemished, wrinkled, whatever. Standing in line at the grocery store, she had imagined the things the teenage box boy could do to her. She hadn't even minded his zits or spiked hair. She had sought out and located his good qualities, his large hands, the strong legs that pressed against his jeans. Then there was the middle-aged, pork-bellied mailman who smiled at her every day, and the retired widower across the street who, she was certain, would tend to her as carefully as he tended to his roses.

Good lord, what had happened to her? She had been such a good wife, so conservative, polite, inhibited. Then she met James Arlington. Ever since James . . .

Well, ever since James she had become an entirely different person. She had fed on his wildness and gone slightly crazy. The thing was, though, she liked being crazy. She lived to be crazy now. She lived for those moments when Elliot was out of earshot and she could scream and laugh and pound her feet into the floor. She kept wondering how she had stood it all those years before, how she could not have realized that she was boiling inside. Now, it was as if she were a mad pig let out of the pen. She shot across the corral, banged into walls, ran and squealed and would probably keep right on running and squealing until she was dead.

The three minutes were up and Elliot walked out of the bathroom. His hair was wet and neatly parted on the left side. It looked thicker and browner when wet, but when it dried she would notice the thin spots and the gray that streaked it. He was wearing blue jeans and a white T-shirt that showed off the one part of his body that was always tanned: his arms. She noticed his jeans were getting tight around the middle, that he'd put on another pound or two in his gut. Yet, despite all that, all the weight and thinning gray hair, age sat well on him. He had been gangly at twenty, still unsure at thirty, too stiff at forty. At fifty-six, he was beginning to look like someone's distinguished grandfather. And she wondered why his good looks didn't move her at all.

He smiled at her and sat down while Leah got the pancakes out of the oven and brought them to the table. She hurried back to the pantry for the syrup and brought that, too.

Elliot served himself in silence. Leah sat stiffly, precisely, in her wife mode. It had come to the point where she had to consciously define who she was at every moment. She had to look at her surroundings, the man sitting opposite her, and think either, *I'm with Elliot. I'll be quiet and decorous*, or *I'm with James. Thank God*

I'm with James. It doesn't matter what he does to me because I can laugh and shout and cry as loud as I want and no one will tell me to calm down, to get a grip on myself.

She didn't mind the dual life so much, as long as she got it straight. She should not have danced earlier; she would have to be more careful in the future. Dancing was only allowable with James. Elliot did not understand rock music, or cutting loose. She was glad she hadn't even brought the cigarettes she smoked in front of James because she was certain she would have been tempted to smoke one in front of Elliot. No, she didn't mind her duality, but it was getting harder and harder all the time to keep her lives separate, to remember what she had told James and what she had told Elliot, to not slip up.

She glanced up at Elliot. Her gaze was drawn, as always, to his eyes, to the saucerlike brown orbs with those outrageously long lashes around them. Baby eyes. Eyes to die for. They were what she had noticed first when they met thirty-eight years earlier. Why was it that in the three years since she'd met James, Elliot had become the only man she couldn't fantasize about? It was as if James's bad streak had made her ridicule Elliot's goodness. Even Elliot's eyes were no longer enough to spark her interest.

She wondered if Elliot ever fantasized about her. Instantly, with an excruciating exhalation of breath as if her bones had collapsed in on her lungs, she knew he didn't. She wore cotton pajamas instead of silk teddies and he never said a word. She took off her makeup in the evenings and he looked at her the same as always, as if he'd never known she'd been wearing it in the first place. She no longer even dressed up when they went out to dinner, just as Elliot had stopped dressing up years ago. What was the point, if they were just going to come home and take it all off again anyway?

She knew she should appreciate that she could be

so relaxed with her husband, that he didn't demand she wear uncomfortable clothes or difficult hairdos. But instead, Elliot's acceptance made her feel inanimate, like an old shirt he wore because it was broken in and didn't chafe his skin. Their relationship had been nearly platonic for months, years. She never complained, because a good wife didn't and she still believed in being a good wife. Elliot never said a word about their lack of a sex life, and she wondered if he didn't care, or if he lived under the assumption that good husbands don't complain, either.

"You're up early," Elliot said. These were the kinds of things he said now, nondescript things, things that didn't mean anything, but filled up the empty air. She used to intentionally try to draw him out. She'd talk about the good, early years of their marriage and how things had changed, but somehow Elliot always adroitly steered the subject back to the weather, to the news, to his particular kind of nonsense. Now that she had James to talk to, though, she hardly bothered with Elliot at all. Mostly, she parried empty word for empty word, until they were practically smothered with pointlessness.

Leah took one pancake and stared longingly at the maple syrup. Instead, she patted her stomach, took a thin sliver of low-calorie butter, and ate the pancakes dry.

"I couldn't sleep."

Elliot looked up. "Why not? Too hot? Too cold?"

Leah shook her head. "No reason. Nerves, I guess."

Elliot returned to his pancakes. He ate precisely, never clanging his utensils, always setting his fork down after every bite. His flawless manners had, at first, surprised her because he had not been raised in a family that had any regard for etiquette. His mother had been gruff, uncultured; his father had not been around enough to teach him anything. But Elliot had always been the kind of man who thought things like the way to hold a fork and swallow quietly were important.

"The weather is nice today," Elliot said.

"Yes, beautiful."

"Probably hot back in Sacramento. What do you think? Close to one hundred?"

What Leah thought was that she didn't care if the sidewalks were melting back home. She didn't care about the weather at all, period, and could hardly believe that they had talked about little else for years.

"Maybe high nineties," she said.

They were quiet for a moment and then Leah couldn't help asking, "What do you think this Dylan will look like?"

She had started guessing last night right after Samantha's phone call.

"Who knows?"

"Yes, but what do you think Samantha's type is? Dark or blond? Mysterious or open?"

Elliot glanced at her quickly and then looked away. He clutched his stomach, as he always did when something upset him. After thirty-seven years of marriage, Leah no longer had any real desire to ask him what the trouble was. She knew that was harsh, but she couldn't help it. His problems all had to do with work and she had almost no interest in that. It was almost as if she had worked at that insurance office with him for thirty-six long years, and now she was sick of it. He must have picked up on that indifference because, in the last few years, he'd stopped telling her anything anyway. He always said he was fine, not to worry, and then he sneaked into the bathroom and finished off another bottle of Maalox.

"I haven't a clue, Leah," he said.

Leah looked back down at her plate and noticed

her hand was shaking. She set down the fork and forced herself to relax and sit back in her chair.

"I'm just curious, that's all," she said. "Our little baby is in love."

Elliot clanked his fork against his plate and Leah's head shot up. Their gazes met, Elliot mumbled an apology—as if a bit of unintentional noise was the worst thing in the world—and finished his pancakes in silence.

As they did the dishes together, the way they always did, Leah was more aware of him beside her than she had been in years. She felt his heat, heard him breathing, and realized she had been tuning him out for years, the way you tune out the sounds of traffic after living in the city for a few years. It saddened her to remember that once, at the beginning, her body had sung for him. She had written him bad poetry and touched him almost constantly, afraid that he might vaporize if she let go.

Leah dropped the plates in the soapy water and turned to her husband.

"It's not so bad," she said, smiling. "You didn't want her single and lonely forever, did you?"

"Samantha wasn't lonely," Elliot said. "Did you, even once, hear her complain about being alone? She was good on her own."

Leah said nothing, but inside she was thinking, *Of course she was lonely. She just never understood about love. First love. Oh God, to be her when she walks in that door. To be starting over.*

She said none of this, though, and smiled the way she always did, in the slick, superficial manner she had learned from James. She handed Elliot the plates to dry.

"Let's just wait until we meet him," she said. "Maybe you two will hit it off."

Elliot grunted and dried the dishes.

2

There was no drive that could match it, Samantha thought. First they had to fight traffic through the congested streets of Sacramento, then hook up with I-80 and begin the slow rise out of the smoggy city, into the green hills of Auburn. Then they twisted up, up, up over the spine of the Sierra Nevada Mountains, through the maples and oaks, then up into pines, where the air was so fresh and cool and startling that Samantha gasped at it. It was like living underwater and then, finally, coming up for air and seeing the sky.

She had always loved this drive. As a child, she had sat in the backseat and bounced from side to side as her father took the turns at a much too safe speed. Now, she was in the driver's seat, and she pressed down on the accelerator and sped into the fast lane.

"You're a wild woman, Samantha Shaperson."

Samantha looked at the man beside her and smiled. It was still so strange to see Dylan there, to turn and find anyone there at all. She was used to putting her briefcases and papers on the passenger seat of her Honda sedan, not to reaching over there and touching flesh. Hot, solid, delicious flesh. She did it now, touched him, ran her fingers over the bones in the back of his hand.

"None of that," he said. "We're going to see your parents, remember? No touching or kissing for two weeks."

Samantha laughed and put her hand back on the wheel.

"If I thought you were serious—" she said, but could not complete her sentence because Dylan was suddenly all over her, burying his lips in her neck, nibbling her ear, running his hands down her ribs to her hips. Samantha swerved and the driver behind them honked. She pulled into the slow lane and pushed Dylan off.

"You're crazy," she said, glad that he was, glad that he was everything he was. Dylan Price. Last night, she had said to her father, "I want to bring the man I've fallen in love with." The man she loved. My God, she loved someone. It was possible.

She had abhorred the thought of love at one time in her life, actually at most times of her life, but now she could not get enough of it. It was almost as if Dylan carried some sexually transmitted parasite and it had infiltrated her bloodstream, consumed her cells. It was a horrible vision, and yet Samantha could not tolerate the thought of it ending, as if this were what she'd always wanted, to be eaten alive by passion.

Dylan slipped back into his seat and ran his fingers through his long hair. Samantha teased him that that was the only reason she'd fallen for him, because she'd finally found someone with hair nearly as long as hers. Hers was red-brown and wavy, and fell halfway down her back. His was dark brown and tightly curled, falling just past his shoulders. He usually wore it in a ponytail, but for now he had left it loose and the breeze from the open window swatted it against his face.

He was a gorgeous man. There was no mistaking that. Samantha, who usually didn't bother with people's looks, had noticed that straight off three months ago, when she first met him. She had been in Congressman Hastings's office, going over strategy for the upcoming election, when Dylan had barged in past the secretary, dressed in jeans and a Save the Whales sweatshirt. She, who always had something to say, had been speechless at the sight of him.

"Congressman," he had said, ignoring her completely, "did you get our letter?"

The congressman had smiled, as if he were, unfortunately, well used to intrusions like this.

"Of course, Dylan," he had said. "You know how sympathetic I am to the environmental movement."

Dylan smirked and moved a step closer to him.

"You know I could rip your environmental record to bits," he said. "All I'm asking you now is this: are you going to do something about that Japanese barge carrying nuclear waste straight past the California coast, or will it be up to us?"

The two men looked at each other and Samantha knew she not only felt invisible, to Dylan she was invisible. Immediately, she disliked his arrogance, his aggressiveness, but she was hard-pressed to get past his looks, all that long hair pulled back in a ponytail, those green eyes flecked with yellow, that wind-burned skin, the hawkishness of his features. He hovered around six feet, was very thin but muscular. Samantha took in all of these things and then turned away and smiled, because there was nothing else you could do but smile when you looked at a man like that.

"Look, Dylan, my hands are tied."

"Bullshit. You know what happens when that barge

hits a reef, or makes one little slip-up in navigation? We're all dead, that's what happens. There's enough nuclear waste on that death trap to fry every man, woman, and child from San Francisco to Los Angeles. Are you telling me you're just going to sit there and let some asshole dump his radioactive crap in your front yard?"

Dylan was leaning over Congressman Hastings's desk, his hands spread apart and his knuckles white as he pressed them into the desk. His eyes were fiery, his face red, and Samantha realized that after eleven years in politics, he was the first man she had met who she knew, without a doubt, was sincere.

"First of all," Samantha said, "crude remarks don't make the grade here." Dylan jumped back abruptly at the sound of her voice, as if he had not realized she was there. "Second," she went on, "don't you think you're overdramatizing the situation?"

Dylan looked at her critically, and Samantha mentally went over her appearance, her gray eyes, makeupless face, brown skirt, white blouse. She rarely wore makeup and, for the first time, she wished she'd taken the time to put on a little lip gloss.

"And don't you think you're sticking your head in the sand?" he queried back. "Do you think all this nuclear waste is just going to disappear? If it doesn't spill off our coast, if, by some miracle, it reaches Antarctica where the bastards intend to dump it, what do you think is going to happen to it? Do you expect the ice to just melt it down? Radiation doesn't melt. It destroys. It's going to kill every living thing down there. Then it will slip into the ocean, get mixed in with the currents, and come back up here, or to Africa, or to Asia. Don't you understand that we're killing ourselves? Don't any of you people get it?"

By the end of his speech he was shouting, and he banged his fist on the desk. Congressman Hastings stood up, but Samantha dove right back into the argument.

"I understand," she said, "that you are trying to do a good thing. I understand that you're scared about your future, the world's future. I'm scared, too. But we've got nuclear waste and it has to go somewhere. We've got a hole in the ozone layer and a rapidly shrinking rain forest and neither of those problems are going to disappear overnight. We've got to work together to try to fix what we can, not threaten decent congressmen who are trying to make a difference."

Dylan stared at her a long time and Samantha forced herself to keep her hands at her sides, to not fidget. Finally, surprisingly, he backed away.

"I'm trying to make a difference, too," he said. "EarthAlert is out there every day, *doing* things when everyone else is just talking."

"Look, I admire what you do," Samantha said. "But you've got to work within the law. There's a system for—"

"Fuck the system," Dylan said. "The system is what's killing us. The system is what puts off the cutbacks on CFCs for another year. The system protects big business at the expense of the planet. The system is a bunch of gray-haired suits in Congress who will be dead before the mess they've caused kills the rest of us, so what the hell do they care?"

He spoke with his hands as well as his mouth, and Samantha was electrified listening to him. She did not tell him that she agreed with him or that she admired what he did. And she did admire it. He stood on the front line while she fumbled around in the back.

"What's your name?" he asked her at last.

She was startled by his question, but didn't show it.

"Samantha Shaperson."

He repeated the name silently, as if encoding it in his memory, and then turned back to the congressman.

"EarthAlert's flagship is docked in San Francisco and ready to head out today."

"Dylan, don't," Hastings said. "You're not going to stop them. And someone could get hurt."

Suddenly, Dylan was energized again and he strode to the door.

"Like hell we won't stop them," he said. "And if anyone's going to get hurt, it's the goddamn Japanese." He slammed the door and stomped down the hallway.

Samantha listened to him go, heard him shout something at one of the secretaries, then she turned back to the congressman. He laughed and rubbed his chin as if Dylan had just punched him there.

"Dylan Price," he said, in answer to her unasked question. "The head of EarthAlert."

"The radical environmental group?"

"The very one. They've thrown themselves in front of whaling ships, rammed their boats into tankers, chained themselves to old-growth trees to prevent anyone from cutting them."

Samantha shook her head. "I've seen some of their exploits on the news. Now that I think of it, I remember seeing a long-haired man knocking out a poacher with a solid kick to the groin."

Congressman Hastings laughed. "That's our Dylan. The thing is, I'm on his side. But I've got to work within the law. I've got constituents to think about. You've told me yourself that it's political suicide to come across as too radical."

"And I was right," Samantha said, although she was thinking about the kind of world they might have if everyone was as impassioned as Dylan Price, if everyone was willing to go to such extremes to make things right.

Now, sitting in the car on the way to her parents' cabin, Samantha smiled.

"You're thinking of seducing me," Dylan said.

Samantha laughed. "Hardly. I'm thinking of the day I met you, in Congressman Hastings's office."

Dylan did not laugh with her. He set his jaw and looked out the window. "The bastards rammed our boat, although everyone believes we went after them first. We've been in dry dock ever since, while they've been sailing their goddamn waste around the globe."

"You'll get her up and sailing again soon," she said.

"It's frustrating as hell not being out there, doing something. It drives me insane, twiddling my thumbs with paperwork, making the rounds of senators and congressmen, trying to drum up support, to get somebody, anybody, to take a stand. They're all such cowards."

"You've got to admit it's better now," Samantha said. "You've got the White House on your side."

"It's not enough!" Dylan said, slamming his hand down on the seat. "Any proposal with muscle in it is ripped to shreds by the business advocates in Congress."

They drove in silence. Samantha suddenly felt a little queasy and she rolled down her window. Strange how the same event had been viewed so differently. She would always remember that day in Congressman Hastings's office as the beginning of their relationship. He had remembered her name, looked up her number, and, after the uproar over the encounter with the barge had died down, asked her out for coffee.

Dylan, on the other hand, remembered their first meeting as the day his EarthAlert flagship was rammed by an irate barge captain. She fell in love with a passionate radical, and he lost his battle to stop a nuclear-waste shipment.

She had not wanted to love him. She had thought all loves were like her parents', cozy but dull, quietly accepting, uninspired. Why hadn't anyone told her that love could be like *this*? Physical, as if her skin had tripled its elasticity and made her limber as a dancer. As if every nerve cell sped to the spot Dylan touched and writhed in ecstasy. Whenever he left the room, she wanted to pound her feet on the floor like an impatient, spoiled child waiting for him to come back.

She was not herself, she knew. She had cut back on her hours at work. Overtime could not compare to lying in bed with Dylan. She had stopped taking paperwork home when she knew she would see him. She had put her friends on standby. But no one could blame her for going a bit overboard. Who wouldn't, with a man like Dylan? Besides, it was only temporary. She and Dylan had said from the start that their relationship would remain free of strings or promises. Eventually, they'd go their separate ways, with a few passionate moments to add to their memories. No harm done, she told herself, then gulped up the air from the open window.

"Dylan," she said.

"What?" he asked, not turning toward her. He looked out the window, brooding, thinking, she knew, of everything but her, of endangered species and ozone holes and chlorofluorocarbons. Three months since they met and Samantha could hardly think of anything but him.

"Nothing," she said. "Nothing."

Dylan got the suitcases out of the car as Samantha ran up the steps to the cabin and embraced her parents. It was a nice-looking cabin, Dylan thought, better than he had expected. This area was called Dunnigan Creek by the few families who had cabins here. It was sixteen miles northwest of jam-packed Lake Tahoe and cut off from nearly everything by the walls of granite mountains on all sides. To get here, they'd had to drive up and over one of those enormous batholiths on the skimpiest dirt road left in civilized California. During the last ten minutes, they had passed only one other house.

Dylan walked up to the front door and found the three of them staring at him. He stood up straight and laughed.

"Dylan Price," he said. "Ready for inspection."

Samantha and her mother laughed, but Samantha's father did not. He stood back and kept his hand on his stomach, as if he had a gun stashed there that he'd pull in a second if Dylan made the wrong move. Samantha took Dylan's hand. He was surprised that her palms were sweaty.

"Mom, Dad, this is Dylan Price. Dylan, these are my parents, Leah and Elliot Shaperson."

Elliot hung back, said nothing, but Leah quickly closed the gap between them and kissed his cheek. He was surprised by her perfume, the same as Samantha's. She was shorter than Samantha, curvier, with eyes more blue than gray. She was pretty and young-looking and unmistakably vibrant.

"It's so good to have you here," Leah said.

"Thanks," Dylan replied. He turned to Elliot and extended his hand. Elliot shook it and Dylan noticed that his palm too was slightly damp.

"I know you weren't expecting me," Dylan said. "I'm sorry if I've cramped your style."

"Of course not," Leah said, jumping in between them. Dylan looked at her, wondered if her hair was dyed, and how often she had to go to the gym to keep a nice figure like that.

"Come on in," Leah said. "Elliot, bring the suitcases. Oh, Samantha, it's so good to see you. I love that skirt."

Leah put her arm around her daughter's waist and led her inside. Dylan reached for the suitcases, but Elliot was already there.

"I've got them," Elliot said, and took a deep breath

before lifting them both. Dylan held the door open for him and then followed him inside.

The cabin was not phony rustic, the way the socialites on the lake in Tahoe built their homes, but nearly primitive. Wood floors and ceiling, a fireplace for heat, no vents or central air that Dylan could discern. A main living room/dining room/kitchen, a loft upstairs, a single bedroom and bathroom down the hall, and a bookcase jammed with books beside the fireplace.

"Do you two want something to drink?" Leah asked. "How was the drive? Traffic? Was it hard to get the time off from work, Samantha?"

Samantha laughed and walked into the kitchen. She got two beers out of the refrigerator and opened them. She winked at Dylan as she handed one to him. She wandered around the cabin, touching the walls and paintings.

"I've missed this place," she said. Elliot dumped the suitcases in the loft with a thud and then came down the stairs. He stared at the beer in Dylan's hand as if it were a piece of silverware he had just stolen and then turned to Leah.

"Any lemonade?" he asked.

"I'd have to make it," Leah said, telling him with her eyes that she would do no such thing.

"I'll make it," Elliot said.

He walked into the kitchen and found the frozen lemonade in the freezer. He searched the cupboards for a pitcher, slamming each door and grunting when he couldn't find one. Finally, Leah went into the kitchen.

"For Pete's sake, Elliot," she said. "I hear you. Let me do it."

Elliot moved away without argument and Dylan and Samantha smiled at each other.

"Traffic was terrible in the city," Samantha said.

"You use my map?" Elliot asked. "It showed how

to avoid the capital traffic. It's three point two miles longer, but saves ten minutes, twenty at rush hour."

"Yes, Dad," Samantha said, walking over to him and slipping her arm through his. "I used your map. Now sit down and talk to me. I haven't seen the two of you in weeks."

Weeks, Dylan thought and almost laughed. He hadn't seen his parents for fourteen *years.* And he could go another fourteen or, preferably, one hundred and fourteen and that would be just fine with him.

He looked at Samantha sitting on the couch with her father, still touching him, picking the lint off his T-shirt. Dylan's father never had lint on his shirts. Everything was laundered daily, ironed perfectly, and hung up by the maids. Dylan had grown up not understanding what dust was, not knowing that if you didn't have a barrage of servants, there would come a time when there would be a coating of dirt on the furniture. Now, though, he understood that fact of nature very well. He got tremendous pleasure out of watching how thick the dust could get if he left it alone. He found that there really was no limit; it could build to one or two inches deep.

"Tell me how the insurance business is," Samantha said to Elliot.

"Oh, you know. The same."

"No, I do not know. Tell me, Dad."

Elliot turned away for a moment. Dylan watched his eyes, the way he always watched people's eyes, seeing if he could spot sincerity in them. He considered himself a good judge of truthfulness; it was one of his few talents. He had not had the discipline to finish college, or the rigidity to stand a nine-to-five desk job. But he did have a passion for the earth, and an eye for honesty.

Elliot wrung his hands a little, clutched his stomach. Dylan's gut instinct was that he was hiding something, but he had to be mistaken. From what Samantha had told him, Elliot was a devoted husband, an insurance salesman, a loving father. What was there to hide in a life like that?

Elliot turned back to his daughter, smiled, and launched into the story of his latest clients, referred from people he'd covered for twenty years. It was amazing, he said, that people still trusted him enough to refer their friends to him. Even though his company's rates were slightly higher, people liked the service he gave them.

"Of course they stick with you," Samantha said. "Anyone would be a fool not to stick with you."

The pitcher of lemonade slipped through Leah's hands and slammed against the counter. They all looked up and Leah searched for a sponge to clean up the small spill.

"Sorry," she said. "My hands were wet."

Samantha and Elliot nodded and went back to talking, but Dylan kept his eyes on Leah, watching her sponge up the mess with shaking hands. She looked up suddenly and met his gaze. She blushed like a schoolgirl, then poured her husband his glass of lemonade.

While Samantha and Leah were in the kitchen, making dinner, Dylan stood at the railing of the deck, looking out over the amazingly unblemished forest. The treeless granite peaks disappeared into the clouds; beneath them, the mountainside was so thick with pines, he could not see even a touch of light through the branches. At the valley floor, aspens and cottonwoods were scattered along streams, twirling rounded leaves the color of a tropical sea.

Elliot was sitting in the chair behind him, and Dylan could feel his gaze piercing the back of his head like a surgeon's probe. Dylan's scalp tingled, as if Elliot had already worked a scalpel into his gray matter and were trying to dissect the workings of a long-haired, radical, left-wing hippie like him.

"Goddamn amazing," Dylan said, turning around.

Elliot's eyes widened and he gripped the metal edges of the chair. Dylan had figured out in three seconds that Elliot was not a man who tolerated cussing well. And so Dylan accentuated every cuss word he uttered and delighted in watching Elliot flinch.

"I beg your pardon?"

"I said it's goddamn amazing that this forest hasn't been logged or sold off. So few places like this are left. Every time I pass through one, I want to get down on my knees and kiss the ground."

Elliot was watching him, his mouth hanging open, and Dylan laughed.

"It's my work," Dylan went on, "to save the places like this that still exist. To go after the bastards who want to kill the rest of them off. I'm the head of EarthAlert. Ever heard of it?"

Elliot shook his head. He was still gripping the chair tightly, as if he were struggling to sit still through an earthquake. Dylan paced across the deck while he spoke.

"Four of us started it. The other organizations are too goddamn publicity oriented. They spend more of their time drumming up contributions than they do getting out there and doing things. Do you know how much the fuckers spend on advertising?"

Elliot had gone white, but Dylan continued.

"About a fifth of their budgets, that's how much. A few years back, one of the most prominent groups spent six million of their fifty-million-dollar budget on goddamn stamps! It's probably worse now. They've got a lot of support, that's for sure. They play on that liberal guilt and even get a few snobs in upstate New York to put their stickers on their bumpers. They know how to play the game and come across as radical, too. But we didn't want to play any games. All we wanted was to get out there and start doing something."

Dylan stopped pacing abruptly and caught his breath. He looked out over the forest again and thought of the sixteen acres in Connecticut that had been completely wooded with maple and birch trees until his parents got their greedy hands on it. Once the plans for their mansion were finalized, they immediately ordered in two bulldozers. They wanted all of the trees removed except for a thin line of maples around the perimeter. Dylan was eight at the time and his father brought him to the site to see the clearing. Dylan had put his hands over his ears as the screeching dozers wrenched each root from the ground. He screamed when the trees fell slowly and stiffly, like old men dying. He sobbed and grabbed the back of one of the bulldozers, trying to stop it, until his father yanked him away.

"Stop it this instant!" his father had shouted at him, pushing him back into his Mercedes. "This was supposed to be fun for you, to watch them clear the site. All little boys like heavy equipment."

"But they're killing the trees," Dylan had cried.

"For God's sake, they're just trees, Dylan. We'll put a lovely lawn in. You'll like it much better."

His parents put in their acres of lawn and flower beds and built their mansion, but Dylan never forgot the trees. His parents saved a portion of them for firewood, but Dylan walked out of the room whenever they threw a log on the fire.

"People think I'm crazy," Dylan said to Elliot now. "Maybe I am. Not because of the things I do, but because I want to do them, because I have hope."

He whirled around and stared at Elliot.

"I'm not an idiot," he continued. "I'm not going to save the world. But maybe I'll save one tree. Maybe I'll drum up enough support to kill one nuclear power plant. And maybe, if there are enough people like me working in every corner of the globe, we'll still have a planet in another hundred years."

He watched the color slowly come back into Elliot's face. Dylan sat down in the chair beside him.

"What kind of insurance do you sell?" he asked.

Elliot reached for his lemonade, but had finished it long ago. He set the empty glass back down.

"All kinds," Elliot said, but his voice broke. "All kinds."

"Like what? I'm not up on insurance. Don't have any that I know of."

"What?" Elliot said, sitting forward. "You've got to have car insurance. It's the law."

"Not if you don't have a car, it's not. Did you know that at current vehicle-emission rates, the potential incidence of cancer from those emissions alone is thirteen to twenty-three thousand cases a year? And that's just in California! Makes me sick, all these selfish bastards driving around in their Buicks every day, when they could get rid of their fat asses if they'd just walk or ride."

Elliot rubbed his hand across his forehead. Dylan noticed he was sweating.

"You'd put me out of business," Elliot said.

Dylan threw back his head and laughed. "Not in my lifetime, unfortunately. No, Elliot, you're safe and sound. Life insurance, health insurance, that's the field to be in with all the crap in the air and water. You're gonna see people dying like never before. AIDS, cancer, radiation, chemical poisoning. Hell, I'll be amazed if any of us are left standing in another fifty years."

Elliot stood up abruptly. "Leah! Leah, come here."

Leah rushed out, with Samantha close on her heels. They both looked from Elliot to Dylan and back to Elliot again.

"What is it?" Leah asked.

Elliot clutched his stomach. "I . . . I think I'd like a cocktail," he said.

Leah's eyes widened. "A cocktail? But Elliot, you never—"

"A screwdriver. Can you make one of those?"

"Yes, but—"

"Make it. Please."

Leah stared at him a moment longer and then walked back into the house.

"Is everything all right?" Samantha asked.

Dylan looked up and smiled.

"Perfect," he said. "Your dad and I were just talking shop."

Samantha seemed unsure, but finally she nodded and followed her mother inside. When Leah came back out with the screwdriver, Elliot grabbed it from her. He waited until she had gone back inside, then he swallowed half of it at once. He stared down at Dylan.

"There's something I need to say."

Dylan leaned back in his chair. He smiled because he knew what was coming, the don't-hurt-my-daughter speech.

"It's about Samantha," Elliot went on. "I hope you understand how special she is. She's my only daughter. I simply won't allow you—"

"Dinner's ready!" Leah interrupted, peeking her head out the door. "Come on, you two. Pork chops are on the table."

Dylan stood up and squeezed Elliot's arm.

"Not to worry, Elliot," he said. "I know she's special. What she and I have is special. I've never known anyone quite like Samantha. She's liberal, open-minded, and independent as hell. She'll be fine. Me, on the other hand . . ."

Then he laughed and, as he went inside, felt Elliot's eyes boring through the back of his head again.

Leah sat across from her husband, with Samantha and Dylan on either side. She made sure they all had enough pork chops and applesauce and rice and salad, and then she leaned over to Dylan surreptitiously and drank in the scent of him. Why did men under forty always smell so delicious, so sensual and musky, while men over forty smelled, well, over forty? Like their father's after-shave.

"So, tell me, Dylan," Leah said, "how did you and Samantha meet?"

Dylan flashed her his smile and she sucked in her breath. My God, he was a beautiful man. It had taken all of her willpower not to blurt that out when she first saw him. Her mouth had formed the word "oh" when she saw all that hair, those green-yellow eyes, the jagged lines of his face, but she had managed not to actually say it. She had been too aware of Elliot beside her, watching her reaction.

Even Elliot could not take his eyes off this young man, although she knew it was for a different reason. He kept staring in amazed disgust at Dylan's hair, probably devising a plan to sneak up to the loft at night with a pair of scissors and cut it all off. Elliot was not a man who understood about men with long hair.

Leah stared at Dylan, drank in the scent of him, and wondered what he and her daughter were doing beneath the table. Every now and then, she felt a foot rush past her on its way to another.

"I was on a tirade as usual," Dylan said, laughing. He ate heartily while he spoke, which Leah liked. "As I recall it, Samantha was helping Congressman Hastings with some details of his campaign and she came in just after I'd burst in and let Hastings have it."

Samantha set her wine glass down. "Actually," she said, "I was there when you walked in."

Dylan looked up blankly. "You were?"

"Yes. I was standing right beside the desk when you barged in. You must have been too engrossed in your battle to save the California coast to notice."

Dylan thought about this for a minute and then shrugged.

"If you say so," he said. Leah turned to her daughter in time to see her face fall. She reluctantly pulled out of Dylan's hemisphere and reached for her daughter's hand. She wanted to tell her that men were always like this; they did not bother with the details of even the most important occasions.

"What happened after that?" Leah asked her.

Samantha smiled again and Leah felt her reach her foot out to rest it between Dylan's legs. How quickly all was forgiven when love was new, when touching each other was so much more important than words.

"He called me three days later," Samantha said. "Of course, I knew at once who he was, but I pretended not to. He asked if I'd like to go out for coffee. We met, started talking, and didn't stop until two in the morning. We've been together ever since."

"Of course I noticed she was beautiful," Dylan interjected, staring only at Samantha. "But beauty doesn't do it for me. What really caught my eye was her strength. She stood up to me, tried to make her point, although she was wrong and I, of course, was right."

Samantha laughed and threw her napkin at him. Leah watched them, saw they had forgotten about her and Elliot entirely for a moment. She leaned back in her chair and took a deep breath.

"Where do you live, Dylan?" Elliot asked.

Dylan finished his wine and poured himself another full glass. "Over by Old Sacramento. Not a very good part of town, I'm afraid."

"Doesn't chasing down oil rigs make you a very good living?" Elliot asked.

Dylan stared at him. "I'm not in it for the money, Elliot," he said. "I've never been interested in money."

"Money is a reality," Elliot said.

"More of a reality for some than others. I make enough to eat and sleep and pay my bills, most of the time. Beyond that, money just gets you things that never really make you happy."

"This cabin makes me happy," Elliot said. "It cost—"

"Too much," Leah broke in.

Dylan smiled. "Look, I'm not saying money isn't important to some people. My parents think money is everything. All I'm saying is it doesn't matter to me."

"More wine, anyone?" Leah asked, changing the subject. No one answered and when Leah turned to Samantha, she found her sitting back, a small smile playing on her lips as she stared at Dylan. Her long, red-brown hair was pulled forward over one shoulder and her gray eyes, in the fading light, were luminescent. Whenever Leah looked at her daughter, really looked at her, she was dumbfounded. How could someone so beautiful, so sure of herself, have come out of her?

"In a business like insurance—" Elliot began.

"You're dealing with people's life savings," Leah finished.

Elliot nodded, and as he went on to explain what money could mean to people, Leah leaned over and whispered in Samantha's ear, "I think Dylan's wonderful. Your father needs a little shaking up."

Samantha smiled wider and kissed Leah's cheek. "Thank you, Mom."

After dinner, Leah and Elliot insisted on doing the dishes and Samantha and Dylan went for a walk. They walked down the steps of the deck and out into the woods. As soon as they were out of sight of the cabin, Dylan took her in his arms.

Samantha still could not get over the feel of him. The dark brown hairs on his arms, the ripple of the muscles in the back of his thighs, the indentation between his shoulder blades. She felt nearly primal when she was with Dylan, scratching and clawing and screaming to keep him touching her.

He led her farther into the forest and then pulled her down on the ground. Samantha reached for the buttons of his shirt. They both watched her hands, slowly unbuttoning, her fingertips stopping often to twirl the hair on his chest. When she had his shirt open, he reached for her. He raised her arms up and slipped her shirt over her head. She wore no bra beneath and he smiled as he tweaked his thumb across her nipples.

Then, all at once, he was on her, tugging at her skirt and his pants. When they had their clothes off, he pushed her down into the pine needles. They scratched her back and bottom, but then Dylan touched her again and she lost awareness of everything but him. His fingers caressed her; so did the wind and his lips, and she felt as if she were being touched everywhere at once, by a million tiny fingers.

She spread herself out for him and was ready immediately. She pulled him close, took him deep inside of her, and then did what she loved to do. She spread her fingers wide through his hair, fanned it out around his face, and kissed him.

He pulled her up on top of him. She wrapped her legs around his hips and arched back, swishing from side to side until he pulled her close. She felt the tautness in his arms and legs, the quick beating of his heart against her chest, and then she let go, too, and cried out his name.

"I love you, Dylan," she said.

Her voice had broken and he pulled away, setting her down beside him.

"You remember our rules, or our lack of them, right? No strings. No commitments. No plans. No talk of marriage or what we owe each other."

Samantha looked away. She found her clothes and got dressed. From the very beginning, Dylan had made it clear that he couldn't offer her anything but the moment, and she had been certain that was all she wanted.

"I remember," she said, brushing pine needles from her hair.

"No requirements of each other," Dylan went on, pulling on his pants. "I don't know what I'm going to feel a month from now. I'll run the second I feel cramped. I hate pressure. I just want to be up-front about this."

Samantha blinked until her eyes were dry and then turned to him. She forced a smile.

"I feel the same way. I've got my career and my friends. I've got my whole life. I won't let a man take it away from me."

They smiled at each other and Dylan kissed her.

"We've said from the start that we should be able to see other people," he said.

"Of course." She meant it. Monogamy was for people like her parents. For people without much passion left, who got their fill of excitement from TV and novels.

"I'm still a little concerned about AIDS," she said.

"Not to worry. Condoms are required."

Samantha nodded. It was really all very civilized and adult. So why, then, did she feel that there were a million unsaid words beating against her chest? Why, when she had things exactly the way she wanted them, did she feel as if she were out of control? Despite her best intentions, she had not been able to limit her emotions to a casual kind of passion. Passion was never casual, she realized. It had its own heartbeat, with a steadily intensifying rhythm. Each morning when she woke up in Dylan's arms, she thought, *It would be so much easier if he'd left yesterday.* And then, a moment later, she'd whisper, *Thank God he's mine for another day.*

"I want you to understand," he went on, "that I can't give you what all the other guys can. I'm not a lifer. I don't believe in happily ever after."

She didn't believe in happily ever after either, but

she did believe in this, this intensity, this burning in her fingers to touch him.

"I don't, either," she said. "At least, not for me. If you're trying to prepare me for a letdown, don't. We'll stay together as long as we're both happy. I don't come with any strings, Dylan."

He smiled at her so widely that Samantha laughed. She believed it was their freedom that made them so passionate. They had no holds on each other, and so they clung tighter, to squeeze all the pleasure they could out of every moment, knowing it wouldn't last.

"I do love you, though," she went on. "No strings. No requirements. Love does not have to be my parents' kind of love."

"Do they love each other?" Dylan asked.

"Of course. They're married."

Dylan laughed. "Don't be silly, Samantha. Marriage doesn't have the slightest thing to do with love."

Samantha stared at him. "Why such a strong aversion?" she asked.

He shrugged. "I've just never seen a good marriage," he said. "Your parents probably come the closest, at least in terms of longevity, but it's the quality, not the length, that really matters. Do you know of any quality marriages?"

"What about your parents?" Samantha asked. "You've never told me about them."

"Never mind about them," he said. "They're inconsequential."

"No parents are inconsequential."

"Mine are. And that's not what we're about, anyway. Whispering secrets. I'm not into baring my soul."

Samantha turned away, stung. How quickly he shifted from one extreme to the next. From making love to her to shutting her out.

She started for the cabin, but Dylan pulled her into his arms. She had her back to him and he wrapped his arms around her waist, buried his face in the nape of her neck.

"I'm sorry, Sam," he said. "My parents bring out the worst in me. They always have. They're wealthy and snobbish and cold. I got away as soon as I could."

"What are their names?"

"Alan and Sophia."

"What do they do?"

"Nothing. Everything. My father retired from banking years ago. He makes money with investments. More money than he'll ever use. My mother has her clubs, her charities. She spends an inordinate amount of time putting crap on her face."

"How often do you see them?"

"Never. When I was eighteen, I chose a college in California to get away from them. I left while they were on vacation in Australia. They sent me a postcard, saying goodbye, and I haven't seen them since. I didn't even tell them when I dropped out and I don't think they have a clue what I do now. They call once a year, on Christmas, and we talk for three minutes about my mother's charities and my father's investments. When I started talking back and growing my hair out, they looked at me kind of blankly, like I was someone else's son."

"They sound awful," Samantha said.

"They are. They're nothing like your parents. They couldn't sit around a table and have a pleasant conversation if their lives depended on it."

"You thought our conversation was pleasant?"

"I like the way your parents finish each other's sentences. They anticipate what the other is going to say."

"Do they? I hadn't noticed."

"That's because you're too close. Step back. Take a look at them."

"I would think you'd be scornful of that kind of thing," she said.

"Just because it's something I'll never have doesn't mean I can't admire their companionship. The problem is, they've combined themselves, taken on each other's characteristics. I could never do that. I can't stop and think about the repercussions of my actions on someone else. My style is to act without thinking about anything or anybody."

He pulled back, shrugged as if that would take the import from his words, and Samantha knew what she was supposed to do now. Lighten the mood so he wouldn't worry that he had said too much. They would both pretend that he hadn't given out any secrets, that they were no more intimate than before. Amazing, the lies such generally honest people told when they were dancing around love.

"What about my parents?" she asked lightly. "Think you'll be able to stand them for two weeks?"

Dylan smiled, literally let his breath out as if he'd been expecting her to pry, to demand more.

"I'm sure I can," he said as they headed back toward the cabin. "The question is, can they stand me?"

4

When Elliot walked into the bedroom, Leah was sitting up in bed, reading her latest romance novel. She had pulled her short hair back with a ribbon and was scrubbed clean of makeup. He was still shocked when he saw her like this, though he never let on that he was. In the early years of their marriage, she had never washed her makeup off until after he went to bed. She was up long before him in the morning, as well, and when she came out of the bathroom, she was done up as always, with rouge and mascara and pink lipstick, and her bobbed hair sprayed to sticky perfection.

Yet recently, as if in retaliation for all those years beauty held her hostage, Leah had begun taking off her makeup earlier and earlier. First, an hour before they went to bed. Then before they watched their evening television programs, so that she looked pale and almost childlike in the blue light. Then, a few months ago when he got home from work, she was standing makeupless in the doorway to the kitchen, her hands on her hips, daring him to say something. For a moment, he entertained ideas of what he could say, discussions they could get into about the things women had to go through to be beautiful, how marriage should be a haven from that. He could remind her of the times she looked absolutely perfect with no makeup on at all—after Samantha was born, every time she stepped out of a swimming pool. But somehow he knew those discussions would lead to others, to how things had changed, to how they felt. She'd ask him questions he wouldn't have answers to, or he'd be tempted to tell her what he knew. The thought of delving into all that had literally made him tremble. So he had merely smiled at her instead and walked into the bedroom.

Elliot got into bed beside Leah now and glanced down at the page she was reading.

> Roarke pulled Chanel to him tightly. Her heaving bosom pressed against him deliciously and he could feel her wild heartbeat. She struggled against him for a moment and then suddenly, breathlessly, gave in to him. She leaned her head back and he needed no more invitation. He bent his head to hers and kissed her. Her ruby lips opened and their tongues touched wildly, passionately, until . . .

"How do you say that name?" Elliot asked. "Is it 'Chanel,' as in 'chair'? Or 'Shanel,' as in 'ship'?"

Leah put her marker into her book and looked up. "It's 'Chanel,' like the fragrance," she said.

Elliot shook his head. He liked straightforward names. If he wrote a book, his heroine would be Jane Smith and his hero Michael Johnson. When Samantha was born, he had wanted to name her Sarah, but Leah had been adamant. "I want a strong name," she had said. "I want her to be somebody." Elliot had gone home to pick up a few extra things for Leah and by the time he came back, Leah had put Samantha May Shaperson on the birth certificate. He clearly remembered what happened after that, how he had walked to the window in Leah's hospital room and stared down at the parking lot for forty-five minutes. He had ignored all of Leah's questions, even her tears, until all his urges to argue had passed, until he turned around and smiled and told her names didn't matter to him in the slightest.

Now, Leah set her book down on the nightstand and pulled her legs up beneath her.

"So?" she said. "What do you think of Dylan? He's certainly a passionate young man."

"Passionate" was not a word Elliot could comfortably use in conjunction with his daughter. He had spent his whole life making sure everything he did and said to Samantha was nonsexual. When she was four, he stopped giving her baths, at eight he stopped taking her onto his lap. When she was fourteen and took to wearing T-shirts that barely reached her thighs to bed, he never looked lower than her face. At sixteen, when she stripped down to her bikini every hot summer day, he hardly looked at her at all. His thoughts were strictly of a fatherly nature, so that in his mind she remained ten years old forever, straight as a board and sexless.

"He's a radical," Elliot said.

"I believe Samantha is, too."

"She is not!"

"Maybe not in action," Leah said, "but in ideas. She's always been an environmentalist. You know that. She's never voted anything but liberal Democratic."

"She is nothing like that young man."

"What scares you so much about him?"

Elliot folded his arms. This was another discussion he'd rather not have. He was not certain what the right answers were, what Leah wanted to hear. He was not certain that he could keep everything in check.

"I am not scared," he said.

"You are. You can't stand him. He threatens you."

"If I'm scared, it's because I'm afraid for Samantha. Dylan is exactly the type of man who could hurt her. He's excited by her now, but once that wears off, he'll leave her. He's not interested in commitment. He's interested in causes, in saving the whales."

Leah stared at him in surprise. He had raised his voice and he almost never did that. He calmed himself and spoke more softly.

"I've never seen her look at anyone the way she looks at him," he said.

Leah closed her eyes. "I know."

"I can remember when she was five years old and I was tucking her in. She looped her arms around my neck and told me she was going to marry me."

Leah smiled and looked at him. "She adored you. She still adores you."

"No. I'm just her dull, old father. And Dylan is. . . everything she's denied herself before. She'll go crazy over him. I know it. I saw my mother do the same thing over my father."

"Samantha is not your mother, Elliot," she said.

Elliot looked down, noticed their hands were touching. He had not felt that happen. There was so little pleasure in it, it was almost like touching himself.

"My father had the key to my mother," he said. "I don't know where he got it. I don't know why she didn't do something to get it back. They ignited each other and then blew each other up."

"That was a different situation," Leah said.

"Maybe. But it began the same way. With passion. They were radical, too. Dad was going to make a fortune on the drug industry. He thought he saw the wave of the future, when marijuana and all that was to follow would be legalized and end up in everybody's medicine cabinets. Mom went along with him, mistook his foolish ambition for greatness. And then it all went to hell. Dad invested all he had in pharmaceutical stocks and went broke. He left because he couldn't stand to see his defeat reflected in Mom's eyes and Mom followed that up with a great succession of men who used up the rest of her soul. Dad would come back every once in a while and they'd have tremendous reunions and battles. *That* was what passion got them."

Elliot set his jaw and turned away. He had said too much. He rarely, if ever, said too much, but as he watched Dylan and Samantha tonight, as he saw them come in from their walk, their skins red from rubbing, their pupils dilated from sex, he had felt the terror well up inside of him. It was like watching his parents again, as if he had not escaped at all.

He remembered one of those nights when his father, Steven, came back after a six-month disappearance. Elliot and his sister, Meredith, had been playing cards when Steven simply sauntered in.

Before stomping out of the room, Meredith had given Steven a stare that would have burned the skin off a real father, but which merely made Steven laugh. Meredith was thirteen at the time, disgusted by all the comings and goings, and on the verge of hating all of them. In three more years she would say, "See ya, Mom," and walk out the door with a suitcase full of blue jeans and T-shirts to go live with a friend.

"Oh well," Steven had said after Meredith left. He turned to Elliot. "Come give Daddy a kiss."

He started toward Elliot, but Elliot stepped out of reach. He had cried for six days when Steven left the first time, but when he realized his tears meant nothing to anybody, he never cried again. He didn't want anything from his father anymore, except for him to go away for good.

They heard shuffling in the hallway. Elliot's mother, Joann, came into the room and gasped.

She and Steven stared at each other the way they always did, with love and anger and passion and fury, with everything they felt bubbling right at the surface.

"You bastard," Joann said and then Steven laughed and swept her up into his arms. They kissed passionately and Elliot turned away. Before Steven left the first time, Elliot had loved to see them kiss, because it meant that they were happy, that they wouldn't fight for a while. But now he hated it because this time it meant that his mother would take his father back again.

That reunion lasted seven days. After day two, they started fighting. By day three, Joann wanted to know how Steven was going to support them. By day four, Steven was hatching new schemes, talking about some mob connections he had, a smuggling ring he knew about in Florida. By day six, they were fighting as much as they were making love and by day seven, they only fought. His mother broke every dish she had replaced after Steven came home the last time. At midnight, she screamed at him to get out.

"I'd be happy to," Steven shouted back. "And don't expect to see me again."

But of course they did. They always did.

Elliot related this story to Leah now and Leah leaned her head against his shoulder.

"I didn't realize you still thought about your parents so much," she said.

"I don't. I haven't, until tonight. Mom's in Miami. Do you realize I haven't seen her for eight years, since Dad's funeral, or spoken to her for three? Amazing how easy it is for us to be cruel to each other."

"You could call her . . ."

"No. It's better for me to keep it a clean break. I vowed I would never make the same mistakes Mom and Dad made and I haven't. We've had a good life, Leah.

A long, calm, content marriage. If Samantha has to get married, that's what I want for her."

Leah pulled away. She turned off the light and lay down. The room was bathed in moonlight from the curtainless window. The wind brushed a branch against the panes.

"Samantha isn't you," she said finally.

"No, but she can learn from me. She can—"

"She has to learn for herself. And you're wrong if you think all passion is bad. Your father had some harebrained ideas and, when they didn't work out, he couldn't take it. Dylan is not your father."

"He's got his own harebrained ideas," Elliot said.

"Yes, but you have to admire his spunk."

"Do I?" Elliot said.

Leah adjusted the covers around her and sighed.

"Go to sleep, Elliot," she said.

Elliot tried to do as she said, but instead he lay there, listening for the sound of his daughter and her lover above him, sure that whenever he heard the floor settle, they were making love in the bed.

The next morning, after breakfast, Leah grabbed her purse off the counter.

"I overlooked a few things at the market," she said. "More orange juice and eggs, and mushrooms for the spaghetti sauce. I'm going to run into town and pick them up."

"I'll go with you, Mom," Samantha said.

Leah found her keys. "No, dear. You stay here and keep the men company. I'll only be a little while."

She raced out before Samantha could argue and got into the car. She started it and headed down the long, dirt drive, then took the road that led to Lake Tahoe.

It was a half-hour drive, up over the mountain and through the back roads, but Leah welcomed every second of it. She had to plan exactly what to say, how to explain. She laid her arm on the open window.

"James," she would say, "I'm sorry. I didn't mean to lie . . ."

Oh no, he would rip that one to shreds. He was a psychoanalyst with years of training, several of which in his own personal psychotherapy. He'd been a practicing Freudian psychoanalyst for twenty years and could see past every façade straight to the heart of a problem.

Leah turned onto the main highway leading into the northwestern edge of Lake Tahoe. There was no getting around the fact that James had asked her not to go on this vacation and she had gone anyway. On the night before she left, he had said in his very proper, very affected British accent that he had cultivated over the years, "If you go, Leah, I'm not sure exactly what I'll do."

They had been lying on the floor in his office. Leah had told Elliot she was going marketing for the vacation and it would probably take her a good deal of time. He had nodded and gone back to watching a *Matlock* rerun, and she had hurried out to the car, where the groceries she had bought earlier were already sitting in the trunk.

She had driven straight to the tall blue glass building in downtown Sacramento that housed James Arlington's office. She took the elevator to the thirteenth floor—an unnerving coincidence at best, which James dared his patients to complain about—and walked into the empty waiting room. She walked down the hall to James's office, opened the door, and found James standing naked in the center of the room, with every blind wide open, every light on, so that the good people of Sacramento, if they wanted to, could see him in all his glory if they simply looked up.

He was not the most handsome man she'd ever known. When she first came to see him, as his patient, she had found his looks . . . unnerving. Unnatural. Later, when she began exploring him intimately, she discovered the tuck marks behind his ears, the scar along the bottom of his jaw. In the three years she'd known him, he'd gone in for two face-lifts; he was constantly on the lookout for new ways to have his face realigned.

His hair was light blond, box dyed, and straight as a pole. His eyes were blue, vibrant, and often cold. He was thin, with bony hands that were always cool, even in summer. He kept his office at sixty-two degrees to see how his patients responded to physical discomfort.

"Take your clothes off," he had said immediately on that last night. She did as she was told, her heart beating rapidly from both excitement and fear. Even after all this time, she never knew what James had planned, what he was capable of, and that both intrigued and terrified her. She stepped out of her skirt and blouse and shoes and walked toward him.

"Stay there," he said. She stopped. He reached back onto his desk and picked up a thick rope. Leah swallowed hard, but said nothing.

James ran the rope through his hands. He slid it down his chest and then dropped it over his pubic hair. Leah watched him grow hard as the cord touched him. She trembled a little and he smiled.

He walked toward her.

"James, I want to tell you—"

He ran up to her and grabbed her arm, twisting the skin until it turned bright red and she cried out.

"Shut up," he said. "Goddammit, shut up. You're *ruining* it."

She bit her lip to keep from crying and he let go. She wanted to massage the welt, but she didn't dare move. She had learned early on to stay still, to always let him have his way.

James moved to within inches of her and grabbed her hands. He tied them up tightly behind her, then pulled the rope along to the center of the room. Leah followed, backward, as James lay down on the floor and pulled her on top of him.

After that, the bruise on her arm no longer mattered. Nothing ever mattered—not the occasional welt, not the things James made her do, not the rope in his hands, not the gun in his drawer, nothing—once James started touching her, kissing her. Then, she could only thank God that he wanted her, that he was nibbling her ear, that he was asking her to forgive him for hurting her and making her do all these things because, really and truly, he adored her, he couldn't live without her.

When they were through this last time, however, he had not untied her as he usually did. Instead he stood up, his limp penis right at eye level as she sat on the floor, and said, "If you go on this vacation with your husband, Leah, I don't know exactly what I'll do."

"I have to go," Leah had said quietly.

"You don't have to do anything. You want to go. If you want to go, say it. Don't try to lie to me."

Leah had bit her lip again. She knew she was no match for him. James was so intelligent, had graduated summa cum laude from Yale. He was a good psychiatrist, one of the best in the state.

"I'm not lying," she said. "It's for Elliot. These two weeks are what he lives for."

"Elliot," James said with a sneer. "Elliot hardly lives at all." He roughly untied her hands and let her get dressed.

Leah still did not know why he bothered with her, why she was the one he had chosen. She had been his patient once, although Elliot had never known a thing about it. For years, she had been accumulating a weight of boredom, of discontent, and then in a six-month period, all of her feelings had intensified. She had begun to feel as if she never wanted to get up in the morning. She let the dust pile up on the furniture. She stopped going to the market and made peanut butter sandwiches for dinner instead. She could not get out of her bathrobe. Every morning, after Elliot left for work, she burrowed farther beneath the covers and came out only when she had to eat and go to the bathroom.

Elliot said nothing, did nothing. That had made her furious at first, but then even the fury dissipated and she realized she was dead inside.

Samantha came over once during that time and thought Leah was sick. When she came by again a month later, she pulled Leah into her arms and rocked her.

"My friend has a wonderful psychiatrist," she had said. "She was suicidal for a while, and she says this man saved her life. I don't know his name, but I'll get it today. Go see him, Mom. I'm worried."

Leah went. She was utterly intimidated by James Arlington at first, by the coldness of his office, by the starkness of his eyes. She sat on his couch and could not think of a single thing to say.

They sat in silence for ten full minutes, and then James got up from his desk and sat beside her. He took her hand and it was as if, instantly and completely, he took her heart, too. It was a kind gesture, the only kind gesture, she realized now, that he'd ever offered. She cried and he held her. She didn't say more than ten words in fifty minutes, but when she left she could breathe again.

During the second session, Leah talked about Elliot. She told James everything about him and was shocked that everything took only fifteen minutes. She told him that Elliot sold insurance, that he took sick days only when absolutely necessary, that he watched television every evening, liked fishing on the weekends, and had not taken her on a vacation to anywhere but their cabin for years.

She said all this and then James moved beside her on the couch again. He asked her only a few questions, and then began to touch her. He slipped his arm around her waist. She stared down at his hand and kept talking while she marveled at the strange feel of him.

When the timer went off after fifty minutes, James nibbled on her ear. Leah didn't breathe, didn't speak. Then James stood up, buzzed his secretary, and told her to reschedule his next appointment. And then, without a word, he pulled Leah down on the floor and began to unbutton her blouse.

Leah had stared in amazement at the strange hands touching her. There was no guilt, no worry, only this bewilderment that his hands were so different, that different fingers could elicit such drastically different responses. She had not known her skin could still prickle like that, or seem to rise up of its own accord toward his hands. For years, she had forgotten that she was a person outside of Elliot, that this was her body, *hers*.

James pulled off her blouse and unclasped her bra. He leaned forward and took her breast in his mouth.

Leah had never cheated on Elliot before, never even considered it, and yet there was no hesitation. While James touched her, there was no Elliot at all. She pulled James close to her, arched her back when he wrapped his teeth around her nipple. She slid down beneath him, pulled him over her. She struggled out of her pants quickly and yanked at his. She did not even act like herself. She guided him inside her, laughed when she took him in completely. Even this was different. Elliot was thicker but shorter; she could feel James all the way up inside her. She raised her hips up to meet him, did not care that the secretary might hear her cry out. She bit into his shoulder when she came.

When it was over, Leah sat up. With Elliot, she usually got dressed right away, or he slipped away into the bathroom and took a shower. With James, she sat there naked, surprisingly unselfconscious, miraculously content.

"How did you know?" she asked.

James stared at her with his stunning blue eyes. "It was simple. Your eyes were dying for it. Why would you want to get up in the morning? Who could face a day without any passion in it?"

James slotted her in for every Tuesday and Thursday night, without charge, and Leah went back to making dinner and cleaning the house. Elliot never asked about the change in her, but then he had never complained about the dirty house or cold dinners, either. He had simply waited, in his completely Elliot way, for things to right themselves. And when they did, he went on without a word or any acknowledgment, but with a smug smile that said, I knew I was right.

Now, driving toward Tahoe, Leah thought back over her relationship with James. She had thought they would have a perfect love affair, passionate and pure. Obviously, she had not understood what James was about. It seemed he cared for her; if he went too far, if he dug his fingernails too deeply into her back and drew blood, he always begged her forgiveness, told her he loved her. It was only when he opened that desk drawer, or turned that ice-cold stare on her, or made her . . . No, she wouldn't think about it. She would erase all the bad parts from her mind because the truth was that James made her come alive. He filled her up, just as he had that first time, not just physically, but mentally, too. She was like a pitcher with a crack in the bottom and by the time she was lifted out of James's well, she was empty again.

This had gone on for three years now, two times a week, every week, except for the annual two-week vacation in June, and James's month-long vacation to Europe every August with his wife. She had asked him why he didn't cancel that, if he wanted her to cancel her vacation.

"Because," he'd said, "I go for the culture, to meet other analysts. It's for my career, Leah. Why do you go to your silly little cabin?"

"Because . . . Because . . . that's what we do. Elliot and me."

James had thrown back his head and laughed. "Elliot and you," he said. "That's a good one."

Leah reached the outskirts of Lake Tahoe and traffic started to bottleneck. They were inching up on the Fourth of July weekend, and many of the vacationers had come in early. Leah battled the mob until she reached Safeway, where she pulled into the parking lot.

She got the groceries she had intentionally forgotten to buy and put the bag in her car. She stood inside the market until the time reached five till the hour, and then she walked out to the pay phone, used her personal credit card that Elliot knew nothing about, and dialed James's office number.

His secretary picked up.

"Mr. Arlington's office."

"This is Mrs. Shaperson," she said. "May I speak to Mr. Arlington?"

"I'll see if he'll take your call," the secretary said, the way she always did, the way James had instructed her to. Sometimes he took Leah's call and sometimes he didn't. He told her there were times when she needed to be taken down a notch or two.

This time, though, he picked up. It was Tuesday, she was due at his office at seven o'clock that evening, and of course, she wouldn't be there.

"You are coming," he said immediately.

She could picture him, sitting in his black leather chair, his back to the gorgeous view just outside his window. His blond hair would be neatly combed, his blue eyes alert, taking in everything, his surgically perfected face hard and unlined. His patient would have just left, and he would be putting his notes away in their folder, throwing away any cigarette butts or tissues that had been needed in the past fifty minutes.

"I'm in Tahoe," Leah said, surprised her voice was as strong as it was.

James was quiet for a long time. She hated his silence, hated it particularly when they were making love because it usually meant his mind was curling around some violent idea, some torturous game. Sometimes she thought she was insane to keep coming to him. But even insanity offered its rewards. James was not all bad, not all evil. He offered excitement and passion and moments of euphoria and she had to have that. She had to. Even if it meant humiliation, or raw, ugly bruises on her back that she had to be careful to hide from Elliot. James was like a drug with awful side effects, like bad heroin that made you high but also psychotic.

"I asked you not to go," James said at last.

"I know. But I couldn't disappoint Elliot."

There was the sound of a match being struck and Leah could see him lighting his pipe, the smoke blurring his face for a moment.

"Do you love him, Leah?" he asked.

Leah leaned against the stuccoed wall of Safeway. Vacationers were pouring in and out, loading up with Coca-Cola and Doritos and hot-dog buns. It was hot today, nearing eighty-five already. The sun was directly above her.

"Please, James," she said. "Let's not go into it."

"Why not? Is Elliot there with you?"

"No. I'm alone. I just can't. Not now."

"You're a little girl, Leah," he said. "You can't do anything. You can't function on your own. You can't leave your husband and you can't stand up to me."

Leah closed her eyes. The sun was too hot. She

was breaking out in a sweat all over. She lifted up her arms and saw the two saturated spots beneath them.

"I don't love him the way I love you," she said breathlessly. She pulled her shirt away from her chest; it was drenched with sweat.

"Which is how?" James asked.

"You make me feel things," she said. "Elliot is . . . Elliot is just there when I go to sleep at night. He makes the coffee in the morning."

James was quiet again.

"Elliot is my husband," she said.

"He doesn't have to be. Don't you see that, Leah? Unhappy people get divorced every day. Thirty-seven years of marriage is nothing special, not even something worth fighting for."

Leah opened her mouth to tell him that it was, of course it was, but then she closed it again. He would want her to defend her statement and she could not. What was worth fighting for? The emotionless kisses when Elliot left for work in the morning? The last months without any sex at all?

James waited for her to respond, but when she didn't, he chuckled.

"You'll come home to me and I may or may not want you."

"James, no."

"We'll see," James said. "I'm getting bored anyway. I've got a new woman patient. A beauty. Young. Black. Desperate for a little attention."

Tears streamed down Leah's cheeks. She turned away from the crowds and leaned her head against the phone.

"James, don't."

"She's beautiful, Leah. Striking. Long legs. Marvelous round breasts. She's just come out of a bad relationship. She needs me. And she's wild, Leah. When she opened her purse for a tissue, I saw handcuffs and a dildo thicker than my fist. I'd like to use them both on her. I really would."

Leah cried and waited for him to stop. Later, it would occur to her that she could have hung up on him, told him he was a pig, that she didn't need him. It always occurred to her after she'd seen or talked to James that she had a choice. But when she was with him, she felt powerless.

"Love me, James," she said. She heard him take in his breath. She surprised him, she knew, every time she waited out his vulgarity. It was obvious that he kept expecting her to leave, obvious that no one had ever stayed with him as long as she had, or put up with as much.

"When do you come home?" he asked at last.

Leah breathed again, dried her tears, and knew that, for now, James had given in. Suddenly, she longed for him, despite his penchant for pain and the invasions into her soul. None of that mattered because, when it came right down to it, he gave her life, he picked her up off the grave and made her dance. She longed for his coarseness, his sexuality, his passion, even his violence, because at least when he hurt her, she felt fury and humiliation. No matter what anyone said, that was better than feeling nothing.

"One week from Sunday," she said.

"That's perfect," James said. "My wife has a book convention that weekend. Come to the house."

Leah gripped the phone. Oh yes, this was what she lived for now. This euphoria when James wanted her. This anticipation of his touch. She had never seen the inside of his house. He had driven her past it now and then and they had hidden in the dark car waiting for his wife to pass by the window. When she did, James stuck his fingers inside Leah until she came.

"I'll be there," Leah said.

"Have fun with the hubby," James said. "See if you can't interest him in a fuck. I know it's a challenge, but I'll need you warmed up."

He laughed and hung up and Leah fell back against the wall. A woman asked her if she was through and Leah walked off in a daze. She found her car, got inside, and turned the air-conditioning on full blast. She rested her head on the steering wheel and was certain, at first, that she would not cry again. But then she thought about Elliot, about the fact that he no longer wanted her, and the tears came. For years now, he hadn't come to her, and the last time she'd tried to interest him in making love, he'd gone limp in her hands. He had said it was just tension, problems at work, but neither of them had come near each other since. She cried and then let the air-conditioning dry her tears. She pulled out of the parking lot and started back for the cabin.

5

Dylan's dream jarred him awake on his third morning at the cabin. He slipped out of bed without waking Samantha, put on an old pair of sweat pants and a T-shirt, and walked out into the crisp morning air. He jogged a little, but then decided just to walk, to take in the scenery.

He had been dreaming of his parents. The two of them had been sitting at the dinner table, talking for once, finishing each other's sentences. Dylan had walked in on them and they had wanted to know about his day. He had run across the room and sat beside them, spilling out everything in one long, excited torrent. They had laughed at his stories, then his father had patted his back and said, "Good job, son."

When Dylan awoke, he was smiling. But the smile quickly faded. The truth was that he could precisely pinpoint the last night his parents had been civil to each other. It was the same night they had stopped sleeping together.

It happened on his seventh birthday. Dylan had

woken up to the sound of glass breaking. He had grabbed his teddy bear and run down the hall, thinking his parents were hurt. When he came to their closed door, he stopped.

From behind the door, his mother had shouted, "You bastard! You filthy bastard!"

Another crash had followed and Dylan realized it must be the glass perfume bottles that sat on the vanity. Someone was smashing them one by one.

"All I wanted was a little enthusiasm, Sophia. For God's sake, a little movement. Do you think there's any enjoyment in fucking an inanimate object?"

Dylan had not understood the words, but the heartlessness of the tone had chilled him. He pulled his teddy bear to his chest. He leaned against the wall and slid down to the floor, crying soundlessly.

"How dare you?" Sophia shouted. "You rotten, filthy bastard!" *Crash.*

There was a struggle, something large and bulky smacked into the wall, and then Dylan heard his mother crying. It was the first time he ever heard her cry and at first, because it was so foreign, he thought it must be laughter. The door was flung open and his mother stepped out with a trail of blood on her cheek. She looked at him on the floor and then, without a word, walked to the guest bedroom at the other end of the hall, slamming the door behind her.

His father came out a few minutes later. He lifted Dylan off the floor and walked him back to his bedroom. He put him into bed.

"Daddy?" Dylan said.

"Don't ask questions, Dylan," Alan said. "This is between your mother and me. It doesn't pertain to you at all."

And then he was gone, without a hug or kiss or word of comfort. Dylan didn't see his mother for three days, by which time she had a pink scar on her cheek and a firm set to her mouth that hadn't relaxed, not even on the last day Dylan saw her.

Dylan stopped now and leaned against a tree. He breathed deeply, wondering why that memory had come to him now. He hadn't thought of it in years.

He headed back toward the cabin and then stopped. Elliot and Leah were already up, walking out onto the deck together. From this distance, they could have passed for brother and sister. They moved in unison. Time together always did that, blended personalities, stole every last bit of individuality. He did not understand how anyone stood it.

Dylan stood masked within the trees and watched them. Elliot handed Leah a cup of coffee and she sipped it. They stood side by side near the railing, a thin sliver of light the only gap between them. For the longest time, they said nothing, as if nothing needed to be said, as if the fact that they chose to stand so close together when there was plenty of other space said everything.

Finally, Leah turned her head and said something to Elliot and he smiled. They both sat down in the deck chairs and watched the sun inch up over the trees. Dylan thought about joining them, but instead headed for the other side of the cabin. He felt as if he were intruding on their intimacy, as if he had seen something meant only for the two of them.

Samantha and Leah sat in their bathing suits on the sandy shore of Lake Tahoe. Dylan had rented a jet ski and was doing doughnuts around an anchored motorboat whose inhabitants were trying to enjoy lunch. Someone in the boat was waving at him to stop, but Dylan just kept going round and round, raising havoc and making two-foot waves. Samantha could see the smile on his face as he made the people in the boat sick.

She turned to her mother. "Are you certain Dad won't come down?"

Leah laughed. "And deal with all the traffic? Are you crazy? No, he'll find himself a quiet stream somewhere and sit around until he catches a guppy."

Samantha smiled and looked back out to the water. Dylan had finally given up his sport and headed out to the open lake. It was a majestic summer day. The sky was a vivid blue and the lake, deep as the ocean, was cobalt. The pines came right down to the shore and Samantha was certain there was no more beautiful place on earth.

"He's quite an interesting man," Leah said quietly.

"Dad?"

"No. Dylan."

Samantha nodded. They had been at the cabin for four days now and, so far, things had gone pretty much without incident. Which is not to say that Elliot had accepted Dylan. Far from it. When Dylan started talking about one of his causes, when he quoted statistics and offered his gloom-and-doom predictions for the earth, Elliot practically had a coronary. Last night, after Dylan had stepped outside, Elliot had turned to Samantha and said, "I've tried to be a good man. To leave things better than I found them. Then he comes along and tells me I've actually been polluting the air, contaminating the ground water, setting the stage to kill my grandchildren."

"He's just concerned, that's all. He tries to wake people up, make them see reality."

"The reality is that he's putting the blame on everyone but himself. I'm just trying to live. Everyone's just trying to live the best way they can."

"Dad, please, just give him a chance. I know he's different. But you've got to trust my judgment about him."

Elliot had stared at her as if her judgment had been

suspect for years. And though Samantha knew it didn't matter, that she'd stay with Dylan with or without her father's consent, she longed for him to smile at her and tell her she'd made the right choice, that he was proud of her. She was used to doing things right, winning his approval. She had made the honor roll every semester in school, had been captain of the tennis team, was accepted into three colleges. It was like a habit she couldn't break, doing something and then turning to her parents to make sure they noticed.

"I never imagined myself with anyone," Samantha said to her mother now, lying back on her beach towel.

"Why not?" Leah asked. Samantha followed her gaze as it fell on a couple sitting next to them, smoking cigarettes. Leah's nostrils flared, as if she were trying to get a whiff of the smoke.

"I don't know," Samantha said. "I was always so busy. I had my friends. I had college and grad school and then this job. There wasn't time."

"There's always time for love."

"No. That's not really true. Politics ate me up inside. It still does. If I didn't have to sleep, I could work twenty-four hours a day. I almost did, before Dylan. Now, I've got to sacrifice my work a little to be with him. It's unsettling."

"It's worth it."

"You couldn't have convinced me of that six months ago. Before Dylan, I had control of my time. I could do whatever I wanted, whenever I wanted, without reporting in to anyone. I was just Samantha Shaperson, and I loved it."

Leah shook her head. "You're from a different generation. I don't understand you."

Samantha sat up again. "What's to understand? I'm a person. I'm complete without a man."

"Are you? I know I'm not."

"Are you saying that without Dad, you'd only be half a woman?"

Leah shrugged. She turned her face up to the sun and closed her eyes.

"No one talks about me alone anymore," Leah said softly. "Have you ever heard anyone say, 'Do you know Leah Shaperson?' or 'Did you hear about Leah?' No. They all say, 'Did you hear about Leah and Elliot?' We've been joined at the hip."

Samantha almost said that it was Leah herself who'd done the soldering, but she did not. She tried to spot Dylan out on the water, but he had disappeared around the edge of the bay.

"I haven't been just me since I was sixteen," Leah said, "when I met your father. Oh, he was gorgeous then. I thought he was a college student."

Samantha laughed. "Tell me."

"You've heard this story so many times, Samantha."

"So? It's my favorite. Tell me again."

Leah lay down on the towel. The sun tickled the hairs on her legs as she remembered. It was all so clear, as if she had a photograph of the moment and looked at it daily. She'd been wearing a long white skirt and pink sweater. School had just let out and she was working her way through the mob of students in the hall. When she stepped out into the sunshine, she saw him.

He was standing by the front gate of the school, wearing blue jeans and a denim shirt. He looked older, perhaps he was even a college student. She had never seen him before and she was struck at once by the gauntness of his cheeks and, particularly, his round brown eyes to die for.

"I felt the wind rush out of my lungs," Leah said.

"No."

"I did. I swear it. I couldn't move. When he looked at me, he didn't smile, didn't call me over. He just looked and looked and it was like he was pulling me to him, like I had no will at all."

Samantha laughed and lay down beside her.

"What happened?"

Leah went back, was, for a moment, that sixteen-year-old girl who had never been in love, who had wished for passion so badly she'd made herself sore. That hunger had made her bold and desperate enough to walk right over to the stranger.

"Are you looking for someone?" she had asked.

He had stared down at her. He was at least six inches taller than her and Leah adored that. She loved tilting her head back to look at those wonderfully lashed eyes of his. She knew, from that angle, that he could see the smooth curve of her neck.

"I'm waiting for Principal Skinner," he said. "I'm transferring from Madison High, so I can take the advanced art courses here."

"Oh," Leah said, somewhat disappointed that he wasn't in college as she had thought. She would have loved to get involved with an older man. It would have done worlds for her reputation. She hoped he was a senior at least, a year older than her.

"You're a senior?" she asked.

"Yes."

Leah nodded. She wanted him to go on, to tell her his life story, but he simply lapsed into silence. She looked around, hoping to think of something witty to say, but could come up with nothing.

"Well," she said, "good luck. We're the best school in the city for art. I'm sure you'll like it."

She started to walk away and then, as if she were dreaming it, felt his fingers on her arm.

"Wait," he said. "You didn't even tell me your name."

She would remember the next moment forever,

dream it over a thousand times, because nothing in her experience had ever matched it. Not their first kiss, not his marriage proposal, not their wedding, not the day Samantha was born. Nothing. She had come alive that day, when he first touched her.

She had turned around slowly, his hand still on her arm, and looked up at him. He was smiling at her and she knew, with an instinct perhaps inbred in the species, that he thought she was attractive, that he was interested. It was like boiling water funneling through her veins. Her legs ached to dance, her fingers clutched at her books so she wouldn't clutch at him. She smiled, because it was the one part of her she couldn't hide and he smiled wider, and laughed, and shuffled his feet a little. Then her heart soared, shot up past the school buildings, past the clouds, into the galaxy.

"Leah," she said finally. "Leah McDermott."

He was still touching her and, at the same time, they both looked down at his hand on her arm. He let go slowly and brought his hand to his heart, as if he were protecting it.

"I'm Elliot Shaperson," he said. "I'm so glad to meet you."

Leah opened her eyes now, on the beach, to find her daughter resting on her elbow and staring at her.

"That's what I felt with Dylan the first time we went out," Samantha said. "He called me and we met for coffee. Right away, he launched into a tale about jumping into freezing water to stop a Norwegian from harpooning a whale. I laughed, loving his daring, and then suddenly his hand was on the back of my neck. He had sneaked up and leaned across the table and was only a breath from me. And all of a sudden I thought, *Oh God. Oh God, this is what love is.* I knew it then, knew exactly what he would mean to me, at the very beginning. It was as if Dylan had thrown his own harpoon and lodged it in my chest."

"There's no greater thrill than that first moment when you realize a handsome man wants you," Leah said.

Samantha smiled and sat up once more. Leah watched her tilt her head toward the sound of Dylan's jet ski. Her eyes scanned the lake until she spotted him, jumping wakes, taking it as fast as it could go, mastering it the way he seemed to master everything.

"You're so lucky," Leah said. "You're at the very beginning, when everything he does intoxicates you, when his touch is still new."

Samantha turned and looked at her. "Are you trying to tell me something?"

Leah shook her head. "Only that you should cherish this time. There are other things to cherish later on, of course. Companionship. Being able to get into your flannel pajamas with curlers in your hair and know he won't leave you. But this time, the beginning, is the most special."

Samantha nodded and turned back to the lake. Her eyes once again sought out and found Dylan. They held him until he skied out of sight.

By five o'clock, Leah was feeling feverish from all the sun, and she sat beneath the umbrella. Most of the other sunbathers had left the beach, and Dylan and Samantha were alone in the water, splashing each other like children.

When Leah closed her eyes and listened to their splashing, she was transported back in time. Every summer day, she had blown up the wading pool in the front yard and Samantha and her friends had played in it, slapped their small hands against the water. Those were good years, when Leah was certain of what she was doing, who she was. She was Elliot's wife, Samantha's mother. She had PTA meetings, piano lessons to drive

Samantha to, friends to talk to about the difficulties and joys of raising children.

It was good until Samantha began to need her less. By sixth grade, Samantha was popular in school, had a group of friends, went to after-school choir practice and soccer and tennis games. Leah cleaned the house while she was gone, cleaned and cleaned and cleaned, and left messages for the other mothers, most of whom had found jobs and were no longer around to help guide her. Leah thought about going to work too, thought about it day and night until she was immobilized by fear. What could she do? She, who had never worked, never done anything but be what someone else needed, a faithful wife, a cook, a chauffeur, a good mother.

One morning, when Samantha was in tenth grade, she came into the kitchen and found Leah making pancakes.

"You'll do this all your life, won't you, Mom?" Samantha said, without malice, but without respect, too.

Leah poured the pancake batter onto the griddle, trying unsuccessfully to form it into the shape of an elephant.

"Do what?" Leah asked, although she knew.

"This. Make pancakes. Cook all day. Clean. Even when I'm gone, you'll still be doing it."

Leah slammed the bowl of batter down on the counter and turned on her daughter.

"Don't you dare judge me, Samantha," she said.

Samantha lifted her chin a notch and grabbed her books off the table.

"You think you have nothing to offer," she said. "It's just stupid. You're as smart as Dad. Smarter, probably. All my life you told me I could do anything. Why can't you?"

Leah turned her head away and breathed deeply until she stopped her stupid tears. She hated them, hated the fact that she cried when Elliot pounded his fist in anger. She tried so hard to control herself, and yet the tears were always there, waiting to come gushing out at the smallest criticism or slight.

"I'm happy," Leah said when she had herself under control. She heard Samantha snicker and then slam out of the house. When Samantha left for college, Leah told herself again that she was happy, that she simply didn't need to work. Every morning for the last seventeen years, after Elliot got up and went to the office, Leah had whispered "I'm happy. I'm happy" until she almost believed it.

Leah opened her eyes now and watched Samantha and Dylan in the water. Dylan pulled Samantha into his arms and slid his fingers down her back. He glanced around the beach, did not notice Leah sitting beneath the umbrella, and stroked his hand around Samantha's ribs. He leaned back and traced a finger over her breast. Samantha closed her eyes and pressed her breasts harder against him.

Leah shivered and shifted her weight. She felt the heat between her legs as she watched her daughter press herself into her lover, rub her hips against his. Dylan smiled. God, he had a wonderful smile. His hair was all wet and slicked back. He squeezed Samantha's nipple and Leah had to pull her legs up to her chest to control the tingling.

She closed her eyes, because she couldn't stand it. The thought of never being looked at again, the way Dylan looked at Samantha, was too much. The thought of never soaring, the way Elliot had made her soar that first day she met him, of never being wanted by a new man, never having another first kiss or touch, was like dying. It made her gasp; it sucked the air out of her lungs and stopped her heart.

It wasn't fair. Having a child was almost like being forced to disappear, molecule by molecule. This was supposed to be Samantha's turn for love, Samantha's turn for everything. But Leah was still alive. She still wanted someone to touch her the way Dylan touched Samantha, even if her breasts were not as appealing, if they sagged a little and were disfigured by rivers of blue veins. She was still eighteen inside, had a mind that raged, a body that craved pleasure. The terrifying thing was that she could be ninety, covered in wrinkles and liver spots—hideous to someone like Dylan—and her body would still lean toward his, she would still ache for him to touch her, to want her.

I am not dead, she screamed, trapping the words in her throat before they came out. She turned away from the lovers and angrily packed up her things. *I'm not just somebody's mother.*

That night, after returning from Lake Tahoe and eating a dinner of hamburgers and fried tomatoes because Elliot's excursion to the river hadn't netted any fish, Dylan and Elliot walked out onto the deck.

"You having a good time here?" Elliot asked, not looking at him.

"Great. I rented a jet ski today. Raised havoc all over the lake."

Elliot was quiet and scratched his head. From the very beginning, he had had no meeting ground with Dylan. What made a man devote his life to a cause? What kind of fire raged in his veins? How could he stand all the shouting, the fighting, the confrontations? The thought of spending even an hour in Dylan's shoes made the pain in Elliot's stomach flare up. He would rather die than lead Dylan's kind of life.

"You like selling insurance?" Dylan asked.

Elliot turned to him. "That's what I do."

"Yeah, but do you like it? Did you dream about selling insurance when you were little?"

Before he could regulate himself, Elliot's face clouded over in anger.

"When you were little, did you dream about ramming oil tankers and making hard-working loggers' lives hell?"

"Actually," Dylan said, "I did."

Elliot hesitated, then laughed. "Dylan, you're not like any man I've ever known."

Dylan smiled and Elliot knew that he had taken the words as a compliment. He liked being unlike other men. Elliot twisted his neck because it was so foreign a thought. When he was ten, Elliot had let his hair grow to his shoulders. At fifteen, he occasionally ditched school and went to the park with friends. But by the time he got married and had Samantha, that nonconformity had just seemed silly, out of place. He was a husband, a father, and although his own father had made a farce of his obligations, Elliot would not. He stopped drinking beer, said "darn" instead of "damn," and bought a sedan. He did not think he was a cliché; he thought he took his life seriously. Every night when he tucked Samantha in, he looked at her sweet face and knew he'd done his best by her.

"I like insurance," Elliot said. "It's not glamorous. It's not something I dreamed about. But the truth is, it keeps me humble and grateful. I go out to houses demolished by earthquakes and thank God mine is still standing. A husband comes in in tears to cash in on his wife's life-insurance policy, and as soon as he's gone, I call Leah just to hear the sound of her voice. Maybe it sounds awful, but I compare other families' calamities with the calm of my life and, like it or not, that does something to me."

Elliot gripped his hands into fists. He'd let out one confidence and as if that cleared the way for more, he could feel his secret beating at the back of his throat. Ever since Dylan arrived, Elliot had had the strangest desire to confide in him about his company. Dylan was so different from him, and he had the distance to see the situation clearly. Elliot could not tell Leah or Samantha what had happened; he couldn't let them know how badly he'd failed.

"I want to ask you something," Elliot said.

Dylan stood up straight, as if bracing himself against an interrogation.

"Your . . . organization," Elliot said. "You don't have a lot of money, right?"

Dylan shifted his weight. "Not a lot," he said. "We rely on contributions, and there are not many people willing to contribute to such a radical group."

"Exactly," Elliot said. "So you've got to find ways to keep your company alive, without funds. To cut corners."

"Right," Dylan said.

"Let's say you were in a different field," Elliot said, fidgeting a little. "Let's say, hypothetically, that you sold insurance, like me. That you've got your own company. You've had the same partner for thirty-plus years and then that partner gets himself into trouble and starts skimming off the top. When you finally find out, you're so deep in the red, you're not sure you're going to be able to pull yourself out. If your clients find out, they'll sue your heart right out of you."

Dylan's mouth dropped a little and, for some reason, that made Elliot thrust his chest out. He had thought he would feel both relieved and ashamed when he finally told someone about his partner's embezzlement. But the truth was that, in some strange way, Elliot felt proud. Proud that something monumental, something even criminal, had happened in his small life. Proud that he could shock a man like Dylan. He nearly smiled, then caught himself. What on earth was coming over him?

He hadn't told Leah because he was afraid he'd have to use their life savings to rescue the company and she'd be furious. He hadn't told Samantha because fathers were not supposed to get into jams like this. The situation was awful, horrible, financially disastrous, and yet that smile still danced around his lips and he had to shake his head to be rid of it.

"Maybe I'd turn my partner in and have him take the rap," Dylan said. "Then I could try to build up confidence in myself again."

"This man is your friend," Elliot said, coming back to himself, feeling the weight of his predicament again. "He has been your friend for more than twenty years and though you hate what he's done, it is not within your code of ethics to turn him in. Aside from that, your scheme does not make sense. You would be blamed as much as him for not seeing what was happening sooner."

Dylan turned and leaned against the railing.

"Well then," he said, "the first thing I would do is remove all access to funds from my partner. Everything would have to be funneled through me, every claim, every check, every pencil, for God's sake. I'd fire staff, because it's either me or them, and it sure as hell wouldn't be me. I'd work like hell to get more clients, and never let up on the rotten bastard until he repaid every cent. Then I'd hope to hell he could do it or I'd die before anyone figured out what had happened."

Elliot stood very still, staring up at the stars that were just beginning to appear in the purple sky.

"You are," he said, "very different from me."

Dylan laughed. "That's a very polite way of saying you think I'm a hard-nosed bastard."

Surprisingly, Elliot laughed. "Perhaps."

They laughed together for a moment and that's how Samantha found them.

"Well," she said, "*this* is nice."

She slipped into Dylan's arms and he buried his nose in her hair. They fell together so easily, so naturally, that Elliot stepped back and clutched at his stomach. He knew this was the way it should be, that she was a grown-up who could feel love and passion. He knew it and that knowledge singed his heart; it made him realize his job was done. She no longer needed him. In the way that mattered most to fathers, he had lost her. He turned away and walked back into the house.

"Sometimes I feel as if I've had enough of them to last a lifetime," Samantha said as she watched her father walk away. "Then, a second later, usually when they're gone, I nearly ache for them."

She remembered all the nights she had slept in the loft in the cabin, thinking of her parents below her, being content at their mere presence. Whenever she had heard a strange sound, or an animal outside, she had thought, *No need to worry. My parents will take care of it.* And they always did.

God, she hadn't thought of that in a long time, she realized. She had forgotten there was security better than any lock or a gun hidden beneath the mattress. There were parents who seemed to be there only for your welfare, who slew all the monsters, always kept you safe.

"My parents will outlive me, no doubt," Dylan said. "Their money is an elixir to them. Hell, they might live on it forever."

"Dylan, don't make jokes. I don't think you know how you'd feel if you lost them."

"I do. I'd be glad. Because despite all the money

they've made, they've never done a good thing in their lives."

"Dylan . . ."

He stared at her bitterly for a moment, as if she were his parents, but then his eyes softened, and Samantha stifled the urge to ask him about his life. She knew only bits and pieces of it. She thought of her parents, who knew everything there was to know about each other, who knew whole histories, habits and favorites, dislikes and quirks. God, it would be wonderful to know Dylan like that. For him to know her like that in return, so that she could stop being careful with all her words.

"Let's talk about you," Dylan said abruptly. "You've always been the good girl, done the right thing. I wonder what's going to happen now that I'm such a disappointment to your father."

"Nothing's going to happen," Samantha said. "I don't pick my friends according to their wishes."

"That's because all your friends, before me, were acceptable to them. I've felt a little like an offering. Another item in your list of accomplishments that you want Mommy and Daddy to be proud of you for."

Samantha yanked away from him.

"I'm my own person," she said.

"Are you?"

And in that slight hesitation before she said yes, she realized that she wasn't exactly sure.

Before she could think what that meant, he pulled her to him and kissed her. That kiss made her forget everything but the need to get closer to him. To her, his body was perfect. Not in form, but in the way touching it made her feel. He was thin and tan and chapped; his hair, as always, was wild. She could not get enough of him.

He unbuttoned her blouse and slipped his hand inside.

"Oh, Dylan," she said. "Who knew it could be like this?"

Elliot heard Samantha, and he blanched, then started for the deck. Leah grabbed his hand and pulled him back.

"Elliot, no," she whispered. "Please. Let them be. You'll only embarrass yourself."

He looked at her, distraught, and when Samantha and Dylan came in, hurriedly said good night, and nearly ran upstairs, Leah pulled him outside. He seemed unsure which way to go, and she slipped her arm around his waist and guided him. She felt him shivering beneath her fingers.

They said nothing for ten minutes. They took the path Elliot always took, because Leah knew it calmed him to walk somewhere familiar. She held on to him tightly and, after a while, felt him relax against her. She noticed, as they walked, that their strides were perfectly in step. She remembered, at the very beginning, how Elliot had taken huge steps and she had taken tiny, demure ones, and they had struggled to stay in line. When he had kissed her, they sometimes both leaned the same way and butted noses. But, over the years, he learned to lean to the left and she to the right, he shortened up his step or she lengthened—it was unclear which one of them had compromised—and now it was as if they had been in sync forever.

Her fingers reached only to the edge of his back now, not around his middle anymore. He had been so skinny, that day she met him in high school. He had eaten ravenously for the next few years and never gained an ounce. On the night he had proposed to her, the night he graduated high school—when she still had one year left to finish—he ate three helpings of pasta. They had gone to a small Italian restaurant and just after he took a bite of spaghetti, with a noodle still clinging to the side of his mouth, he had said, "Leah, I love you. I want to ask you to marry me now before anyone else has the chance."

She had wanted to leap with joy, but instead she had thumped her feet against the floor in suppressed victory.

"I have to graduate first," she said.

"Of course," he said, finally realizing he had food on his mouth and wiping it away. "And I'll find a job."

"You know Daddy wants you to go into his insurance firm," Leah said.

Elliot looked down and blushed. "I know. But I'd like to do something on my own first. I'm not sure what. Just something."

Leah squeezed her glass so tightly, she was sure it would shatter. She unhinged her fingers slowly and then laid them on top of Elliot's.

"I love you, Elliot. You know I'll marry you. We'll be happy forever."

Leah smiled now, as she walked with her husband. Such a sweet memory. When people asked her about those first years with Elliot, she always smiled. He had been such a sweet young man. So shy, so gentle, so concerned with doing things the right way. He had allowed her to make every decision about their wedding. He had saved every penny from his job as an artist for a local literary magazine so he could take her on a honeymoon to Reno. The magazine didn't pay him well, but he loved the work, loved creating abstract covers and reading the short stories and then developing illustrations for them. He was good, too, Leah remembered. But then the magazine folded, Leah got pregnant, and Elliot had done, as always, the right thing, and gone into her father's insurance business.

Bill Mangowitz, the son of her father's partner,

joined up a few years after Elliot, and the two of them took over most of the work. After the two senior partners retired, Bill had wanted to change the name of the company from McDermott Insurance to Shaperson and Mangowitz, but Elliot had refused. Leah's father had started the company on his own, built it into what it was, and Elliot was adamant that he always be given the credit for it.

Elliot had been selling insurance now for thirty-six years. After just a few years in the business, he had packed his art supplies away in the attic and hadn't touched them since. In the last few years, he had even stopped doodling on a pad when he talked on the phone.

They walked along Elliot's path, and Leah squeezed Elliot's middle.

"I was thinking about your art," she said.

He stopped suddenly and stared at her.

"Your child is probably having sex right now and you think about my art?"

Leah shrugged. "My grown daughter is definitely making love to a very attractive man and that's her business. We've been walking for ten minutes and my mind wandered. I was also thinking about when you proposed to me and ate three platefuls of spaghetti."

Despite himself, Elliot smiled.

"Best spaghetti I ever had was at Lucini's. It's a shame that place closed."

"You were so sweet. You are still the sweetest man."

He looked at her doubtfully, and Leah's heart broke. So it had come to this, to doubting each other's sincerity. She had friends who had awful marriages, drag-down, knock-out fights. She knew women who hated their husbands, called them bastards and villains.

She knew couples who had lived in silence for ten years because they couldn't stand to hear what the other had to say.

All those people looked at her and Elliot and thought they were the perfect couple. They were polite, courteous, and no one had a clue about her affair. Leah cooked and cleaned, Elliot did the dishes and mowed the lawn. What more could anyone want after thirty-seven years?

Leah blinked back tears. She wanted her husband to believe her when she told him he was a good man. She wanted to make love with him and say, as Samantha had said, "Oh, Elliot. I never knew it could be like this." She wanted to be excited when he came into the room, instead of seeing him the way she saw these familiar trees in this too familiar path, without interest or much care at all.

She wanted to be more disturbed by the fact that she was having an affair. She wanted to be racked by guilt, to give up James in a blaze of tears and agony, and then to run home to the arms of her loving husband.

But Elliot rarely opened his arms to her anymore. She wondered, if he found out about James, if he would even fight for her.

Elliot caught her tears and took a step back. Leah saw, in that movement, everything their marriage had become. When he tried to talk to her, she turned away. When she ran her hand over his hip in bed, trying to interest him in making love, he feigned sleep or pretended not to understand the implication.

Though people thought time together drew you closer, the opposite was true. The day she married Elliot, Leah felt part of him, joined body and soul. But then, as if the following years of marriage had been a steady, slow earthquake, the once solid rock they had been finally split in two.

Oh, she loved him. But what was love after thirty-seven years? Just a faded accessory. Just an undistinguished piece in your repertoire of emotions, with all its vibrancy faded to gray. A stiff offshoot of your heart, like the straight line on the monitor when the patient is dead. It just seemed silly, making love to someone you knew so well.

"Are you all right?" Elliot asked.

Leah nodded, not trusting her voice.

"Well, I'm not," Elliot said, walking again but this time keeping a two-foot gap between them. "I'm on edge. I don't ever remember being like them at their age."

"You were."

"We were younger when we first met. There were more rules about what you could and couldn't do."

"And sometimes we broke them."

"You're her mother," Elliot said. "Doesn't any part of what she's doing bother you at all?"

Leah stopped and touched his arm. He tried to keep walking, but she held him in place.

"It bothers me that you can't let her go. She's thirty-five years old, Elliot. Why do you look at this as if it is a loss to you?"

"Don't tell me that I'm gaining a prospective son-in-law. I don't want that. I want Samantha. I want things the way they used to be."

Leah smiled. "You'd hold her back in time if you could. You'd make her a girl forever."

"I would," Elliot said seriously. "If it meant that she'd never be like this. Have you heard her talk to him about anything important, about her dreams, what's in her heart? About anything other than how his touch makes her feel?"

Leah was quiet. She hadn't heard Samantha and Dylan talk at all. They joked with each other, but when they stole away to be alone together, it was not to stare into each other's eyes and reveal their souls. It was to touch, to kiss, to slip their hands under each other's shirts and touch skin.

"That comes later," Leah said.

"It didn't with us."

He was right. From the very beginning, there had been a mixture of passion and intimacy. She had trusted him with her secrets from the first day. It was only after years had passed that she started to hold back, to keep parts of herself in reserve, as if she were restocking what he had taken from her.

"She's not herself, Leah," Elliot went on. "You know how she usually rambles on about her career, about the latest campaigns, who's planning to run, what chances they have against the Republicans. Since she's been here, she hasn't once talked to us about her career."

"So?"

"So? Samantha always talks about her career. It's what she does. It's who she is. Before Dylan, she was excited about every part of her life. Now she's just excited about this one thing, this one man. He limits her. I know he doesn't mean to, I know he cares about her in his own way. But the truth is that instead of adding to her, he detracts. He makes her less than what she used to be."

"We can't stop her from loving him," Leah said quietly. "If you keep putting Dylan down, she'll only dig her feet in deeper. She'll cling to him no matter what her feelings are, just to spite you, to prove she can control her own life."

"That's just stupid."

Leah laughed. "Oh no it's not. It's what children, at any age, do to their parents. But if you let them be, if you welcome Dylan with open arms, either the two of them will grow together or they'll break up. And eventually, I promise you, Samantha will come back to herself. It's impossible to sustain their kind of passion. We all come back to ourselves, unfortunately."

They stared at each other in the twilight. They hadn't talked like this in years and Leah felt unusually alive. Her hands tingled and she swished them through the air. In the early years, when Samantha was little, the two of them used to lie in bed, unable to stop talking. Leah would look at the clock, feel guilty because Elliot had to get up in a few hours, but then have to share just one more idea with him.

They had never run out of conversation. Even after week-long vacations, when they spent nearly every second together, they still talked about what they'd done, what they felt, what they planned for the future. Gradually, all of that changed. First Elliot began to get more tired. He went to sleep before her and they couldn't talk in bed. Then they took to watching three hours of television at night instead of talking by the fire. Then, at dinner, as if they believed they were boring each other with the details of their daily routines, they began to give only outlines, the barest summaries. Then came the silences, minutes first, then hours of high-pitched stillness that at first disarmed them, but then became routine. There was no tension with Elliot, no need to keep the conversation going the way she had to with strangers, and so, sometimes for days, there was no conversation at all.

"Dylan is trying to make a good impression," Leah said. "You're not making it very easy for him or Samantha."

"How am I supposed to do that when they're screwing in my cabin?"

They both said nothing. As they stood there, twilight faded to darkness. The front edge of a storm was blowing in and it brushed Leah's hair against her cheek. Even in the growing darkness, she could see Elliot's hands shaking.

Elliot took a step toward her, but Leah stepped back.

"Leah, I'm sorry. I don't usually talk like that."

Leah was quiet a long time. She understood now, about Elliot.

"You look at them," she said, "and you see everything we're not. You see their passion and our lack of it. You see their sexuality and realize we never make love anymore. You hear them talking, laughing, and you think 'When was the last time Leah and I laughed?' They've got a new love; it's all shiny and sensual and breathtaking and, when you look at them, you realize you'll never have that again, unless you divorce me or have an affair."

She said those last words breathlessly, wondering if he could look through the darkness and see the truth in her eyes. He was very quiet. She could not even hear him breathing. Something moved in the pine needles behind her and she jumped a little as an animal darted past.

Finally, Elliot simply turned and started back for the cabin.

"You won't even talk to me about this?" she called after him.

"Why should I?" he said over his shoulder, still moving. "You've got me all figured out."

Leah ran up to him and grabbed his arm.

"No, Elliot. That's the trouble. I don't have anything figured out. I don't know anything anymore."

He shrugged her off and kept walking.

"Elliot, stop. Dammit, talk to me."

But Elliot said nothing, just kept walking, and Leah stood in the forest, watching him go.

7

"Too bad my parents didn't want to come," Samantha said as she and Dylan parked outside of Harrah's casino, on the Nevada side of Lake Tahoe. "I told them not to cry when we break the bank and don't cut them in."

She took her money out of her purse.

"I'm only going to spend ten dollars," she said. "All in nickel slots."

Dylan pulled a wad of money out of his pocket and Samantha gasped.

"I thought you were poor," she said.

"I am, most of the time. But if I know I'm coming to Reno or Tahoe to gamble, I save up. This is three months' worth of eating peanut butter."

"How much do you have?" she asked.

"Only three hundred."

"Dylan!"

"Dylan, what? There are few things you can get without working too hard or selling your soul, and I intend to follow through on this one. You play your silly slots and, when you're through, come find me at the roulette wheel getting rich."

As soon as they walked into the casino, Dylan headed for the roulette table and Samantha found a lucky-looking slot machine in the corner. She asked the cashier for ten dollars' worth of nickels and, one by one, put them in the slot and pulled the handle. She never bet more than one nickel at a time and saved all her winnings in a cup. When she was through, just half an hour later, she had increased her ten dollars to thirty-five.

She cashed in her nickels and went in search of Dylan. She found him holding court at the roulette wheel, with a woman on either side of him urging him on. Samantha did not know the rules of the game, but she understood the stack of chips in front of Dylan.

"What do you think, Katie?" he asked, turning to the blonde beside him. She looked to be about thirty-five or forty and was heavily painted. Even from across the roulette wheel, Samantha could smell her perfume. "You're my good-luck charm."

The woman giggled and Samantha stiffened. She noticed that Dylan's arm was around her waist.

"I think," the blonde said, "number eight."

"Eight it is!" Dylan said, putting half his chips on that number. The dealer spun the roulette wheel and Samantha watched the blonde press herself closer against Dylan.

"The number is eight, black," the dealer said, and the crowd let out a cheer. A new stack of chips was pushed Dylan's way and he kissed the blonde, then turned and kissed the woman on his other side, a skinny little brunette who could hardly have been more than eighteen.

Samantha pushed her way through the crowd that had gathered around Dylan.

"Aren't you going to cash that in?" she asked.

He looked up, surprised to see her. There was a look of irritation in his eyes that she'd never seen before. It made her feel ugly, the sour face at his party.

"Are you crazy?" Dylan asked. "I'm on a roll."

"But you've already won," Samantha said. "How much money do you have there?"

"Place your bets, please," the dealer said.

Dylan shrugged her off. "Baby, you're blowing my concentration."

Samantha squared her shoulders as he turned back to his blonde. She told him she wasn't sure what number he should choose this time. Dylan turned to the teenager, who smiled like a girl falling in love, revealing braces.

"How about eighteen?" the girl said. "It's my birthday today."

"Hey, everybody, it's Andrea's birthday!" Dylan said, giving her another kiss. He placed a good portion of his chips on eighteen and Samantha turned away in disgust. As she walked away, she heard the cheer of the crowd as the wheel came up on his number. She stopped and turned back to the dealer.

"How much money has he won?" she asked.

"Close to five thousand now."

Samantha gasped and thought about trying to reason with him again. But when she looked at Dylan's frenetic eyes, she knew he wouldn't listen. He tightened his grip on the women at his sides, while Samantha walked away with as much dignity as she could muster.

She found the bar. She chose a small table in the center of the room and polished off three beers waiting for Dylan to finish his sport. They had a video screen turned on full blast in the corner, so she couldn't hear the cheers or know how well or badly he was doing. She sat and watched MTV, sinking lower with every video, getting angrier with every second. She stared down at the table but didn't see it. Instead, she saw Dylan's hands around those women, his fingers digging erotically into the flesh of their waists.

He had told her he didn't want to be pressured; he needed the freedom to do what he wanted, go where he pleased, with whomever he fancied. It hadn't occurred to her until now that she had agreed to his terms only because she had been certain she was special enough to change him.

She ran her fingers through her long hair and signaled the cocktail waitress for a fourth beer. A man from the bar tried to catch her eye, but she ignored him. A second later, he sat down beside her anyway.

"I like a woman who drinks a good beer," he said.

Samantha looked at him. He was attractive, with short-cropped brown hair and a mustache. But then, she was well on her way to getting drunk and most of the men in the bar looked attractive to her now. She thought of Dylan, his fingers pinching those women's waists, and she smiled.

"I'm Samam . . . Samantha," she said.

"Wayne. You waiting for someone?"

He seemed ready for rejection and that made him more appealing. *This* man would not ignore her. *This* man would tell her his secrets.

"Nope," she said.

Wayne smiled and ordered a beer when Samantha's came. He started talking about his business, a car dealership in Reno, and Samantha struggled to hold the thread of the conversation.

"What did you say?" she asked.

"A convention," Wayne said. "A bunch of Western dealers are here on a convention. Left the wives at home."

He laughed, revealing stained teeth, and Samantha noticed, for the first time, the wedding band on his finger. She stared at it as if it were a hideous tattoo. She could not turn her eyes away. It was thin and silver and she could make out the green of his skin beneath it.

"You all right?" Wayne asked.

Samantha forced her gaze away from the band.

"Why do you wear your wedding band if you want to get laid?" she asked. "Laid" was not her kind of word, and she almost giggled. But she didn't. She felt too old for giggling, all of a sudden.

Wayne seemed surprised for a second, but then he relaxed and smiled. "It turns most of you girls on," he said. "Don't ask me why. You like the rush of stealing some other woman's man."

Samantha felt sick and stood up.

"You ready?" Wayne asked.

"I'm ready," Samantha said, and emptied her beer on his lap.

"You crazy bitch!" he shouted, knocking over the table in his haste to get away from her.

Samantha ignored him. She handed her empty beer bottle to the cocktail waitress and went to find Dylan. She looked around the casino, saw that there was a new crowd at the roulette wheel, and that he and the two women were missing.

There was a lounge filled with couches on the other side of the casino, and Samantha curled up on a sofa in the corner. She must have drifted off, because she woke to Dylan standing over her, softly touching her cheek. She jerked away from him and sat up.

"Where are your friends?" she asked.

He stepped back, glanced over his shoulder toward the casino, and then back at Samantha again.

"Katie went back to her husband a while ago. Andrea. . . is still in her room."

Samantha knew then what he had done, exactly what he was capable of. She sensed it in her bones; they stiffened like old wood on the verge of snapping. She thought she was the worst kind of fool, believing she was adult enough, liberal enough to agree to this kind of relationship. The truth was that if you loved someone, you couldn't share him. Anyone who told you differently was selling something.

She knew what she was supposed to do. She should smile, tell him that she understood completely that he had found another woman attractive, taken her up to her room, removed her clothes, touched her, made love . . .

The wind rushed out of her lungs. She tried to stand but couldn't, and was glad that she could pretend it was the beer she had drunk. Dylan reached for her hand to help her, but she pulled away.

"Where's your money?" she asked, trying to gather herself together, to force her head up, to remember she was Samantha Shaperson, a woman who had done just fine on her own until Dylan came along. He could screw every Andrea in the world and she would still be fine. She would.

Dylan shrugged. "Lost it," he said. "I was on a roll there for a while, but luck has a way of running out."

Samantha finally managed to stand up.

"You lost it all? You had five thousand dollars and you lost it?"

"Toward the end, it was close to seven thousand, actually." He laughed and Samantha stifled the urge to beat him. The tips of her fingers tickled, her feet ached with the weight of that urge. She was surprised by her own fury. Surprised too that she was able to control it, just like she had controlled her love for him for three months, kept it measured and logical and realistic. Kept its intensity hidden. Until now.

"You're a fool," she said, with more menace than she had intended.

He took a step back, as if he weren't seeing her

clearly this close up. He opened his mouth, then closed it. He took her arm and led her out to the car.

Dylan drove home. Samantha was surprised he knew how, because he did not own his own car and, up until now, she had done all of the driving. After tonight, however, she would not be surprised by anything he did. She didn't know a thing about him.

She looked out the window, watched the forest pass by in a blur of black. She could not make out trees or the river that ran along the side of the road. She wasn't sure if that was because of the moonless, cloudy night, or the effects of the beer, or because she felt empty inside and that colored the world black.

"You okay?" Dylan asked.

Samantha did not answer. She could not speak without exploding, and she couldn't explode without losing him. She knew this was how it would be from now on—her holding everything in, pretending an apathy she could never feel while he shredded her soul to bits with his unfaithfulness and indifference. She could leave him, but suddenly her legs felt leaden. How could you leave love, even bad love, when the love itself had tentacles that bound you? It would have been like ripping off her leg, to leave him. She must have told a dozen friends over the years to leave rotten lovers, and they had all agreed with her advice and then done exactly the opposite. She had thought them stupid and weak. Love, she realized now, made you that way. It sucked the strength right out of you.

Dylan rapped his knuckles against the steering wheel.

"You know what happened," he said. "With Andrea."

Samantha nodded; she was too afraid of words to speak.

"I figured you did," he went on. "Thanks for not

saying anything. God, I was afraid you'd blow up, like all the others."

All the others. Samantha dug her hand into her mouth, biting down on her knuckles to keep from screaming. She was the very opposite of special to him; she'd been lumped with all his women, stripped of distinctiveness.

"I'm sorry about this," he said. "I know we both agreed to the rules, but it's hard when you actually test them for the first time. After you've been with someone for a while, it's impossible not to feel a kind of ownership. But that's exactly what I can't stand, the fact that people consider other people their possessions."

Samantha bit down harder and blinked as fast as she could to stop the tears.

"I mean, you and I," Dylan went on, "we had an agreement. Other people were okay. Maybe my timing wasn't so good, though." He laughed, as if it were all nothing, as if he were telling this story to his best friend.

Samantha squeezed her eyes shut. Her mind said, *Stop. Please stop. Don't tell me any more.* But she couldn't take her hand out of her mouth long enough to speak, or the sobs would start.

"I've tried to be up-front," Dylan continued relentlessly, talking in that realistic, logical, completely unemotional voice that devastated her. He might as well have stopped the car and thrown her out. Who knew indifference could hurt so much? It was more devastating than cruel words or pounding fists.

"I never wanted to hurt you," Dylan said. "I never wanted to have to lie about where I was, who I was with. So I was with Andrea. It was no big deal. She's only eighteen, for God's sake. I won't be seeing her again."

The funny thing was, as Dylan was ripping her heart out, she was thinking also of Andrea. The girl probably thought she and Dylan had the romance of the century, that he would call, send flowers. Samantha, at least, had something to fall back on. A career. Her family. Friends. At eighteen, a girl had so few defenses, so little strength to withstand the Dylans of the world.

She finally retracted her fist from her mouth. She turned to him, saw the smug, satisfied smile on his lips, and dug her hands deep into the seat.

"You're a bastard, Dylan," she said. "A rotten, selfish bastard."

His face went white for a second and then he swerved to the side of the road and cut the engine. He turned to her.

"What?"

"You heard me. You're disgusting. It's not enough that you have to satisfy your male ego by fucking another woman under my nose. No, you have to pick a teenager, a girl who probably has visions of marriage by now. You're the worst kind of man because you have no idea what you're doing to the women you touch."

He stared at her, obviously stunned by her anger, and she hated him. Hated his surprise, hated that he could not see what he was doing to her. She hated him for not being the hero she thought he'd be, for not being gentle beneath his bravado. He was all bravado; there was no soft core beneath it and that was not fair. She'd thought there would be more to him.

The fury rose up from her stomach and shot into her fists. She pummeled them against his arms and chest. He didn't strike back, or try to stop her; he only protected his face and let her have her fill. She kept on hitting.

Finally, her arms felt leaden. She dropped her fists, put her head in her hands, and sobbed. She thought of Dylan and Andrea in a bed on a floor above the bar where she had sipped her beer. She thought of Dylan touching Andrea's wrists, sliding his finger along her collarbone, chilling her, drawing her out—doing all the things he'd done to Samantha with the same enthusiasm and emotion, as if a body were just a body and the soul inside of no consequence to him.

Dylan slipped his arms around her and, despite everything, Samantha let him hold her. She really was no good to anyone anymore, least of all herself. She should make him leave, but she couldn't. She should push him away, but her body rebelled and held on.

"I'm sorry," Dylan said. He pulled her tighter and Samantha buried her face in his chest. She curled her legs up on the seat as Dylan rocked her.

"I didn't know it would hurt you this much," he said. Samantha leaned back to look in his eyes. She wanted tears, but he didn't offer them. She could not find any hint of insincerity in his eyes and she didn't know if that was better or worse, if he was rotten enough to hurt her intentionally, or stupid enough not to understand that sleeping with another woman right in front of her was, at the very least, the worst insult a lover could give.

"I can't regulate my feelings," Samantha said. "I can't stop them at a certain point and not allow them to become more intense. I can't stop myself from feeling jealous."

"I can't be who I'm not," Dylan said. "I can't be normal and monogamous and your Prince Charming."

"I don't want that."

"Sam, I think you do. I made it all clear at the beginning, didn't I? This is how it has to be with me. I'm sorry."

Samantha pulled away and dried her cheeks. Dylan slipped back behind the wheel.

"I think you're scared," she said.

Dylan shook his head. "I'm not. It's not fear, it's a choice. I've seen marriage, I've seen long-term relationships, and they always end the same way, in silence and disappointment. I'd rather have beginnings over and over again. I'd rather leave when I'm just beginning to fall in love."

"What if it goes too far?" Samantha asked. "What if you fall in love too hard and then can't leave?"

She said this breathlessly, with her gaze turned away, and she waited an eternity for him to answer. Finally, he said, "That won't happen, Sam. Please don't wait for it to happen."

She had no air left, no strength in her arms, no words left in her vocabulary. She looked at him, sitting with his eyes closed, gripping the steering wheel. She wished to God that she knew what he was thinking, that, just once, she could be like her mother looking at her father and knowing everything there was to know. She wished she wasn't always guessing, shooting in the dark, taking steps in the wrong direction. She wished they were past this already, well into the stage when commitment and fidelity were accepted and expected, when faithfulness was what you gave freely, out of your heart.

Finally, Dylan opened his eyes. "I say all that," he whispered, "but I don't want to lose you, either. I've never known anyone like you."

The air rushed back into Samantha's lungs. Thick, warm, oxygen-rich air that she gulped. She tried to hold back, but could not. She reached out for him and Dylan held her, more tightly than she could have hoped. She gripped him, molded him to her, wondered if the trembling was coming only from her, or if it was possible that he was trembling, too.

"What will we do?" she asked, but Dylan did not answer, just went on holding her, breathing life back into her with his touch.

Dylan and Leah walked out the front door of the cabin, their hiking boots on. Samantha was lying down with a rare headache and Elliot had left at dawn to try his luck at fishing again. Leah stepped off the porch, spun around three times, then pointed to the west.

"That way," she said and laughed.

"Lead the way."

She started off, her feet skipping like a child's. Dylan had spent ten days with her, and she had not skipped before. When she walked with Elliot, her steps were slow, contained, matched perfectly to her husband's.

Leah ran into the forest, latched one arm onto a tree trunk, and spun herself around it. She swung from one tree to another, as if the trunks were hands she grasped in a playful square dance.

Dylan followed her, smiling. Ever since the episode at the casino two nights ago, his relationship with Samantha had been strained. And Elliot had not even attempted to warm up to him. It was strange, though, how easy things were with Leah.

She wanted to talk. Desperately. She had led him on three walks already, talking constantly as soon as they were out of range of the cabin. She had spoken a little about Elliot, a little about Samantha, but mostly about herself. On and on about love and passion and ambition and motherhood, as if no one had ever listened before.

"I never had any goals," she said abruptly today. She always started conversations like that, leapt right into the middle, as if she'd already carried on the first part of the discussion in her mind.

"Any goals for what?" Dylan asked, following her up the side of the mountain.

"For myself. For a career. Not like Samantha."

"So don't be like Samantha."

She stopped for a moment, looked back at him and smiled.

"I'm not," she said.

She did not follow any particular path through the woods. She carved her own, pulling herself up boulders and racing down hills.

"But I want something to look forward to," she said, checking left and right and then choosing a path through the trees to the right. "It's important to look forward, to plan for something. Don't you think?"

"I suppose."

"Dylan, it is. Let me tell you, it is. Otherwise you get into a rut. You stop caring. You can't get out of bed in the morning."

She did this all the time, acted as if she were talking in generalities when really she was giving him clues to herself. He never pried, never asked for more details; he wasn't sure if he even wanted to know.

"I don't have any goals," Dylan said, following her.

"Unless you can count getting through the day as one." He hoisted himself up on a rock and then down the other side. The sun was high and strong, but the forest shielded them from the worst of the heat.

"You do have goals. You just don't recognize them. You want to save the world. What bigger or better ambition is there than that?"

She stopped abruptly and whirled around to face him. She had been climbing and walking just as fast as him, but she was hardly even sweating.

"Do you work out or something?" he asked.

Leah tossed back her head and laughed like a reckless teenager. She had never laughed that way before.

"I go to the gym three times a week," she said, "for an aerobics class and a round of workouts on the equipment. Then I have a couple of smokes before I shower the scent of tobacco away so Elliot won't smell it. What do you think of that?"

She had her hands on her hips and a look of triumph on her face. Dylan had no idea what to make of her.

"I think that's an act more suited to a rebellious but scared teenager than a wife," he said. "Just smoke in front of him. Who the hell cares?"

Leah started up the mountain again.

"I like to get lost," she said, as if this were part of the same conversation. She did that too, went from subject to subject and expected him to keep up. She seemed to be miles ahead of him, in thought, in experience, in stamina.

"How come?"

"I don't know," Leah said. "I haven't really thought about it. Maybe because, no matter how hard I try, I always know where I'm going."

She turned around, smiled briefly, sadly he thought, and then went on again. Her short hair swished from side to side. Her shoulders were wide set, like Samantha's. She was trim, except for her waist, with wonderful, rounded hips and slim thighs. With the bounce in her step, it was hard to believe she was fifty-five.

They maneuvered through the woods, going up, coming down, hitting a dead end at the top of a cliff and having to backtrack to pick a new route. Leah talked almost constantly, flitting from subject to subject.

"Maybe I'll go back to school," she said. "Become a lawyer."

"I can't picture you as a lawyer."

"Why not? I've got the brains for it."

"Sure you do. But not the heart. Or the lack of one."

She laughed and moved slower as they traversed up the side of a granite mountain. She kicked out rocks beneath her as she climbed, all the while throwing out suggestions for careers that would never suit her.

"An accountant, maybe?" she said.

"Too dull."

"An actress?"

"Too self-indulgent. Besides, why do you have to do or be anything?" he asked. "Not everyone puts a career on the top of their list. I don't."

"But you love what you do," she said, stopping and taking a breath. Dylan saw her goal, the precipice, and the two of them determined the best way to get there. They'd have to make a sharp turn on the right and then zigzag up the granite face.

"I do love it," Dylan said, "but it's not a career. Not really. I didn't sit down and plan out what I wanted to achieve. I just loved the earth, and this was a way to help it."

"So are you saying I should just do what I love?"

"Why not?"

Leah shrugged and looked up toward the precipice. "Because I haven't a clue what I love, Dylan."

She started up the granite face. Dylan followed close behind, looking down occasionally at the valley spread out dizzily below them. He was mostly silent, concentrating on keeping his footing. Leah, however, went on talking, oblivious to the risk of falling.

"What do I love?" she asked herself aloud. "I don't know. Music, maybe. But I can't sing or compose. I love to dance, but I'm not very good. I love shopping. I love clothes. I love Samantha's clothes. I love those fabulous leggings they've got now, the ones with the stirrups. And big, man-sized, outrageously designed sweatshirts."

"So buy some."

"And wear them where? Elliot would laugh me out of the room if I came in wearing teenagers' clothes."

"I doubt that."

"What else?" Leah asked, still climbing, carving long switchbacks across the face of the mountain. They had to backtrack twice, when the route became too steep.

"I love romance novels," she went on. "But I can't write. Never could. The funny thing is, I loved math in school, just like the boys. I adored numbers and formulas and statistics. That's why I love it when you quote all those horrible cancer rates and the percentages of the rain forests that are being demolished yearly. I can understand it, when you put it like that."

"So come work for me," Dylan said without really thinking about it. "Be our statistician. God knows we need one, to update the information that comes in every day."

They were almost to the top of the precipice, but Leah stopped. She turned around and stared down at him and he realized his mistake. He could not have the mother of his girlfriend working with him. That would only add complications, more ties he would have to cut later on.

"You really need a statistician?" she asked.

Dylan put his hand against the mountain and leaned in to keep from falling. Looking at the valley hundreds of feet below him made his head swim.

"Well, we could use one, sure. But I'd have to clear it. We'd have to find the funds, create the position, check your qualifications. And it would be shit work. I shouldn't have said anything."

She stared at him until he finally met her gaze. He'd had her pegged as the soft one, but now he realized his mistake. She was tough as nails, and could see right through him.

"No," she said, "you shouldn't have said anything if you didn't mean it."

She whirled around and made the rest of the climb to the top of the mountain. Dylan followed after her and then they stood side by side and stared out over the majestic Sierra Nevada mountains.

On all sides, there were pines topped by granite mountains and bright blue sky. The wind whipped at them, threatened now and then to knock them back down the way they had come. Dylan sat down and, when Leah remained standing, testing her strength against the wind, he took her hand and pulled her down beside him.

"I'm sorry," he said.

She shrugged and held on to his hand. She moved her thumb over his knuckles.

"Whatever," she said. She was hardly sweating, while he was coated in moisture. He laughed.

"You've got more strength and stamina than I do," he said. "And more courage. You came up that mountain like a goat."

She pressed her thumb down hard on his knuckles and then let go. She dangled her legs off the side of the cliff.

"I'm fearless here," Leah said. "I'm not afraid of

heights or getting lost, and I'm sure as hell not afraid of anything in these mountains. But at home? I don't know."

For the first time, they lapsed into silence and Dylan remembered the sight of her and Elliot standing close together in the morning light. He had thought of Leah as a mother up until then. That was the first time he'd considered that she was somebody's lover.

"Do you love her, Dylan?" Leah asked suddenly.

Dylan was not surprised. He had felt Leah's questioning eyes on him from the moment he arrived. Whenever he and Samantha went out for a walk, the hairs on the back of his neck stood on end until they were out of sight of the cabin. He knew it was Leah who'd been watching them.

He slipped the rubber band out of his ponytail and shook out his long hair.

"I'm not the love type," he said finally. "I care about her. Samantha is . . . everything I could ask for. Beautiful, smart, strong. I should love her."

Leah turned away and looked out over the west ridge. A hawk soared above it and then dove into the trees.

"She loves you," she said.

Dylan nodded. He waited for Leah to tell him how unkind he was, leading Samantha on. Instead, Leah touched his arm. She ran her fingers down his forearm and rested her hand on his wrist.

"You've made her explore herself," she said. "She's never done that before, never really been introspective at all. God, you don't know what that was like for me. I've analyzed everything I've ever done, every word I've ever spoken. I'd ask her what she was feeling and she'd tell me nothing and mean it! It made me crazy."

Dylan laughed. "I've never thought much about my feelings, either."

"I don't understand that. Feelings are everything.

They're what life's about. Don't you look at Samantha and think, 'What do I feel for her? What is it exactly?' "

Dylan shook his head. "No. I just let it happen. I'm with her when I'm with her, but when she's gone, that's it. I go on by myself."

Leah kicked the backs of her heels against the cliff.

"Samantha doesn't," she said. "Not anymore. She never wanted to be emotional. She never wanted to be like me. I was the crier. I was too soft, too easily hurt. Samantha focused on Elliot from the beginning. He knew how to handle himself. He was practical, logical, and she emulated him. She's always been ambitious. Never had a soft bone in her body. The boys lined up for her, but she was oblivious. And then you came along and stabbed her through to her soul, and I don't think she knows exactly what to do."

"You sound pleased."

Leah turned and fixed him with a radiant smile. He sucked in his breath because, all at once, she was beautiful, young again, and deliciously devilish.

"Oh, you bet I am. This is my vindication. They've put me down, she and Elliot. They thought I was too histrionic, too feminine. But feelings aren't feminine, you know. You've got them. Elliot's got them. And now, by God, Samantha's got them. I want her to feel what I've always felt, know what it's like to drown in them."

Dylan stared down at her hand on him. Her nails were painted bright pink and she stroked her index finger back and forth across his skin.

"It sounds like I hate her," Leah went on. "But I don't. I just want her to live completely, experience everything. I love her more than anyone. I'd run through fire for her. I swear to God, I'd give up my life. Do you know what being a mother is like?"

Dylan shook his head and waited as Leah traced the bones in his fingers.

"It's like looking through a one-way glass," she said, "falling in love with the person on the other side and knowing they'll never see you or return the affection. It's a completely different thing, being a parent and being a child. Children rebel, they break away; parents don't. They can't untie their own chains. I'm bound to her, I adore her, I dream of her. But to Samantha, I'm just her mother, someone to be tolerated because she's family."

"She loves you," Dylan said.

"Of course. In the way a daughter loves a mother, with compassion and gratitude. But not with that burning around her heart, not the way I love her."

Leah slipped her fingers between his and squeezed.

"I don't want you to hurt her," she said. "I know you think you will. You think you'll tire of her and have to break her heart. But I'm older and wiser and I've seen something you haven't."

"What?" Dylan asked.

"I've seen how you look at her. I've seen love in your eyes."

Dylan tilted his head back to take the sun in completely. He closed his eyes.

"You may think so, Leah," he said, "but you're wrong. I care about Samantha. I'll do my best not to hurt her. But it's not love. Not your kind of love, anyway."

She jerked her hand away. He opened his eyes as she stood up, holding her arms out to the sides to catch the wind.

"Let me tell you something, Dylan Price," she said, practically shouting it down the mountain. "You don't know a damn thing about my kind of love."

She started back down the mountain, kicking up rocks and sliding more than walking.

"Leah!" Dylan called after her, but she didn't listen. She made it down in just under ten minutes and then was lost in the forest. Dylan inched his way down slowly, feeling shaky all of a sudden and clubfooted.

That night, Elliot dealt the cards for a game of hearts. Samantha had the low score, as she always did. She was a better bluffer than anyone. She'd show just the right amount of concern while she was picking up all the hearts and then, before they could stop her, she'd nab the queen of spades too and they'd all be stuck with twenty-six points and a yearning for revenge.

Elliot loved playing hearts. He loved playing gin rummy and old maid and crazy eights and Monopoly and Life. Thanks to abominable television reception, he and Leah and Samantha had sat at this table nearly every night they came to the cabin, playing games, laughing. Often, over the years, he would catch Leah's eye and smile, and she would smile back, and his heart would leap. If he'd had the words, he would have told her how happy she made him, how good his life was, how proud he was of her and his daughter.

Tonight, he looked over his hand and knew his best bet was to pass his three aces to the right. He did that, and then Samantha passed him three low spades and he figured she was going to try to shoot the moon again.

"Two of clubs starts," Elliot said, as he said every hand of every game, as if someone might have forgotten. Dylan had never played the game before tonight, so Elliot said this mostly for his benefit. He was sitting to Elliot's right, deep in concentration, looking at the cards Elliot had just passed him.

Leah threw out the two of clubs and they began. Elliot tapped his foot on the wood floor, as if there were music playing. The others had been noticeably quiet throughout the game, but he didn't mind. He didn't even mind Dylan being here tonight. It was nice to have a foursome. It was nice playing cards, eating popcorn, having his family around him.

The round intensified as Samantha started picking up hearts and feigning concern.

"You're going for it," Elliot said.

"Of course not, Dad," she said. "I haven't got a chance in hell." Then she laughed, full and deep, and Elliot stiffened.

He had heard that laugh before, a long time ago, in Leah. She had been a real laugher at Samantha's age. She used to throw her head back, stretch her mouth as wide as it would go, and let out a holler that shook the floor. And then once, just once, Elliot hadn't thought before he spoke and had said, "You might want to tone that down a little when people are around, Leah. It's not altogether feminine." Leah had stopped abruptly and had never done it again, not when he had bombarded her with jokes he learned at the office, not even when he pushed his own laughter louder in the hopes that she would join in. He was never able to undo the damage of his words. Every time Leah laughed a small, decorous, subdued laugh, he cringed.

Elliot forced his concentration back to the game. He wished now that he had saved one of his aces, so that he'd have a shot at stopping Samantha himself. He looked at Dylan, wondered if he understood the rules of the game completely.

"We can't let her get all the hearts again," he said.

Dylan shook his head. He seemed annoyed, intense. "Of course not."

Elliot sat back in his chair. He and Dylan and Leah were supposed to work together. Their scores were inching toward one hundred apiece while Samantha only had sixteen. The game would be over unless one of them stopped her.

Samantha threw out the king of clubs. Leah looked

at Samantha and then tossed out the three of hearts. Elliot's heart raced. He knew Dylan had the ace of clubs. He'd play it, pick up a heart, and Samantha would finally get some points against her.

Dylan looked over his cards, hesitated, and Elliot sat forward. Dylan reached for a card and threw it out. It was the ten of clubs.

"Are you crazy?" Elliot shouted.

Dylan threw down his cards and stood up.

"Look, I don't know what you want from me."

"I want you to play the ace of clubs and take a heart. She's shot the moon practically every time. Don't you understand the rules?"

"Obviously not."

"Let me explain them again," Elliot said through clenched teeth.

"Christ," Dylan said and then stomped out of the cabin, slamming the door behind him.

The room was suddenly quiet. Leah blinked back tears.

"What?" Elliot said. "You can't say that was my fault. He had absolutely no idea what he was doing. It wasn't fair to the rest of us."

Samantha stood up. She came around behind him and rested her chin on the top of his head.

"You can be such a silly man," she said.

She kissed his cheek and then went out after Dylan. Elliot sat opposite his wife at the table. He stared at her, but she did not meet his gaze.

"I just wanted him to play the ace of clubs," he said. "I knew he had it. Any fool would have known—"

Leah waved his words off. She sat motionless and his right arm began to shiver. He held it with his left.

"What are our plans for our thirty-eighth anniversary?" she asked.

"I beg your pardon?"

Leah looked up. He had looked into her gray-blue eyes for so many years, and yet now they looked completely strange to him.

"I want to know what we're planning to do," she said. "We passed by our thirty-year anniversary as if it were nothing. Thirty-eight years would be a big deal to some people. Are we going to go to Europe, take a cruise, what?"

Elliot shook his head. Now his left arm began to shiver too and he couldn't control it, either. He stood up and paced around the floor. He could sense the beginnings of something bad, something he might not be able to control. Leah's voice had an edge, his arms were shaking, the room had suddenly turned ice-cold. He thought, briefly, of fleeing, but then he realized how ridiculous that would be, a man running from words as if they were bullets.

"It's not until next April," he said. "I hadn't thought about it."

Leah slumped into her seat. From this angle, Elliot could see the gray roots in her hair. He never told her when he saw them; he knew she couldn't stand her signs of age. He never mentioned the wrinkles around her eyes either, or the extra weight in her stomach she never lost after Samantha, or, especially, the things he knew about her.

"Then I suppose it won't be Europe," she said. "That takes a little bit of planning."

"Leah, what are you saying?"

Leah's body went rigid, like steel piping, and her mouth tightened into a firm line.

"I'm saying," she said, "that we will have been married for thirty-eight years next April and I think that deserves something. Not a dinner out. Not flowers or a goddamn bracelet. Something more. Something!"

She kicked her chair back and stood up and Elliot had the craziest notion that, over the ten days of this vacation, she had altered every cell in her body. Every morning, she was a little different. Her eyes were set farther apart, her fingers were a little bit longer. Pretty soon, she would walk into the room and he wouldn't even recognize her.

She stormed toward him and he stepped back. His heart was beating so frantically, it vibrated his chest.

"I want to go to Europe," Leah said. "You know I've always wanted to go. I want to stay in fancy hotels and eat out for every meal and spend tons of money. I want to see Paris and dance in a fountain and be your lover again."

She said this all in one breath, like a round of automatic gunfire, and the rapid-fire beating of Elliot's heart bruised the inside of his chest. Leah seemed so young again, vibrant, and he felt so old.

"Leah, honestly, we don't have the money for all that."

"Like hell we don't. What have you been working for all these years, if not to live a little now and then? What is the point of wealth if you never use it to be happy?"

She reached out and gripped his shoulders. He stared at her tanned arms, wondering when they had gotten so dark. He noticed too that her muscles were well defined, chiseled, not the arms of a fifty-five-year-old.

He thought of the money in their savings account, the money he had been planning to pour into his company to make up for his partner's indiscretions. All the secrets he'd kept, all the lies he'd whispered in exchange for a smooth life, nearly overtook him, like the shadow of an oncoming train while he stood waiting stupidly on the track.

"I am happy," he said, trying to soothe her, to bring

back the woman he knew. "I'd love to take you to Europe. Maybe two years from now, for our fortieth. We could—"

She stepped away from him and wrapped her arms around her stomach. He took a step forward, then stopped when he saw her shiver.

"You have no idea what's happening to us, do you?" she asked.

Elliot shook his head. He really didn't. Everything had been fine; they were happy, content. He had made sure their lives were peaceful. She didn't complain and he didn't come clean. As long as nothing was said, it was possible to ignore the facts, to pretend everything was as it should be. It was a precarious balance, he knew, but he had kept it.

Then they had come here to the cabin, that damn Dylan had unbalanced them, and now he wasn't sure what was going on. Leah was angry, he was feeling things he never had before, Dylan could not pick up a simple game of hearts, and no one was explaining anything to him.

"No, Leah," he said quietly. "I'm at a complete loss."

She turned around suddenly, gave him a little smile that touched his heart, but then set her mouth in a firm line again.

"You wanted a calm, passionless life and that's what you've gotten. You won't have it any other way."

"You wanted that, too," he said.

"Oh no. I wanted you. I wanted passion. I still want it. I want tons of it, in fact. I want to breathe it morning, noon, and night."

Elliot stepped away from her. He could not stand it when she talked like that. It ripped a hole in that cover over his heart.

"You don't sound like you," he said.

Leah shook her head furiously. "This is me. This

is what I feel. I've never told you before. I've hidden everything inside. I've . . . had outlets."

Breathe, he told himself. *Breathe.*

"And then we came up here with Samantha and Dylan," Leah went on, wandering around the living room, touching objects, smiling strangely. "I've had to watch them. They've ignited me somehow. They can scarcely control themselves. All they've got is passion. It's so heady, they lose their minds. They say and do things they shouldn't. They fight, they make love."

"It sounds awful," Elliot said.

Leah laughed. "Oh, it is. And it isn't. It's glorious *and* brutal. We had that too, Elliot. Don't you remember that year before we married?"

"We didn't fight," Elliot said.

Leah walked over to him and grabbed his hands.

"You had a girlfriend before me. Lydia."

Elliot closed his eyes. Lydia Sculler. He hadn't thought about her for years. Lydia, with long blond hair and legs that drove him wild. Lydia, who did something with her tongue that turned him to jelly.

"After you proposed to me," Leah said, "you met with her one night, for old time's sake. I'm still not exactly sure what you two did."

Elliot opened his eyes and stared at her.

"I'd forgotten."

"I know it. But we fought, Elliot. Don't you remember? My friends told me they'd seen you and Lydia together and I waited at your house until you came home. I wanted to claw your eyes out. I think I tried to. I hated you, and I loved you. I cried, and you cried, and you promised you'd never hurt me again. I hit you and you pulled me into your arms and I screamed and you begged and the making up was glorious."

Elliot's stomach tightened. He remembered that night with Lydia. He had never doubted his love for

Leah, but he had doubted his wisdom in marrying her when he hadn't slept with anyone else. Lydia had been willing to solve his problem for him, but he had pulled away at the last minute. The act of sex was nothing, he had realized. Just a few moves anybody could do. But when you coupled it with love, well then, that's when you had something nearly magical. That's what he used to have with Leah.

"Look at me," Leah said. He looked into her eyes. How funny that the eyes never change. The face decays around them, the hair turns gray, the body disintegrates. But the eyes stay exactly the same shape and color, revealing the same soul.

"We fought like Samantha and Dylan, we loved just as passionately as they do. You slipped in my window one night. Remember?"

Elliot nodded, although the memory was gray.

"You crawled into my bed," she went on, "and begged me to let you make love to me before the wedding. You touched me and kissed me so perfectly. I can still remember. I can still feel it, if I close my eyes and lie perfectly still."

"I felt out of time," Elliot said, smiling, remembering clearly now for the first time in years. "I thought I would die when I touched you, because you were so soft, and so beautiful."

They stared at each other and then Elliot reached out and touched her arm. He waited for the same emotion, the same awe, but it was not there. She was still beautiful, still soft, but she was just Leah now, and he had been touching her for thirty-eight years.

She saw the disappointment in his eyes and looked away. She blinked back tears and then finished the story.

"My father walked down the hall and broke the spell. He said, 'Leah, are you all right?' Your erection instantly disintegrated."

Elliot laughed a little and Leah brought his hands to her chest. "The day you got the job at the literary magazine," she said, "you drove up to school and stole me out of class. We drove to—"

"To San Francisco," he finished. "We rode the cable cars and I bought you a silk scarf, and then we crossed the Golden Gate and found that beach in Sausalito and you dared me to go in the water."

"And you did, Elliot. You dove straight in and practically got frostbite. God, I loved you that day."

He stared at his wife. "You've been remembering these things all these years," he said.

"Yes."

"You knew I'd forgotten, didn't you?"

"Yes. Because you've made yourself believe that passion is bad, that it's what your parents had and it only leads to heartache. But that's not true. Our passion led to love, Elliot."

Elliot pulled his hands away. He walked to the window and leaned his head against it. His arms stopped twitching now that he knew he had to tell her the truth, but that was because he was too frightened to move. He was a logical, down-to-earth man, and yet just before he spoke, he sensed the ghost of his father passing just behind him.

"I can't take you to Europe," he said. "Bill Mangowitz has been embezzling from the company. I've got to replenish the funds with our savings. Otherwise, there won't be any company."

He heard Leah gasp, but he didn't turn around.

"When did you find this out?" she asked.

"Six months ago."

Leah started crying and when he turned around, she was leaning against the back of the couch.

"You had no intention of telling me," she said.

"What was there to tell? That I had been a fool? That I might be out of a job?"

She shook her head in disbelief.

"All these years," she said, "I thought the one thing we had left was trust. But we don't even have that. You couldn't tell me your biggest secret and I—"

Just then, Dylan and Samantha came in through the front door. Samantha stopped when she saw her mother.

"Mom?" she said, coming toward her, but Leah ran to the bedroom before she could reach her.

The really scary part, Elliot thought, was that he had finally told his secret, but he felt no relief. What he did feel was that he'd just opened up a hole in himself wide enough to get words through. He felt like a champagne bottle someone had started to uncork and then forgotten about, with all that harnessed pressure working on the small air leak until, one day, it would shatter the glass with its eruption.

Samantha was staring at him, waiting for him to explain. The truth was, Elliot would have liked someone to explain it all to him. He squeezed Samantha's shoulder going past, then went after Leah.

Late on their last night at the cabin, Samantha slipped out of bed and crept out the front door. It was raining, and she turned her face up to the black sky to take the pelting raindrops in her eyes and nose and mouth. She twisted her neck, loosened the stiff joints that had plagued her since she and Dylan went to the casino together.

She was about to step back inside when she noticed a light on the deck. She walked quietly around the side of the cabin and saw her mother standing near the railing, smoking a cigarette under the shelter of the overhanging pine trees. Samantha stopped abruptly, literally did a double take. She had done the same thing this morning when she came down for breakfast and found her mother drinking gin straight from the bottle. Leah had put the bottle back beneath the sink before she noticed Samantha watching.

Now, Leah inhaled deeply on the cigarette and then blew the smoke out in a furious gust. Samantha was about to step back into the shadows when Leah spoke.

"What is so goddamn awful about having a cigarette?"

Samantha walked up the steps to the deck. The wood was slick now, from the rain, and she gripped the railing. She stood beside her mother, or whoever this woman was who'd invaded her mother's body.

"What's going on, Mom?" she asked, although the truth was she really didn't want to know. She just wanted her mother to fix it, to patch things up with Elliot, to crush her cigarette out and toss away the bottle of gin and go back to being who she was supposed to be.

Leah shrugged and took another drag. Samantha watched her, amazed that the act of smoking could so drastically transform a person. When Leah sucked on her cigarette, she scrunched her face up to keep from getting the smoke in her eyes, and in that act she looked old and tough and completely alien.

"I'm just sick of it all," Leah said, waving her cigarette in the air and leaving trails of red light in the darkness.

Samantha turned her head away. Her forehead began to throb and she massaged her fingers against her temple.

"Your father's partner has been embezzling from him," Leah went on. Samantha whirled around and stared at her.

"Bill?"

"Yes, Bill. And Elliot will not turn him in. He wants to use up our savings to pay the company back."

Samantha stood there, stupefied, feeling as if she'd swooped down on a strange, new family and set herself in the center of lives she didn't understand.

"When did this happen?"

"Six months ago. The bastard didn't even tell me."

Leah crushed her cigarette beneath her toe and then paced around the deck. She was wearing one of Elliot's work shirts and it dangled just above her knees. Her hair was loose and every time she walked away from the shelter of the trees, rain plastered it down.

"He probably thought he was protecting you," Samantha said.

Leah stopped and glared at her. "Do I look like I need protecting?"

Right now, she did not. But until two weeks ago, Samantha would have answered that Leah needed the utmost protection. Samantha could still remember her mother lying in bed three years ago, unable to get up, do anything. What had happened to that woman? Did two therapy sessions really cure a depression like that? Did cigarettes and gin give you this much courage?

"No, Mom," Samantha said.

Leah nodded and started pacing again. She clenched and unclenched her fists; she stomped her small feet into the deck; she tossed her arms about. Samantha had the strangest feeling that Leah was erupting right there in front of her.

"You go on and on and you think it's worth it," Leah said. "You pretend and smile and make jokes about things that kill you inside because it's the right thing to do."

Samantha glanced at the house. She wanted to run, wanted to flee and then come back and change this scene. She did not want to be surprised by the passions her parents were still capable of. Truthfully, she didn't want them to be passionate at all. It seemed silly, her mother flailing around, smoking and drinking, acting like a teenager.

"And then," Leah went on breathlessly, grabbing Samantha's arm and peering into her eyes, "and then you wake up." She snapped her fingers and smiled strangely. "You wake up and realize you can't stand it. You're still alive but you're dying inside. You know you'll kill yourself if you can't break out and *live* a little."

"I don't know what you're talking about."

Leah released her grip and stepped away. She leaned against the railing again, slipped her hand into Elliot's shirt pocket, and pulled out another cigarette.

"Don't think I don't love him," Leah said, lighting her cigarette. Samantha realized then that her mother was talking to herself, working things out in her mind. She stepped away, shivering. The rain had soaked her shirt and chilled her. She glanced up at the window of the loft, thought of Dylan sleeping inside. No matter what he'd done with that girl, no matter how confused she was about him, she longed to be back in his arms.

"I'm tired, Mom," she said.

Leah waved her away and then went right on talking.

"I love him. I do. But what is that, after thirty-eight years? It's nothing. It hardly moves me at all."

Samantha turned her back on her and forced herself not to run inside. She reached the sliding glass door and could hardly open it because her hands were shaking so badly. Finally, she got a grip and slid the door open, then hurried up the stairs to the loft.

She peeled off her wet clothes and, naked, got into bed beside Dylan. He mumbled something in his sleep until she pressed her cold body against him. He opened his eyes, stared at her, and then kissed the tears that mingled with rainwater on her face.

"What is it?" he asked.

"Just make love to me," she said.

He hesitated, then kissed her, and Samantha took him into her hungrily.

• • •

The four of them packed in silence. Dylan and Elliot took the bags down to the cars while Leah and Samantha vacuumed and dusted and pulled the sheets back over the furniture. Samantha put her hand on Leah's shoulder.

"You all right?" she asked.

Leah turned to her daughter. Last night was mostly a blur. She had sneaked down after everyone had gone to sleep and finished off the bottle of gin. Then she had walked outside and stood in the rain, smoking the entire pack of cigarettes she'd driven to Tahoe for that afternoon. At some point, Samantha was there, and Leah had said things she shouldn't have. She couldn't remember exactly what. So many thoughts had been running around in her brain, she wasn't sure which she'd spoken and which she'd only thought.

"All right?" she said. "What does that mean?"

Samantha stepped back. "I don't know. Last night you just seemed . . . not yourself."

Leah laughed gruffly. "Not myself. That's not really possible, is it, Samantha?"

Samantha dropped her hand from her shoulder.

"Are you angry with me?"

Leah nearly stomped her foot. Of course she was angry. Who wouldn't be angry at a daughter who did not understand that her mother had feelings. She was a person, not just a shoulder for Samantha to cry on, or a bank account she could draw on, or a sage there for advice to help her with *her* life.

Leah walked away without answering and checked the kitchen cupboards again to see if they'd left any food behind.

"Did you and Dad make up?" Samantha asked.

"Make up for what? We never fight. You should know that by now."

Samantha's jaw slackened and Leah waved her off.

"Please stop being surprised by me," Leah said. "What do you all think, that I'm dead inside?"

"No, Mom, I just . . ."

Dylan and Elliot walked back inside, glanced at them, and then took off to their respective bedrooms to look for something else to do. Leah started the vacuum and headed for the living room.

She was boiling inside. Her blood was bubbling and simmering and steam was rising toward her nostrils and ears. Pretty soon, she'd either start screaming all the things she'd held in over the years, or she'd grab Elliot as he passed and start pummeling him. She wanted to beat him senseless, so that for once he would understand her; he would know what it was like to live a life without any sense in it.

Suddenly, Leah remembered James. His wife was out of town and she was going to his house tonight. She could fling off her clothes and make him do the things *she* wanted him to do. She'd grab him before he reached for his rope and gadgets and show him that she was exciting enough on her own.

Leah pushed the vacuum cleaner faster, imagining James's hands on her, his lips on her neck. How much longer? She stared at the clock. Seven hours until she could be with him. She vacuumed wildly, flinging the machine up and back.

Over the hum of the motor, she heard Dylan come down the stairs. He said something to Samantha and Samantha laughed. Leah rammed the vacuum cleaner into the wall.

Suddenly, there were hands on her shoulders and someone pulled the plug on the vacuum. Leah turned around, furious, to find Dylan standing behind her and smiling.

"You look like you're ready to go forty rounds with someone," he said.

Leah did not smile. They were teasing her. She

looked at Samantha and saw the sparkle in her eyes. Even after last night, Samantha did not understand. She wanted to believe Leah was just having a bout of temporary insanity. But the real insanity had come before, when Leah had pretended to be subdued when really she wanted to dance and shout and let loose. It was insane to think she could fake it forever.

"Don't patronize me," she said to both of them, wrapping the cord.

"Mom, we're not," Samantha said.

"Like hell you aren't. Take your grand little passion and go," she said. "I'm sick to death of watching you."

The two of them looked at each other and then Dylan headed for the door. Samantha, though, came over to Leah and put her arm around her.

"Have I done something?" she asked.

"You've taken all I used to have."

"You're talking in riddles. Tell me what you mean."

The boiling stopped for a moment and Leah fell against her daughter.

"Nothing. I'm sorry. I've lost my mind."

"If you're worried about Dad and the company, don't be. He always works things out."

Somehow, Leah found it within her to laugh. "You are so amazingly naïve when it comes to us," she said. "Sometimes even fathers can't work things out. I swear, Samantha, I think Elliot and I did you more damage than good by being happy and stable while you were growing up."

"How can you say that?"

"Because you have no clue that we struggled for it, that we're still struggling. You're so surprised when we're unsure, or when bad things happen to us, as if you're the only one who's allowed to be confused or to suffer or feel ecstasy. We're still people, even if we are parents. We go on living until we die."

"I know that."

"No, Samantha," Leah said, "I don't think you do."

They finished cleaning. Elliot and Leah made their last pass-through, avoiding each other by at least three feet whenever they crossed paths. Leah checked all the drawers and closets while Elliot fastened the locks on the windows.

"I think we're ready," he said, when they finally met again in the living room.

"Fine."

"Leah . . ."

She looked up and saw him struggling. He was pale and she knew he, like she, had not slept last night. She thought about helping him out, giving in, smiling. Then the boiling erupted in her veins again and she stood up straight.

"It's nothing," he said. "Forget it."

They locked the front door and stood with Dylan and Samantha on the porch. They were quiet, and though this was usually the moment when Leah shone, when she put everyone at ease, told them all what a great time had been had, this time she was silent.

"You won't go through Tahoe on the way back, will you?" Elliot said to Samantha. Before she could answer, Leah jumped in.

"For God's sake, Elliot, Samantha can find her own way. Leave her alone."

Elliot turned away and Leah watched both Samantha and Dylan lower their heads.

"What is it with all of you? Can't you stand a little honesty?"

Dylan was the only one who looked up and he did it only for a second, to wink at her. The gesture shook her, sent the boiling blood into her breasts and down between her legs.

"We probably should just go," Samantha said.

She walked over to Elliot and held him tightly. Leah looked at Dylan. He was staring longingly at the car, obviously eager to get away. And that, she thought, was what she wanted more than anything. To get away. To see something new, be something new. Dylan looked up, caught her eye, and held it. She felt that tingling again.

Samantha came over to her next and hugged her.

"I'll call you when I get home," she said, as if Leah had asked her to, the way she usually did. Leah nodded. She waited eagerly for Dylan to come to her.

Dylan shook Elliot's hand, muttered a thank-you, and then turned to Leah. Her body jerked as he leaned forward. He kissed her cheek and the heat rushed to her head, made her dizzy. She slipped her hand around his waist, squeezed him, managed to get one finger up beneath his shirt. His skin was hot, on fire.

"Well," he said, stepping back. "Thank you both. You have a beautiful cabin and we had a great time."

Then he and Samantha were off and Leah cringed at the sight of his arm around Samantha's waist. He led her around to the driver's side and closed the door after she got in. Then he waved once more, got in the car, and they were off.

Leah turned to Elliot.

"I want to get home right away," she said.

Elliot seemed startled that she had spoken.

"What? Why? I thought we'd make our usual trek through the back roads. Stop at the river you like so well. I already made the sandwiches."

But Leah was shaking her head, thinking of the heat of Dylan's body, thinking of James standing naked in the center of his office, the rope in his hands. She ran her fingers down her hips, hardly able to stand it. She was going to his house tonight. He'd stop the boiling, or heat her up so majestically that she'd finally erupt.

"No," she said. "I'm not in the mood. I've got plans for tonight. With a friend. Let's get out of here."

She walked down to the car, felt Elliot hesitate and then, as if he had no choice, follow her.

Samantha followed Dylan into his apartment and collapsed on his opened sofa bed. He had a small studio, with hardly enough room for the couch bed and a coffee table. He walked into the corner of the room designated as the kitchen, with a half-sized refrigerator, two electric burners and no oven, and took out a bottle of whiskey. He poured her a drink and handed it to her.

She downed it all at once, coughing from the heat, and asked for another.

"You survived," he said, pouring out more whiskey. "Hell, *I* survived. That's the real feat."

Samantha sipped the second glassful. Dylan sat down beside her and slipped his hands up beneath her shirt. He had a quick vision of Leah's finger sliding across his rib, but he pushed it away.

"Come on," he said, "three times in two weeks is like nothing at all. I've been going crazy wanting you."

He took her drink away and pushed her down. He was surprised at her stiffness, but he figured he could ease that away. He kissed her neck, slipped his hand down over her breast. She shivered a little, but then she went stiff again.

"Is there a problem?"

Samantha stood up abruptly and grabbed her drink. She downed it and then held on to the kitchen counter.

"Your arithmetic is off," she said. "I believe you had at least four fucks in two weeks. That is what you call them, right? Fucks? I suppose the word suits what you do."

Dylan sat up. "All right," he said.

"You wore a condom with that girl, right?" she asked.

"Yes."

"Well, at least you had some sense. I'm surprised by that."

Dylan stood up. This was unbelievable. These last two weeks were unbelievable. He had done what he never did, agreed to meet a woman's parents, agreed to spend two fucking weeks with them, and all it had gotten him was screwed. Samantha's father hated his guts, her mother was either psychotic or hot for him, and Samantha had suddenly become demanding.

"Don't be like this," he said.

Samantha's face fell. She started for the door, but Dylan grabbed her hand. He spun her around, but she yanked herself away.

"Don't grab me like that," she said.

"Don't treat me with contempt," he shouted.

"I will as long as you deserve it."

They stared at each other and Dylan had the strangest sensation of sinking. He tried to hold onto Samantha, but the feel of her skin made him fall faster, and he pulled his hand away.

"This is what I hate," he said. "We start to mean too much to each other and, with that, comes all these strings and conditions and rules. People are better to one another as acquaintances than they ever are as lovers."

Samantha turned and started for the door again.

"Samantha," Dylan said, his voice hardly sounding like his own. It was weaker, softer. "Don't go."

She stopped. She touched the door, leaned her forehead against it. Her long hair spilled all over her back.

He came to her and wrapped his arms around her waist. He dipped his nose into her hair and held her tightly. He thought back to that night at the casino. He couldn't even remember why he had taken Andrea up to her room. He hadn't found her particularly attractive. He wasn't even in the mood. But when he had watched Samantha walk away from the roulette wheel, disgusted with his desire to gamble, he had wanted revenge. She'd had no right to judge him. No right to try to control what he did. She was not his mother, or his wife. He had given more to her than to any other woman. Why the hell couldn't she see that?

He had steadily lost all his money, then grabbed Andrea's hand and asked her what room she was in. She had said, hesitatingly, "My parents have room 1103. They said they'd be out until midnight."

He pulled her up to room 1103, took her clothes off, and wondered what the hell he was doing. She was thin as a board, still undeveloped at eighteen, and scared shitless. He was thirty-two, completely unaroused, and a total bastard. She lay there, stiff and unmoving, like the terrified, completely inexperienced girl that she was. He squeezed his eyes shut and pretended she was Samantha. He spent half an hour wishing her breasts were shaped more like Samantha's, that she would give something back, the way Samantha did, talk to him the way Samantha did, laugh when he touched her beneath her arm, the way Samantha did.

He went through with it because he always went through with what he started, and because this was a lesson for himself as well as for Samantha. There were other willing women in the world. Tons of them.

Now, Samantha turned around in his arms and suddenly kissed him. He was surprised and then awed by her power over him, how she used her lips like a net to capture him. He felt the tears on her cheeks and he kissed them.

"Don't cry," he said. "I'm sorry. I'm sorry for

everything. I don't know what to do with you, Samantha."

"Love me," she said, kissing his neck, slipping her fingers up under his shirt.

He was lost again, beneath her touch, under her lips. He hardly noticed when he said, "I do. You know I do."

Elliot sat in the den, listening to Leah bump around in the master bedroom. She was rummaging through her closet, trying things on, taking them off. He pressed his fists together until they turned white.

He had been sitting there since they got home from the cabin, two hours earlier. Usually, Leah immediately started unpacking and doing the laundry, but today she had simply walked into their bedroom, locked the door, and begun getting ready.

Elliot stared around him. He and Leah had painted this room a dark hunter green and then Elliot had built in bookshelves on two walls. The shelves were filled with novels and history books and those glorious, glossy art books Leah had given him when they were first married.

Finally, the noise in the bedroom stopped. Leah had decided what to wear. She had not told him where she was going, or who the friend was she planned to see. But he knew. He had always known. She thought he was an idiot, but he was not.

The man's name was James Arlington. He was a psychoanalyst with an office in downtown Sacramento. He was married, with no kids. He made one hundred thirty thousand dollars a year, had had five plastic-surgery operations, one to tuck his chin, one to lengthen his nose and jawbone, and three standard face-lifts. He took a vacation to Europe with his wife every August, and had two other lovers besides Leah, although Elliot was certain she didn't know about them.

Elliot stayed very still while he listened for sounds from his wife. Three years ago, he and Samantha had discussed Leah's depression at length. Samantha had known of a good psychiatrist and they had agreed that it would be best if Samantha was the one to suggest that Leah see him. Elliot had thought it important that he remain as he'd always been, supportive, loving, slightly removed. He didn't want to make Leah defensive, or self-conscious about her actions.

Leah had not confided in him. She had told him she was meeting friends every Tuesday and Thursday night rather than admit she was seeing Arlington. Elliot was hurt by the lie, stunned that she was so good at pretending, but the main thing was that she had seemed better almost immediately. He was surprised, then, when she kept her twice-weekly appointments. Even more surprised when Samantha mentioned that Leah had told her she'd stopped going to the psychoanalyst after the second session.

That was when Elliot began following her. He trailed way behind her and parked down the street from Arlington's office building. First he just sat in the car. The next time he walked into the lobby. After that he took the elevator to the nearly deserted thirteenth floor.

The fourth time he followed Leah, he finally had the nerve to walk down the hall to Arlington's office. He opened the door and found the place dark, except for a light beneath the doctor's private office.

Elliot had taken three deep breaths and then walked down the hall. He put his ear to the door. For a long time, he heard nothing, and then there was a crack, a soft moan. Elliot was about to barge in when he heard Leah say, "Oh, James. God, yes. Right there."

For a moment, he felt nothing. No pain. No anger. Then it all rushed in, all the fury and violence he'd tried so valiantly to remove from his life. He ran out of the office and pounded his fists against every door he passed. He flung open the door to the stairs and strode down two steps at a time, stopping at each landing to kick the wall, ram his knuckles against them. When he reached the third floor, nausea hit him and he threw up twice.

He ran out of the building and headed straight for the metal lamppost. He pulled back his hand and threw his fist against it. He grimaced at the pain, but smiled at the blood. It was the first time he'd ever intentionally hurt himself and, for some strange reason, it felt good.

He drove home and left a note for Leah.

> *Emergency at the office. Need to drive out to San Francisco to check a claim. I'll be home tomorrow.*
>
> *Elliot*

He jumped back in his car and drove the Sacramento streets until his tank was empty. Then he filled up again and actually did drive to San Francisco. He parked at Golden Gate Park and walked to the bridge. He hiked its auburn expanse three times, until his legs were throbbing, until the earlier pain he'd inflicted on himself finally broke through his consciousness. Until his knuckles burned and, when he tried to wiggle his toes, realized he couldn't; he'd probably broken a few of them kicking the walls.

He drove toward home slowly, stopping at a gas station to clean up the blood he'd let dry on him. After he got back in the car, he still felt undecided about what to do. One half of him hated her, literally felt sickened, infected by what she had done. The other half grasped at explanations the way a man drowning at sea flails at driftwood. Leah had been lonely since Samantha moved out. He was too wrapped up in his own life. She'd always needed more than him: more sex, more fun, more life.

He thought about murdering her, then shook himself to chase the incredible notion away. He thought about confronting her, shouting at the top of his lungs, making her cry and beg him to forgive her, and then he realized that when he pictured the scene, his mother and father were playing his and Leah's roles.

He pulled into his driveway, and cut the engine. He sat in the car for a long time, unable to get out but also unable to drive away. He looked up and saw Leah standing on the porch, watching him warily.

He stepped out of the car, surprised that his legs didn't buckle, that he was able to move at all when everything inside him felt broken. He walked up the path to her, hiding his bruised knuckles behind him. He could hear the fight within him almost like voices. "Go. Leave. Stay. Shout. Keep quiet." He made the decision that if Leah smiled, or made any reference to seeing her "friend" the night before, he would leave her.

He reached her and they stood on the porch in silence. She toyed with her robe and stared out over their well-manicured lawn. Elliot had always taken great pride in having the best-kept grass on the street.

"I was worried about you," Leah said at last.

He stared at her and knew she wasn't lying about that, at least. She worried about him and she came home to him. She always came home to him. Wasn't that enough? Or, if it wasn't, wasn't he good enough at lying to pretend that it was, to keep everything smooth and quiet?

He knew then, as all his logic and inaction and fear settled down on him like extra, weighty layers of skin, that he couldn't leave her. He could not move unless pushed, he could not pack his bags unless Leah handed him the suitcase. He hung his head as he decided that he was a completely inept man. He could rationalize his way out of any courageous act.

He hired the private investigator two months into Leah's affair. He wanted to know about James Arlington, what type of person his wife wanted. When he got the facts, he was more perplexed than anything. Besides a good salary, what did James Arlington offer her? Elliot stared at the picture of James the investigator had taken and thought his looks were too phony. He wondered why, when the man had been deciding which portions of his face to change through plastic surgery, that he hadn't chosen to thicken his lips. They were mean looking, thin and bloodless.

As Leah continued her Tuesday and Thursday meetings with James, Elliot was amazed that he was able to tolerate it. It was like torture that hurt so badly he eventually became numb to it. The strange thing was, as time went by, Elliot actually got better at pretending. It became almost like a perverted game to him, seeing how well he could keep his misery from her. He began a tally of her lies and, as of now, she had reached one thousand seventeen.

The only thing he couldn't fake was his own erection. The moment he found out about Leah and James, he couldn't hold one, could not even arouse himself. Leah became almost ugly to him, like a used piece of furniture, a ratty old couch someone had thrown out on the porch.

The ironic thing was that he had vowed this would never happen to him. His father had cheated on his mother numerous times before he left. The first time his mother had found out, Elliot walked in on them in the living room and found every piece of crystal shattered and his mother slicing one of the shards down her arm. It was Elliot who grabbed the glass away from her, who held her while his father called her a crazy bitch and went off to sleep with his mistress.

Elliot had promised himself that the same thing would never happen to him, that he would find a loving, faithful wife. He thought he had. Like a fool who refused to acknowledge when he had lost, he still thought of Leah that way. Every time she went to James, he had this crazy idea that it was all some kind of mistake.

Now, he heard Leah open the bedroom door, then hesitate outside the door to the den. Finally, she knocked.

Elliot released his fists and sat up straight.

"Come in."

She walked in, dressed beautifully in a silver pants suit. She had swept back her hair, added an extra touch of rouge and perfume. It was always like this. For James, she wore the kinds of clothes she never wore for him. Everything shimmery and satiny and soft.

Elliot gripped the desk and forced a smile.

"I'm leaving now," she said.

Elliot's heart raced; it always did. Every time, in these last minutes before she left, he entertained the thought of telling her what he knew. He imagined himself blurting it out, laughing devilishly and watching her face go pale as he shouted, "I know! I know! I've been following you for three years!" He imagined pouring out the details, maybe even picking up something breakable and shattering it against the wall. He imagined grabbing her roughly, shaking her, perhaps even spitting in her face.

He imagined all of this and then sank lower in his chair and never said anything. He would not be like *them*, his parents. They had been barbaric in their passion, primitive in their lust and violence and fury. Elliot's calm, his silent suffering, his civility, would triumph someday. This affair would pass and he would be the victor. Leah could not stay with a man like James Arlington forever. Elliot would not believe that of her.

"When will you be home?" he asked.

"I'm not sure. Late. Don't wait up."

Elliot nodded. Leah hesitated and then came forward and kissed his cheek, as she always did. He started to lift his hand up to hold her there, but she pulled away before he could touch her. He didn't think he would have followed through with the gesture anyway.

She walked away quickly, humming as she let herself out the front door. Then, tiredly, Elliot stood up and grabbed his keys. As always, he counted to ten and then walked out the front door. He waited until she was halfway down the street, then stepped into his car and followed her.

10

Leah tore through the streets to James's house like a criminal on the loose. She ran four red lights, took every turn too fast and left skid marks. It wasn't until she reached the final hill that led to James's mansion that she got herself under control and slowed.

She looked over the other large houses, set behind expansive lawns strung with motion detectors and Malibu lights. She would have gone to James even if he was poor, but it was an added thrill that he wasn't. He lived in the nicest neighborhood in Sacramento; his house was huge, probably dustless and temperature controlled.

She drove up the hill and turned into the last driveway. James's house was set back, an imposing Tudor structure of stone and stucco. Leah got out, took a deep breath, and started for the door.

A car drove past as she reached it and she waited until the headlights had passed her before she knocked. It took a good two minutes for James to answer.

When he did, he was dressed in a silk robe. He had tied the sash loosely around his waist, so that the robe fell open, exposing his naked body beneath.

"Leah," he said. "I'm so glad you could come."

She walked into the marble entry, where a huge crystal chandelier hovered overhead. She looked around, through the double doors to the right that led to a dark, masculine study, and to the left into an airy, feminine sitting room. In front of them, an opulent marble staircase ascended to the second floor.

"Drink?" James asked.

Leah nodded. She followed James through the sitting room, under an arched doorway, and into a long, elegant living room with a bar at the far end. Past the bar were two more doors and to their right another staircase. The house felt borderless, nearly lifeless. Every step Leah took echoed across the marble floor.

James handed her a straight gin and she drank it quickly. He stood by the bar, smiling, his blond hair perfectly combed, every piece of him flawless except for his opened robe that exposed his flaccid penis.

"You're staring at me," James said.

Leah blushed and turned away. She took a step, but her heels clicked so loudly on the floor that she stopped. She heard a clock ticking from somewhere, but she couldn't locate it.

"How was your trip?" James asked.

"Fine. Samantha came with her boyfriend."

"Really? I didn't know she had one. When did this happen?"

"A while ago," Leah said. "We didn't find out until this vacation."

"And what is the man like?"

Leah walked back to the bar and James refilled her drink. She noticed a cut across the back of his hand and wondered how he'd gotten it. He didn't cook or garden or do anything rougher than lift a notebook, and mess around with her.

"He's attractive," Leah said, biting her lip to keep from adding that he was the most handsome man she'd ever met. "He's an environmentalist."

"I get so tired of them, don't you?" James asked. "They've got no regard for hardworking businessmen. They'd put every man in the nation out of a job if it would save one of their precious trees."

Leah said nothing. She rested her hand on the bar two inches from James's hand. She wanted to touch him so badly her fingers twitched, but she restrained herself.

"And where does Elliot think you are tonight?" James asked.

"With a friend."

"Which friend?"

"He didn't ask."

James stared at her with his psychoanalyst's stare, unblinking, making her search out answers for herself.

"Are you suggesting that he should ask?" she said.

"Wouldn't you?"

Leah didn't know. She had never really thought about it. She had only been relieved when, night after night, Elliot had let her go without any hassle. She could hardly stand the lie as it was. If it took any more elaboration, she didn't know if she would be able to pull it off.

"Do we have to talk about Elliot?" she asked.

"No. Of course not."

He took her drink away and grabbed her hand. He pulled her after him, slipping through doors, up stairs, down hallways. Leah tried to look around, to take in all the lavishness, but she could not get past the ecstasy of finally touching James after two long weeks. He was like food she had been starving for.

James opened a final door and took her into a feminine bedroom. It was painted light pink, with stenciled flowers along the tops of the walls. The large bed was covered in a white lace canopy, the comforter decked out in a Laura Ashley print.

"Is this your room?" Leah asked.

"No. My wife's. I've never fucked in here before."

Leah cringed a little, although whether from revulsion at his crudeness or excitement, she couldn't tell. She only knew that, somehow, James split open her body and all her boiling blood rushed out like lava. He made her heart pound and prance and skip beats. He made her soar and fall and scream and cry and laugh, and all of those things felt equally good, because they were all real, and strong.

James walked over to the bed and ran his hand over the comforter.

"She sleeps in here. Elaine. She hasn't come to my bed in over seven years. I've never pressured her. She's a beautiful woman, but not at all my type. She's too stiff."

Leah watched him. He was sliding his robe down his shoulders, revealing his perfect arms, his chest covered with blond hairs, his rock-hard stomach.

"She stopped coming to me when I suggested we try something different," he went on. "She took one look at my whip and ran screaming down the hall."

He stopped the robe just above his waist and Leah raised her gaze to meet his.

"I'm glad you're not so squeamish, Leah," he said. "It was hell for a while, not having anyone who understood my needs."

He dropped the robe. Leah's mouth was bone-dry. James smiled and walked over to her. She arched her back when he extended his fingers, but his hand did not touch her. He reached past her and opened the top drawer of his wife's dresser.

He pulled out a handful of black net stockings. He

rubbed them across Leah's cheek and she closed her eyes. He stroked her for a moment, moving in closer, until she could feel that he was no longer flaccid, but thoroughly excited.

The stroking ended abruptly, and he yanked her to the bed. She said nothing as he laid her down in the center and spread her arms and legs wide. It never got too bad, as long as she was quiet.

James tied her arms and legs to the bedposts with the stockings. Then he walked over to the chair in the corner and picked up the horse whip he must have put there earlier. Leah shuddered a little. She had fantasized about this night for two weeks. She had hoped that James would simply hold her, make love to her without any toys or violence at all.

"Couldn't we just—"

"Shut up," James said, as he always said whenever she protested. He was breathing hard.

A draft came up over the bed and into the crevices between her legs. James marched around the bed, sliding the length of the leather whip up and down his palm. Leah knew what this was about. She had left to go to the cabin and now James would punish her. He had punished her in the past too, when she was late for one of their meetings, or said something to make him lose his erection. He had hit her, pinched her, once even poked the tip of a knife into the flesh of her buttocks until she bled. She could take it because, afterward, he was always more gentle than ever.

"You shouldn't have gone," James said, more like a child than an adult. She looked at his eyes and was stunned to see tears in them.

"James, I'm sorry."

"No you're not." He ran his fingers down her throat and then, in one quick motion, ripped her shirt down the center. He yanked her pants and underwear down below her knees. Leah cried out a little, but then bit her lip to keep quiet.

James stared down at her. He shook a little; the whip in his hand vibrated.

"I'm treating an abusive man now," he said. "Do you know what's funny? I'm helping him to learn how wrong violence is, that you should never take advantage of another person that way, just because you're stronger. And he's getting better."

A tear slipped out of the corner of Leah's eye. "That's not funny," she said. "You're a good analyst."

He was. All his patients thought so. He had stepped over the doctor/patient line with her, but only because he'd seen what no one else had, that only passion could save her.

"I am a good analyst," James said. "And what nobody understands is that that doesn't have a damn thing to do with the kind of man I am. All the logic and theories and techniques in the world won't save me. I'm so far past logic it's frightening."

He stared at her again and Leah shivered. There was a definite draft in the room, as if he'd put a fan beside the bed. She listened carefully and did hear a hum.

James lifted the whip up slowly. The whole time before the whip sliced into her skin, she was watching his face, the tears on his cheeks, and thinking, *He won't do it. This is where he'll draw the line. He'll just give me a light tap, a small welt.* Instead, he cracked the whip down over her stomach the way a jockey flailed a slow horse, with full, furious strength. Leah screamed at the pain, tried to yank her arms and legs free to protect herself, but James only cried harder, and whipped her again.

She screamed at him to stop. She flung herself against her binds until the one around her right arm started to loosen. James raised the whip again, but just as it came down, Leah got her hand free and tried to catch it. It stung her hand and ricocheted onto her hip. She cried out again and, as if she weren't afraid of him at all, yanked the whip away.

They both watched it fall to the ground. Leah wrenched her feet free and managed to release her other arm. She stared down at her body, at the bloody marks across her stomach and hip. She could not believe it. Even now, when the pain was so intense it made her dizzy, she could not believe this was happening, that she had let it happen, that James was just standing there, crying, dazed.

She tried to walk to the bathroom, but her legs buckled. James was suddenly beside her, helping her, and though it made no sense, she let him guide her.

"I love psychology," he said, simply picking up the conversation where he'd left off, as if what he'd done in between was just part of a strange intermission. "I love it because, even if I can't stop myself, I can understand. That's why I went into it, to try to make sense of all these senseless parts of me."

"How can you make sense of this?" she asked, crying as she stared at her bloody wounds in the bathroom mirror.

James stepped back and cocked his head. He dried his own tears and seemed on the verge of hardening himself when he answered, "My years of training tell me it's because my father got his kicks out of molesting me. He'd slip into my room at night, make me take his dick in my mouth, or up my ass. He'd laugh when I screamed. He started tying me up when I got too strong."

Leah stared at him, horrified. She could not even imagine it. What the hell was wrong with people? It got worse every day; human genes were mutating instead of evolving, breeding atrocities rather than extinguishing them. The moment Leah had held Samantha in her arms, she had known she would lay down her life for her. She had thought that feeling came with parenthood, that there was something in the blood that kept you from hurting your child.

"My mother knew about it," James went on, "but she was too terrified of him to do anything. It went on until he died, when I was sixteen. That natural death was fortuitous for me. Otherwise, I might have killed him."

"Oh, James," Leah said.

James shook his head and then literally did harden himself. He straightened up, his eyes turned cold. He became the man he showed to the world, the calm, closed-off psychoanalyst.

"He died," he said, "and at eighteen I went away to college and found my salvation in psychology. I could understand then, you see. I could put a label on him, turn him into something sick, rather than something evil. And when I started to feel the same tendencies in myself, this need to play out on other people what he'd played out on me, well then, I could look that up in the book, too. It made everything seem all right, somehow. I could classify myself as having a psychosexual disorder brought on by years of child abuse combined with sexual assault."

Leah shook her head as James cleaned her wounds, bandaged the worst parts.

"Maybe if you found your own analyst . . . " she said.

James shook his head. "During my seven years of psychoanalytic training after medical school, I went through my own analysis. But I didn't come out any better. I recognize that about my profession. There are some people you just can't cure."

Leah knew she was insane to feel pity. But lately

she'd been on familiar terms with her own insanity. She lifted a trembling hand to his cheek.

"Your father took your soul away," she said.

James stared at her for a long time. He shivered a little beneath her hand and then, finally, broke away.

He found one of his wife's coats and slipped it around her shoulders.

"Tell Elliot you were cold and a friend let you borrow this," he said. "Take what's left of your pants suit and throw it out in someone else's garbage, so he won't see it. And for God's sake, Leah, don't let him see your stomach. Elliot is not the type of man who would understand this."

Leah almost laughed. Elliot would take one look at this situation and head for the hills. His wife was having an affair with a lunatic, and she couldn't walk away. She came home stiff and sore and bloody, and still this man did something for her, plugged some hole in her heart, and that was worth it. God, how little her life must be worth, if being with James was worth something.

They walked back down the halls and stairs the way they had come and reached the front door.

"You'll come Tuesday," James said.

Leah nodded. She felt depleted, exhausted, defaced.

"Good," James said, his composure back, his earlier confidences forgotten. "I've got a yen to play Russian roulette again. You'll do it, won't you, Leah? With lives like ours, we've got to add what sport we can. We need to walk along the edge."

And though Leah wanted to deny it, to run home to Elliot and be simple and happy with him, she knew James was right. She was obsessed with the edge, the tightrope she danced on, even this sad, sadistic man. She would come on Tuesday. She would play James's games.

She walked away and stepped gingerly into her car.

One of her cuts started bleeding again as she drove slowly back home.

Samantha felt a rush of adrenaline when she walked into the office for the first time after her two-week vacation. Four months remained until the next election, and things were crazy. Her boss, Amy Tarkington, was marching around shouting orders, candidates nervously paced the halls, the consultants met with them in various conference rooms, trying to calm their nerves and get them to agree to a winning strategy for November.

Samantha stayed late that first night, going through the seventy-two messages that had been left for her in her absence, trying to work out a counterattack to a sleaze campaign directed at their first real hope for a Democratic seat in solidly Republican Orange County.

She stayed late the next night too, and the next, filling the long days with meetings and phone calls and paperwork. She felt again that wonderful sensation of losing herself in work. There was so much to do before November, so many publicity campaigns to organize, rumors to stop, rumors to start.

It had been a long time since she'd been swept up in it, and for three days, she hardly thought of Dylan at all. He didn't call and she didn't worry why not. She left no messages for him and felt good and strong again, as if she didn't need him at all, as if these last three and a half months had been a dream.

At the end of her third day back, when work had taken her well into the evening, she hung up her suit and changed into her cycling shorts and T-shirt. She walked down the nearly empty corridors of Democratic headquarters and took the stairs down to the parking garage where she kept her bicycle.

She strapped on her helmet, pulled on her gloves, and rode out into the waning sunshine. All through the summer and fall, she rode to and from work on her bike.

She had bought this mountain bike last spring and had already put two thousand miles on it.

She was tired, and had a headache, but she didn't want to go home. Home meant the answering machine and the chance that if Dylan hadn't phoned, she wouldn't be able to stop herself from calling him. Home meant time to think about what had happened at the casino. At Dylan's apartment, after they got home from the cabin and made love furiously, Dylan had said to her, "About Andrea . . . If it happens again, I'll use a little more discretion. It wasn't right, to do it right in front of you."

She had smiled and said thank you, and thought, *If it happens again, I'll kill you.*

Now, she rode hard through the Sacramento streets, past traffic at a standstill and sparkling new buildings mixed in with decaying ones. She rode past the fields south of Sacramento. She looked down the rows of lettuce, wilting in the hot July heat. She pedaled harder, until the fields were just a blur, until her mind had only one concern, not to fall.

She rode clear to Lodi and back, coming home in pure darkness. She slowed her pace for the last ten miles, reveling in the touch of the wind on her skin, the muscle-weary tingling in her legs.

She rode to the west end of Sacramento, where her apartment was. When she finally turned onto her street, she glanced down at her watch and saw that it was ten-thirty. She had been riding for four hours.

She locked her bike up in her garage and walked upstairs. She knew, before she even put her key in the lock, that Dylan was inside. She could sense him, smell the molecules of his scent still clinging to the air. She opened the door.

Dylan was sitting on the couch, a bowl of popcorn and a beer beside him. He stood up abruptly.

"Where have you been?" he asked.

She looked down at her sweaty clothes and laughed. Her heart raced, then nearly soared up into the sky. He was worried. He was here.

"Riding, obviously," she said.

He stomped over to her and she realized he was far past fury into some new emotion she'd never seen before.

"I've been sitting here for three hours waiting for you," he said. "I called the office, but they told me you left at six-thirty. Hell, I even called your father and had to deal with his crap about me having a key to your apartment. What do you think went through my mind?"

Samantha reached out for him, but he pulled away. She set her helmet down on the entry table and took off her gloves. Love was just a game, she realized in that instant. Dylan responded to her only when she failed to respond to him. How ridiculous! As if someone who loved you openly was not as desirable as someone who treated you with contempt.

"I'm sorry, Dylan," she said, smiling as if she weren't really sorry at all. "I guess I didn't think about it. I had a headache and needed to ride. It was such a beautiful night . . ."

He turned and walked into the kitchen. She watched his back, saw it rise and fall heavily as he tried to control his breathing. She expected him to laugh at any second, to tell her he was just feigning concern, that in a relationship like theirs, no explanations were required.

Instead, when he turned around, she was struck by the agony in his eyes. *Hold back,* she told herself. *Ignore him. You're winning.* But she could not resist him. She closed the gap between them quickly and pulled him into her arms.

"I'm sorry," she said. "I honestly didn't think you'd worry."

He held her tight and Samantha heard his heart racing. She thumped her foot against the floor a little, delighting in her victory.

"Don't . . . Don't do that again," Dylan said, his voice catching.

Samantha turned her head so he wouldn't see her smile. Oh yes, she would do that again. She would do it again and again as long as it evoked this reaction, as long as it woke Dylan up to the fact that he loved her, too.

11

*Two weeks later, Dylan whistled as he walked into a restau*rant on the wharf in San Francisco an hour late. Samantha was already sitting at a corner table, sipping a glass of wine. She'd had business in the city and Dylan had ridden with her, not telling her that he had business of his own. An hour ago, he'd stood on the bow of his rebuilt *EarthAlert 1* ship.

He quickened his pace, so excited by the prospect of setting out to sea again that he didn't notice the man sitting opposite Samantha until he was standing right over him. Samantha looked up, startled, as if she had forgotten he was coming.

"Oh, Dylan, what time is it?" She looked at her watch and then shrugged. "Sorry. Lost track of time. This is Michael Munsen. Michael, this is Dylan Price."

Michael stood up. He was as tall as Dylan, with a quarter of Dylan's hair. Light brown, it was cut well above his ears. He wore wire-framed glasses over his brown eyes. He had a firm handshake and a warm smile, and Dylan immediately disliked him.

"Nice to meet you," Michael said. "Samantha has been telling me all about you and your organization."

Dylan nodded and then slipped into the booth beside Samantha.

"Can you believe it, Dylan?" she said. She was slightly flushed and, when he reached for her hand, he could feel her sweaty palms. "I was just sitting here waiting for you when Michael walked in. We haven't seen each other in years."

She looked up at Michael and he winked at her. Dylan let go of her hand and rapped his knuckles against the table.

"I'm attending a seminar at San Francisco State," Michael said. "My practice is in Sacramento."

"It's so funny to hear you talk like that," Samantha said. " 'Seminar.' 'Practice.' You sound like such an adult."

"Samantha and I have known each other since elementary school," Michael said to Dylan. "Third grade."

"Second," Samantha said.

"Samantha was the best handball player in school."

"Michael was the second best," Samantha said. "We'd team up and nobody could beat us." They smiled at each other and Dylan searched the restaurant for a waitress.

"I'm afraid I had a terrible crush on her," Michael said.

"It was mutual," Samantha replied, and then laughed to cover up her embarrassment. "We dated for a while, off and on."

Dylan pulled out the rubber band holding his hair back and ran his fingers through his hair. Goddammit, where was that waitress?

"Michael was the most popular boy in high school," Samantha said.

"No way," Michael said. "A little geeky, as I recall. Glasses were not in back then."

"I was crushed when Michael went away to Stanford," Samantha said.

"Good school," Dylan said, because it was something to say and he realized he hadn't said a word since he'd sat down.

"It is," Michael said. "Expensive, though. I'm still paying off my loans."

"Michael's a surgeon," Samantha said.

Dylan's head jerked up involuntarily. God, he hated words like that. "Surgeon," "corporate executive," "civil lawyer." Solid, substantive words that conjured up such respectable images.

"Why did you two break up?" Dylan asked. He emphasized the words "break up," just in case they'd forgotten. He tried to catch Samantha's eye, but she ignored him. He wished now that he had sat beside Michael, so that he could see her eyes.

"We didn't really," Samantha said, toying with the rim of her wine glass. "Michael got accepted at Stanford. I decided to go to UCSF. We thought we could make it work long distance."

"But . . ." Dylan said, filling in the words for her. She was speaking so slowly, staring at Michael after every word, as if she needed his approval for each of them.

"But it was too hard," Samantha finished finally. "Six months into college, Michael drove to my apartment in the city and stayed the weekend. We decided to just be friends."

A man and woman can't be just friends when they're sleeping under the same roof for a weekend, Dylan thought. It wasn't possible.

He thumped his hand on the table, to get a waitress's attention. Finally, a very grumpy one came and he ordered a scotch, straight up.

"Breaking up with Samantha was the hardest thing I ever had to do," Michael said to Dylan, as if Dylan were his best friend. "But I got a first-year scholarship to Stanford for premed and I couldn't pass it up. After a while, I realized Samantha needed to be free to see other people. She forgot me sooner than I forgot her, I'm sure."

Samantha laughed again. The waitress brought the scotch and Dylan gulped it. He let it burn his throat and then unclenched his fist, trying to relax. Suddenly, he couldn't wait to get back on his boat, to get in somebody's way, raise a little hell.

Michael reached into his pocket and took out a card. "I have to be going," he said, standing up. "But this is my office phone. Let me write down my home number, too."

He did that and handed the card to Samantha. Reluctantly, Dylan stood up and shook his hand.

"Nice meeting you," Michael said. "You're one lucky man."

Dylan said nothing as Samantha pushed past him and hugged Michael tightly.

"It was so good to see you and to talk," she said. "I can't believe we haven't gotten together since college. That's much too long."

"I know. I'm sorry."

"I didn't realize I'd missed our talks that much."

"Remember?" Michael asked.

Samantha nodded. "Yes. I remember."

Samantha watched him leave the restaurant and then, almost reluctantly, she slipped back into the booth. This time, Dylan took the seat across from her. He quelled the urge to shout or make her explain. He mentally glued his feet to the floor so that he wouldn't run out after Michael the surgeon and beat his pretty face to a pulp.

"Guess what?" he said.

Samantha, still looking where Michael had been, slowly brought her gaze around to him. "What?"

"*EarthAlert 1* is ready. We're heading up to Alaska in two weeks. Our target is Vanguard Oil. They've started a run of commercials in the last few months, touting themselves as the petroleum company that cares. I'm curious to see how well that statement holds up when we block their tanker's path."

"You're leaving?"

"Yes. I'll be gone for two or three weeks. We're going to make it tough as hell for those bastards to get their oil."

The waitress came back. Dylan ordered another scotch and swordfish, then glared at Samantha when she asked for salmon.

"You're creating a demand for an endangered species," he said.

"Good God," Samantha said. She turned to the waitress. "I'll take a steak instead."

When the waitress left, Samantha said, "As long as we've got a lot of cows, it's all right to kill them. Is that what you're saying?"

Dylan ran his fingers through his hair.

"Let's not get into it," he said. "I want to talk about my trip. I've been itching to do something again. It's been too long."

Samantha sat there, silent, until the waitress brought their salads and Dylan's second scotch. She toyed with her food.

"I wasn't sure when the boat would be finished," Dylan went on, wondering why he was struggling for conversation, why he didn't just let it drop. "Thank God we're ready now that Vanguard wants to make their run."

"I had no idea you were even thinking of going," Samantha said.

Dylan sipped his scotch. He looked around the restaurant, trying to find another pretty woman to lock his gaze on. None of the women in the place caught his eye, though.

"This is what I do," he said quietly.

"Say what you mean," she said, setting her mouth in a firm line. "You didn't tell me until now because you didn't think it was any of my business."

"It isn't."

They both sat very still. Dylan listened in on conversations around him. Lovers were arguing. A mother hissed at her daughter to keep her voice down.

"Samantha—"

Samantha held up her hand. It was shaking and Dylan resisted the urge to grab it and hold it tightly.

"Sometimes," she said, "I have no clue why I'm with you. I want to walk away so badly, but I don't have the will to do it. I can't stand that about myself."

Dylan did not know what to say. Samantha was the first woman who had ever left him speechless.

"I thought, at first," she went on, "that I was better with you than without you. But that's not true, is it? I'm less when I'm with you. I'm not even half of what I usually am."

"Don't lay this on me, Sam," Dylan said.

"Who's laying anything on you? God, Dylan, even when I try to be honest with you, you turn it all around. I'm talking about me, not you."

"Look, I'm going to Alaska. That's all there is to it. Catch up with your old friend while I'm gone."

The words came out biting, not at all smoothly, as

he had intended. Dylan had not thought he was capable of jealousy. He had not thought he was capable of a whole realm of emotions until he met Samantha. He didn't particularly enjoy finding out that he was so ordinary.

"Do you want me to see Michael or not?" she asked.

Dylan waved his hand. "I don't care. You know the rules. You can see whoever you want."

Samantha stared out the window. The houseboats in the dock had their lights on and looked like floating carnival rides.

"We can always change the rules," she said.

For a moment, Dylan entertained the thought of taking her up on her offer, but then he laughed at himself. He was feeling a momentary pulse of jealousy. It would pass. He would head out on *EarthAlert 1* in two weeks, do what he did best, raise some havoc, screw up some corporate asshole's plans, and by the time he came back a few weeks later, he'd have his feelings for Samantha under control. It was what they needed, a little time apart.

"No," Dylan said. "Rules are rules. You do what you want with your friend. It's no skin off my back. I'll be busy with my work. We've still got a little time together before I leave and then, if things haven't changed too drastically in the meantime, we'll get together when I get back."

Samantha stared at him until his skin burned. "God," she said, "why on earth do I love you?"

Samantha dropped Dylan off at his apartment that night and then drove off with a skid. She sped all the way home, dodging traffic, plowing through yellow lights where she usually stopped. She made it home safely, luckily, and stomped up to her apartment.

She slammed the door shut and immediately dialed Michael's number.

"Hello," Michael said.

Samantha gripped the kitchen counter and took a deep breath.

"He's such a bastard," she said.

Michael laughed. "Samantha. It's so good to hear from you again."

"You saw him," Samantha said. "He was jealous. He was up to his eyeballs in jealousy."

"Yes, he was."

"And then do you know what he tells me? He tells me he's leaving in two weeks to save the Alaskan coast. He couldn't have cared less that you and I met up again. He even told me to go ahead and see you while he was gone."

"So our plans were for nothing."

"Not *our* plans. Mine. I'm sorry I dragged you into this."

"You're a sneaky woman, Samantha," Michael said. "But I didn't mind. It was nice to see you again, even if I was only a pawn to make your boyfriend jealous."

The plan had come to Samantha a week ago. Coming home late from her bike ride had worked so well that she had decided to take things a step further. She would not only make Dylan worry, she would make him jealous.

She had thought of Michael Munsen. He was not really an old boyfriend, more an old boy *friend.* He had been a handball teammate and study partner rather than a first love, but Dylan would never know that. She tracked Michael down through a friend and called him. It took her half an hour to work up the nerve to ask him to meet her at the restaurant and pretend it was an accident. It took another half hour of pleading, of playing their old game of what will you do for me if I do this for you, for Michael to agree. She would have to counsel a friend of his who was thinking of running for mayor of San Jose, but that was a small price to pay for making Dylan jealous.

"It was obvious that he cares for you," Michael said.

"Was it?"

"Yes. His fists were clenched so tight, I thought he'd erupt. I'd be the first doctor to treat the human eruption."

Samantha laughed. She had been surprised that she was able to laugh so easily with Michael. All those years apart should have made them awkward, but though Michael had grown into himself, become more sure and confident, inside he still was the gawky, shy boy she had taken under her wing. He was just as funny as he used to be, just as gentle. His eyes had twinkled when he met her in the restaurant.

"My love," he'd said, taking her in his arms and kissing her neck ravenously. "I've missed you. I've never stopped loving you."

The other customers had looked at them while Samantha laughed.

"Sit down, you idiot," she said. "At least wait until Dylan gets here."

Saying they had dated off and on was only a little bit of a stretch. They had taken each other to dances when there was no one else to go with. They had experimented on each other, tried out French kissing and what this kind of touch felt like on that part of each other's body.

He had been a good friend and, instantly, he was a good friend again. That was the thing about people you had known since childhood. It took so little time to slip back into the old patterns of friendship.

And yet, there had been something else there tonight, too. When Michael had kissed her neck, she realized he wasn't joking. And from the moment they sat down, she had known that he wanted her.

"So how long will lover boy be gone?" Michael asked.

"Two to three weeks. He leaves a week from Friday."

"Good. That gives me almost enough time."

"Almost enough time for what?" Samantha asked, although she knew.

"To make you forget him," Michael said. "And start loving me instead."

Elliot fixed himself a vodka martini. He could feel all of their eyes on him, but he ignored them. He had never drunk much before but since they'd been back for three weeks from their vacation in the mountains, he found he couldn't get through the day without a martini or a stiff shot of gin.

He finished the drink and turned around. Like a fool who didn't know when she'd had enough, Leah had invited Samantha and Dylan over for dinner. Leah and Samantha were sitting on the couch; Dylan was in Elliot's wing chair. That left the hard rocking chair Elliot could not stand, but he walked over and sat in it anyway.

"I'm really excited about Sharon Mulligan's chances," Samantha was saying to Leah. "She's a liberal Democrat, prochoice, pro-ERA, proenvironment. Two years ago, we wouldn't have had a chance of pulling her through, but the polls tell us we're running only six percentage points behind. It's making us almost giddy, finally having a chance to win."

"That's wonderful, Samantha," Leah said, although Elliot could tell right off that Leah did not think it was wonderful, that she was hardly listening at all. She had been strangely silent and pensive for the last three weeks. She walked stiffly, as if she were hiding something in her coat pocket. During that time, Elliot had cut off a number of his thoughts in mid-sentence and she had only tilted her head and said, "That's nice, dear."

"Dylan's going to Alaska in a few days, Dad," Samantha said. "Did I tell you that?"

"Yes, you did," Elliot said. *Thank God,* he added silently. "Where are you headed exactly?" he asked Dylan.

Dylan shrugged. He too had been quiet since he'd gotten here. He had just stared at Samantha hard enough to read her thoughts.

"We're not clear on that yet," Dylan said. "We're after an oil tanker, and wherever they go, we go."

"You can't stop them from taking their oil," Elliot said. "People have to drive, you know. And the oil companies own rights to their fields, don't they?"

Dylan finally wrenched his attention away from Samantha and turned to him.

"We've got rights to clean water," he said. "All the birds and fish and sea lions in Prince William Sound had the right to live, but the Exxon *Valdez* didn't give a shit. Someone's got to give a shit, Elliot."

Dylan stood up and walked to the fireplace. He propped his elbow on the mantel and ran his fingers through his long hair.

Elliot was very quiet. He was not as taken aback by Dylan's language as he had been at the cabin. Actually, though he would never admit this to Leah or Samantha, he had been fishing for a way to get Dylan fired up, to ease the awkwardness that had fallen over the four of them since Dylan and Samantha arrived an hour ago. Even a little tussle was better than total silence.

"You're a vigilante, Dylan," Elliot said. It wasn't so bad, he realized, to raise his voice a little, to have a little conflict. Nothing crazy, of course. Just a little provocation, a few biting words here and there. He was surprised how easy it was to bait Dylan, even more surprised by how much he liked doing it.

He hadn't gone as far as he had in his dreams—yet. Ever since they got back from the cabin, his dreams had been filled with shouting. Arguments, condemnations, even fistfights with Leah. Sometimes, just after he woke up, he nearly shoved Leah out of bed, thinking he'd already kicked her out and she'd had the nerve to sneak back under the covers. Then he remembered he'd dreamed their fight, and was surprised by his own disappointment.

"So?" Dylan asked.

"So, that's not right," Elliot said. "Even you have got to see that without rules, without regulations, without order, we wouldn't be a society at all. We'd disintegrate into tribes again. There'd be murder and mayhem ten times worse than what we've got now and nobody would give a hoot about your precious trees and water and rights then. We'd all have survival to worry about."

"Elliot, please," Leah said.

Elliot turned to her. "Please what?"

"Please stop. Dylan's a guest."

"I don't mind, Leah," Dylan said, smiling. "I can fight my own battles."

"But you shouldn't have to. Not when you're in our home."

Leah stared at Elliot and he was struck by the same feeling he'd had daily since they came back from the cabin. Apprehension. As if he were the last strong brick in an old house and everything around him would crumble if he fell apart.

He had followed her to James Arlington's house the night they got back from the cabin. He had passed down the street just as Leah reached the door. He had stopped and turned off his lights and was able to make out James's limp penis peeking out of his robe.

As soon as Leah had walked inside, Elliot turned the car around and skidded down the hill. He stopped at the first bar he could find, ordered a martini, and then another, and another. By the time he got home, just ten minutes before Leah, he realized he'd found a way to numb the misery.

He continued to numb it daily. Leah still went to James's office every Tuesday and Thursday night. Everything was the same as it had been for the last three years except that Elliot drank now and seemed to have crossed over an invisible line. He was no longer just impotent; he couldn't touch Leah at all anymore. He crept to the very edge of the bed while they slept and prayed she would not get cold during the night and cuddle with him.

He could not meet her gaze head-on for more than a second or two. He could not compliment her on her outfits or cooking, could not make light conversation while they sat together at dinner. He lengthened his days at the office and did not give an explanation why.

He realized, as he stared at his wife now, that he was on the verge of hating her. For three years he had been on the verge of hating her, but it wasn't until now that his control had started to slip and he was falling over the edge.

"Dylan, walk with me," Elliot said. "I need some air."

Both Leah and Samantha looked up in surprise, but Dylan only smiled. God, Elliot admired his courage. He might be an irresponsible, left-wing hippie, but he was fearless, and that was something.

"Let's go."

It was muggy and hot outside, an awful July night, but they walked quickly anyway. They reached the end of the block, where Elliot usually turned left to make a quick jaunt around the neighborhood.

"Let's go that way," Dylan said, pointing toward an alley across the street. Elliot hesitated. He did not take alleys. They led to other alleys and walkways and streets he'd never heard of.

"I'd rather not."

Dylan had already started across the street, but he came back again.

"Why not? This is a good neighborhood. I doubt you've got any criminals hanging out in your alley."

"It's not that." Elliot looked up into the night sky. A Sacramento night appeared like twilight, with all the city lights tempering it. Only a few stars were even visible through the haze. That was another reason he loved the mountains, because he could make out the constellations he had studied in school.

"I got lost once," Elliot said. "As a child. My father had taken me to a carnival and then left me to go chase after women. I wandered away when he didn't come back. I was lost for two days."

"Two days!"

"I wandered out of the carnival, thinking my dad was waiting in the parking lot," Elliot said, remembering. He had been five years old, without a dime in his pocket, without a clue as to which direction was home. He had searched for the car and, when he couldn't find it, figured his father had already headed home.

"I walked," Elliot said. "Just walked and cried. I stayed up all night, afraid of every shadow. I finally wore myself out. In the morning, I ended up in a park somewhere and slept for ten hours under a tree. When I woke up, there was a blanket over me and an apple near my hand. I have no idea who gave it to me."

"Good people," Dylan said.

"I ate the apple and started walking again. I suppose I drew attention to myself with that blanket wrapped around me. A police officer found me and after a couple hours of questioning, helped me to remember where I lived. The cop wanted to knock the daylights out of my father, but Dad just laughed and said it did me good, being out on my own."

Dylan stared at him for a moment and then tilted his head toward the alley.

"Come on, Elliot," he said. "I'll be right beside you."

Elliot grabbed his arm. "I never told Leah that story."

"Why not?"

"I don't know. Crazy, huh? As if she'd care one way or another."

Dylan pulled Elliot across the street. They reached the border of the alley and Elliot hesitated.

"Did I tell you about my adventure in the Amazon two years ago?" Dylan asked, starting into the alley. Elliot took a deep breath and followed him. The alley was dark, long, and narrow, and dogs barked at them from behind wood fences.

"We thought we could bring the government of Brazil around to our way of thinking," Dylan went on. "But they wouldn't even listen. The rain forests are essential to their economy. They'd cut them all down in a second if they could make a buck. They laughed when we started talking about the ozone hole in Antarctica. They honestly didn't think it had anything to do with them."

Elliot listened to Dylan's strong voice and relaxed the tension in his neck. He realized Dylan was telling him this story to take his mind off his fear and, strangely enough, it was working. Dylan led them out the end of the alley, picked another one down another street, and led them to it.

"So we took matters into our own hands," Dylan

said. "We put up road blocks on the logging roads. Spiked the trees, did anything we could think of to make them worthless to the ranchers and loggers. I hate to say it, but we even poisoned a cattle herd, so the rancher could not tell the government he needed more forest razed for grazing land."

"You killed cows?" Elliot said. "Doesn't that go against everything you stand for?"

"No. Sometimes sacrifices have to be made for the greater good. Five hundred cattle for a forest."

"I don't know that I agree with your logic."

Dylan laughed. "That's all right. I'm not sure I always agree with it, either."

They walked down five different alleys. Elliot's step slowed toward the end, when he realized he didn't know where he was. It was dark, there were no streetlights, and his sense of direction had always been poor. But Dylan walked on confidently, and Elliot ignored the quick pace of his heart and followed him.

"The thing about getting lost is," Dylan said, when they emerged from the fifth alley and looked around the quiet residential street, "you can't do it very well anymore. There are too many maps, too many people to ask for directions. You can use a calling card if you don't have change to make a call, or just dial the operator and do it collect. The thing is, Elliot, it's pretty near impossible to get yourself lost. No matter how hard you try."

Elliot realized, as Dylan spoke, that his heart rate was decelerating, that the sweat beneath his arms had stopped pouring out. He looked around, recognized the house on the corner, the neighborhood market down the street. They had come only five blocks, and he had driven through this area years ago because one of Samantha's friends lived here.

"We just go back that way," Elliot said, pointing

right. "Turn on Dearborn Street and then make a left on Ensenada."

Dylan smiled. "Lead the way."

Dylan took his plate of barely touched veal parmigiana into the kitchen. Leah was already at the sink, doing the dishes, and she looked down at the plate.

"You hated it," she said.

"No. I'm just not much of a veal fan. I think of the calves and, well . . ."

Leah nodded and tossed the remaining veal into the trash can.

"Let me help," Dylan said.

"You can clear the rest of the table," Leah said. "And then you can dry."

He did as she asked, peeking in on Samantha and Elliot, who were huddled together in the living room.

It had been an awkward dinner. Samantha had carried most of the conversation, talking about work, about her friends, even, briefly, about Michael the surgeon. Dylan had pressed his fingers against his fork until she finished the story about how they had met up again and were going to get together. He had smiled as nonchalantly as he could.

Now, he cleared the table and walked back into the kitchen. Leah had already washed most of the pans and handed him a towel to dry them.

"What are they doing?" she asked.

"Talking."

"About us, no doubt," Leah said. "Probably about how fast things change. Everything seemed fine between me and Elliot when we got to the cabin, and then, over the span of two weeks, I lost him. He lost me. It's been even worse since we got back. I can't connect with him now."

"Leah—"

"I thought it was something I'd done," she said, rinsing the plates and handing them to him. "I thought he was picking up on my feelings, but that wasn't it at all. It's all him. He's changed. I don't know if he knows it yet, but he has."

"Changed how?"

"He's feeling things. He makes himself a drink first thing every night. He can't control himself. That was always the biggest thing to Elliot, to be in control."

"I'm sure you'll be all right," Dylan said.

Leah splashed her hands back into the water and stared at him.

"Why? Because we've been married for so long? You think we should just stay together because we've stuck it out this long and it's not like we could find anyone else to love us?"

"That wasn't what I meant."

"Wasn't it? Don't you and Samantha just sit around and laugh at us? You think our passions are ridiculous, that we should just curl up and die and leave the living to you two."

Dylan put the towel down.

"What are you so goddamn angry about?" he asked.

Leah shook her head and Dylan saw tears in her eyes. He almost comforted her, but then decided he'd had enough.

"I'm getting out of here," he said.

He marched out of the kitchen and into the living room. Elliot and Samantha broke apart from their confidences and stared at him guiltily.

"Thank you for dinner, Elliot," he said. "And for the walk. Samantha, I think we'd better go."

She stared at him, started to protest, but then thought better of it. She said goodbye to Elliot, then to Leah, and the two of them got into her car.

"What was that all about?" she asked.

"I've just had enough of your parents and their little spats," he said, more roughly than he had intended. "What the hell was I doing there? They aren't my family. It's not my problem. I'm sick of being dragged into it."

Samantha gripped the steering wheel.

"You're right," she said, "we're not your family."

"Let's just go home."

"We don't have a home, Dylan," she said. "You live on one side of town and I'm on another."

"For God's sake, Sam. Just come home with me. We've only got a few days left before I leave for Alaska."

Samantha took a deep breath and Dylan could not help admiring how she pulled herself up, stopped her tears, and met him eye to eye.

"No," she said. "I don't think I'll go home with you. I think I'll drop you off and go back to my apartment and call Michael."

He knew it was a dare, a test. If he cared about her, he was supposed to respond, get angry. And though inside he did respond, his heart practically leapt to his throat, he did not give away anything. He hated tests; he failed them just to prove that he would not be manipulated. He lifted his chin a notch.

"Fine," he said. "That's probably a good idea."

Samantha's hand shook as she started the car. At every stoplight, Dylan nearly broke his silence and told her what he really felt. He did care about her parents; how could he not? They were the opposite of his own parents; they were what parents were supposed to be.

As they inched closer to his apartment, he almost told her that if she started up with Michael, he'd go crazy. He nearly said that he loved her. But then he came back to his senses. He had always believed he was a step ahead of the game because he knew what was coming. He knew that no matter what he felt for Samantha now, it would pass. Romeo would have tired of Juliet eventually. One day he would have gotten frustrated with all her *words* and called her a garrulous Capulet, she would have cried and told him he had only loved her when she was young and pretty, and then not even the excitement of their forbidden love would have saved them. Maybe the two of them had had the right idea, taking themselves out at the height of their passion, not lingering long enough to be disappointed in each other.

Samantha pulled up in front of his apartment and sat with the engine running.

"Samantha—"

She held up her hand to stop him. She was shivering and a tear slid down her cheek. He lifted a finger to wipe it away, but she pushed him aside. He opened the car door and stepped out.

On the last Thursday in July, two days before James left for his month-long trip to Europe with his wife, Leah walked into his waiting room. She ran her hand down her stomach as she always did now, feeling the scabs beneath her blouse. The scars would never heal completely. There would always be a thin white line over her hip and across her stomach, where the worst of the blows had struck her. She had worried at first about keeping the evidence from Elliot, but that was ridiculous because Elliot did not come near her anyway.

She walked down the hallway toward James's office. When she opened the door, she found him seated at his desk, his Smith and Wesson revolver already in his hands.

Leah clutched at her stomach. He had been trying to get her to play Russian roulette since she got home from the cabin, but so far she had managed to avoid it. She had played the game twice before, when James had threatened to leave her if she didn't, and both times she had come home with urine stains on her underwear. For days afterward, she had nightmares of guns going off into her temple, of James handing her his revolver and saying, "Fire it. Come on, fire it."

He stood up from behind his desk and she started crying. She didn't know why she came here. Since that night he whipped her, she cried nearly every time she saw him. She still responded to his touch, but it was paired with a shiver of fear and revulsion. She had stopped looking in mirrors; she had no desire to see the kind of person who allowed this to happen.

It had all been clear in the beginning; she needed passion and he gave it to her. He added a little bit of pain and humiliation along with it, but she could take that, as long as he gave her what she needed.

Then the fear began to grow, the humiliations got worse, and still she couldn't stop herself. She knew exactly whom she resembled: those women on Oprah and Donahue who wouldn't leave abusive husbands. She shouted at them, "Get a life! Find some self-esteem and leave the jerk!" But they never did. Leah had thought they were weak, stupid idiots, and now she knew they thought that of themselves, too. She thought it of herself.

"Please, James," she said. He watched her cry. She waited for him to soften, the way he had after he whipped her, but he did not.

"I've let you weasel out of it the past few times," he said. "But not tonight. I've got an itch for it. Don't you?"

No! Leah shouted in her mind, but the word didn't come out. This was all she was now, James's plaything, the dog he kicked. Elliot had stopped looking at her, stopped talking to her, stopped touching her. When she came out of the bathroom and he came in, he sucked in his belly to keep from brushing against her. He wouldn't look at her and only spoke when spoken to. He made her feel hideous, the monster he was forced to live with.

It was only here, with James, that she felt alive. And that was only because he frightened her into breathing again.

"You know I always go first," James said, coming over to her with the large, glossy revolver in his hand. "If I can do it, so can you. I'll blindfold myself and let you spin it."

Leah cried harder, but she did not turn and run. She could not understand why her feet stayed rooted there, why she let him do this. She wished someone would tell her what was wrong with her.

He pushed the gun into her hand. It was cold and heavy and she thought wildly about aiming it at him and pulling the trigger until she shot him with the single loaded bullet. She could take him out and this would be over. But, without him, she would be dead, too. She'd have to go home and live with a man who never looked at her, never made love to her, never really faced her head-on. No one did, except for James.

James walked back to his desk and took a blindfold out of his top drawer. He wrapped it around his eyes and tied it in the back.

"Come, Leah," he said. "Spin it."

Slowly, nearly hypnotically, Leah did as he asked. Holding the gun as far from her as possible, she opened the cylinder. She squeezed her eyes shut as she spun the chambers and snapped the cylinder shut, not wanting to see where the single bullet landed.

She handed the gun back to James. It had been awkward and heavy in her hand, but in his the revolver seemed like a toy, small and featherweight. He even tossed it once and then caught it tightly in his grip.

He took a deep breath and lifted the revolver to his right temple.

"God, this is stimulating," he said, and then pulled the trigger.

Leah jumped back, ready for blood to splatter her, but there was none. James laughed and tore off his blindfold.

"I never lose," he said, triumphant. His face was bright red, his eyes wide open and half mad. "Now let's see how your luck holds out."

He put the blindfold on her and then handed her the gun. In her mind, Leah was saying, *I won't do it. I won't do it.* And yet she raised the gun to her head, almost as if James had taken control of her arm.

Her hand shook badly, and suddenly James's hand was there, holding the barrel steady against her temple.

"Do it," he ordered.

Tears streamed down Leah's cheeks. Twice before, she'd pulled the trigger. Twice, she'd been lucky. But luck always ran out. She imagined Samantha and Elliot finding out that she had killed herself in a game of Russian roulette. They would know all there was to know about her then. There were two kinds of people in the world: those who would play this game, risk their lives for sport, and those who would not. God, they would never forgive her.

Leah almost regained her sanity then, nearly put the gun down. But then James's free hand clamped down on her shoulder.

"Come on, Leah," he said. "You know you want to do it. Live on the edge. Stare death in the face and knock it down."

Leah squeezed the trigger before she could think. She waited for the impact, was certain she'd shot herself, that she was falling over, but then James pulled the gun away and whipped off her blindfold.

He was breathing hard and he stared at her. He put his hand underneath her chin.

"You've got guts, Leah Shaperson," he said. "I'll say that about you. You've got a hell of a lot of guts."

He kissed her and Leah waited for the passion to take hold, the way it always did, even at moments like these. This time, though, she could not get past the shivering. She had wet her panties again, and the urine seeped down her inner thighs. James slipped a finger in her waistband and Leah stepped away.

"I've got to go," she said.

James blinked twice, disbelieving.

"I beg your pardon?" he said.

"I can't stay tonight. I'll see you when you get back from Europe. Goodbye, James."

She ran out, half expecting to feel a bullet in her back. But she made it to the door safely, and then out into the hall. She pushed the elevator button, but when it didn't open right away, she ran to the stairs and raced down thirteen floors.

She did not go into the underground parking lot, but instead rushed out into the street and gulped at the air. She bent over, trying to catch her breath, to force oxygen into her lungs. She was still crying when two men approached her.

"Lady, are you all right?"

She ran away from them, into the street, and a car blared its horn. She stared at it, thought for a crazy moment that it was her car, that Elliot was inside staring at her in horror, but of course that couldn't be right. He was at home, watching television, unsuspecting. She ran on, feeling James's eyes on her from the thirteenth floor of the building, still feeling the rush of air at the side of her temple where a bullet might have entered.

The next day, Elliot sat in his office, one hand holding up his head. He was exhausted, but he didn't let that slow him down. He spent sixteen hours a day here now. He arrived at six in the morning and didn't leave until ten at night. He ate his meals here, changed clothes here, sometimes slept here, all in an attempt to avoid Leah.

He ran his fingers over his forehead. He was sweating, although the air conditioner kept the office cool. His secretary talked on the phone in the other room; his partner, Bill Mangowitz, skulked around the halls, trying to keep hidden. Elliot had let him stay on, had given him the opportunity to right what he had wronged, but he was beginning to think he'd made a mistake. Bill spent more time out of the office than in it, and Elliot knew he was going to the track, trying to hit the big jackpot so he could pay off the debt in one fell swoop instead of eating away at it a little at a time. Elliot was beginning to hate him. It seemed as if he were beginning to hate everyone.

The phone rang and Elliot answered it.

"Elliot Shaperson," he said.

"It's me."

Elliot stiffened. "What is it, Leah?"

She was silent for several seconds and he could picture her standing in the kitchen, sipping a drink and blinking back tears. Lately, he was rough with her every time he spoke to her, as if he'd finally admitted what others had always known, that time together gave a person license to be mean.

"I just wanted to know what time you'd be home," Leah said.

"Late. Don't hold dinner."

"I wasn't going to," Leah said sharply. "Dylan left today for Alaska. I asked Samantha over."

"Good. Tell her she's better off without him."

They were both quiet and Elliot looked down at his hand. It was shaking wildly, jerking its way across the desk. He had no idea what was happening to him.

"I'll tell her what I want to tell her," Leah said finally.

"Fine. Good night."

Elliot hung up and sat back in his chair. They were hardly even civil to each other anymore, and the frightening thing was that civility was all they'd been surviving on for years. Leah had slackened off three years ago, when she started up with James. Until now, Elliot had been kind enough for both of them.

He had done so well for so long, and now it seemed he'd simply run out of gas. There was nothing left inside of him to be kind to her with. All he could do was avoid coming close to her, because he knew he was about to explode.

Leah lay beside her husband, listening to him breathe. He was the steadiest breather in sleep. In and out, four seconds for each intake and exhale. She turned toward him and raised herself up on her elbow. She watched him, saw his eyes flutter behind his lids, his fingers reach out for some object in his dream. She slipped her finger into his fist and he clutched it like a baby.

A tear slipped down Leah's cheek. James had been gone for a week and the terror of that game of Russian roulette was finally beginning to fade. That night, she had run through the streets until she was exhausted and then come home early. Elliot had looked at her strangely when she walked in the door.

"That was a quick dinner," he had said.

"Everyone had to leave early," she said. "We decided to do the same as last year and take August off from our dinners. Everyone's on vacation. Besides, it will be nice to spend some time with my husband."

She had waited for his reaction and nearly started crying all over again when he glared at her, as if spending time with her was the last thing he wanted. She knew he had been avoiding her. How could she not notice the way he worked from dawn till way past dusk, the way he slept on the edge of the bed? The worst part was, all of a sudden she missed him. She missed his tenderness and concern. She missed knowing for certain that he loved her.

She slipped her finger out of his grip and Elliot turned on his side toward her, as if he could sense her pulling away. She quietly got out of bed and walked into the living room.

She sat down in Elliot's chair. He sat in it every night, when he watched television or read the paper. She wiggled into the indentation he had left that evening, smiled when she saw he was wider than she by at least four inches. She smiled and then she cried, and she knew she was positively insane.

Elliot was good and kind and she loved him. James was vicious and cruel, and would probably end up killing her. Yet if James called her now, she would go to him, she would chance it. She would risk her life if only to feel young again, to walk on the edge. That was how important it was to her.

She stood up and walked into the bathroom. She turned on the light, blinked at the brightness, and for the first time in a month, stared at herself in the harsh, unforgiving florescence. She was getting old, nearing sixty. Her eyes were cynical and their spirit was broken. The face that looked back at her was not worth saving, and that, really, explained everything about James. She just wasn't worth anything better.

She turned off the light and stepped out of the bathroom. She jumped back, surprised to find Elliot standing in the hall, staring at her.

"You're up," Leah said.

Elliot said nothing. He stared at her, seemed to stare right through her, and then turned and walked back into the bedroom. He stood looking at the bed, as if he didn't recognize it. Leah's heart immediately softened. Despite it all, it was still her job to take care of him. It was the one thing she knew she was still good at.

"What is it?" Leah asked softly. She reached out for his arm, but he stepped aside when she got close. The air went out of her. Elliot had never done that before. She had not even known he was capable of it.

"Every night since we got back from the cabin," Elliot said, "I've lain in bed, staring at the ceiling, wondering what to do."

"What to do about what?"

"For three years I've done nothing. I know you think that's wrong, that people should get things out, talk about their feelings, but I never believed that. You just make things worse when you talk about it. What good does it do you to accuse someone and then have them admit it? Words, even apologies, don't change anything."

Leah stepped back until she reached the wall of the bedroom. She leaned against it, tried to breathe.

"Elliot, what are you—"

"Then, when we got back, when you left that first night we got back, I started feeling something I hadn't before. I started feeling . . . abused."

Leah's heart was beating so loudly, she could hear it in her head. She thought of the car headlights that had passed her just as she walked up to James's house, how the roar of the engine had sounded familiar. She thought of running out of James's office last week and thinking she saw Elliot in a car that passed by.

"I don't understand," she said, although she did.

"I know," Elliot said. His voice was hoarse and the words were garbled.

"What?"

"I said I know," Elliot said, turning to her. He showed her a face she didn't recognize, red with suppressed rage. She clutched her nightgown to her chest.

"You know what?" she asked. She would make him say it. She still could not believe he knew. No one could know and not say anything. He had come home on time tonight and they'd had dinner together. How could he sit through a whole dinner with her and not say anything? How could he have sat through so many dinners, gotten through so many days, and still kept quiet?

Elliot stepped toward her, his face and neck blistering from rage, and Leah saw James's face in his. She saw the recklessness, the fury, the need to lash out. She stepped back, but then Elliot turned from her and lunged for the bed. He yanked the blankets off and threw them on the floor. Then he grabbed the pillows, flung them hard against the mattress, then hurled them across the room. He stared back at her, burned her with his gaze, then, in one viciously graceful move, swiped his arm across the dresser, knocking over frames and perfume. Glass shattered on the hardwood floor and liquid seeped into the wood, bombarding the room with fragrances.

Elliot looked around wildly. He started toward her and Leah jumped back, but then he turned and ran to the closet. He flung open the door and grabbed one of Leah's blouses. He ripped it off the hanger, then hurled it at her face.

Leah watched this man, this alien man, as he ripped off blouse after blouse and flung each one at her harder than the one before. She did not back away when the clothes hit her. She took every shot, was somehow relieved at the stinging on her cheeks, as if, after all, she was getting what she'd always thought she deserved.

She stood in silence, in awe, in dreamlike fear. Elliot went through the entire closet, ripped out every piece of her clothing. When he was through, he picked up her shoes and sailed them right for her head. Leah screamed and ducked and then, for the first time, understood that he hated her and ran out of the room.

He was faster and he grabbed her before she could get to the bathroom to lock herself inside. He pulled her into the kitchen, flipped on the glaring fluorescent lights, and fixed her with a stare that chilled her.

"I know you've been seeing James Arlington for three years," he said, the words straight and precise as arrows. "I know you've gone to him every Tuesday and Thursday night and screwed his brains out in his office. I know you went to him the day we got home from the cabin."

Leah slumped, and, as if every word were fists pounding on her head, she fell toward the floor. By the time he was through, she was down on her knees, crying. He stared at her, seemed to finally see her through his fury, and then pushed her away in disgust. She had to brace herself to keep from crashing into the kitchen cabinets.

"I've always known!" Elliot shouted. "You thought I was a fool, that I'd stopped looking at you. But I was always looking. Always!"

"So why didn't you do anything?" Leah shouted back up at him.

His eyes were wide, frenzied, and Leah pulled herself up. She backed into the corner of the kitchen.

"Because I loved you," he said, his anger turning to pain. He started crying, miming sounds with his mouth. Leah was both repulsed and drawn to him. She didn't know a thing about him, she realized in that instant. She had not known he was capable of shouting, of going crazy, of ransacking their bedroom. She had not known he could feel so much pain, that he must have been feeling it all along.

"Because," he went on when he could, "I thought it would pass. I thought you'd come back to me."

"I never left you," Leah said.

Elliot's head jerked up and his tears stopped abruptly. The knives sat on the counter by his hand and he pulled out a steak knife. Leah's eyes widened as he fingered the blade.

"You think I'm crazy," he said. "You think I'd hurt you."

"I don't know what to think."

He stepped toward her, smiling, the knife still in his hand. She raised her hand to her mouth, and then Elliot quickly turned and threw the knife across the room like a carnival performer. It landed in the sofa and stuck out like an extremity.

"I saw him open the door to you," Elliot said, grabbing her arm. "His fancy silk robe was hanging open. I could see him from the road. I kept thinking, 'She won't walk in. Leah would be sickened by a display like that.' But you weren't. You were eating it up."

"He makes me feel things!" Leah shouted. She was the one who was crying now. "He wants me. He's excited by me. You can't even—"

They stared at each other and, for a moment, Elliot came back to her. His face crumbled, the anger disintegrated, and she saw him, her husband. She touched his cheek.

"Oh, El, we've got to stop this."

He jerked away at her touch and stood up straight.

"I couldn't perform after the first day I found out you were with him," he said. "Every time I'd try, I'd imagine the two of you and it made me go limp."

He turned around and walked back to the bedroom. He looked at the mess in confusion as if he couldn't remember what he had done. Then he walked to the closet, pulled out the suitcase, and opened it up on the bed.

Leah came in and stood by the door. She thought, *I'm dreaming. If anyone's going to leave, it will be me.* But as she thought this, Elliot packed his underwear and socks and shirts and pants in his suitcase and then snapped it shut.

He walked past her without a word. He set the suitcase down by the front door and then walked into the dining room. He took his briefcase off the table and then walked back to the door.

He opened it. Leah expected him to stop, to lose his nerve. At any moment, she would come up with the perfect explanation, the exact words that would bring him back to her. She imagined telling him about James's cruelty, but that would only sicken him. She could lift up her shirt and show him her scars from James's whip, but then he would wonder what kind of a woman would take that. She tried to put together the words that could explain all she'd been feeling, her need to be seen, to be wanted, to live, to cry, to shout, but they wouldn't come together right. It didn't make sense, even to her.

Elliot stepped through the portal and out into the night.

"You're leaving me?" she asked finally.

"Yes. I guess I am."

"But Elliot . . ."

He looked back at her and seemed unsure for a moment. "I tried so hard not to be," he said, "but I suppose I'm my father all over again."

"Where will you go?" she asked.

"To Samantha's, I think."

"Oh, Elliot, no. This will kill her."

His anger was back instantly.

"You should have thought of that before you started screwing your psychiatrist."

"I needed to be wanted again. It wasn't James I wanted. If it could have been any other man, believe me, it would have been. But he was the only one who offered."

"Great. My wife would spread her legs for any man."

Leah pounded her fist into the door. "Dammit, at least try to understand me. I felt as if I were dying inside. I had nothing to look forward to, no real reason to get up in the morning, except to make you your breakfast and get you off to work. I was terrified of getting a job. My friends had dwindled away. I was alone, Elliot. Can't you understand?"

Elliot stared at her a long time. Then he shrugged.

"No, I can't understand. I loved you. I loved our life. I felt more alive with you than with anyone else. But if it was passion you wanted, a new man, then that's what you've got. Arlington can screw you all he wants now. But don't count on that being too much. He's got two other lovers besides you, Leah. I'm not even sure if you're first on the list."

Elliot turned and walked to his car. He drove away slowly, calmly, the way he always drove. Leah stood in the doorway, hollowed out, breathless. She had been crying earlier, but now her eyes were dry. She stared at Elliot's fading taillights, reached out as if she could catch what was left of his spirit in the air. But he had taken it all with him and, when she closed the door, she was completely alone.

13

Dylan had come back from Alaska, fully changed. He went straight to Samantha's apartment, told her he loved her, that he wanted to marry her. Then someone started beating on the door. Dylan asked, "Are you going to get that?" and Samantha said no and started crying. With every knock, Dylan was fading, until she could see right through him. She reached out to hold him, but her fingers touched only air. She screamed, and then opened her eyes. She was lying in bed, alone, and the knocking was real. It was one-thirty in the morning.

She grabbed her robe and hurried to the door. When she opened it, her father was there. Her first thought was that her mother was hurt, or dead, and Elliot wanted to tell her in person. Instead, he swung a suitcase out from behind him, and set it down in her living room.

"I've done it," he said. "I've become my father."

Samantha let him in and closed the door. She kept glancing down at the suitcase, not understanding what it meant. Was he going to some insurance convention? Taking a trip he hadn't mentioned to her?

"Where's Mom?" Samantha asked. She was still groggy from sleep, still upset about her dream, still missing Dylan who had not yet come back from Alaska, and still wondering if it was smart to be spending so much time with Michael, as she'd been doing since Dylan left. She hardly had any room left in her mind to think about her parents.

"She's at home," Elliot said. "I've left her."

At first, she thought it was a joke. "I've left her" were the three words she had been absolutely certain she would never hear her father say. And yet, Elliot's eyes were cold and determined and completely serious.

She tried to grip the wall to steady herself, but she was too far away to reach it and she stumbled. Elliot led her to the couch and, a moment later, came back from the kitchen with a glass of water.

She drank the water greedily; his words had left her parched. She'd thought she'd known him, but she'd known only the father in him, the part that made him rush out into the street after her when she wasn't careful, tutor her in math and drive her to friends' houses for sleep-overs. She had never known the man, just as she had never known the woman in her mother, what they thought and felt, what they were capable of.

Finally, Samantha said, "You did what?"

"You heard me right," Elliot said. "I left her. Don't ask me why. I'll never tell you."

Samantha gathered her nerve and stared at him. She did not recognize one single thing about him. His brown eyes were too dark, his usually neat hair messy. He shook when she had never seen him anything but steady.

"You must be kidding," she said. "You'd never—"

"I did," Elliot said. "I'd like to stay with you for a

little while. Just for a few days. Until I can find an apartment."

"I don't understand this," Samantha said.

"What's to understand? It's over."

"Why?"

"I can't tell you."

"How is Mom?"

"I don't really know," Elliot said. "Obviously, I don't really know anything."

"Dad . . ."

Elliot shook his head. He walked to the window and looked out. He put his hands in his pockets, jingled the coins there.

"You love her," Samantha said. "This just isn't possible. You two have been together for so long."

"Just because your mother and I have been married for thirty-seven years doesn't mean I'm dead inside. She can't run all over me and expect me to just get up afterward and brush myself off. I did that for years, but no more. Tonight I woke up and knew I couldn't do it anymore. It was the strangest thing."

His eyes darted around the room, he licked his lips; he did not look like anyone's father or husband. He glanced down at himself, seemed surprised to find his same body there, as if he were as awed by the changes in himself as she was.

"Mom loves you," Samantha said.

Elliot turned back toward the window. "No, I don't think she does. I don't think she has for a long time."

Samantha stood up. She took a step toward him, then stopped. Took another step and stopped again. Then the tears came. Elliot walked over and took her in his arms.

"I know this is hard for you," he said. She snuggled into his warmth and held on as tightly as she could. She had not clung to him for years. She hadn't even allowed herself the indulgence of a long hug. Her parents' comfort had seemed like an affront to her independence. Whenever she touched them, she did not hold on long enough to even notice what they felt like, if they had gained weight or changed smells.

Now, she held on tightly and noticed everything. Elliot smelled precisely the same. Oh God, she had forgotten that smell, the mix of sweat and after-shave and soap. She buried her head in his neck and wiggled her fingers around his thick middle. He had always been so solid. She remembered that. She remembered playfully beating her hands against his chest, asking him if he were made of wood. She remembered thinking he was impenetrable, not like other men. He could stop cars and bullets, she was certain.

"It will all work out," Elliot said. "Not like before, but in some different way that we can all live with. You're an adult now. You've got to understand that you can't stay with someone out of habit. There's got to be more there. Your mother and I lost something. I'm not sure when or how. But it's over."

He pulled away from her and Samantha stifled the urge to yank him back, to take him with her everywhere. She smiled at herself; it was a ridiculous thought, dragging her father around to business meetings and dates. She had thought she was so independent, so strong, and yet as long as her parents were alive, she would always be somebody's daughter.

Elliot had been sleeping on Samantha's couch for two nights when Michael called. Elliot answered, and as if they'd always been the best of friends, they spoke for twenty minutes before Elliot finally handed the phone over to Samantha with a smile.

"It's that surgeon," he said, smiling, jabbing the phone at her, and Samantha laughed.

"Obviously," she said.

Right away, Michael said, "Your dad told me what happened with him and your mom. I'm sorry. Is there anything I can do?"

Samantha closed her eyes for a moment. "It's all right," she said. "I'm fine. Are we going to dinner tonight?"

"If you're up to it. But if you'd rather spend time with your dad . . ."

Samantha looked at Elliot sitting on the couch. "Would you mind if I went out with Michael?" she asked him. "It would just be for a couple of hours."

"Are you kidding?" Elliot asked. "Go. Stay out as long as you like. It will be nice for me to have some quiet time anyway. I've got tons of work from the office."

"Did you hear that?" Samantha said to Michael.

"Yes. I'll see you at seven. Dress up a little. I'm taking you to the nicest place in town."

Samantha hung up the phone and stared at her father. He was grinning from ear to ear and she laughed.

"You'll love him even more when you see him," she said. "He's got very, very short hair and a BMW. He's the antithesis of Dylan."

Elliot stopped grinning and looked away. "I never said I hated Dylan. But I could tell right away that he wasn't serious about you and you were head over heels for him. It scared me."

"Since Dylan's been gone," Samantha said quickly to deflect her father's words, "Michael has bought me flowers, taken me to dinner, called every time he said he would."

"He sounds perfect," Elliot said.

"No. He sounds dull. He sounds like someone who's already fallen in love with me, and so where's the challenge in winning him?"

They stared at each other a long time and then Elliot shook his head.

"I don't understand you women," he said.

"Do you think we understand ourselves?"

Samantha went out to dinner with Michael and had fun, and ate well, and wondered why she couldn't get excited over the man sitting opposite her. He was so distinctly her friend, she found it nearly impossible to imagine him as anything more.

She came home late and didn't sleep well. Early in the morning, she heard her father scuffling around in the living room. She got out of bed, put on her robe, and walked into the living room. Elliot was there, bent over his briefcase, arranging papers. He had already showered and dressed and shaved, and was ready for work. The sun, however, had not yet risen. Samantha glanced at the clock in the kitchen; it was not quite four in the morning.

"You can't go to work already, Dad," she said.

Elliot jumped a little at her voice and then snapped his briefcase shut.

"I might as well. I've got some paperwork to catch up on anyway."

Samantha watched him ready himself. She knew every move he would make before he made it. Her mother had craved sleep, so Elliot used to be the one to get her up and ready for school every morning. Every day, at seven AM, she had sat at the kitchen table eating cereal and watching her father stand by the counter, tightening his tie. All of his ties were solid colors, blue, red, black, gray, and he tied them exactly the same way each time, staring at his reflection in the toaster while he did it.

Then he slipped his keys into his pants pocket, his wallet in his jacket pocket, and jingled the coins he kept in his pants for sodas. She'd heard those sounds for years and become nearly deaf to them, but now, suddenly, the clanking of his coins sounded lyrical, nearly operatic.

She moved up behind him. "Dad, please. Stay a little while. Let's have a cup of coffee. I can't go back to sleep, either."

He turned to her, nodded, and she went off into the kitchen. She poured the coffee and turned on the air conditioner to battle the August heat that wouldn't let up, even at night. She brought the coffee mugs into the living room.

They sat down side by side on the couch.

"How was your date with Michael last night?" Elliot asked.

"Good. We went to La Frite, that fancy French restaurant downtown. Don't ever go there. Nothing on the menu is under thirty dollars and you get about a quarter serving of everything."

"But was it good?"

"Nothing is that good."

"How was Michael?"

Samantha touched his arm. "He was fine, Dad. Pleasant as always. I'll be seeing him again tonight, if that makes you happy."

Elliot pulled his arm away and stiffened. "Stop treating me like I'm an old fool. I know a lot more than you, whether you believe that or not. I know that love can blossom out of friendship if you just hang in there long enough."

Samantha squelched the desire to argue with him. Didn't he think she was trying? If she could force herself to love Michael, God knows she would. Just as she would have forced herself to be attracted to the computer nerds in college who would go on to earn six-figure incomes, or the class valedictorian in high school who was brilliant but covered with acne. Instead, her heart only raced for the rebels, the motorcycle riders and bad boys who would never go anywhere or do anything but look good.

"I called Mom last night," Samantha said, to change the subject.

"Oh?" Elliot's expression was blank, he gave away nothing in his eyes. Samantha shifted on the couch.

"Yes. From the restaurant. Michael convinced me she'd want to talk. She didn't sound very good, Dad. She said she's not eating. She rarely goes out of the house. At night, she can't sleep very well because she's scared of someone breaking in."

"She's just making a bid for sympathy. Leah will be fine."

Samantha stared at his hard profile. She knew it wasn't possible, yet he looked younger. It was the firm set of his jaw that did it. The resolve in his eyes.

"You still won't tell me what happened?" Samantha asked, although she knew the answer she would get. Last night, she had asked her mother the same question.

"He left me," was all Leah had said. "I can't tell you why."

"Why not?" Samantha had asked.

"A marriage has got to have some secrets, doesn't it? Even a bad marriage."

"But Mom—"

"Don't 'but Mom' me. And don't tell me you have a right to know. You don't. This is between Elliot and me. I know you think we've done you some wrong, but we haven't. We stuck together while we raised you and now you're a big girl. We have no duty to stay together just so you can have your illusions about marriage. You can deal with this just fine."

"But I can't deal with it just fine," Samantha said. "You two were the one thing I always depended on. There was no doubt in my mind that you would stay married forever."

Leah hesitated, and Samantha could hear her taking

a drag off a cigarette. Samantha was certain that the house was filled with cigarette smoke now; the moment Elliot left, Leah would have started smoking full-time. Samantha could almost see her, sitting at the dining table, the ashtray overflowing, the television going in the background, the cupboards nearly bare of food, and the front door bolted shut.

"I'm sorry," Leah said. "But what's done is done. Elliot left and he's not coming back. I'm sure of it."

Now, Elliot set his coffee mug down on the table. "I can't tell you what happened," he said. "Your mother and I have separated, but that doesn't mean I want to hurt her."

"How can telling me what happened hurt her? I'm your daughter. Don't you think I have a right to know?"

Samantha realized she was dangerously close to crying. She stood up and took her mug to the kitchen, tossing the coffee down the drain. She took a few deep breaths to steady herself, but when Elliot came into the kitchen, she let the tears go.

Elliot pulled her into his arms. He rubbed her back, the way he always rubbed it, in smooth, circular, fatherly strokes. He patted her, touched her hair, did all the things she remembered and yet she still felt as if she were losing him, as if he were slipping right through her fingers.

"Don't do this," Samantha said, still crying. "Please, Dad. I need you two together. I can handle everything else if I know you two are steady."

Elliot pulled away and dried her tears.

"You're old enough to realize that what happens between your mother and me has nothing to do with you."

"No, I'm not old enough to realize that. Is anyone ever old enough to realize that about their parents? What you two do has everything to do with me."

"Samantha, please."

"I don't understand," Samantha said. "You were fine at the cabin. You were just like always. You took walks together. You were fine!"

Elliot stepped away. Outside the window, dawn was just beginning to paint the sky.

"Things happen," he said. "I know this hurts you. I know you deserve more of an explanation, but I can't give it to you. If your mother wants to tell you, fine. But the fact is that I left her. I'm not going back. I won't ever go back."

"But why not, Dad? You love her."

Elliot turned around and Samantha was struck by the fire in his eyes. Every second with him now was a surprise to her.

"You told me yourself once," Elliot said, "that our kind of love wasn't enough. That it was boring, mundane, not worth fighting for."

Samantha hung her head. "I was wrong."

"No you weren't, Samantha," Elliot said, shaking his head vigorously. "You were right."

Leah sat on the floor in her living room. She had not sat on a chair or the sofa since Elliot left, two weeks earlier. She spent most of her time in the living room, in front of the television, hunched forward on the floor like a monk in deep meditation.

She went out only for cigarettes and orange juice. She smoked continually, lighting one cigarette from the stub of another. The only thing she could get down was orange juice; she drank ten glasses a day.

She could not eat. It was strange and, actually, kind of wonderful, this nausea. She had lost eight pounds in fourteen days and was considering writing a book on the ruined-marriage diet.

She left the answering machine on loud and listened to the messages, picking the phone up only if

Samantha called. A couple of friends called to tell her they were shocked to hear Elliot had left, the dentist's office wanted to confirm her appointment, someone asked if she'd like her bugs exterminated. She kept waiting for the lawyer to phone, to tell her that Elliot had started divorce proceedings, but so far that had not happened. At first, she thought Elliot might call to check in on her, but now she knew he never would. Elliot did not make decisions lightly or easily, but once he made them, they stuck.

Leah stared at the television, but did not recognize the program. It was some soap opera, obviously, but she didn't know which one. After she had watched Elliot drive away two weeks ago, she had walked back inside, flipped on the television, and had not turned it off since. She could concentrate for only five minutes at a time, so she kept the remote handy and bounced from sitcom to drama, world news to unintelligible movies of the week.

She was surprisingly calm. Aside from not eating and not being able to sit on the furniture, she was actually completely normal. She got up every morning, put on her makeup, got dressed. Then she walked into the living room and sat on the floor.

She didn't feel anything. Not anger or sadness or regret. Not relief or confusion or guilt. Nothing. If she died now and the coroner did an autopsy, he would find her hollow inside.

The night was the only bad time. She heard sounds she'd never noticed when Elliot slept beside her. The house creaked, people slammed their car doors down the street. When the wind brushed a tree limb against the house, she imagined someone scratching on the outside of the window, trying to get in. She felt certain that someone was watching the house, that they knew she was alone inside, without a man to protect her.

During the day, her biggest challenge was to deal with Samantha. Her daughter had waited two days to call after Elliot left, and then, as if making up for lost time, had bombarded Leah with phone calls and visits. Leah knew what she was after. Samantha was logical, straightforward, with a black and white way of seeing the world that she'd inherited from Elliot. She wanted a *reason.* She wanted information, explanations. She thought it would make her feel better if she could just understand *why* Elliot had left. She had no idea how wrong she was. Whys didn't do crap for you. They just gave you facts you were happier not knowing.

Leah was surprised that Elliot hadn't already told Samantha the truth. If the situation had been reversed, Leah would have. She would have told every moving object that Elliot was the villain, that he had cheated, that he had done this despicable thing to her. But Elliot, of course, was still Elliot, and he had left it up to her to tell Samantha. He was an idiot, though, if he thought Leah would ever come clean.

The handsome man on the screen stuffed newspapers beneath the door of his old lover's house and lit them with a match. Leah watched, mesmerized, as the flames caught and the house went up in smoke. The man cried when his lover screamed.

The doorbell rang and Leah stood up. It was probably Samantha, wanting more information. Leah walked slowly to the door, turning back now and then to watch the fire on the television. The actor was still crying, but he was smiling, too. Leah opened the door.

James stood there, dressed in a fancy three-piece suit despite the heat. Leah blinked once, then twice. He was supposed to be in Europe for at least another week. He had never come to her house before. She hadn't even realized he knew where she lived.

"Aren't you going to invite me in?" he asked. As always, when he first came back from Europe, his phony

British accent was even more accentuated, as if he had been practicing on every street corner.

Leah nodded and let him in. He looked around the room and she saw her things through his eyes. Her house was nothing like his; it probably wasn't worth even a tenth of what his cost. The furnishings were comfortable and unassuming, taken right off the showroom floor. She expected James to smirk at this, but he did not.

"What are you doing here?" Leah asked. "I thought you were still in England."

"Elaine got a terrible case of strep throat two days after we arrived. We tried to stick it out, but she was not getting better and neither of us trusts socialized medicine. We decided to come home early."

James turned around and smiled at her and Leah felt a quiver of revulsion. That had never happened before. Usually, when he smiled like that, she wanted him.

"How did you know where I lived?" she asked.

James laughed. "It doesn't take a detective to look up patient records and find your address. Besides, Leah, I know everything about you. You know that."

Leah walked away from him. She reached for the cigarettes on the coffee table and lit one. Her hand was shaking badly.

"I'm not really up to this today," Leah said, surprising herself that she could say it. "Maybe on Tuesday."

James walked up behind her. He didn't touch her, but she could feel his breath on the back of her neck, making the hairs stand on end. She stared at her lit cigarette, realized that, if she needed to, she could shove it in his eye. She shivered, wondered what was wrong with her, why her mind was working this way.

"Today," he said, "when I got into the office, I had the strangest message on my answering machine."

He still breathed on her, then abruptly stepped away and sat down in Elliot's chair. Leah cringed. Even after what had happened, James should not be sitting there. She almost leapt forward when he leaned his head back. A few of Elliot's gray hairs had stuck to the upholstery and she didn't want any of James's blond hairs mingling with them.

"It said," James went on, " 'This is Elliot Shaperson. I've left. You can have her.' Tell me, Leah, what does that mean?"

Leah's legs buckled and she tried to sit on the couch. Again, as if she were not good enough for softness, she could not. She fell to the floor and brought her knees to her chest. She sucked the cigarette down quickly as she spoke.

"He's always known," she said. "That's what he said. He's been following us. He followed me when I went to your house. And I think I saw him that night, after we played . . . after we played Russian roulette. I ran out into the street and he practically hit me with our car. I looked at him, thought it was him, then assured myself that I was crazy. Then he simply exploded. He walked out."

She could feel James's eyes on her, like probing fingers, but she didn't look up. She heard the screaming on the television and longed to see what was happening, but she was afraid to glance at it. She finished the cigarette and reached for the ashtray on the table. She ground the butt out on top of the stack already in there.

"I'm not usually surprised," James said. "But this surprises me. Where is he now?"

"He found an apartment and moved in last weekend. He'd been staying with Samantha before that."

"How does that make you feel?"

This time, Leah did look up.

"How do you think it makes me feel? I've lost my

husband. No matter how much you mocked my marriage, it was my life for thirty-seven years."

"I never mocked it. You did."

"Oh, for God's sake. Don't start playing the analyst with me. I've had it. I've had it with all of you."

She stood up, but so did James. He grabbed her arm and twisted it behind her, kissing her at the same time. Leah did not want him, did not feel in the least bit sexual, but she let him kiss her. She knew better than to pull away, knew that James liked nothing better than a rousing game of rape.

"I missed you," James said, pulling away for a minute and panting. "You're the only woman I've ever missed. It's really quite extraordinary. But you realize, however, that I can't leave my wife for you."

Leah laughed. God, this was really ridiculous. Her whole life was ridiculous. If she could, she would rewind the tape, send herself back three years, and find another analyst. She would go back to being just Elliot's wife; she'd be calm, subdued, apathetic. And if she lacked passion, well then, so what? Was it really so great a price to pay for a stable life? It didn't seem so, now. Passion was not worth anything now.

"Do you really think I want to marry you?" Leah asked. "To have to play with your little gadgets every night? To get beaten up and whipped and forced to put a loaded revolver to my head? To suffer so you can have your mixed-up revenge on your father? Are you *crazy*?"

James's eyes hardened and Leah realized her mistake too late. Until now, she had always been careful with her words. James was not a man to toy with. He had always scared her, even at the height of their lovemaking. It was what made him so exciting, not knowing exactly what he was capable of.

She realized now what she should have recognized three years ago: she was messing with the wrong man.

He dug his fingers into her flesh. She tried to pull away, but he only dug in harder.

"Just who the *hell* do you think you're talking to?" James shouted.

"I'm sorry, James," she said, trying to smile. "I shouldn't have said that. I'm on edge. I'm—"

He hit her before she could respond. He swung his hand back and smacked her with his knuckles, slicing her cheek with his wedding ring. She screamed and backed away, but he came at her again, hit her again, and sent her flying into the wall.

She crashed to the floor, crying, and he stood in front of her, the tips of his shoes inches from her face.

"I thought you understood," he said. "I thought you had some *compassion*."

"Compassion for what?" she cried. "For your brutality? You know better, James. That's the worst part. Your father was an ignorant, vicious man. But you've got all that psychology and knowledge at your fingertips. You've got no excuse for the things you do."

James pushed the tip of his shoe against her cheek.

"I wouldn't touch you again if you were the last woman on earth," he said. His voice was calm, composed, and that scared her more than if he'd shouted. "You never were any good anyway."

He pulled back his foot and Leah, transfixed, watched him use all his force to swing it toward her. It landed dead in her stomach and the air rushed out of her lungs.

"You're nothing to me," he said. "Not a goddamn thing."

She gasped for air. From somewhere far off, she heard the clicking of James's shoes on the floor, and then the creaking of the front door.

"You watch your back, Leah," James said. "You never know who might be lurking there."

Then the front door slammed and Leah managed

to get to her knees. She bent over, blood spilling off her cheek onto the floor.

She knelt there for a long time, hunched over like a dying woman. She ran her fingers over her ribs, flinching at the slightest touch, wondering if they were broken. Finally, she pulled herself to her feet. She twisted and, though the pain raged through her stomach, she didn't think he had broken anything.

She walked gingerly into the bathroom and looked at her face. Her cheek was already bruised, and there was a two-inch gash down the side. She put a washcloth under the hot water and flinched when she held it to her face.

She cried while she tended her wounds and put a bandage over her cheek. She cried while she walked stiffly around the house, trying to loosen up her joints, refusing to simply lie down and die. She kept right on crying until Elliot called. She stood over the answering machine, listening to him talk stiffly, unemotionally, telling her that he had contacted his lawyer and was ready to start divorce proceedings. Then all her tears dried up.

She grabbed the phone before he hung up.

"You're a bastard, Elliot," she said. "A goddamn bastard."

She flung down the phone and grabbed her purse. She thought about going to Samantha, but knew that she would not want to take sides against her father. She thought about all of her friends, the ones who had phoned to offer their sympathy and then most likely hooted to one another about her misfortune. Then, finally, she thought about the man who had been on her mind since she came home from the cabin. She opened the front door, walked to the car, and went out searching for Dylan.

14

When Leah walked out the door of her house, Samantha was sitting across from Michael in an elegant restaurant on the other side of town. Beside their table, a bottle of the house's best champagne was chilling. Michael had ordered steamed oysters as an appetizer, and as Samantha ate one, the butter dripped down her chin and she laughed.

Michael reached across the table with a napkin and wiped her chin. Then he dropped his hand and smiled at her.

"Do you like it?" he asked.

Samantha nodded. She liked everything he ordered. He had exquisite taste in wine, in food, in cars, in clothes.

"Good," Michael said. "I aim to please."

The waiter came and poured the ice-cold champagne and then Michael raised his glass in a toast.

"To that torrid love affair we had in high school," he said.

"Oh, Michael," Samantha said, laughing. They clinked their glasses and Samantha looked around the restaurant. It was a ritzy seafood place, Samantha didn't even remember the name. The prices were only on Michael's menu and, at first, she had taken offense at that. But then, after thinking it over, she realized he made five times as much money as she did and fair was fair.

"I'm so glad you agreed to come tonight," Michael said. He pushed his wire-frame glasses back on his nose and smiled shyly at her. He was suave one minute, modest the next. He still seemed surprised that she was spending time with him, even though they'd been out together nearly every night since Dylan left for Alaska.

"Of course I agreed," Samantha said. "You're one of the few people who isn't screwing me over."

The minute she said it, she regretted it. She sounded so bitter these days. Every morning, she woke up angry. She had headaches all the time. Her father had found his own apartment and begun divorce proceedings. Her mother seemed to resent her calls and questions. Dylan should have been back in town days ago, if he'd held to his original schedule, but he had not called. She had not called him, either.

Michael leaned across the table and took her hand. His fingers were lean and small and delicate, and Samantha could imagine them holding his medical instruments, making precise, careful movements to clear someone's clogged arteries.

She smiled at him and he smiled back and Samantha could not stop the thought, *This is too easy.* She did not have to make him love her. She did not have to search for searing political commentary to keep the conversation moving; Michael didn't care what she talked about. She did not have to wear makeup or fancy clothes; Michael liked her in anything.

He had always been this way. When she had first

met him, in elementary school, he had been the quiet boy in the corner, the one with his hand raised to every question the teacher asked. The other students had hated him. Samantha had walked up to his desk one day and said, "It's good to be smart. Just give everyone else a chance now and then, all right?"

He seemed shocked at first that anyone had spoken to him, and then nearly cried with gratitude. He dropped his hand for every other question and clung to Samantha's heels from then on.

Samantha took him under her wing, taught him how to mess his hair, make the best of the awful, polyester clothes his mother dressed him in. She yanked him out onto the soccer field and forced him to play.

"You're too hard on me," he said over and over, but he never walked away. He learned to play soccer and pestered his mother into allowing him to pick his own clothes. He could not get accustomed to contacts, but he did trade in his old tortoise-shell glasses for wire frames.

In junior high, he began to grow, and grow, and he shot up past everyone. Samantha encouraged him to try out for the basketball team and, much to his own surprise, he was good at it. He continued on teams all through high school and college.

He was shy with nearly everyone except Samantha and his friends on the basketball teams. But by high school, he was no longer the tallest boy in school, no longer the most reclusive and gawkiest. He was handsome. At sixteen, he bloomed into the kind of boy girls loved to be seen with, rather than the kind they were embarrassed by. He came into his own and Samantha couldn't help it, she took pride in what he'd accomplished, who he'd become.

She remembered clearly the day he told her he was going to be a doctor. They were sophomores in high school, sitting on the football field, eating their sack lunches. It was a cool autumn day, and red and brown leaves from some far-off tree danced across the gridiron.

"Sam," Michael had said, lying on his back and staring up at the sky, "do you think anything is possible?"

She had lain down beside him, so that their arms and legs were touching. They always touched, she had realized, and everyone thought they went together. But it had never been that way. There had been kisses here and there, experiments on each other's body parts, but for the most part they were just friends. Wonderful, inseparable friends.

"I suppose so. Within reason. You can't fly to Saturn or walk on water."

"I know that. But within reason, within the bounds of reality, do you think you can do anything you set your mind to?"

Samantha pulled herself up on her elbow and stared at him.

"What do you want to do?" she asked.

He took a deep breath and then gave her a smile that knocked the wind right out of her. She had never seen it before, never even had an inkling of all that he would become.

"I want to be a doctor. A surgeon, really. A heart surgeon, I think. I want to be the best there ever was."

She didn't laugh. With anyone else, she would have smirked at their silly intensity, but there was nothing silly about Michael. She knew he would do whatever it took to make his dreams a reality. She leaned over until their faces were inches apart.

"Why don't I love you?" she asked him.

He was not surprised by her question. She realized then that he had probably been asking himself the same thing for years.

"I don't know. I wish you did."

She kissed him, hoped that, just once, sparks would fly. But they didn't. She pulled away, smiled at him, and sat up.

"I have no doubt that you'll be a surgeon, Michael," she said. "A great one."

He studied for thirteen years to become that surgeon. And he'd proven her right—he was a great surgeon.

"Dylan's back from Alaska, right?" Michael asked now, breaking her reverie. He blushed a little and turned away, and Samantha knew that he loved her. It was not the play kind of love they'd had as children, but the real thing. He saw her differently now, the way a man sees a woman, while she was still in the past, staring at her best friend on that football field, asking him why she couldn't love him. She had tried to make it clear the first time they went out that they could only be friends because she was in love with Dylan. Yet she knew she was sending mixed signals. It was too easy to lean against Michael when they walked, to let him put his arm around her. She liked the feel of his lips on hers at the end of the evening, even if it was only for a chaste kiss. It was too wonderful being wanted, being the only one in Michael's life. It was intoxicating and she wanted to suck up every second of it that she could, because she knew she would never get the same thing from Dylan.

"Yes, I suppose," she said. "He should have been back sometime this week, although I haven't heard from him."

Michael squeezed her hand and then pulled away. He sat up straight, shook his head as if to shake away his unwanted thoughts, and then smiled once more.

"I'm sure you'll hear from him. He's probably calling you right now."

The waiter came back and Michael ordered for the two of them. Samantha watched him, saw the respect he commanded. The maître d' had seated them in the dead center of the room after Michael announced that Dr. Munsen and his guest had arrived.

The corners of her mouth tilted up as she watched the boy she'd known since grade school act completely the man. She loved the fact that she'd known him when he had braces, that she'd beat him up twice, seen him when he was covered with acne. She loved knowing him, knowing the child within him, and not having to guess about his history.

When the waiter left, Michael looked back at her.

"What are you staring at?" he asked.

"You. I was just remembering who you used to be. You've come so far. You've made so much of yourself."

Michael hesitated a moment and then slid his chair beside hers. He was close enough that she could feel his hot breath on her cheek. Samantha's heart started racing, not out of fear or excitement, but out of curiosity.

"So have you, Samantha," he said softly. Then he leaned forward and kissed her. His lips were feather soft, warm, and tasted of champagne. Samantha slid her fingers around his neck and pulled him closer. She opened her mouth and heard him sigh as he opened his.

It was not like kissing Dylan. She could tell that right away. Dylan was always sure, always took the lead. Michael held back, was hesitant, waited for her to make the moves. When she touched him, he touched her. When she pressed harder, so did he. She smiled a little as she kissed him, because it was a nice change to have control of her senses.

When she pulled away, he kept his eyes closed, as if he were reliving the kiss, imprinting it on his brain. Then, finally, he pulled back and looked at her.

"We never kissed like that as kids," she said.

"How could I?" he asked. "You always made it perfectly clear that you were using me as an experiment, so you'd know what to do when a real boyfriend came along."

Samantha noticed the hurt in his eyes and she grabbed his hand tightly.

"You are not an experiment now," she said. "And you're not just a pawn to make Dylan jealous."

Michael stared at her so intently, Samantha felt a little queasy. Was she lying? She wasn't even sure of her own feelings. He might just be a pawn. Or maybe she was hoping for what her father had told her was possible, a love that grew out of friendship.

All she knew for sure was that love was shaky; even thirty-seven years together did not guarantee success. You'd be a fool to squander even a second of love, whatever its quality or type, because it might be all you'd ever get.

"I mean it, Michael," she said. "This is about you and me. It has nothing to do with Dylan."

He kissed her again, more strongly this time, and then the first course of their six-course meal came and they pulled apart to eat. Three hours later, when they were through, they walked out into the warm August night.

"Shall I take you home?" Michael asked, although the quiver in his voice told her what he really wanted.

Samantha debated only a second. She wanted to rush home and see if the light on her answering machine was blinking, if Dylan had called. But she hated that part of her, hated the weakness Dylan brought out in her. She rebelled against it, just to prove that she could.

"No," Samantha said, and was blinded by Michael's smile. "Take me home with you."

At his apartment, Dylan pressed the redial button on his phone. A few seconds later, he got Samantha's recording for the tenth time. The recording said, "Hello. You've reached Samantha Shaperson. Please leave your name . . . " He had stopped leaving messages after the second call.

He slammed down the phone and stomped around his small apartment. While he'd been sailing the coast of Alaska, he'd come back to himself. He had missed Samantha at first, but then, as the days passed and he woke up every morning to the same gray sea, her face had faded. He had gotten his sea legs again and also his passion for confrontation. His mind became focused on the hunt, with the Vanguard oil tanker as his prey. The two ships had met up on their third day and, rather than risk a high-profile confrontation, the oil company had backed down and the tanker had slunk home. *EarthAlert 1* had spent the next three weeks sailing the Alaskan coasts, on the lookout for whale hunters. They chased two small fishing boats away from a pod of whales and came home feeling victorious. This time.

By the time the trip was over, Dylan felt completely recovered, as if Samantha had just been a sickness inside of him and the clean air had flushed her out. When he got back to Sacramento, he spent the first day tracking down reporters and urging them to do a story on EarthAlert's victory over Vanguard Oil. Today, he'd gone to the office, worked on lousy paperwork, and held three meetings to try to decide who they'd go after next. He'd been doing fine, just fine, until he came home to his apartment and looked at the phone. Before he even knew what he was doing, he was dialing Samantha's number.

He made his first call at seven o'clock. When she didn't answer, he figured she was having dinner with her parents or a friend and would be back by ten or eleven. Now, it was one-thirty in the morning and her recorder still answered for her. Where the hell was she?

Dylan walked into the kitchen and took out a beer. He searched for something to eat, but there was nothing in the refrigerator but a carton of bad milk, a browning head of lettuce, and a wedge of indistinguishable cheese. He slammed the refrigerator door shut.

He wiped the beer bottle over his forehead. It was hot and unusually humid for late August and what he really needed was a cool shower and a good night's sleep. He'd deal with Samantha tomorrow. Or not. Maybe by tomorrow, he'd feel differently, he'd have no need to call her. He laughed at the thought because it was obvious now that time wouldn't make a bit of difference. She had hooked him.

It did not feel good to fall in love. That's why they called it falling. He had tried to pull away from her, but this love had hidden traps, steel teeth that had caught him. Even if he walked away, he'd walk with steel around his ankles to remind him of what he'd left behind.

Dylan was turning to walk into the bathroom when the doorbell rang. He slammed his beer down on the counter and rushed to the door, certain it was Samantha. But when he opened it, he stopped in shock. Standing there, a gash on her cheek, her face bruised, was Leah.

"My God, what the hell happened?" Dylan asked.

Leah's pulse quickened. She had been searching for him all day, since James stormed out. She knew he lived in Old Sacramento, but beyond that he was unlisted and there were too many apartments in the area to go door to door. She had gone to EarthAlert's headquarters, but they had all been out celebrating their victory over Vanguard Oil. Finally, a few of them had straggled back to the office and, when Leah told them she was Samantha's mother and they took one look at her beaten face, they gave her Dylan's home address. Then she had sat in her car in front of his apartment building for five hours, feeling like a fool, like a crazy old woman. By the time she finally worked up the nerve to come up, it was two o'clock in the morning. The light, though, was still on in Dylan's window and occasionally she'd seen him pass by.

Dylan pulled her inside and took her straight to the bathroom. He touched her cheek with his fingers, poking, prodding. He hurt her, but Leah didn't flinch. She welcomed his touch.

"Don't tell me you fell," Dylan said. "I won't buy it."

Leah shook her head. She had promised herself she wouldn't cry, and yet now she couldn't help it. She started softly, but as soon as Dylan saw the tears and pulled her into his arms, the sobs intensified. At first, she cried because of Elliot and James, but then she cried because Dylan's hands felt so good, because he was so young and strong and beautiful, and she was old and battle-weary and undesirable to him.

She pulled away and walked out into the main room. She saw the beer on the counter and took a sip of it.

"I'm sure Samantha has told you the whole story," she said.

Dylan said nothing. He sat down on his rickety dining table—stacked cinder blocks with a heavy plywood top—and watched her. Leah walked around the room, touching walls, objects. It was an awful apartment. The walls were paper-thin; she could hear the television in the apartment next door. The furniture was old and ratty, yet she loved it all. There would be nothing for him to miss here if he just ran away. She marveled at the freedom that must give him.

"I've been having an affair," she said. She waited for the gasp, the expression of shock, but Dylan gave away nothing. She rushed on. The words felt so good coming out, as if her throat had been clogged with everything that had remained unspoken and now she had finally cleared a passageway. It was amazing how easy it was to talk to this man, this stranger, her daughter's lover.

"His name is James Arlington," Leah said. "He's an analyst. He was my analyst for two sessions, until he decided he'd rather be my lover."

She looked back at him, saw that he still wore no expression. God, he was wonderful. She spoke quickly, dramatically, wondering why she hadn't realized before that all she needed was to talk, to tell someone. None of it had seemed real because she'd never shared it. Having an affair was despicable, yet it was something to be proud of, too; it was proof of her sexuality, her desirability. At times, she'd wanted to shout it to the world.

"We saw each other every Tuesday and Thursday evening for three years," she said. "I was certain Elliot never knew. But he did. He followed me."

"He's known for three years and never said anything?" Dylan asked. There was no surprise in his voice, no accusation, and Leah walked back to where he sat, his legs dangling off the edge of the table. She stood directly in front of him. She reached out, hesitantly at first, and then, because she couldn't help herself, touched his legs. They were rock-solid; she could feel the heat of his skin through his jeans. He looked down at her hands, but didn't move away.

"No. That was Elliot's way. To let things slide. To say nothing and let things realign themselves naturally."

"So what happened to change that?"

Leah ran her hands farther up his thighs and felt him tremble beneath her. She looked up at him, caught him watching her, and pulled her hands away.

"The night we got back from the cabin, I went to James's house. I think that was too much. Elliot followed me and saw James open the door to me. James was only wearing a robe, loosened enough to show his . . . you know. Elliot saw."

"So? If he knew you were having an affair and had

been following you, he must have caught glimpses of this man before. He's no idiot. He knows what an affair entails."

"I don't know, Dylan. He changed in the weeks after we got back from the cabin. He started avoiding me, getting up before dawn to go to the office and not coming home until I was in bed. He slept as far away from me as possible, never touched me, never looked directly at me. You saw him that night you and Samantha came to dinner. He was different."

Leah turned around and finished off the last of Dylan's beer.

"He held out for a month," she went on. "I think he probably thought he would come back to himself, be able to sweep this all under the rug again. But then he broke. I really think that was what happened. He woke up late one night and it was as if he'd sliced himself right down the middle and let out everything he'd jammed inside. He was angry, actually angry. He even flung a knife across the room and it landed in the sofa."

Dylan's eyes widened, but he said nothing.

"You're surprised," she said.

"Yes. That he had it in him."

"Oh, he did. He ransacked the bedroom, threw my clothes at me. Then he left."

"Amazing. What even modest people are capable of."

"Elliot's not as dull as he appears. He once worked as an artist, you know. He had dreams of being a great one someday."

"And your cuts and bruises?" Dylan asked. "Is Elliot a closet wife abuser, too?"

Leah laughed harshly. "No. Elliot would never hurt me. This was James's doing. I didn't tell you about James. He's into bondage and pain. Into things like Russian roulette and horse whips."

Dylan stared at her. "And I take it you liked that kind of thing?"

Leah started crying again. "It was never a matter of liking it. It was all part of the package, part of getting what I needed. I know it doesn't make any sense. When I look back, I can't understand why I didn't walk away. It's so clear in hindsight. But it wasn't then. It was all confused. Good and bad, humiliating and liberating at the same time."

"It was worth it to you," Dylan said.

Leah nodded. "Yes. The violence wasn't so bad in the beginning. It was mostly bondage, a few welts here and there. Then it escalated. When I made him mad, he had to punish me. My fear of him started to overtake my excitement. Finally, when he came to the house today, there was no excitement left. I was scared, but mostly disgusted. Like a fool, I didn't tread very carefully. I stood up to him. Told him I didn't want to play any more of his games. He let me know what he thought of that."

Leah cried harder and, this time, Dylan hesitated before he came to her. She saw that hesitation and cringed, knowing what she must look like to him. She must seem old and ridiculous, trying to save her youth by toying with a cruel man, demeaning her marriage.

Dylan held her and Leah collapsed against him. She knew nothing could ever happen. She knew Samantha loved him, and that, despite what he said, Dylan loved her, too. But for just a second, she had such an intense longing to be young and desirable again that she couldn't resist. She pressed herself against him, felt his hardness against her softness, and raised her head up and kissed him.

He let her do it. He was too decent to pull away. She kissed him and opened her mouth, and her tongue searched all over his. She ran her hands down his ribs, over his hips, scooped them around his buttocks and over the front of his thighs. She worked her fingers over the fly in his jeans, felt no hardness there, and quickly moved them up to his chest, to his neck, to his face, to all that wonderful, thick hair. She did all this quickly, in a split second that imprinted every sensation on her brain. He was a sweet man, she knew then, as sweet as Elliot. He was giving her his body on loan, letting her use it. She hated to give it back, but she did. She pulled away.

"You must think I'm ridiculous," she said finally. She sat down on the sofa and hid her face in her hands. He sat down beside her and pried her hands away. He looked right at her.

"You're a flesh-and-blood woman," he said. "You want love and lust and passion and commitment. You want what you're entitled to. That's what I think."

Leah stared at him, saw in his eyes what she had once seen in Elliot's, a youthfulness, a hope for the future, ambition, fire.

"Dylan, I don't know what to do."

Dylan ran his fingers through his hair.

"I'll tell you the truth, Leah," he said. "Neither do I."

15

Elliot sat in his office, staring blankly at a pile of overdue bills. Utilities, client refunds, supplies, even last week's staff salaries. Only the office supply company had been lenient with them, because they had always been good customers. But even they had their limit, and McDermott Insurance was reaching it fast.

Elliot had not taken Dylan's advice and wrested financial control out of his partner's hands. He had set up a monthly payment plan with Bill, so that he could repay the missing company funds. And he had allowed Bill to go on paying the company's bills, as he'd done for thirty years. Elliot had gone overboard to be fair, believing that anyone, if given the chance, would take the opportunity to redeem himself. Now, as he stared at the stack of demanding, demeaning overdue notices that Bill had jammed into the back of his desk drawer, he realized he'd been as wrong about human nature as a person could be.

Earlier this morning, the phone in Bill's office rang

while Bill was out again on some unexplained errand. Elliot rushed to answer it, knowing that by doing so he was facing the truth he had avoided until then. He wasn't sure what came over him, except that all at once, as had happened with Leah, he just wanted all the lying to stop. He couldn't stand his own naïveté a second longer.

He did not even have to say hello. The bookie at the other end immediately started shouting that Bill had worked up a seven-thousand-dollar debt and he wanted it paid now. Elliot had been fairly certain that Bill still went to the horse track, hoping to hit the jackpot. Now it was obvious that he was still using every cent he could get his hands on, whether it belonged to him or this company, to bet on horses that never won.

Elliot hung up on the bookie without saying a word and searched through Bill's desk. He found the overdue bills stuffed in the bottom drawer beneath books and a flask of whiskey. He took them back into his office and closed the door. He drew the blinds, leaned forward over his desk, and tried to breathe. Ever since he'd been living alone, in the furnished apartment he found three miles from his old home, the pains in his stomach had intensified. He could not understand that. He had removed himself from the problem, rid himself of Leah and her infidelity. He should be cured.

But he was not. He reached into his top drawer and took out the container of antacid tablets. He chewed up four of them and waited nearly an hour for some effect.

For a man who liked to avoid conflict, he had certainly picked the wrong friends and family. Both Leah and Bill were like street kids itching for a fight. Leah would have flung James in his face eventually; Bill would have ripped money out of Elliot's back pocket. It was as if the crazy fools had wanted to get caught.

He heard shuffling in the main office and knew that

Bill had come back from his three-hour business errand that really meant he'd been at the track. Elliot pulled himself up straight and wondered if it was true that every man had his limit. Once pushed just a hair too far, he went wild; he was capable of anything. Because suddenly Elliot felt capable of anything. Of violence, of fury, of revenge. Suddenly, he didn't care anymore about restraint or kindness. He understood about his father now, drawn away from his family by his lust for excitement, yanked back by passions he couldn't control. He'd been sucked up into his emotions as if they were the winds in a cyclone. He'd left destruction everywhere he went.

Bill scuttled past his office door, but Elliot called out, "Bill, come here please."

Bill stopped and walked back to the door. He opened it and stepped inside.

He was a small man, five feet six inches, almost completely bald now. He was soft-spoken, articulate, well read. He had been Elliot's best friend for thirty years, but that meant nothing now. Years together were no guarantee of loyalty or love or anything.

"Bill . . . " Elliot said and then stopped. Another stomach cramp came on and he chewed two more tablets. When the spasm had passed, he looked at his partner.

"You know I've been more than fair," Elliot said.

Bill nodded. His face was red and, when he started to cry, Elliot turned away. Bill had a wife and two teenagers to support, but Elliot couldn't help that. He didn't want to help that. Suddenly, he didn't care very much at all.

"I know where you've been. What you've been doing, where the money's gone."

"Elliot—"

"Don't try to deny it," Elliot said, holding up his hand. "I know. You won't be getting your hands on any more of the company money. You won't be coming within miles of this office."

He picked up the stack of unpaid bills and let them drop. Though they were just paper, they crashed as loud as bricks.

"I'd like you to clear out," Elliot said, and Bill's head started bobbing up and down in rhythm to his tears. "You can have everything in your office. I'll even give you a severance pay and let your family keep on with the company insurance. But I'm telling you, Bill, there's no way in hell I'm going to let you take my company away from me, too."

Elliot looked up, watched Bill nodding, crying, and realized his stomach had relaxed. He stood up, stretched out, felt surprisingly good for the first time since he'd walked out on Leah more than a month ago. He walked around his desk and touched Bill on the arm.

"You've got a problem," he said. "Get some help."

Elliot walked out of the offices of McDermott Insurance and into the hot sunshine. He loosened his tie and then took it off completely. He walked over to his car and threw the tie in the backseat, then his jacket. He rolled his sleeves up, unbuttoned the top two buttons of his shirt, and took off walking.

He went where he never had before. Usually, for lunch, he walked down the main road to Burger King or Taco Bell, but today he turned at the first residential street he didn't recognize. He made rights and lefts, took alleys, tiny walking paths. As he got farther from his office, he picked up his pace. He walked past a housing project, where children jumped rope and teenage boys stared at him with suspicion. He walked past brand-new apartments built with glass blocks and metal and wondered how people could stand to live behind such sterile walls. He started up a hill that took him out of the slums and up into the part of town where restored

Victorian and Craftsman-style bungalows and town homes lined the streets.

Elliot walked until his feet were burning in his shoes, until his armpits were drenched with sweat. He walked and walked and knew he'd never be able to find his way back and, all the while, he was smiling. He was thinking about his days at the literary magazine, about his dreams of being an artist. He was thinking about Leah, when he first met her, how beautiful she was, how thoroughly she had excited him, and how good it had felt to be excited, as if he were not quite attached to the ground and could sail away at any moment.

He reached the top of the hill of stylish homes and stopped. There, he had a commanding view of Sacramento, of the capitol, the high rises and shops and homes and parks. Through the smog, he could see the foothills of the Sierras, where, within their protective womb, his cabin sat alone and still.

He sat down on the curb. Cars drove past, but he didn't notice. He took off his shoes and socks and wiggled his toes in the sunshine. He laughed at himself and then he cried. He thought perhaps he'd gone insane, simply split himself off from who he used to be and created a new personality. He certainly didn't recognize any of his actions. He didn't know who the man was who'd walked out on Leah, who'd started divorce proceedings, who'd told his best friend and partner to get out. He had no idea who he was anymore. Then he stopped, thought about it, and realized that was not true. He was his father.

The heat finally began to subside in mid-September. A breeze picked up on the mountains each morning, laced itself with the scent of pine, and then blew down from the Sierras. Tonight, in particular, there was a chill in the air and Samantha gladly reached into the back of her closet and took out a cardigan, draping it around her shoulders before she stepped outside.

It was near midnight, but her mind was set. She was going to Dylan's.

He had left messages for her the night she stayed at Michael's. She had come home in the morning, seen the red blinking light, and known it was him. She had hesitated before pushing the rewind button, not knowing what she wanted to hear. Did she want him to tell her he'd missed her? Or to hear him tell her it was over, so that she could officially grieve and let him go? She wasn't sure which alternative would leave her better off.

Dylan did neither of those things, however. He left two messages, telling her he was home, that he just wanted to say hi, to give him a call if she had the time. There was no gentleness in his voice, nor any bitterness. No inflections to read, no catch in his throat. She stormed away from the answering machine hating him for his nonchalance, hating herself for caring so much.

She did not call him back. For three weeks, she'd gone to work, thrown herself into the quickly approaching November elections, and lost herself in paperwork whenever she felt the urge to call. She went out with Michael every evening, went home with him nearly every night, and squeezed her eyes shut when he made love to her, trying like hell not to wish he was Dylan.

She managed not to call Dylan and yet, all along, she could feel herself slipping, as if she'd tried to climb away from him, but the hill was too steep. Tonight, Samantha walked through the darkness and knew she had lost. She could not replace him with Michael, no matter how hard she tried.

As she neared Dylan's apartment, her feet picked up their pace. She tried to hold herself back, but she had missed him too much while he was away. She felt literally starved for the sight of him; her stomach rumbled, her legs were weak.

She was prepared to knock, sure that she would rouse him from sleep, but surprisingly the door was already cracked open. She stepped in to surprise him.

She heard laughter first. Female laughter. She stood completely still and, when it came again, she realized it was intimately familiar. She took quiet steps into the room and looked around the corner to the kitchen. Her mother stood in front of the stove, whipping up some kind of pasta sauce. Dylan was right beside her, his arm around her waist, and as Leah laughed, Dylan leaned over and kissed her cheek.

Samantha shook her head, as if that would erase the image, make everything right again. But they were still there, her mother and her lover. She cleared her throat.

"Excuse me," Samantha said.

Leah jumped and spilled spaghetti sauce down the front of her shirt. Samantha looked from her to Dylan, who was merely smiling, as if this were all perfectly normal.

"Sam!" he said. "Leah, look who's here."

He walked over to her, bent to give her a kiss, but Samantha pulled away. She felt hot, and sick, and wanted Michael so badly it hurt. She wanted him beside her, his small, warm hand around her waist. She wanted him to whisper in her ear, 'Let's go, Sam. I won't let them hurt you anymore.' She would believe him, trust him, let him lead her away into his nice, neat, orderly little world.

She backed toward the front door. She had left dozens of messages for her mother over the last few weeks, but Leah had returned very few of them. Had she been here? What the hell was going on?

"Samantha," Leah said, coming after her.

"Don't," Samantha said. "Just don't say anything."

She turned and bolted out into the night. She ran

as fast as she could to her apartment garage, where she strapped on her helmet and hopped on her bike. She would ride until her legs burned. Maybe she would never come back.

Three hours later, Dylan slammed the phone down and paced across his living room. Leah was sitting on the very edge of the sofa.

"She's still not home," he said.

Leah wrapped her arms around her stomach. They had been calling Samantha every five minutes for three hours, leaving messages, begging her to let them explain. Actually, Leah had been begging to explain. Dylan's messages had been terse and frustrated. He just wanted her to call, to let them know she was all right.

Oh God. What had she done? Why hadn't she said something to Samantha three weeks ago, when all this started? Leah had wanted to, but when she heard the way Samantha still talked about Dylan, she couldn't do it. Leah knew what young love did; it made you jealous of innocent affection, jealous of a lover's time spent with others, jealous even of things, of fabric against his skin, the bike he rode, the places he visited. There was no way in hell Samantha would not be jealous of Leah.

She knew now that she had been right. She had seen Samantha's face when she walked in on her and Dylan tonight. Her daughter had been appalled, disgusted, and devastated. At first, Leah had felt furious. Furious that Samantha could not see her as anything but old and motherly, as if it were impossible that Dylan could want her. But then those feelings had faded and she had just wanted to take Samantha in her arms, to explain that things were not what they seemed.

Things were never what they seemed. James, for instance, had always seemed so strong and in command of himself, but since he beat her and stormed out of her house, he had begun leaving messages on her answering machine. At first, they were demands that she come back, play his games again. Then, when she made no response, he started threatening her. He told her he would kidnap her if she didn't come, that he'd punish her as she'd never been punished before.

He did this every day at noon, while Leah stood directly over the recorder, trembling, but unable to walk away. Today, she had heard the panic in his voice. In a strange way, she had felt sorry for him. She knew what it was like to need something so badly and not be able to get it. She knew what it was like to border on obsession for someone. She had, at one time, felt that way about him.

He had said, "Leah, I know you're there. Listen to me. This is what is going to happen to you someday if you don't come back. You'll be all alone in your house and a man will sneak in. He'll have a mask over his face and a knife. He'll put it to your throat and rip off your clothes. But he doesn't want to fuck you, Leah. He wants to slice off one finger at a time. Then he'll move to your chest, take the knife, and—"

Leah had ripped the machine out of the wall before he could finish. Then she locked every window and secured the dead bolt on the front door. She would not answer the phone during the day anymore.

Only Dylan knew what James was doing. He had listened to a few of the messages and told her to call the police. When she refused, when she told him that she didn't want to chance Samantha or Elliot discovering what kind of man she had been involved with, Dylan had glared at her.

"You make yourself a victim," he had said. "You were his victim when you let him beat you and you continue to be his victim. You've got to do something."

He was right. But Leah wasn't sure what that something was. If she pushed James any further, she was afraid he would break, start acting on his threats. She knew he was capable of it. She had meant it when she told him his father had stolen his soul; he had no conscience to guide him. She called the phone company and got an unlisted number. That was all she could do, that and hope his obsession had limits, that under all the obscenity, he was still thinking straight.

That's what Leah had been dealing with these last three weeks. That's why she hadn't returned very many of Samantha's calls. But she couldn't explain that to her daughter. Nor could she explain about how she'd been spending most of her time with Dylan.

It had started that night she first came to his apartment. After she had humiliated herself by trying to make Dylan want her, to force herself into her daughter's skin, the two of them had sat on his couch.

She had said, "I'm crazy."

Dylan had laughed. "No, Leah. You're the least crazy person I know. You know what I think you are?"

She looked up at him nervously. "What?"

"I think you're young at heart. That's all. I think you like to skip like a child and get lost in the woods and dance until your legs ache. I think you are what we all should be, ruled not by your physical age, but instead by what you feel inside."

She had stared at him, drunk in every hawkish feature, the yellow flecks in his green eyes. She'd been tingling, just sitting beside him, and for the first time she realized it wasn't because she wanted him to touch her, but because, with him, she felt eighteen again.

"I love Elliot," she had said quickly, breathlessly. "I've always loved Elliot." She had not confessed that to anyone, not even to herself.

"I know you love him. I could see it at the cabin.

I thought it was incredible, how in tune you two were, as if you always had the same melody playing in your heads."

"I thought you were laughing at us," she said.

"No. Why would I laugh? You two had something I knew I would never achieve."

"In the last years," Leah rushed on, "we became so old, so sedentary. I'd make dinner, we'd eat, then we'd watch television or read. We never did anything. Never traveled anywhere exotic, never made love anywhere but in the bed, and even that faded away in the end."

"So you started up with James."

"Yes. I guess. I don't remember actually thinking 'I'm unhappy with Elliot so I'll go have an affair.' It just happened. James touched me and there was no way I could refuse. He felt so good. I felt so wild again. So young and reckless."

Dylan stared at her and then gingerly touched her cheek.

"You were reckless," he said.

Leah blinked back tears. "I can't explain it to you. You hear women talk about staying with abusive husbands and you just want to slap them silly."

"Then it happened to you," Dylan said.

"Yes. No. I mean, I always thought my situation was unique, that James was really kind underneath all the violence, that things would change. I suppose that's what every woman thinks."

Dylan took her hand and pulled her up. She winced a little from the pain in her ribs.

"You won't take him back again, will you?" he asked.

"God, no. I swear it."

He studied her eyes and then nodded. "Good. Now, we need to go out."

Leah touched her cut cheek. "I can't. I look terrible."

"You look as if you've been in one hell of a fight. People will love it. They'll think you're a female boxer."

Despite herself, Leah laughed.

"Out where?" she asked.

"Just out. Let me show you Sacramento at night. Let me reacquaint you with the eighteen-year-old Leah Shaperson."

He did. He took her to three bars, sat her at the counters where she'd never dared to sit before, and ordered her beers, which she had never drunk until that night. He danced with her—fast, wonderful dances that made her giddy. Then they walked everywhere, past shops and coffee houses and through a red-light district where the prostitutes owned the streets. When their legs rebelled, they found a dark spot on a walking bridge over the Sacramento River and sat there until the sun came up, until Leah said, "That's it. That's what I've been wanting. To see the sunrise."

Dylan smiled and held her hand. "There's one every day, Leah," he said.

Nearly every night since, Dylan had taken her out, reintroduced her to her youth, to her craziness, to her daring. As her end of the bargain, Leah cooked him dinner, helped him with some of the paperwork for EarthAlert. She felt alive again. She had a purpose again. Dylan told her about the state of the earth and, for the first time, Leah listened. She realized there were things to do, and she wasn't too old to do them. With Dylan, she didn't feel old at all.

In these last three weeks, Leah had told him all her secrets, laid herself bare in front of him, and he had rejuvenated her, given her back her youth. She had thought it was about sex, but it wasn't. Dylan made her feel young again without even touching her. He treated her with respect, brought her out into the night, expected her to get wild, and that, *that* was what she had wanted so desperately, for someone to realize that she could get wild, still. That under her wrinkles and graying hair, she was the same as she'd always been.

That was what she would have liked to say to Samantha, but she would never have gotten all the words out. Samantha was her daughter, not a confidant. Samantha could be sixty and Leah eighty, and Leah would still protect her, still hide the ugly truths from her because that's what mothers did.

"Samantha probably went to a friend's," Dylan said now, as he paced across his apartment and Leah sat nervously on his couch.

"What if something happened to her on the way home?" Leah said. "You saw how upset she was when she saw us."

"We could call the cops, but they won't do anything until tomorrow or the next day. I have a key to her apartment."

Leah looked up at him. "Yes. Go, Dylan. Explain to her. It would be best coming from you."

"Explain what? Why the hell do I have to explain anything? You're my friend. I'm allowed to have women friends. If she thinks she can—"

Leah stood up and grabbed his hand.

"You can be such a fool," she said.

"Don't try to make me feel something I can't."

"But you do feel it, Dylan. You love her. And that love terrifies you for some reason I can't quite understand. It makes you angry as hell."

Dylan pulled away and walked to the window.

"I will not be controlled by her," he said.

Leah shook her head. "You already are."

"Look," Dylan said, "I'm going over there. Not because I have to explain, but because, first, I need to know if she's all right and, second, she and I need to have it out. It's not working. She expects too much."

Leah nodded. "I'll go with you." She grabbed her purse off the couch.

"No," Dylan said. "I think you should call Elliot. Maybe she went there."

Leah froze. Call Elliot. How easy that should be. But the strange thing was, she felt guiltier now than she had while she was sleeping with James every Tuesday and Thursday night. The talks she had with Dylan, their laughter, their journeys through the wilder side of Sacramento seemed much more intimate than anything she and James had ever done. And, however strange it sounded, she couldn't bear to hurt Elliot with another secret. Because that was the worst part of all of this, the fact that she had hurt Elliot.

"You call him," Leah said.

Dylan stared at her. "Leah, this is no time for histrionics. Elliot will probably know where Samantha is. We've got to clear things up, now."

Leah nodded and stood up slowly. Her heart was racing. Who knew that her heart was even capable of racing because of Elliot?

She took her address book out of her purse and looked up Elliot's new number, which Samantha had given her. He answered on the first ring and his voice was hoarse from sleeping. Leah had not even realized that it was three o'clock in the morning. She took a deep breath.

"El, it's me," she said. He gasped a little and Leah felt a pang in her heart. She could see him, his hair in his eyes, red lines across his cheek from the pillow.

"What is it?" he asked.

"Is Samantha there?" she asked.

"No. Why should she be?"

"She ran away. We're . . . I'm not sure where she is."

She could hear him sitting up, trying to come out of sleep enough to understand her. She imagined he was wearing his white and blue pajamas, that he had a sheet and a thin blanket over him.

"Why would Samantha run away?" Elliot asked. "What are you talking about?"

Leah leaned against the wall and closed her eyes. *I'm sorry, Elliot,* she thought. *Isn't it funny that I'm sorry now, when it's much too late to mean anything?*

"I was at Dylan's," she said. "She saw us together and ran out. She hasn't gone home yet, or she's not answering her phone. Dylan's gone over there. I just wanted to tell you first, before you heard it . . ."

Her voice trailed off and she realized that Elliot had not said a word. She could hear him breathing unevenly. She wanted to shout out all her explanations, but she knew he wouldn't listen. Why should he, after all she'd done?

"Well, now I know," Elliot said. "You've taken up with your daughter's lover. That's fabulous, Leah. Great news."

"Oh Elliot, wait," Leah said, but he didn't. He slammed down the phone.

16

*It was three-thirty in the morning when Dylan reached Sa*mantha's apartment. He had ridden his bike, passing only one motorist who was swerving from curb to curb. He left his bike in a heap on the grass and ran up the steps to the apartment.

Immediately, the hairs on the back of his neck stood on end. Her living room window that faced the outdoor corridor was open, and a curtain billowed out. The lights were off.

Dylan jiggled the front door, but it was locked. He knocked, but no one answered, and then he opened the door with his key.

The room was pitch-black and eerily quiet.

"Sam?" he said, but there was no answer. He slid his hand along the wall until he found the light switch. He flipped it on.

He blinked once, twice. He fell back against the wall and tried to catch his breath.

The living room had been torn apart, thrashed and

stripped and decimated. The couch was slashed in bold, ugly strokes, its stuffing scooped out and strewn across the floor like snow. The wing chairs that had sat on either side of it had had their legs cut off and the extremities had been scattered around the room. The glass coffee table had been shattered; shards lodged in the walls and carpet.

The phone had been ripped from the wall, its cord cut into a dozen pieces. The bookcase along the far wall had been knocked over, its shelves torn from their hinges like dead branches. Samantha's precious books had been raped, their bindings cut, their pages shredded and littered on the floor, a few of them burnt to black ashes and still smoldering in the carpet.

There were burn holes in the carpet in the shape of a happy face. A bottle of red wine had been overturned and splashed around the room in some kind of brutal artistry. The room smelled of vinegar, sweat, and smoke.

Dylan's stomach turned. He faced the open door and breathed deeply, sucking up the cool air. When he was steadier, he took a first step into the room. Glass shards crunched beneath his feet and the sound was like nails on a chalkboard, chilling him. He moved slowly, until he looked toward the bedroom door. Samantha. He rushed into the bedroom and flipped on the light.

His first feeling was one of relief that she wasn't there. But then that relief turned to horror as he looked around. Samantha's white sheets had been spray-painted red. The walls too were covered in gruesome red paint. Dylan stared at them, at the pictures someone had drawn in a childlike scrawl, and shivered at the thought of the kind of mind it must have taken to do this.

The pictures were of women and children lying decapitated on the ground, surrounded by men with knives in their hands and hugely disproportionate penises. They were of giant, unidentifiable animals forcing themselves on tiny creatures, of helplessness and mercilessness, of rape and murder.

Dylan closed his eyes. He bent over, as if someone had kicked him in the gut. He was not religious; he doubted if there even was a god. But now he prayed to every god he could think of, to Allah and Zeus and guardian angels that Samantha was safe, that she hadn't been here when this happened, that she was not out there somewhere with the psycho who'd done this. He prayed so hard his teeth hurt, his ears rang, and then he cried because he was certain that this would be his punishment for not believing. Something would happen to Samantha.

He stood up straight, opened his eyes, then quickly closed them again. The pictures burned his heart, wrecked his soul, and he could not stand to look at them anymore. He was turning to walk out when he heard footsteps in the other room, followed by a scream. He ran out.

Samantha stood in the center of her living room, pale as the moon. Her bike helmet was in her right hand, and her clothes were drenched with sweat. She turned slowly toward Dylan, her eyes questioning, pleading, and he would have given all he'd had to turn back time, to be lying in wait outside of her apartment when the bastard who had done this arrived. He wouldn't have even waited for an explanation. He would have killed him before he made a move.

Dylan closed the bedroom door behind him and walked toward her. He moved slowly because he could see her trembling, because he was afraid that sudden movements would set her screaming. She tried to speak, but she could not make any sounds.

He reached her and carefully wrapped his arms around her shoulders. He waited for her to cry, but she did not. She trembled violently, and he clung to her tighter to keep her steady. She tried to look around, but he pulled her face back to his chest, to shield her.

Finally, she found her voice, but the sounds she made were guttural, indistinguishable. She pulled away and started for the bedroom.

"Sam, don't," Dylan said. He was the one who was crying. He had not cried since the trees came down on his parents' property and yet now he could not stop the tears. He never wanted to let Samantha out of his sight again. He never wanted to be out of her sight. He suddenly felt small and defenseless and utterly defeated by a world that created people capable of such abominable acts. It took all of his hope away. It made his fight for the future of the planet seem absurd.

"Please don't go in there," he said.

Samantha ignored him and opened the door to her bedroom. The light was still on, and he heard first a cry, then a thump as she sank to the floor. When he reached her she was sobbing, shaking so badly she seemed to have lost control of her body. He scooped her up into his arms. She clung to him and buried her face in his neck as he carried her out of the apartment.

Elliot and Leah sat at the dining table in the small furnished apartment Elliot was living in. All of the walls were white and stark and empty, except for one awful picture of a bloated gray fish, its eye resting too far back over its gills, that sat above the blue canvas sofa. The apartment came fully equipped with a stained coffee table, an outdated RCA color television, and a loudly humming refrigerator. Through the door to the bedroom, Elliot saw his unmade bed covered with an orange comforter that had a musty smell, like the interior of his mother's old Cadillac, that he couldn't get rid of.

Elliot looked across the table at Leah. She had arrived two hours earlier, banging on his door as if a mob were after her. He had been up since her phone call, up and vacillating between hating her and worrying about Samantha. He had opened the door and glared at her.

"Just let me in," she had said. "I'm worried about Samantha."

He had stepped aside as she marched in and then waited for her excuses about what had been going on between her and Dylan. So far, however, she had offered nothing. She had simply stayed near the phone, calling both Dylan's and Samantha's apartments every few minutes. She did this again now, dialed Dylan's number and let it ring six times and then dialed Samantha's. Nobody answered at either location.

He was surprised by everything about her. Surprised that she'd had the guts to come here, surprised at what she wore—tight blue jeans and a large black sweater. He was even surprised at what she looked like; there was a dimple in her cheek he'd already forgotten about.

He stood up and walked to the sliding glass door. It opened onto a rail-thin balcony that overlooked the parking lot. He had thought he'd stumbled onto a great deal when he found this place. The apartments were all furnished, quiet, somewhat cocoonish in their dark, cramped confines. The manager had told him that he got a lot of divorced men—men who had left their furniture at home, who had no clue how to go about restocking themselves with pots and silverware and towels. He had not told Elliot that the very impersonality of the place would eventually make even the strongest man want to shrivel up and die.

Leah got to stay in their house, see the same pictures on the walls, sleep in the same bed, while he got three mismatched plates, an ugly fish picture, and a rusted electric skillet that never got hot enough to cook meat through. Leah was only getting divorced from him, but Elliot was getting divorced from his house, his neighborhood, his *things*. He missed his chair, dammit. He missed his reading light and the wine glasses with the blue stems and the cushioned toilet seat that had seemed such a ridiculous extravagance when Leah bought it.

"Goddammit," Leah said, "why don't either of them answer?"

Elliot said nothing. The sun was beginning to rise over the city. The sky was orange and blue, and Elliot smiled a little thinking God was a Denver Bronco fan, filling the heavens with old players and coaching scrimmages at dawn. Thin lines of clouds, like yard markers, were just beginning to be visible.

"Elliot, tell me what to do," Leah said. "Please."

Elliot turned around. For the first time in years, Leah looked her age. There were dark, baggy circles beneath her eyes and she'd been hunched forward since the moment she arrived here, as if she were afraid he'd reach over and punch her in the stomach.

He was glad that she felt miserable, glad that she was wringing her hands, feeling responsible, guilty. It was hard to believe how good it felt to see her suffering. Beneath all the morality and phony goodness, he was just as mean and despicable as anyone.

He walked back to the table and sat down. He picked up his cold cup of coffee and drank what was left of it. Leah had gone into the kitchen to make coffee almost as soon as she arrived, but Elliot had jumped in front of her.

"I'll do it," he had snapped and then nearly laughed in pleasure when Leah jumped back. She was scared to death of him, he realized. Scared to death of what he would say about her and Dylan. He wanted to draw the suspense out, not say a word about any of it so that she'd have to sweat a little.

Now though, Elliot was the one who could no

longer stand the suspense. He leaned across the table and stared at her.

"I'll tell you what to do," he said. "Tell me the truth for once. Were you and Dylan in bed together when Samantha walked in?"

Leah jerked, and went pale, and Elliot realized his stomach was not cramping at all. How strange. At one of the worst moments of his life, when he was on the verge of discovering the treachery his wife was capable of, he was perfectly calm.

Leah did not meet his gaze. She shifted in her chair, took a moment to formulate her answer. It was as if he'd fitted a noose around her neck and was slowly tightening it.

Finally, Leah met his gaze. "No, Elliot," she said. "Dylan and I have been spending time together these last few weeks. We go out dancing, to bars. I won't even try to explain why. I was cooking him dinner tonight and he leaned over to give me a friendly kiss on the cheek when Samantha walked in."

Elliot stared at her and, for the first time, noticed a scar on her cheek that hadn't been there before. She saw where his gaze landed and turned her face away, so that he couldn't see it.

"I want you to explain it to me," he said.

"No."

Elliot was taken aback by that. She did not whine or try to plead her case. She sat stiffly and calmly and refused him.

"Why not?"

"Because you won't understand. Because you'll mock me."

He almost said "I won't," but then she fixed him with a stare that kept him silent. He had thought he held all the cards when she walked in, but now he realized they were split fifty-fifty. He had guilt to hold over her head, but she still had secrets he'd never penetrated, and she was not willing to give them away for free.

He wanted to attack her story, find the flaw in it, but somehow he knew she was telling the truth.

"Could Samantha have misconstrued what she saw?" he asked.

Leah nodded. "Yes. I suppose infidelity includes many things besides sex. I stole Dylan's time away from her, his interest. That was as much of an adulterous act as anything."

Her honesty shocked him. He stood up, walked around the room, stared at the horrible picture of the fish on his wall. He found, each time he looked at it, that he could make out more flaws in its execution. The gills were out of proportion to the body, the fin was angled the wrong way, the colors were unrealistic and ugly. He found himself, more and more, studying the piece as an artist, as he would have studied it thirty-six years ago when he was painting illustrations at the literary magazine.

"I can't tell you what to do, Leah," he said, still staring at the picture. "You've dug your hole, so to speak. Now you'll lie in it."

"Oh, for God's sake," she said, "don't start preaching to me now. Samantha is out there somewhere, thinking the worst. She already feels betrayed because you and I are breaking up. I just don't want her to think I've betrayed her again."

"But you have."

Elliot whirled around and they stared at each other. He expected to feel his heart racing from the confrontation, but actually it had slowed to a snail's pace. He usually had to struggle for the simplest word, but now they all came easy. He could bait her, demean her, chastise her. He still knew her vulnerable points, exactly where to stick the knife to avoid her armor, and she had the same knowledge about him. That was the risk you took with marriage: if it failed, you'd have enough weapons to destroy each other.

"If she's hurt," Elliot went on, "I'll hold you responsible."

Leah moved her hand to her throat.

"You've never been this way before," she murmured.

Elliot laughed bitterly. "No. Not until you showed me who you really are."

The phone cut through the bitter air and they both jumped. Leah reached for it, but Elliot was quicker. He grabbed it and said, "Samantha?"

There was a hesitation on the line and then Dylan's voice.

"No, Elliot. It's Dylan."

Elliot gripped the edge of the table. He was torn between anger and worry, but then worry won out.

"Where is she? Is she all right?"

Dylan sighed. "Yes. She's all right. We're at the police station. There was a . . . break-in at her apartment." He lowered his voice and went on. "It was pretty bad, Elliot."

Elliot hardly knew what he was doing. He reached for Leah's hand out of habit and, out of habit, Leah held it.

"Samantha's place was burglarized," Elliot said to her. Her face paled and he squeezed her hand tighter.

"Not burglarized," Dylan said.

"What, then?"

"Someone vandalized the place. Tore up her furniture, burned the carpets. They . . . " Dylan's voice got even quieter and Elliot had to strain to hear. "They spray-painted some pretty gruesome pictures on the walls. Sadistic things. Thank God Samantha was out when it happened, but she won't go back there."

Leah had leaned in to hear what Dylan was saying and her face drained of color. She pulled her hand away from him and walked slowly through the apartment. She stopped at the far wall and leaned her head against it.

"Can I speak to her?" Elliot asked. He felt big and bulky and despairingly incompetent. He wished he were anything but Samantha's father. A friend, a distant relative, even a stranger. Someone who could not be held responsible. A father was supposed to protect. He should love too, and give advice and driving lessons, but safety was his main concern. Elliot had failed the one job he'd been given. Someone had sneaked around his outstretched arms and hurt his child.

"She's in shock, Elliot," Dylan said. "I can't get her to talk at all. I think you and Leah ought to get over here and take her home. I'm going back to the apartment with the police."

"All right," Elliot said. "Which station are you at?"

Dylan told him and Elliot hung up. He stood very still for a moment, staring at nothing, remembering how, when Samantha was young, he had told her over and over that she didn't have to be afraid of anything, that she was as strong as any man. He had taught her to sleep beneath the stars and throw a baseball like a boy and walk without fear. But he had not taught her the most important thing: to be careful. He had wanted her to be hopeful, to have faith in people, to believe in goodness. He had not prepared her for the real world. He had not explained that sometimes people did unexplainably bad things.

He looked over at Leah, who was still standing facing the wall. He walked over to her and put his hand on her shoulder.

"You heard what Dylan said, about her apartment."

Leah nodded and shivered.

"He wants us to come to the police station," Elliot went on, hearing the tremor in his voice and feeling

Leah tremble beneath his hand, as if the same faulty wire were strung through both their bodies. She turned around and stared at him. "She's in shock," he went on. "She won't go back there. She—"

He started crying and Leah slipped her arms around him, the way she always had. She pulled him to her breast and Elliot clung to her, crying loudly.

"We did our best," Leah said. "She lives on her own now. We can't shield her anymore."

"She's the only person whose pain I'd take on gladly," he said.

Leah held him as he cried. He lifted his head up, so the tears would go back down the way they had come. Eventually, they subsided. He breathed. He went on living even though his body was filled with rage and helplessness and he was thinking that being a parent was both the best and the worst thing in the world.

Samantha blinked when her parents walked into the police station, holding hands. She had almost gotten used to seeing them separate and their intertwined fingers held her mesmerized. She tried to say something, but nothing emerged.

Leah saw her first and rushed forward, but Samantha leaned away from her embrace. Dylan, who had been sitting beside her the entire time, stood up and touched Leah's arm.

"Tread easy," he said.

Samantha wanted to tell him that he was being ridiculous, that she was fine, just fine. But her vocal cords were still not working, had not been working since she looked up to the bedroom wall and saw what was painted there.

The police had asked her questions, and Dylan had answered them for her. They had deduced that the break-in had occurred around two o'clock, when her answering machine stopped answering. They had nothing to go on, no clues as to who had done the damage. Dylan looked down at her now and spoke to her as if she were a child.

"I'm going back to your apartment now," he said. "I want you to go home with your mom."

Samantha wanted to scream at him that she was an adult, she could handle this by herself, but again she was mute. He stared at her longer and more intensely than he had for weeks, and then left with the policemen.

Samantha stood up and walked to the window. It was morning now, a clear, wonderfully cool September day. She should have never gone home last night. She should have ridden all the way across the country, found some abandoned cottage in the woods of Maine, and outfitted the door with seven dead-bolts. She should have stockpiled enough food to last for months and never come out once.

Someone touched her and Samantha jumped. She turned around to face her parents.

"Honey, I'm so sorry," Elliot said. He tried to hold her, but again she pulled away. She did not want to be touched by anyone. After Dylan had carried her out of her apartment and taken her to the police station, she hadn't let him touch her, either. She was walking on very thin ice, she realized. One touch and she would start screaming again, the images on her walls would reappear and she wouldn't be able to stand it.

"I want you to come home with me," Leah said. She was nervous and stiff, as if she were expecting rejection. Samantha remembered walking into Dylan's apartment last night, seeing her mother and Dylan together, but all of that seemed like years ago. Why had she been so upset? What was a silly kiss compared to what had happened to her home?

Samantha shuddered. She saw it again. The crude drawing of a decapitated woman, her long hair flailed around her bloody neck, the disjointed body showing mismatched breasts and snakelike pubic hair. She saw the other images too, the men-beasts raping children, the big triumphing over the small. And she had seen what Dylan hadn't noticed, what had been written on the wall next to the bed: the words "Watch your back, Samantha."

Whoever had done this knew her. It was not a burglary at all, but an attack aimed directly at her. If she had been home, she would certainly have been part of the carnage, decapitated just like that picture and left as evidence of the destruction man could do.

Her father reached his arm out, then drew it back. But this time Samantha wanted him. She fell against him, buried her face in his chest. Elliot held her, tried to soothe her, but could not even come close this time.

Elliot led her out of the police station, with Leah trailing behind. He took her into the backseat with him and Leah got in the front and drove them home.

When they arrived at the house, Elliot walked her into her former bedroom. He put her into the bed which always had fresh sheets on it, as if Leah had been expecting something like this to happen for years. Elliot tucked her in and sat on the bed beside her, holding her hand.

Samantha struggled for her voice and finally found it.

"Can you stay?" she asked.

Elliot turned away. "For a while," he said. "Not overnight, I don't think. Nothing's changed between your mother and me. We just . . ."

Samantha nodded. It didn't really matter anyway. He could be sitting right next to her and someone could still attack her. There was evil strong enough to sneak around fathers and it had homed in on her.

"I'm so sorry, Samantha," Elliot said, rubbing his

eyes. "I'm just glad that you weren't there when it happened. The thought of you . . ."

He stood up and took a deep breath. Samantha squeezed her eyes shut to try to stop the images.

"Get some rest," Elliot said at last. Samantha nodded, and kept her eyes closed tight.

Dylan walked through Samantha's apartment with the three detectives assigned to the case. They all had the same reaction he'd had when they first saw the damage; they gasped a little and stopped in their tracks.

"Jesus Christ," one of them said.

Dylan walked straight into the bedroom and forced himself to look at the pictures. This time, he felt less disgust and more fury. How dare someone do this? How dare they take the filth out of their own minds and impose it on someone else?

Dylan looked over the bed, pulled back the spray-painted top sheet. On the bottom sheet, a human figure had been drawn and encircled with a red line, like the chalk mark drawn around a dead body in a bad movie. Dylan threw the sheet back down, covering it.

He raised his gaze and saw what he had missed before, the words on the wall beside the bed. A chill ran through him.

"Detective!" he called out. Detective Polk walked in and Dylan motioned toward the wall.

"The guy knew her," he said.

They stared at the words. "Watch your back, Samantha." Dylan gripped his hands into fists, wanted to start a manhunt, bring in every suspect, torture them all until he got some answers. He wanted to do something, not just stand there like the helpless man he was.

"He could have seen her name on her mail and copied it," the detective said.

"He?" Dylan asked.

"You ever see a woman draw something like that?"

Dylan looked back at the pictures and then checked out the rest of the apartment. The kitchen had mostly been spared, except for the spilled bottle of red wine. Dylan watched the detectives take their pictures, make their reports, move all too slowly.

"What are you going to do?" he asked. "Nothing was stolen. It's obvious the guy did this for kicks. You've got to do something before he tries something else."

Detective Polk led him outside the apartment.

"Look," he said, "we'll dust for fingerprints, but it's not likely we'll find any. We'll talk to the neighbors, see if anyone saw anything. When Miss Shaperson's ready, we'll talk to her, see if she can think of anyone who might have done this. And then, frankly, we'll just have to wait until something else happens."

"You saw what was written on the wall. Someone's after her."

"Maybe. And maybe someone gets off on drawing sick pictures. Maybe someone saw Miss Shaperson leaving her apartment at midnight and saw his chance to do a little damage. Maybe she's just an unlucky victim."

Dylan whirled around and stared out over the street. He scanned the faces of people walking by, searching every one for a sign of guilt.

The detective touched his arm.

"I know how you feel," he said.

Dylan jerked away. "You don't know anything."

He stormed down the steps and out onto the street. He had driven over with the cops, but now he ran, pounded his feet into the ground and ran as fast as he could. He bolted into oncoming traffic and down threatening alleyways. He prayed someone would get in his way, or pick a fight with him, so that he could let all this fury out. His knuckles ached to hit something, to split skin, touch bone.

He ran all the way to his apartment, ten miles away,

ignoring side aches and burning feet. He slammed the door once he was inside. Then he sat down on his couch and put his head in his hands.

Since the day he'd met Samantha, he had struggled to keep his emotions in check, not realizing that he'd never had any control. He was not the man he had thought he was. He had not been valiant enough to save Samantha, and he was not strong enough to save himself. Despite his best intentions, despite all his grand promises, he had fallen in love with her anyway.

Elliot sat at his old dining table in his old house. It felt strange to see him there, Leah thought, as if nothing had changed. They had sat in silence for nearly an hour after they brought Samantha home and since then they had whispered. Samantha had been asleep for five hours. They could not stop themselves from checking in on her every fifteen minutes or so, as if they'd gone back thirty-five years, and she was that new baby they'd just brought back from the hospital.

Dylan had called a couple of hours ago, to tell them that the police were finishing their search, and that there had been words on the wall, words that were hauntingly familiar to Leah. "Watch your back, Samantha." James had said, "Watch your back, Leah. You never know who might be lurking there."

Leah knew, without a doubt, that James had done this. She had known from the moment Dylan told them there were sadistic pictures on the walls. It was almost as if she'd been there with James, felt his fury, heard his cries mixed with laughter. She imagined him standing over the carnage, a can of red spray paint in his hand, feeling both exhilarated and disgusted with what he'd done.

What this did to Samantha was inconsequential to him. It was Leah he was after, and he knew that this was the best way to get to her, through her weakest spot, through her daughter. And suddenly, with a clarity that should have come to her years ago, Leah knew he would never stop terrorizing her until he had destroyed her, just as he had been destroyed by his father.

"I'm going over to the apartment tomorrow," Elliot said.

Leah nodded. She should go too, but she already knew what it looked like. She knew, better than anyone, how James's mind worked, how he liked to shock people, how violence thrilled him.

"It won't be easy," Leah said.

"It wasn't easy for Samantha."

They were quiet again and Leah wished he would hold her hand, as he had earlier, when they had walked into the police station together. It had been so easy, for a moment or two, to comfort each other, to fall into the old habits of kindness. She hadn't realized, until then, that some old habits were good ones.

"I'm going to ask her to stay for a while," Leah said. "Maybe to even think about staying on permanently. It . . . would be good for both of us."

Elliot nodded and turned away.

"I should go," he said.

Leah bit her lip to keep from begging him to stay. Despite their circumstances, it felt good to have him here, to be able to slip into the shower and know Elliot was guarding the door. To make sandwiches for two instead of one. To let him check on Samantha once in a while, share the burden.

"All right," she said.

Elliot stood up. "Lock the door behind me," he said. "Keep it bolted."

Leah nodded. Her mind was screaming, *It was James! It was James!* But of course she couldn't tell him. What would he think of her then? She had not only cheated on him, but cheated on him with a psychotic man. He would realize that, in an indirect but no less lethal way, Leah was responsible for what had happened to Samantha. She had brought James into their world. She had let a madman loose.

If she told the police, they would blame her. They would tell Samantha. Even worse than Elliot knowing was Samantha knowing. Leah knew exactly what she would see in Samantha's eyes when her daughter heard the truth: horror, repulsion, and disbelief. A mother was supposed to be motherly, to at least know the difference between right and wrong, good and bad. Leah had never been honest with Samantha, not really. Not about what she felt on the inside, not about the wild ideas and feelings that lurked within her. She was certain that her own mother had never been honest with her either, or her mother before her, or any mother.

"Will you be all right?" Elliot asked, studying her face. Leah turned away, hid her eyes so that he couldn't make out the fear mixed with resolve in them. This was her battle, not Samantha's, not Elliot's. She knew exactly how she had to fight it, on James's terms, on James's level.

"I'll be fine, Elliot," she said. "Samantha will be, too."

She walked him to the door and opened it. He turned back and stared at her.

"I'll call tomorrow, after I see the apartment."

"Fine."

He walked away and got into his car. Leah watched him go and then closed the door. She locked and bolted it, and then sat down on the couch and began formulating her plan.

Samantha began to wake up, but then pulled herself back toward sleep. She saw light through her lids, but did not welcome it. She burrowed farther down beneath the blanket and pretended it was night forever.

She smelled soup beside her: cold chicken noodle. Her mother had probably left some sandwiches and low-fat milk, too. Samantha's stomach growled, but she ignored it. She would not get up.

She tried unsuccessfully to force herself back into her dream. She'd been on a brightly painted carousel. At first, there were children too, but then, one by one, they got off, and the carousel went faster and faster. She began to get dizzy and fell onto the dirty metal floor. And still the merry-go-round kept spinning and she was crying so hard she couldn't crawl to the edge to leap off.

It was a horrible dream, but still better than this, than waking up and remembering.

She slowly opened her eyes. The sun nearly

blinded her and, for a moment, she couldn't make out the figure sitting in the chair beside her bed.

"Dylan?" she asked.

"No, honey. It's Michael."

She blinked a few times to clear her eyes. Michael came slowly into focus. First the short brown hair, then the wire-frame glasses and sweet smile. She held out her hand and he grasped it. She was remarkably glad to see him.

"What time is it?" she asked.

He looked at the clock on the wall. "Ten-thirty."

"What day? Wednesday?"

"No, sweetheart. Friday. You've been lying in bed for two days. Your mother's practically going crazy with worry."

Samantha shook her head to clear the cobwebs, but that only brought back the memories. She saw the apartment again, felt that same streak of pure terror run through her, like ice-cold water running into an empty stomach. She gripped Michael's hand.

"It's all right," he said. "I'm here."

"I won't ever go back," she said.

He nodded. "You shouldn't. That apartment can never be what it was before. The horror of what was there will always overshadow the good times before it."

Samantha settled back into the pillows and stared at the ceiling. She still held Michael's hand, heard the ticking of his watch. She could not hear her mother in the other room, but knew she was out there.

"Can you tell me what you feel?" Michael asked.

Samantha smiled. Even when he was trying to help, he was polite, undemanding.

"Not really," she said. "Just that everything's different now. You hear people talk about feeling violated when their homes are broken into. This goes beyond that, into terror, into a kind of catatonia." She thought about each ruined object in her apartment and it was as if those bedroom walls had been her skin, the shredded furniture her limbs, the ruined books her organs. She was actually sore from the devastation; her bones ached, her skin felt raw and chapped.

"I can't imagine I'll ever have the nerve to leave this room," she said.

Michael nodded. They sat in silence a long time, holding hands, looking up when a bird fluttered its wings against the window.

"Your dad went to the apartment," Michael said at last. "He said it was pretty bad."

Samantha closed her eyes. "Can we not talk about it?" she said.

"Of course."

They were quiet again and Samantha was surprised that the silence was so easy, that she wasn't concerned with how long it lasted, or what Michael thought. It was never that way with Dylan. Then, each silence was filled with thousands of halted words.

There was a knock on the bedroom door and Leah peeked her head in.

"You're up," she said.

Samantha stiffened. At the police station, the relationship between her mother and Dylan had seemed unimportant. But she was losing her grip on that apathy, just as she was losing her nerve to get out of this bed. Samantha remembered the kiss between them, the laughter. She remembered that her mother had not returned her calls for a few weeks before that; she had probably been spending all of her time with Dylan.

"Yes," Samantha said. "Obviously, I am."

Leah walked in and stared at the tray of untouched food on the nightstand.

"We've got to get her to eat," she said to Michael.

"I'm sure she will when she's hungry enough."

Samantha smiled at him. Leah saw it and took a step back.

"Dylan called earlier," she said.

Samantha was surprised that she could be angry, that there was anything left inside of her to be angry with. She seemed all hollow inside.

"For you?" Samantha asked.

Leah straightened her back. "No, Samantha. Not for me. He called to ask how you were doing."

Samantha felt Michael's grip tighten on her hand and she squeezed him in return.

"What did you tell him?" Samantha asked.

"That you were resting. That everything was going to be fine."

Samantha laughed harshly. Michael stood up and let go of her hand.

"Leah," he said, "do you mind if I talk to you outside for a minute?"

Leah nodded and walked out of the room with him.

When they had gone, Samantha slowly pulled back the covers and slid her legs to the edge of the bed. Her muscles were tight and achy from disuse. Two days and she had hardly moved at all. She pulled herself up to a sitting position and stared around the room.

Hardly anything had changed since she had moved out seventeen years earlier. The walls were still that awful shade of lavender that she had loved as a five-year-old and then hated by age eight. She had wanted to paint the walls royal blue and fill them with pennants of the baseball teams she loved, but her mother had adamantly refused. "You're a tomboy now," Leah had said to her when she first broached the subject. "But you'll grow out of it and then what will you do? No teenage girl wants a room with blue walls. It's just not feminine."

Samantha had argued then and a year later and every year after that with no results. Her mother gave her the same response every year, that she would eventually outgrow her boyishness, that she would end up hating sports and royal blue. Samantha never had. Until her apartment was invaded, she had had her baseball pennants hung on her bedroom wall. Whoever had scribbled those pictures there had ripped them off and left them in shreds on the floor.

Samantha longed to lie back down, but she had the sense that if she didn't get up now, she never would. She slowly got to her feet, gripping the bed to help herself up. When she was steady, she shuffled over to the window. It was covered with a horrible, flowery purple curtain that matched the bedspread. Samantha had petitioned against both of them again and again, begging for miniblinds and a plain blue and white striped comforter. Her mother, again, had refused.

Samantha pulled the curtain to the side and looked out. The leaves on the liquidambar tree in the front yard were already tinged with vibrant shades of orange. The branches swirled in the autumn breeze, swatting the tips of their leaves against the glass pane.

Autumn was Samantha's favorite time of year. In each of the last few years, she had made a solo pilgrimage to her parents' cabin during the last weekend in September. She left the paperwork at the office and took a stack of novels she hadn't had time to read all year. She took long walks and cooked herself gourmet meals and read until her eyes burned.

Now, there would be no way she could go. She couldn't imagine ever having the courage to be alone again. Not in her apartment, not here in her parents' house, not even at the cabin she loved. Even in this room, this haven, she shuddered when she realized her window faced the street, that someone could simply break the glass and be on her before she'd have a chance to get away.

From now on, she would be constantly on the lookout for danger, wondering if that person was after her, or that one, if that madman would sneak into the house after she was gone and rip it apart again, or if he would come after *her* this time. She was certain that that was the whole point of the attack on her apartment, to serve as a warning of things to come, to teach her that the world was not what she had thought it was. It was not kind and hospitable; it was mean and terrifying and behind normal-looking faces lurked vicious minds you could never fathom.

Samantha shivered and wrapped her arms around her stomach. The door opened and Michael came back in. He walked up behind her, but didn't touch her. Samantha still shivered and Michael hesitantly reached out and touched her shoulder.

Samantha leaned back against him. She couldn't cry, even though she wanted to, even though she thought that if she could just cry herself out, she would be all right again.

Michael's arms came around her waist, unassuming, undemanding, just there, holding her. He dipped his face into her hair.

"Oh, Sam," he said.

She squeezed her eyes shut, trying to force tears. She wished she could be her mother for a moment, emotional, vociferous, bleeding hard but then scabbing quickly. For once, Samantha was angry that she was so like her father; she seemed stoic even to herself.

"I've always been so strong," Samantha said.

"I know."

"Now, I feel nearly weightless. As if that breeze outside could just pick me up and carry me away."

Michael held her tighter, as if he were holding her down.

"It was naïve of me to think that nothing bad would ever happen to me," she went on. "I lived alone and never once worried about being robbed or attacked. And then, someone just waltzed in. Opened a window and tore up everything I had. He didn't even take anything, Michael. At least he could have taken something, the television or the stereo. If it could have been just a robbery, and me just an unfortunate victim, it might be all right. But this was intended for me, and I have no idea why."

Michael rocked her back and forth. He must have come to her from the hospital, because his hands still smelled of rubber gloves and antiseptic soap.

"I suppose," he said, "that this will take a long time. There aren't any words for me to say that will make it any easier."

Samantha turned around in his arms and buried her face in his neck.

"You feel invincible," she said.

He laughed and rubbed his hands down her back. "No. But I'm strong enough to carry you for a while, if you'll let me."

Samantha pulled away and looked up at him. She waited for the comparisons to Dylan to start up in her mind again, but when they did come, they were all in Michael's favor. Dylan had only called and Michael was here. Dylan had kissed her mother, while Michael had taken her mother out of the room to get her to back off.

She kissed him softly. "Can you stay with me for a while?" she asked, used to hearing Dylan say that he couldn't, that he had things to do, causes to fight for.

"Of course," Michael said. "Just let me call the hospital and get someone to fill in on my rounds."

• • •

Four days after the break-in, Michael called Elliot and suggested the two of them clean up the apartment. Elliot took a half-day off work and met him there.

"God," Michael said when he first looked around. The police had left the place untouched. They had dusted for fingerprints and come up with nothing. They had searched for hairs, pieces of clothing, but had very little to go on. No one had noticed anything suspicious the night of the attack. Detective Polk had told Elliot that, unless something new happened, it was next to impossible that they would ever find the man who had done this.

They walked around the apartment. Elliot had come before, taken one look at the pictures on his daughter's bedroom walls, and run to the bathroom. He had retched twice, then flushed cold water on his face. His arms had felt prickly, as if his skin had been infested with mites. He forced himself to look around, to search for clues, but after a few minutes he realized that he was the last man who'd be able to find them. Doing something like this was so far beyond him, he still had trouble believing it was real, that someone wasn't just playing a trick on them.

Michael came out of the bedroom pale, then handed Elliot a large can of white paint.

"Try to cover it up," he said. "I'm not sure how many coats it will take, but do whatever it takes."

Elliot nodded. Michael was twenty years younger than he, but there was a command to his voice. It was Michael, not Dylan, whom Elliot would champion for his daughter. A man like Michael would make sure that nothing like this ever happened again.

They worked for five hours, painting the walls, dragging the ruined furniture out to the trailer they'd rented to take everything to the dump. Samantha had said that she didn't want anything, no pots or pans, no dishes, no clothes other than the ones Elliot had already picked up for her.

"Burn everything," she had told Elliot over the phone this morning. "Burn the apartment down if you can."

Elliot and Michael hauled everything out and then Elliot went down and spoke to the manager.

"She's got three months left on her lease," the woman said.

Elliot took out his checkbook and paid her off.

"Nothing like this has ever happened here," the woman went on.

"Of course not."

They drove the furniture and ruined books to the dump, then dropped off Samantha's unwanted clothes and kitchen items at the Goodwill.

They returned the trailer and then drove back to the apartment. Michael's BMW was still in the parking lot. They sat in Elliot's sedan for a moment, with the engine running.

"Could you tell me," Michael said, "about Dylan?"

Elliot rapped his knuckles on the steering wheel.

"What's to say?" Elliot said. "He's a radical. More concerned with the planet than with people. She loved him much more than he cared for her and I think she sees that now. He came through for Samantha when this . . . this happened. He's been calling her since, but she doesn't want to see him."

"Why not?"

"Dylan and Leah had been spending time together, and neither of them bothered to tell Sam about it. She's hurt. And I think she realizes that she and Dylan were never headed anywhere. They're on their last legs, if you ask me. Winding things down."

Michael nodded. He adjusted his glasses on his nose and opened the car door.

"I'll be over to see her tomorrow," he said.

Elliot nodded, waited for Michael to get in his car, and then drove back to his apartment.

Dylan had had it with calling and was on his way over to see Samantha when the phone rang. He almost let it ring, but then he thought it might be the office with news of another environmental disaster.

Instead, it was an unfamiliar voice, marred by static.

"Could you say your name again?" Dylan shouted into the phone. "We've got a terrible connection."

"Daniel Schwartz," the man said. "Your parents' attorney. I'm afraid I've got bad news."

Dylan knew right then. He had seen the footage on the news last night. The commuter plane between Hartford and New York City had missed the LaGuardia runway by thirty yards and ended up in the river. Only half of the passengers survived. He had known that his parents often took that flight to New York to spend a couple of days in the city, but he also knew that his parents were indestructible. Only the good ever died young.

"Did you hear about the plane crash last night?" Daniel Schwartz was asking him. "I'm afraid both of your parents were on it. They didn't make it. I'm terribly, terribly sorry."

Dylan was surprised to look down and see his hand shaking. He felt nothing. He could not fool himself and say that he had really loved them after all. He did not feel cheated because he hadn't had a chance to patch things up. Even with all the time in the world, he and his parents would never have found their way back together.

Still, his hand shook, and his legs felt tingly, as if he'd hiked too far and his muscles couldn't settle down. The apartment suddenly felt hot and devoid of oxygen.

He took the phone with him to the window and opened it.

"Are you there, Mr. Price?"

"Yes," Dylan said. "I'm here."

"They had a tremendous estate, as I'm sure you know. We plan to read the will on Friday. Can you be here?"

Dylan laughed. He knew he shouldn't have, but he could just imagine his father cackling as he wrote out his will. For a moment, Alan had probably felt like God, doling out so much here and so much there. Dylan was certain he hadn't been left a cent. Alan knew how much Dylan had detested his wealth. His father had probably only wanted him to fly out so he could be made a fool of. He'd be given some trinket as a show of Alan's limited affection.

"I don't have the cash to fly out," Dylan said. "Sorry."

"Actually, your parents provided a fund for that. Everything is already taken care of."

Dylan shook his head. He stared out over the parking lot of his apartment building, and then beyond that to the family-run grocery store across the street. He had made Sacramento his home. Sometimes, on an Indian-summer day like today when the lawns were brown and dying, he almost forgot how green the hills of Connecticut were. It was only in his dreams that he remembered the beauty of the first snowflake that landed in the tree outside his old bedroom window, or the wide streets and colonial houses set behind maple trees the size of skyscrapers.

"When's the funeral?" Dylan asked.

Daniel Schwartz sighed in relief and Dylan knew then that his father had warned the lawyer about Dylan's recalcitrance. The man had probably been expecting much more of a fight.

"It will be Thursday at eleven at your parents' church. I'll send your plane ticket overnight to your office."

"Fine," Dylan said, and hung up.

He pressed his hand down flat on the windowsill until it stopped shaking. He thought perhaps some sweet memory would come to him, something he'd forgotten, a night when his mother had tucked him in or his father had pointed out constellations. But his mind was empty; nothing like that had ever happened. And that, actually, made him sadder than their deaths did. They had given him nothing good to remember them by and, when that plane had gone down, he was certain they had not thought of him.

Dylan did not get to Samantha's until the next day, and by then the Indian summer heat had broken. The early October afternoon was cool and breezy, with a faint scent of smoldering oak from someone's chimney that signaled the approach of winter. Or as much winter as Northern California ever got.

As he rode his bike to Leah's house, he thought about all the money his parents had and how they would have distributed it. Sophia had been awash in charities and she had probably convinced Alan to leave a large sum to a few of them, so that she could be memorialized, get her name on some buildings and streets. He tried to figure out what they'd left him, and he deduced that it must be the Connecticut house. They knew how much he hated it, and so that would be their revenge for having such a difficult son.

He reached Leah's house in fifteen minutes. He leaned his bike against the garage wall and walked to the door. Leah answered his knock at once.

"You look terrible," she said.

He smiled. "Thanks."

He walked inside. She stood by the front door,

watching him, and he nearly told her what had happened to his parents. But then he stopped himself. He felt silly baring his soul. He had never done it before, didn't have the slightest clue how to go about it.

"She's in her room," Leah said finally. "Watching television. I can't stand it. She hates television. All her life she ridiculed me for watching soap operas. She was a reader, a doer. Now she sits in there with that damn thing humming all day. She never takes her eyes from the screen."

Dylan walked over to Leah and touched her arm.

"This is not your fault," he said.

Leah turned away and wiped her sudden tears. "I should have been up-front with her from the very beginning about you and me. I thought she wouldn't understand, that she'd think you were pitying me."

"I wasn't," he said.

They were quiet for a minute and then Dylan said, "When will she go back to work?"

"Who knows? She's got over a month of sick time saved up and I think she intends to use every second of it."

"And the apartment? Any ideas who did it?"

Leah turned away and, in that motion, Dylan saw exactly what she was trying to hide.

"It was James, wasn't it?" he said.

Leah hesitated and then looked straight at him.

"I thought so, at first. But he has an airtight alibi. He was out of town that night."

"You're sure?"

Dylan probed her eyes. At first he thought he saw lies, then truthfulness, and he realized he couldn't make out anything anymore. His hand started shaking again, as it had yesterday when the lawyer called. He dropped it from her arm and held it behind his back.

"Yes," Leah said. "I'm sure."

"Well, then," he said, "I guess we're back at square one."

Dylan walked to Samantha's bedroom door. Without turning around, he asked, "Is she in love with Michael now?"

Leah sighed. "The only thing I know for sure is that Michael is definitely in love with her."

Dylan walked into the bedroom without knocking. Samantha was sitting up in bed, the remote control in her hand, and a soap opera on the screen. She glanced at him, widened her eyes for a second, but then went back to her program.

Dylan marched across the room and yanked the remote away. He turned off the television and threw the remote to the far corner of the room.

"So some nut vandalizes your apartment," he said. "So what?"

She clenched her jaw but said nothing. Dylan sat down on the side of the bed and she slid away from him.

"You weren't there," he went on. "The guy probably made sure you wouldn't be there. No one touched you. You're safe. What the hell is your problem?"

Samantha looked up at him with tears in her eyes. Dylan nearly faltered; he'd thought that was what she needed, a strong push, heartless but honest words. But now he wasn't so sure. He felt as scared as she did. He was certain that his plane would go down on the way to the funeral, or that Samantha would be attacked while he was gone. It felt like earthquake weather, unstable, charged, hot then suddenly cold. Without parents, even bad ones, it seemed as if anything could happen.

Dylan almost leaned forward, took her in his arms as he longed to, but somehow he held back. That was what Michael was for, obviously, coddling her, soothing her into playing the weakling.

"You . . . saw it," she said.

"You're right. I did. I saw that some pervert scribbled his trash on your walls. Ripped up your sofa cushions. Tore out some pages. Big deal. Some women get their bodies thrashed by people like that, rather than their apartments. Some children—"

"Don't trivialize what happened to me!" she shouted.

Dylan grabbed her by the shoulders and stared at her.

"I'm not," he said. "But someone could break in here just as easily as they broke into your apartment. And if you're just lying here, acting helpless, they'll get you. You've got to start fighting again. You've got to get up, Samantha. Face what happened and get on with it."

Samantha jerked away from him and sprang up from the bed surprisingly quickly. Dylan noticed that she'd chewed her nails to the quick, and that she must have lost five pounds in the ten days she'd been home.

"I've faced it," she shouted at him. "Every night, right before I go to sleep, I see those walls again. I see those words, 'Watch your back, Samantha.' I try to watch it, but I don't always know what's back there."

She started crying then, big, gasping sobs that jumped through the air and attacked his body, first with a sharp pain in his head, then a punch to his stomach, a slice across his thigh. He stood up and went to her, but she pushed him away.

"I don't want you here," she said.

"Why not?"

"Because of this," she said, gesturing to the tears on her face. She cried harder, wrapped her arms around herself as if there were no one left to hug her. She turned her back to him and leaned her head against the wall.

He put his hand on her shoulder but she jerked it off. As his hand hit the air, it started shaking again.

"My parents died last night," he said.

Samantha turned around quickly. His body moved in rhythm to her tears, as if that was the only way he could cry, through her.

"The plane crash," he said, and then both hands started shaking. His legs trembled and he reached behind him for the bedpost. He sat down on the edge of the bed.

She came to him and wrapped her arms around his neck. Her tears soaked through his shirt to his shoulder.

"I hated them," he said, wondering whose voice was speaking, why it sounded so broken.

She pulled away just enough to look at him. "So?" she said. "They're dead now. What good is hatred going to do you?"

Dylan stood up abruptly and walked to the window. He shook out his arms, tried to calm the twitching. He breathed deeply and, as if they were connected somehow, Samantha calmed her crying.

"That's not what I came here to talk about," Dylan said. "I want to get you out of this bedroom. I want to help you."

Samantha shook her head vigorously. "You can't help me. You just make me crazy. You love me one second and then you stop. You give me a part of yourself and then you take it back."

Dylan turned around. He thought she'd stopped crying, but there were tears streaming down her cheeks.

"If you care about me," she went on, "stay here. Be with me every day. Sit by my side, help me through this."

"Sam, I can't. I've got to fly to Connecticut. And then there will probably be things to handle with my parents' estate and—"

"And then there will be another environmental crisis," Samantha finished for him. "And then another and another. How do you expect me to believe in you, to trust you, when I can't even get a hold on you? Can you guarantee me that you'll be here tomorrow, or five years down the line?"

Dylan said nothing. He wanted to guarantee it. For this second, at least, he could not imagine being without her. But his plane might go down in a river somewhere. Or Michael the surgeon might suddenly propose. Their passion could cool, or their chemistry falter. There were a million things that could go wrong and Dylan's problem was that he knew all about each of them.

"You can't," Samantha said. "I thought I could live with that. I thought it was all right. But it's not. Not now. I just don't want to be alone anymore."

Her voice cracked and before she could stop him, Dylan had rushed back to the bed and pulled her into his arms. She struggled for a moment but then she gave in to him, in to her tears, and cried against him. It took him a while to realize that, this time, he was crying, too.

His worst fear was of living a mediocre life, having a mediocre love. Right now what he felt for her was awe-inspiring, but if the passion ebbed, if they compromised, he just didn't think he could stand it. He would rather go out in a blaze of glory than have to watch a love so breathtaking gradually become common.

"I'm sorry," he said. "I can't stay. I've got to go to Connecticut and then I don't know. I can't guarantee anything."

She yanked herself away from him and stood up.

"I love you," Dylan said softly. She stood perfectly still for a moment, but then the air rushed out of her and she wilted. Her shoulders collapsed and her head curled downward.

"I think you love touching me," she said. "And being touched. But you don't know me enough to love me. A few months together does not qualify us for intimacy. If it did, you'd stay here with me, you'd understand what I'm feeling. Or, if you had to go, you'd take me with you. You'd let me in on your past."

"You don't want to go to Connecticut," he said.

"Why not?" she asked, turning around to face him. "I want to go where you are. I want to see the house you grew up in, the parks you played in, the school you went to."

Dylan leaned back, as if her needs were hands grabbing at him. He didn't want her to see any of that. *He* didn't even want to see it. He wanted to forget he'd ever been a boy. He wanted to take whatever measly inheritance his parents had left him and then get the hell out.

Samantha saw his hesitation and shook her head.

"You're afraid to give me anything, even a scrap of you," she said.

"I just need time," Dylan said.

"I don't have any more time. I'm scared *now*. I need someone *now*. Right this minute. I lie here every day, staring at the television, trying to convince myself that people are still good, that things are normal. You'll laugh, but I watch *Sesame Street*, because it's so pure. Everything there is so nice."

"I'm not laughing," Dylan said.

"My mother thinks I hate her. My father thinks I'm crazy. Only Michael understands that I'm trying to save myself."

Dylan turned away at the sound of Michael's name. Samantha got back into bed. She pulled the covers up to her chin.

"I can't worry anymore," she said, "about whether or not you love me, whether or not you'll be here tomorrow. I'm just trying to survive, Dylan. To put my heart back together. I can't fight for you anymore. Go to the funeral, and then go off on whatever expedition inspires you. Be a hero. I don't care. Just leave me alone."

Dylan sat very still. It had taken so much for him to admit that he loved her. He had never said the words before. If she would only give him time, let him ease into this feeling. When he looked at her face, though, he knew his time was up. He could see her falling toward Michael as clearly as if the surgeon were standing beneath her, his arms out to catch her.

Dylan walked to the corner of the room and picked up the remote. He handed it to her.

"Do you love Michael?" he asked.

Samantha flipped on the power and the soap opera bloomed back into life. A couple was kissing while a woman peeked through the window and watched them.

"He's a good man," she said. "He comes every day, and he'll keep coming for the rest of his life. You can ridicule that kind of commitment all you want. But some people would kill for it."

Dylan nodded and walked to the door. He felt her eyes on him and, though a hundred reasons for staying crossed his mind, he knew what he was and was not capable of.

"Goodbye, Sam," he said, without turning around.

He heard her crying again as he walked out.

18

The amazing thing, Elliot thought as he walked through his old neighborhood, was how impossible it was to get lost. Every day at lunch, he stepped out of his office and picked a new direction to go in. But even when he wasn't sure of the street he was on or where it would lead him, he always had a sense of direction, of the way home. Though that should make him happy, the truth was that it did not. He had spent so many years in fear, losing out on all kinds of new sights because he took the same roads to the same places every time. Now that he was finally willing, even determined, to venture out of bounds, to lose himself, he couldn't do it.

Every day after another unsuccessful attempt to get lost, he headed toward his old home to visit Samantha. She had been staying with Leah for three weeks and had not yet left her bedroom. He did not know what to make of his daughter.

His daughter, who had shunned every television program except documentaries on PBS, was now watching *Wheel of Fortune* and *Married With Children.* She smiled whenever she saw him, but she could hardly sustain any conversation.

He had tried to talk to Leah about it, but she had only said, more angrily than he thought necessary, "She's an adult. I can't do a damn thing about it."

Today, Elliot reached his old house and stood in front of it on the sidewalk. He stared at the yellow paint that had chipped off the edge of the siding. He noticed the azaleas were dead and rotting and the chrysanthemums were on their last legs. The lawn needed a good, even cutting and trim and the liquidambars should be pruned for winter. These were all of the things he used to do, and he wondered if Leah would just ignore them now, let the grass grow up around her and the trees sprout weighty limbs until they fell over.

He walked up the path, feeling more like a solicitor than a man who used to live here. There was always the urge to just walk in, to claim what was still rightfully his until the divorce went through and Leah got the house. But, as always, Elliot resisted the urge and knocked instead.

Leah answered. She was not wearing any makeup. Elliot looked down at her clothes and wondered when and where she had gotten them. She wore black leggings and an oversized, jersey-type sweatshirt. She had brushed her hair forward in a girlish kind of style, with little wisps scattered across her cheeks and chin. She looked thirty-five, forty at the most.

"Hello," Elliot said, realizing after a moment that he'd been gawking at her.

"They're just clothes, Elliot," Leah said. "There's no law that says I can't wear them."

She let him in. Elliot studied her from the back, noticed the outline of her well-toned legs in those tight pants.

He walked over to the dining table. The day's mail was still on it and he noticed the bills Leah would eventually send him and expect him to pay. Money was tight now that he was paying for his apartment and this place, Leah's groceries and his. He felt unnaturally angry that Leah had not offered to cut back or help him out, that she was being so stiff and unrelenting in the divorce agreement.

He flipped through the bills and came to a manila envelope addressed to Leah in a childlike scrawl. He started to lift it up when Leah yanked it away.

"That's mine," she said, clutching it to her chest. She walked to the kitchen and laid the envelope down on the counter. Elliot clenched his fists against his sides. She was still hiding things from him, even when there was no longer any reason to. If he discovered that she was a closet stripper, a porno star, a prostitute, he wouldn't be all that surprised.

"Fine," he said. He walked to Samantha's bedroom door and knocked.

"Come in," Samantha said. He opened the door.

Samantha was in bed, watching television. Elliot saw her every day, but he was still shocked by the gauntness of her cheeks, the paleness of her skin. His daughter was hearty and athletic and tanned. This woman was a stranger to him.

He sat down in the chair beside her.

"You've been walking again," she said, noticing the sweat beneath his arms despite the cool October afternoon.

"Yes."

"Still trying to get lost?" she asked.

"Yes. No luck, though."

"I told Mom what you were doing and she couldn't believe it," Samantha said, her gaze trailing back toward the screen. "She said you were terrified of getting lost."

"I used to be," Elliot said. "It's become a kind of

challenge, to see if I can bring things back to the way they were."

Samantha said nothing, but he noticed she stiffened up.

"Hey, how about you and I go for a walk?" Elliot said. "It's a gorgeous day. You love the fall. The leaves are starting to turn and drop. We could crunch them beneath our feet. Remember how we used to do that? Then I'd rake them up into a pile and you and your friends would jump in."

He watched her, waited for some hint of enthusiasm, but got only a sigh.

"No, I don't think so," she said.

Elliot turned away. More than anything, he wanted to make her get up, force her to walk again. He had been there for her first step. He could remember it clearly. Samantha had been less than a year old and he had been holding out his hands to her, urging her on. Leah had just stepped into the bathtub, so it was just him and his daughter.

Samantha had let go of the coffee table and fallen. Elliot picked her back up, then held out his hands again.

"Just one step, Samantha," he said. "You can do it."

She looked up at him with her trusting gray eyes. She slid out her pudgy foot, still clinging to the coffee table. When she didn't fall, she got bolder. She let go with one hand, then the other. Elliot reached his hands out a little farther, so that she had to take only one step.

"Come on, sweetheart," he said. "Just one step. Come to Daddy."

Then, suddenly, like the daring, impulsive woman she would become, Samantha leapt at him. She took one step and he moved back so she could take another. Then he caught her and swept her up, and they both laughed and danced their way into the bathroom.

"Your daughter just took her first step," Elliot said

to Leah proudly, as if he had done it himself. In some way he didn't understand then or now, he *had* done it himself. He'd said his first word with her, ridden his first bicycle, gone to school all over again. He'd always felt as if he saw out of one of her eyes, as if one of her hands were connected to his nerve endings. Yet he knew she would reject such a notion. He wanted so much to be a part of her, and she, like every child, had striven all her life to be separate.

Samantha reached out and took his hand, though she kept her eyes fixed on the television screen.

"I just need to stay inside for a while," she said.

Elliot nodded and blinked back tears. He looked at her pale hand in his and then turned away.

Leah had been a saint. She knew she had. Samantha had hardly said two words to her in the entire time she'd been staying here, but Leah had not gotten angry. She had passed on Dylan's phone messages that had stopped abruptly after he showed up here last week. She had let her daughter lie in bed, staring at that damn television, and had not said one word.

But even sainthood had its limits. Leah had thought it would be wonderful to have Samantha back at home. She could be a mother again, a job she knew she was good at. But Samantha wanted very little mothering. She wanted very little to do with Leah at all.

Leah ran her hands over the manila envelope that came in the mail yesterday. Elliot had picked it up, but she had yanked it from him before he could see what was inside or match the childlike scrawl on the front with what he'd seen in Samantha's apartment.

She had opened it when he left. Her hands had shook as she looked at each photograph, but beyond that she gave nothing away. She slipped the pictures back inside the envelope and waited for a chance to burn them.

James had sent them, of course. There was no return address, no note, but the photos made it obvious. There were eight of them, all of men overpowering children, beating them, raping them. She had to believe the poses weren't real, that James had doctored them, and that the tears on those children's faces were painted on. If she didn't believe that, she couldn't go on, she would just break down in hysterics right there.

She did not have to convince herself that this was her responsibility. She had gone as far as telling Dylan that James had an alibi for the night of the break-in when, of course, he did not. But Dylan was the type of person who would take matters into his own hands and Leah couldn't have that. This was her problem.

Tomorrow, she would stop this. Tomorrow, she would demand retribution for the fact that her daughter would not get out of bed. Tomorrow, she'd stop worrying about her soul and take whatever punishment God gave her because something simply had to be done. She was amazingly calm about her decision. In fact, ever since she had made up her mind, she had felt stronger than ever. When the plan first came to her, she had raced to the mall and bought three pairs of leggings and five bright, oversized tops to go with them. It was rejuvenating, exhilarating, finally realizing that there was something she could do.

Leah walked to Samantha's door and waited. She heard the television still humming and she knocked.

"Come in," Samantha said.

Leah walked inside. She smiled every time she entered this room. It was almost exactly the same as it had been when Samantha left for college. The old desk they'd found at a flea market stood in the corner, with Samantha's array of stuffed animals on it. The bedspread and curtains were a matched set of purple and blue flowers. It was a little girl's room and if Leah tried really hard, she could almost imagine Samantha as her little girl again, with her long hair in pigtails.

"What time is it?" Samantha asked.

Leah looked at her watch. "Ten to six. I've got spaghetti cooking."

Samantha nodded. She pried herself up and Leah quickly reached in and plumped up the pillows behind her. Samantha leaned away from her fingers, but Leah was used to that by now. Samantha looked away from the television for a moment and around the room. She closed her eyes.

"That godawful lavender gives me a headache," Samantha said.

Leah was dumbstruck. "You love lavender. It's your favorite color."

"Was my favorite color. When I was five. Don't you remember, I wanted to paint the walls royal blue but you wouldn't let me? You told me it was a boy's color."

Leah did have a vague recollection of that. But mostly she remembered the day they had bought this lavender paint. Samantha had been five years old and the two of them had gone to the paint store and looked through dozens of samples of various shades of purple and pink. Finally, they had chosen this soft lavender and had shown it off proudly to Elliot that evening.

"I always thought you liked it," Leah said.

Samantha still had her eyes closed, but she smiled. "Yes. Just like I liked the flowery bedspread and curtains you picked out."

"I did not pick them out. You did. You wanted ruffles and lace and—"

Leah stopped when Samantha opened her eyes.

"Mom, it doesn't matter." Samantha's attention fell back to the television, as always, and Leah walked to the window. She fingered the curtains she had been so certain Samantha had loved. Then she remembered Samantha as a teenager, when she had been such a tomboy, bringing home bruised knees and black eyes instead of corsages. She remembered now. Along with those royal blue walls, Samantha had wanted a plain blue and white striped comforter and drab miniblinds on the window. Leah had refused. A girl's room should be soft and feminine, she had told her. She could still remember the bitter laugh Samantha had given her, and then the silent treatment that followed for days.

Leah turned back around.

"Do you want some spaghetti?" she asked.

"No," Samantha said, "I'm not hungry."

Leah put her hands on her hips and stared at her daughter.

"I've been more than fair," Leah said. "I've given you enough time to sulk around."

"I'm not sulking," Samantha said.

"You are. You won't go to work, you won't even go out of this bedroom, and you sure as hell won't talk to me. I want to know, are you and I going to have this out or not?"

Samantha stiffened and then, for the first time, flipped off the television. She turned and fixed Leah with a stare that both chilled and electrified her, because she knew it was the first time in her life that Samantha was really seeing her.

"Yes," Samantha said. "We are."

Leah walked to the chair at the side of the bed and sat down. She waited for Samantha to begin.

"Are you having an affair with Dylan?" Samantha asked immediately.

Leah nearly clapped her hands with joy. So, Samantha did think it was possible. A woman of Leah's age was capable of sex. Leah hesitated a moment, drawing out the suspense because she couldn't help it; in that silence she felt beautiful. Then, finally, she answered.

"No. He and I became friends."

Samantha laughed a little and the pain shot back into Leah's heart.

"What do you mean, friends?"

"I mean," Leah said, standing up, "that he and I spent time together, did things together. I needed him, and he was there."

She stared down at Samantha, daring her to meet her gaze. Samantha did. She held it for so long that Leah had to force herself not to look away.

"There are a lot of things you're not telling me," Samantha said at last.

Leah thought of James, of what he'd done to Samantha's apartment, of what she planned to do. She couldn't imagine ever telling Samantha any of that. And she realized, in that instant, that no matter how hard she had tried to be different, to be fully passionate and free, there was one bind she couldn't break. She was a mother, and that was as far from free as you could get.

"You're right," Leah said. "Believe it or not, I've got some secrets left. But I am telling the truth about Dylan. He wasn't cheating on you and I wasn't betraying you. Your father had left and there were things going on with me. I needed someone to turn to."

"Why not me?" Samantha said softly.

Leah shook her head. "I don't know how to be friends with you, Samantha. You expect things of me, certain ways of behaving. I expect them of myself, when I'm with you."

Samantha leaned her cheek against the pillow.

"I don't expect you to be anything but you."

"That's not true. I know it's what you'd like to feel, but the truth is that you've always been the daughter and I've always been the mother, and that's the way it will always be. I make the rules and you break them. I conform and you rebel. When I start rebelling, it just confuses us both."

Samantha stared at her in wonderment. "Sometimes I look at you," she said, "and I realize I don't know anything about you, except what you're like when you're mothering me. Dad, at least, knew you as a wife, a lover. Your friends had your companionship. Now I find out that even Dylan knows more about you than I do. I want more. Why can't you understand how much I need you?"

Leah stood very still. Finally, things were the way they were supposed to be. All her life, Samantha had been the strong one, while Leah was weak. Over and over, Leah had wished that Samantha would come to her, want *something,* need advice or sympathy. Instead, Samantha had grown up at lightning speed, pulled away before Leah even had a chance to kiss her goodbye.

Leah walked over to the bed and took Samantha's chin in her hand.

"Can we start over?" she asked her. "Like friends, just starting out."

Samantha smiled and put her hand over her mother's.

"Yes," she said. "Oh, yes."

That night, after Samantha went to bed, the phone rang. Leah had been reading on the living room couch and by the time she stood up, Samantha had woken up and picked up the extension. Leah sat back down.

It took only a moment for the hairs on the back of her neck to stand on end. She looked at the clock, saw that it was eleven-thirty, and was certain that only one person would call at that hour of night. She ran to the phone in the kitchen.

When she picked it up, she heard Samantha's voice first.

"Who are you? Why are you doing this to me?"

There was a laugh, a familiar, horrid little laugh, and Leah clenched the phone tightly. It was James, of course, with his pathetic British accent.

"You just watch yourself, Samantha," James said. "I had such a good time in your apartment. Maybe I'll come over to your mother's house next."

"Hang up, Samantha," Leah said forcefully.

"Mom?"

"Hang up. Now." Samantha replaced the receiver and Leah picked up one of the knives on the counter. She ran the blade over her palm.

James laughed. He used to chill her with that laugh, but now it turned her stomach. She pressed the blade against her skin, leaving a pink indentation when she pulled it away. How nice it would be if she could just stab it through the phone and rip out James's mean little heart.

"You won't do this to my family anymore," Leah said. She stared at the knife, liked the gleam of it, the serrated edges. It made her feel better, just holding it.

"What am I doing? I just called to talk."

Leah dropped the knife back on the counter and stood up straight.

"How did you get my number? It's unlisted."

"There are ways of getting anything, Leah," he said.

"You're a coward, you know that?" she said. "You, with all your training, don't even see how sick you are. You attack helpless women. You hold your power over your patients like a master teasing his dog with a bone. You aren't even brave enough to have this out with me, so you stoop to terrorizing my daughter."

James breathed deeply and Leah knew that if he were in the room with her, she would kill him. She'd stab that knife into his chest again and again until he was as mutilated as those pictures he'd drawn on Samantha's walls. She shivered, wondering how she could stomach the vision so easily, why James's death was the only death that didn't disgust her.

"Leah," James said, in that phony accent that she once found so authentic and stimulating. "Let's not fight. I happen to know that Elliot is still in his silly little apartment. You must be lonely." His voice slowly rose in timbre until he was practically screeching. She had to hold the phone away from her ear.

"I, for one," he went on, "would be willing to stop all this nonsense if you'd just come to your senses. Come to the office tonight. It can be like old times. Please come, Leah. I need you."

If Leah had had any sympathy left, she would have felt it then. But the moment he'd hurt her daughter, it was all over. She was no Freudian analyst, like him. She did not believe that you could pin all of your faults on a bad childhood. Every person had the will to choose their own life, to change the old patterns, to be better than what they had come from.

She picked up the knife again and ran it across her palm. She would always remember how clear her mind became then. How all of her plans fell right into place. She knew what she was going to do was right. It wasn't good or moral, but then, she was living in a world where the good and moral got trampled.

"I'll never come to you again," she said quietly, clearly, as if she were someone entirely different, someone strong and unafraid.

"Leah—"

"Let me tell you something, James. It's time you started watching *your* back."

She hung up the phone and put the knife back in its holder. Then, very slowly, Leah walked into Samantha's bedroom to explain.

"His name is James Arlington," Leah began. "He was my lover for three years."

She sat on the edge of Samantha's bed. Only the

light on the nightstand was on and Leah was glad that Samantha could not see her eyes clearly, or read the regret and humiliation that was in them.

Leah, however, could see Samantha's eyes. In them, she saw first disbelief, then horror, and Leah tried to imagine what it would have been like to find out her own mother had had an affair. She tried to picture it, but all the images were comical. She could not even imagine her mother having sex with her father, let alone with anyone else.

Leah glanced at the clock. It was just after midnight and the house and street had fallen into its intense suburban silence. She pulled her feet up beneath her and then reached into her shirt pocket where she kept her cigarettes. Samantha had made it clear, without words, that she didn't like Leah smoking. But what did it matter now? Smoking was the least of her sins.

She lit her cigarette and watched Samantha's back stiffen.

"The man who just called was James Arlington?" Samantha said. "The analyst? I don't understand."

Leah took a deep drag and blew the smoke up toward the ceiling.

"Just listen," Leah said. She took a deep breath and then went back to the beginning, to the first two sessions she'd had with James.

"You recommended him to me, remember?" she said. "The thing is, I know he's good. I've talked to a couple of his patients and they swear by him. As for me, he saw that what I needed was sex and he gave it to me. In his mind, he was doing his job."

"He could lose his license for having sex with a patient," Samantha said.

Leah laughed. "He could. But, believe me, the devil won't even add that to his list of accomplishments when he escorts James into hell."

Leah stood up and walked around the room. She

had never smoked in here and it felt strange and liberating, blowing smoke into her little girl's curtains.

"I went to him for two sessions," she said, "and at the end of the second, he started kissing me."

"Mom," Samantha said, cringing, as if her words caused her pain. Leah went on, regardless.

"He kissed me and pulled me down on the floor and it was as if I didn't have any will or choice at all. I'm not saying he hypnotized or forced me. It was just that I was incredibly unhappy, incredibly hollow, and James just filled me up."

Leah took another deep drag. She pushed the curtains aside and lifted up the window to let some of the smoke out.

"I just can't believe—"

"Can't believe what?" Leah said, whirling around. "That I was bad enough to have an affair? Or that someone would want me?"

"Neither. Just that you would do this to Dad."

Leah stiffened.

"Are you still seeing him?" Samantha asked.

"No. It ended a few days after your father left me. James came by and we fought. He had been violent now and then over the years. It escalated at the end. When I told him I didn't want to see him anymore, he hit me badly, cut my face, bruised my ribs. All the passion I'd had for him turned to disgust."

Samantha started shaking and wrapped her arms around her stomach.

"You can't believe it," Leah said.

"No, I can't. How can anyone believe something like this of their mother?"

Leah crushed her cigarette out on the windowsill.

"Some of the sexiest, craziest people in the world are mothers. Goddammit, look at me, Samantha. I'm not old and decrepit. I'm not here only to guide you through. I've got a life, too. My own life. Leah Shaperson's."

"How could you let him hurt you?"

"I don't know," Leah said, opening the window wider and breathing in the cool autumn air. She longed for winter. She longed to live in a place where the snow fell eight feet deep and covered all the cracks and graffiti and weed-ravaged gardens. "Every explanation just sounds ridiculous."

"This is what Dad wouldn't tell me," Samantha said. "This is why he left."

Leah clenched her jaw. Elliot. Everything always came back to Elliot. Leah hated that, hated that he still mattered, that she still thought of him, worried about him. She wondered what he would think of her if he knew what she planned to do tomorrow.

"He knew for a long time," Leah said. "The whole time, I think. It wasn't until after we came back from the cabin that he finally confronted me."

Samantha shook her head. She was still shaking and she pulled the covers up to her chin.

"Dad wouldn't live with something like that," she said. "He always had such definite ideas about right and wrong."

"He did live with it," Leah said. "Stop glorifying him and vilifying me. He's not all good and I'm not all evil."

"If you were anyone else . . . " Samantha said, staring at her with such disgust that Leah felt tried and convicted and sentenced to hang. "But you're my mother. You did this to my father."

"I didn't do anything to him," Leah said sharply. "I did what I had to do for me. And let me tell you something, Samantha, I'm not only your mother, I'm a person in my own right."

They stared at each other a long time, and then Samantha turned away.

"And this James? He's the one who did those things to my apartment."

Leah took a deep breath. "Yes."

"He's out to terrorize me?"

"He's out to terrorize *me*," Leah said. "He's a vicious, bitter, probably psychotic man."

"He's a psychiatrist," Samantha said.

"Yes, I know. His father molested him. He thought going into psychiatry would help him, and because it hasn't, he's trying to beat his frustrations out on me. In his own way, he's remarkably pitiful."

"What did you ever see in him?"

Leah walked back and sat down on the edge of the bed.

"I saw everything I'd never seen in Elliot," she said.

Samantha closed her eyes, as if Leah's words were bright lights that blinded her. She waited a second and then said, "We should call the cops. Tell them we know who broke into my apartment."

Leah shook her head. "There's no evidence. And there never will be. He's too clever."

Samantha paled again. It seemed that with every second, her skin thinned and whitened and, in another minute or two, she would disappear entirely. Leah reached out and touched her hand.

"I'm going to stop him," Leah said.

"How?"

"Leave that up to me. Just do me a favor. If I'm not here, don't answer the phone. Don't answer the door to anyone but your father or Michael."

Samantha gripped her hand tighter. "Mom, how are you going to stop him?"

Leah smiled at her and then stood up. "With his own game," she said.

19

Dylan sat alone in Daniel Schwartz's office. He assumed the others would arrive soon, the chairmen of various charitable organizations, the deans of his parents' pet universities. After five minutes, however, only Daniel Schwartz came into the room.

"Thanks for waiting," he said, shaking Dylan's hand. Schwartz was a small, dark, chunky man with the best office space in Hartford. He was on the tenth floor and had a commanding view of the city and countryside beyond.

"This will go pretty quickly," Schwartz said, sitting down behind his desk. He put on his glasses, opened his file, and quickly began reading.

"We, Alan Reginald Price and Sophia Eleanor Price, of sound minds and bodies, give our entire estate, all our property, real and personal, to our son, Dylan Price. Included in this are: Cash assets of one hundred thousand dollars at First Security Bank. One hundred thousand dollars at Connecticut Mutual. One hundred thousand dollars at Eastern Standard. Seventy-five thousand dollars at Metropolitan Bank of New York. Various mutual funds in excess of two hundred and fifty thousand dollars. Stock assets including two thousand shares in Proctor Steel. Five thousand shares and a controlling interest in Georgia Shipping. Three thousand . . . "

Dylan stopped listening. He stood up and walked to the window. He looked out over the city he had left behind so easily.

"Mr. Price?" the lawyer said.

Dylan waved him on and Schwartz continued with the list of his parents' assets. They did leave him the house, as he had thought. Along with their house in West Palm Beach and the two Mercedeses in the garage. They left him their jewelry and his mother's furs and the priceless crystal. They left him everything and, when Daniel Schwartz was finally through, there was nothing Dylan could do but laugh.

"You're happy, then?" Schwartz said. "I thought you would be. Anyone inheriting a fortune like this must be ecstatic. If you need a lawyer to help you handle it, feel free to call on me."

He handed Dylan his card and Dylan slipped it into his pocket. He walked to the door, still chuckling, thinking what a great stroke of genius this was on his parents' part. They had done the impossible. Made a rich man of someone who was determined to be poor. They must have had such faith in an afterlife, assuming they would be up there somewhere to watch what a person who had vowed to hate money and all its trappings did when he was suddenly given more than he'd ever dreamed of.

"What do I do now?" Dylan asked. Schwartz came to his side and put his hand on his arm.

"I'm currently having all the transfers-of-ownership paperwork drawn up. After you sign all of that, you can quit work, if you want. You can live off the interest of their savings and mutual funds and dividends for a lifetime. You can sell the properties, if you still choose to live out west. Or you can slide right into your parents' old slots. Move into the house, take their places on those committees. You do have a couple of controlling interests in some progressive companies around here. You could fill up an awful lot of time sitting on various boards."

Sitting on various boards, Dylan thought. What does that mean? He said goodbye to the lawyer and walked out of the office. He stepped into the rental car, turned the radio on loud, then screeched out of the parking lot. He headed for the highway, and then for a back road where he could take this damn machine up over a hundred. He rolled down his window, pressed the accelerator to the floor, and took off.

He laughed again, shook his head, and had to, finally, admire his parents. They were brilliant. They had given him what he hated, forced him to either back up his talk with action, or become just like them, a slave to all they'd accumulated. He thought of the money, the stock, the mutual funds, the houses, the cars. He swerved on the road, as if the thoughts were just too heavy.

He raced around the back roads until the needle was on empty, then drove back to his parents' house—his house. He let himself in and walked straight up the stairs to his old bedroom. He turned on the light.

They had changed it the day he left, he was certain. Now, the room was a study, filled with books they probably never read, a desk that looked as if it had never been used. Dylan sat down in the chair.

He wanted to quit work and buy a yacht and sail around the world. And he wanted to donate all the money to EarthAlert and really make a difference. He wanted to show up on Samantha's doorstep with both of those Mercedeses, luring her back with riches. And he wanted to drive the cars into Harlem, leave the doors unlocked and the keys in the ignitions, and see how long they lasted.

He wanted to be good, and he wanted to be bad, and he realized the money had already infected him. All at once, he felt a rush of sympathy for his parents. He had thought they could have controlled themselves if they wanted to, but perhaps not. Perhaps that was the price you paid for wealth: it tricked you into thinking you needed what you wanted. Eventually, you just figured you needed everything.

Leah shoved herself into the back of the supply closet on the thirteenth floor of James's building. She had hoped to be here a week ago, but she thought it wiser to watch James's office for a few days, write down his comings and goings, make sure she picked the perfect time to strike. That time had finally come.

It was Tuesday night and she knew James would be expecting the lover he had replaced her with. Leah had looked up at the office window last Thursday and seen a flash of dark skin pass by the glass. James had always had a lust for black women.

Her watch read six forty-five and, if James kept to the same schedule he always did, in five minutes he would leave his office with his last patient and go downstairs for a smoke before his lover arrived.

She didn't think too much. When thoughts of what she was doing threatened her, she quickly turned her mind to what had happened to Samantha's apartment, and to what that had done to Samantha. Never mind all the tortures James had put Leah through. There had to be retribution for her daughter.

At six fifty-one, James's office door opened and Leah heard James's voice. Another male voice answered and then the two of them laughed. That was strange. She hadn't even known he was capable of that kind of laughter, the friendly kind, the kind without any malice or anguish at all.

The two men passed right outside the storage closet and Leah held her breath. A moment later, when the elevator doors slid closed, she exhaled.

She turned the knob slowly and stepped out of the closet. She knew the routine of this place as well as she knew that of her own home. James kept the latest hours on this floor and would be here, alone with his lover, until eight or nine.

She walked down the hall to James's office. She let herself into the waiting room and then moved quickly down the hallway to James's private office. She opened the door and went in.

Everything was exactly the same, the desk, the two chairs opposite it, the couch in the corner, the windows with the miniblinds pulled all the way up. It was dust-free and cold as ice.

Leah walked across the room. She hesitated only a moment when she reached James's desk. She put her gloved hand on the drawer and then flinched, as if it had burned her. It wasn't right to be so calm. She knew she wasn't insane. And so what did that say about her, that she could be sane and still do this? She was like some character out of a thriller movie, bent on revenge. Only this wasn't about revenge, not really. It was about justice. It was about her daughter. It was about stopping violence with violence instead of screaming and begging for someone to save her.

She watched her hand as she opened the drawer. It did not shake. She found the gun in the back, where James always kept it for his games of Russian roulette. She took it out, opened the revolver, and saw that, as usual, there was only one bullet in the cylinder. She took the bullets she had bought at the gun shop out of her pocket and inserted them into every chamber.

Only then did her hand start shaking. All at once it trembled so badly she could not hold the gun. She dropped it into the drawer, slammed the drawer shut, and ran to the door. She rushed out of the office, down the hall, and crammed herself back into the supply closet. She yearned to run, but she could not chance meeting James. She waited a breathless, endless five minutes until the elevator doors slid open again and James's methodical footsteps traveled back to his office.

Though she thought she would die from suffocation, Leah forced herself to wait another ten minutes. At the end of that time, she heard the elevator doors open again and a softer step, obviously a woman's step, pass by her. She tried not to feel guilty, to wonder what seeing a man blow his own brains out would do to a woman. She only knew that James would go first, that he would put on that blindfold and make the woman spin the cylinder. She was betting that any woman who played the game would be as frightened as she had been and, like her, not have the slightest understanding of guns. James had told her there was only one bullet inside and she had taken his word. He had said "Spin it," and she had, holding it as far from her body as possible.

Tonight, if she was lucky, James would interest his new lover in the game. He would put on his blindfold and his partner would spin the cylinder, then snap it shut. James would point the revolver at his temple, sure of his luck, and then, bam, that luck would run out. Whoever was with him would be as prepared as a person could be for seeing a man die. That was the gamble of Russian roulette.

Leah knew all of this, but still she was crying as she listened to the woman enter James's office. She shoved her fist into her mouth to keep from calling out.

• • •

Late that night, Samantha heard the front door open. She sat up and looked at the clock on the nightstand. It was three thirty-eight in the morning.

For a moment, she thought it was a burglar. She reached for the phone, but then the door to her room opened and her mother peeked her head through.

"Mom?" Samantha said.

"Yes. It's me. Go back to sleep."

"Mom, it's nearly four in the morning. Where have you been?"

Leah stepped into the room. The moonlight seeped in through the window and illuminated Leah's features. Her face was pale, pinched, and her eyes were dazed.

It had been a week since Leah had come clean about James. There had been no more phone calls from the man, but Leah had admitted that she'd seen him driving past the house in the mornings. Samantha was still having a hard time believing any of it.

"Mom?" Samantha repeated.

Leah looked at her, seemed to see her for the first time, and then smiled.

"I was just out driving," she said. "Thinking. Do you know I'm not at all like I used to be?"

Samantha stared at her. "What's wrong?"

Leah still smiled and shook her head. Her right arm was swinging up and back as if she couldn't control it.

"Nothing. Everything's all right now. Go to sleep."

She closed the door and Samantha listened as she walked down the hall into her own bedroom. *I'm not at all like I used to be.* Leah was right. She wasn't. She wasn't even close to being the mother Samantha had grown up with. Back then, Leah had been soft-spoken, old-fashioned, modest. Now she was angry. She smoked. She spoke her mind. She sneaked gin into her room when she thought Samantha wasn't looking. She went out driving until four in the morning. She'd had an affair.

Samantha was still trying to digest that, to figure

how anyone could sacrifice thirty-seven years of companionship and love for a few nights of passion. Didn't she know that what she and Elliot had was precious? God, what Samantha would have given for thirty-seven years with Dylan.

And how could Leah have been with a man like James? A man who would hit her and stoop to terrorizing her daughter. Leah was not stupid. She had to have known who she was getting involved with.

Samantha struggled to a sitting position and then slipped her feet out of bed. Her mother had been out every night this week and what she didn't know was that Samantha had been out, too. The first time, she had only gone as far as the sidewalk before rushing back inside. Then the next night she made it to the corner, then the next around the block. Tonight, she had walked for fifteen full minutes, sucking up the night air as if her lungs had been sealed shut and she'd finally pried them open again.

The shadows scared her, the wind scared her, people she passed scared her, but she kept walking. Michael had told her to take her time, to ease into it, but Samantha had realized that if she eased, she would never make it. Dylan had known that. The last time he'd come to see her—the day they'd said goodbye—it was obvious that he wanted to yank her out of bed and throw her out on the street. She almost wished he had. It would have saved her so much time, so many hours of sitting in bed, terrified, losing her mind to television.

She had been staying with her mother for one month now and it had to stop. It was too easy to slip back in time, to let her mother handle everything, to pretend she had the flu and was too sick to go anywhere. It was too easy to make the mistake of thinking that having a mother around was the answer to everything.

Her sick time was nearly up and she planned to call

her boss and tell her she was coming back on Monday. Tomorrow, she would get dressed and go out searching for a new place to live. She wished she had the nerve to live alone again, but she didn't. Not yet. She'd have to find a roommate.

Samantha stood up. She had grown up, gone to college, found a good job, but when she had come running back here she had become just her mother's daughter again. She had hoped for mother miracles, but they had not come. The truth was, Leah could not bandage her heart, or solve her problems at work, or make her brave again. She could not bring Dylan back; she could not resolve her feelings for Michael. Leah could not, really, do anything that needed to be done in her life anymore, although once she had been powerful enough to do everything.

Samantha walked slowly down the hall to her mother's room. She knocked on the door and, a second later, Leah opened it.

With the light on, Samantha could see Leah's face clearly. Her eyes were most definitely glazed. She smiled too widely and Samantha reached for her hand.

Leah was shaking so badly, Samantha could hardly hold it steady. She pulled her mother into her arms. Leah stood there, shivering, and Samantha felt her tears on her neck although Leah made no noise as she cried.

Finally, Samantha pulled her into bed and covered her with blankets. She brushed the hair off her mother's forehead.

"We'll have to watch the papers," Leah said. "It could happen anytime. I'm not sure who he plays with or how often."

"What are you talking about?" Samantha asked, but Leah just closed her eyes and smiled even while she cried.

• • •

Elliot came over to Leah's to help Samantha move. She had wasted away for over four weeks and then, suddenly, as if God had had enough of her self-imposed seclusion and had shot her spirit back into her soul, she leapt up and took her life back.

Elliot packed her clothes into boxes. She had searched the want ads for a roommate, interviewed a few people, and felt uncomfortable with each of them. She had called Elliot last night and told him she'd found a solution.

"I'm going to move in with Michael," she had said.

"I beg your pardon?"

Elliot had braced himself to hear that she was moving in with Dylan. He had not been prepared to hear that the man he'd championed had won out.

"You know he came over to Mom's nearly every day while I was here," Samantha had said. "I told him I was going to move out and go back to work and he was concerned that I was taking on too much. He thought it would be a perfect arrangement if I came to live with him."

"But I thought you and Dylan—"

"No, that's over," Samantha said stiffly. "I don't know if you heard, but his parents died in that plane crash at LaGuardia. We broke up just before he went to the funeral. He should be back by now, so I left a message on his machine to tell him I'm moving in with Michael. That should ease what little conscience he has."

Now, Elliot helped Samantha pack and wished he could come up with the right words. He wanted to be happy about this move; Michael was the man he wanted for her. He only wished Samantha was happier about it, that her face didn't look the way it used to when she ate some vegetable she hated but knew was good for her.

"That's it," Samantha said, when they had packed up everything. "Michael should be here soon."

Elliot nodded. The two of them walked into the living room. Leah had left early this morning and said she would not be back until noon. She did not like good-byes.

The phone rang and Samantha lunged for it. Elliot was surprised by her eagerness, even more surprised as her shoulders sagged when she heard who was on the other end.

"Oh hi, Michael," she said. "Yes, we're ready. We'll be waiting."

She hung up. "He's on his way over," she said.

Elliot put his arm around her shoulders.

"It's all right to dream of what you'd like to happen," he said.

Samantha shook her head. "No it's not. I sat in bed for four weeks wishing that what had happened to my apartment was just a bad dream, wishing that I could make the world good and safe again. And I've wished, since I met Dylan, that I could make him love me, that I was good enough to change him, but I wasn't. I am so goddamn sick of wishing for things that won't ever come true that now I just want to settle for what I've got."

Elliot stared at her and realized she was exactly like him. He had settled for complacency rather than risk a passionate life with Leah. He had settled for a career in insurance rather than take the hard road back to his art. And now look at him. On the brink of divorce with a company near ruin. Complacent lives always crumbled from lack of maintenance. Nobody worked at things that meant so little.

"Do you love Michael?" he asked.

Samantha pulled away. She moved a few boxes closer to the door.

"I will love him, I'm sure," she said. "He's a wonderful friend."

Elliot blinked back tears at the sadness in her voice. It was Leah's voice, the voice he'd heard these last few years when he suggested that she cook for Valentine's Day rather than going out to dinner, when he bought her a wide-mouthed toaster for her birthday rather than tickets to the ballet, when they took all of their vacations at the cabin rather than flying to France.

He and Samantha sat down on the couch in silence, until the door banged open. Leah walked in, a newspaper in one hand and a cigarette in the other. She was wearing leggings again; this pair was a glittery gold color and her sweatshirt had a loud leopard print on it. She smoked aggressively, blowing the smoke out with a hiss. Elliot stared at her in amazement, without a clue as to who she was or what to say. He felt like an old man beside a vulgar teenage girl, with no bridge between the generations.

"You're still here," Leah said to Samantha.

"Yes. Michael should be over any minute."

Leah nodded and walked into the dining room. She slammed the newspaper down on the table. Samantha leaned over to Elliot and whispered in his ear.

"She's been like this for a week. Furious for no apparent reason. Now you know why Michael will be a great improvement."

They heard Michael's car pull up and Samantha went outside. Elliot took a deep breath and stood. He smoothed down the creases in his shirt and walked over to Leah.

"Are you all right?" he asked.

She stared at him and then blew a gust of smoke over his head. She ground the cigarette out in the ashtray and then walked into the kitchen.

"My daughter is leaving today to go live with a man she doesn't love. No, I am not all right."

She was furious. Elliot could see that in every stiff

gesture, the tightness in her neck, the bitterness in her voice; it fascinated him.

She reached into her pocket for another cigarette and then crushed the pack in frustration when she found it empty.

"I called Dylan, you know," she said, pacing across the kitchen. "I wanted to give him a chance to get his ass over here and fight for her. That bastard hasn't even returned my call."

Elliot stared at her in awe. She was like an entirely new woman, gruff and crude and mesmerizing.

"Samantha said his parents recently died. Give him a little time."

"Don't you dare make excuses for him," Leah said. "You hate him. You should be thrilled that he's letting Michael move in. Michael will make the perfect son-in-law for a man like you."

Elliot turned away. His stomach cramped. It had not done that for weeks, not since he'd begun walking, trying to get himself lost. He sat down at the dining table, then stood up again when sitting only made the pain worse.

Leah stared at him. "You look tired," she said.

He nodded. "I am. I didn't sleep at all last night. I sat on the balcony and watched the sunrise."

"Why?"

"I don't know. I don't sleep well anymore."

"How was it?"

"What?" Elliot asked.

"The sunrise."

Elliot shrugged. "I don't remember."

She started toward him and then stopped in mid-stride. The tightness in her face disappeared and he saw something else, some emotion he couldn't identify.

"You're so sad, Elliot," she said. "But frankly, I don't know if I'm supposed to comfort you. Is there some clause in the divorce papers that says I can't touch you anymore? Is there a law or something?"

She was smiling, teasing him, and Elliot had the strangest feeling that she had whisked herself back in time, become the girl he'd met in high school, while he had aged normally and must look like an old man to her. God knows he felt old. He felt ancient.

"The divorce will be final early next year," he said.

"Yes. I know." She stopped smiling. They were quiet for a long time. There were a million things Elliot wanted to say, but he couldn't articulate any of them. He'd had so many years of filling their conversations with worthless words that now he just felt dumb.

Samantha walked into the house with Michael. They quickly loaded the boxes into his car. They looked right together, Elliot thought. Professional, regal, but still comfortable with each other. Everything was perfect except that Samantha's eyes were hard and unfeeling, and Elliot knew that no matter how hard she tried, she would never love this man.

"Well, we're off," Samantha said when they were done loading. She hugged Leah, who held her too tightly at first and then abruptly walked away. Elliot hugged Samantha and then shook Michael's hand.

"We'll have you over for dinner," Michael said and Elliot knew they would, that they would play at happiness as well as he and Leah had. He nodded and turned away.

20

Elliot had been working sixteen-hour days to turn his business around. He had hired a new agent, despite the company's precarious financial position, to help bring in new clients. He had siphoned five thousand dollars from his personal savings account and, with the help of a local, inexpensive advertising agency, put a pretty fair ad on cable television. He had sent out bulk mailings to all of his loyal customers, telling them they'd get a fifty-dollar discount on next year's premium for every new client they brought in.

He had fired Bill in September and finally, by mid-November, he was beginning to see results. McDermott Insurance had paid off its creditors and could now pay its monthly bills. It would take years to replenish the funds Bill had stolen, but there was enough to cover any claims that came in, short of an earthquake disaster which would take down all of the other insurers right along with him. Elliot no longer felt as if he were standing on the edge of a precipice, ready to fall in.

He thought he deserved a vacation. As he sat on a plane bound for Miami, though, he wasn't quite sure what to do with himself, whether to keep belting down the free wine the flight attendants passed out, or to try to watch the two-year-old movie. He had to remind himself that he was entitled to a little leisure.

If you could call visiting a mother you hadn't seen for eight years leisure.

Elliot had not told her he was coming. He hadn't even known he was coming until a week ago, when he woke up in the middle of the night certain someone was in the apartment. He had gotten up, turned on all the lights, checked behind the drapes. He had been alone, thankfully, but his legs still gave out after he'd finished his search. He fell into a chair and remembered all those nights after his father had left when he'd been certain someone was in the house. He had made his mother get up night after night and check all the closets.

It was one of the few things she hadn't complained about. Even if Elliot woke her up at two in the morning, she got up without a quarrel and checked every door and window, turned on every light. Then she put him back to bed, brushed the hair off his forehead, and said the same thing every time: "Mothers are just as good protectors as fathers. Go to sleep." Elliot often forgot that no matter how often or cruelly his father had left him, his mother had always stayed.

In that middle-of-the-night silence last week, he had realized it was time to face his mother again. Now, he sat on the plane, wondering what he would do when he got to Miami, wondering what he would say to a mother he hadn't spoken to for three years.

His mother, Joann, did not even know that he and Leah were separated. She did not know what had happened to Samantha. He doubted very much if she knew anything about his sister, Meredith. From sixteen on,

Meredith had had no contact with either parent. She hadn't even sent flowers for their father's funeral.

The flight attendant came by and Elliot asked for another complimentary white wine. Half an hour later, he asked for another and, by the time they landed in Miami, he was as relaxed as he could be.

He picked up his bags, rented a car, and bought a map of the city. It had always been Leah's job to navigate through strange places. Elliot had hated new cities, unknown streets. But today, he welcomed the newness, welcomed the eighty-degree sunshine, the rush-hour traffic. He found his rental car and glanced down at the map while he drove, heading south on the freeway for about twenty minutes and then getting off at Emerald. He drove in the direction of the beach.

He found her condominium easily. The street was full of large, ugly buildings that looked like medical offices but which housed thousands of senior citizens. Elliot parked on the street.

He found the right building and went inside. He was immediately assaulted by the smell of decay in the lobby. The furnishings were old and faded; all the curtains were drawn tightly to keep out the smallest specks of light. He ran his finger over a table, expecting to find layers of ancient dust, but it was surprisingly clean.

He walked to the elevator and pushed the button for the seventh floor. The doors closed and the elevator creaked upward. Elliot's nose twitched at the lingering smell of someone's vinegary perfume.

He stepped out on the seventh floor, took a wrong turn to the left, and then found his mother's apartment on the end of the right wing. He stood outside of it for a long time, staring at the door, thinking of a woman inside he didn't know, probably would never know. He prayed that it would never be like this between him and Samantha. He squeezed his eyes shut and begged God not to let him die before Samantha got a chance to know the man her father was.

He knocked. There was silence on the other side and he knocked again, louder. This time, there was a slow paddle of feet and then the door opened.

He knew at once that her eyesight was going and she didn't recognize him. But he recognized her. She was stooped now; her hair was pure white and cut as short as a man's. She wore white polyester slacks and a blue sweater, although her apartment seemed stiflingly hot. She did not look even close to the woman he'd known growing up, except for her eyes. They were long-lashed, round brown eyes to die for.

"Who are you?" she said, squinting.

"It's me, Mom. Elliot."

She stepped back, as if his words had stabbed her. She clutched at her sweater and he thought, for a moment, that she was having a heart attack. But then she dropped her hand and stood up straight. She squinted harder at him. She took a step closer and stood face-to-face with him.

"So, it is you," she said. "You'd better come in then."

They sat on her couch and Elliot unbuttoned his shirt. It felt close to ninety degrees inside.

"I get cold," she said.

Elliot nodded. He looked around the condo. It was hardly bigger than his own apartment, although it was cleaner and more personal. Joann had covered the walls with photographs and two of the watercolors he had painted for her right after he married Leah.

"You still have those seascapes," he said.

She turned, stared in the direction of the waterlors.

"Of course. You gave them to me."

Elliot leaned back into the couch. The smell of the lobby was here, too. As he sat looking at his mother, he realized it was the smell of dust and old skin. Of clothes that had been shoved to the back of the closet for twenty years. Of shampoo found at the bottom of the medicine cabinet, with an expiration date of 1976.

"You're looking good," Elliot said.

Joann laughed. "Don't lie. I look my age. Which, I'm sure you don't know, is seventy-nine."

Elliot reached out and took her hand. It was cool and the skin was nearly translucent, revealing veins and liver spots and a life lived long and hard.

"Mom, can you forgive me?"

She turned away, but Elliot could still see her lower lip trembling. He thought of her here, alone all these years. How could he have let that happen? Why were people cruelest to their own families?

"You ran away," Joann said finally. "Just like Meredith did."

Elliot nodded. "I suppose I did. To tell you the truth, I didn't even realize I was doing it. I forgot how much time had passed since I'd called you. I made myself forget. And then I didn't know how to say I was sorry, so I just stayed silent."

"You always were good at that," she said.

They sat in silence for a while. The sun must have dipped behind a cloud because the room darkened. Elliot inched closer to her, until their shoulders touched.

"Where's Leah?" Joann asked at last.

"I left her."

Only then did Elliot start crying. He had wanted to when he walked out on Leah, and then again when he first saw the apartment he'd be living in, and then when he walked into his old house and saw Leah dressed as someone entirely different. But each of those times, he'd been too much of his old self, still determined to pretend everything was all right.

Now, as if that old self were a balloon full of saline and water, he finally pricked himself and cried against his mother. She didn't put her arm around him and he realized there were too many broken bridges for that. But she didn't move away, either. She leaned her head against his until he quieted.

Finally, she said, "Now you know."

Elliot wiped his cheeks and looked up. "Know what?"

She smiled at him and, grabbing the edge of the couch, hoisted herself up. She walked to the window and pulled back the blinds. The clouds had come from nowhere and suddenly it looked like rain.

"Now you know what I felt for your father."

"I really don't know, Mom."

She turned back to him. "He owned my soul, Elliot," she said softly. "God knows I didn't want him to. I remember how you looked at me when I took him back all those times. You couldn't believe I was such a fool. I couldn't believe it, either."

"Why did you do it?"

Joann laughed. It was a different laugh from what she used to have; huskier, softer, the tail end of a laugh.

"You're not listening," she said. "He owned my soul. I had no choice. I loved him. I hated him. I knew all his faults and attributes. You know how it is when you're trapped in a ferocious rainstorm and then, suddenly, a small hole opens up in the clouds and the sun comes pouring through?"

"Dad was like the sun to you?" Elliot asked.

Joann laughed again. "Oh no. He was the rainstorm. But I suppose, now and then, he was the sun, too. He was everything. All I dreamed of. I don't regret a second of my time with him. I'm sorry that it drove you and Meredith away but, even though this sounds harsh, my love for him came first. It still does, even though he's gone."

Elliot sat very still. His arm twitched occasionally and he held it down. His mother shuffled back to the couch and sat beside him.

"I always knew you loved him far more than you could ever love me," Elliot said.

"Of course I loved him more. He was my grand passion. But I didn't follow him when he left me. I stayed with you and Meredith."

"I know, Mom."

"What will you do," she asked, "about Leah?"

Elliot tilted his head back and closed his eyes.

"I can't go back to her," he said. "She had an affair."

Joann reached out and ran her fingers through his hair. Elliot shivered and thought of all he'd forgotten. All the nights she had soothed him, talked to him, yelled at him, encouraged him. All the nights she'd been there. He opened his eyes.

She was staring at him and smiling.

"What?" he said.

"You're on the verge of discovering exactly how much love can rule your life."

"It's not ruling it. That's exactly the point. Leah had an affair and I will not go back to her."

Joann shrugged. "Suit yourself. But I said the same thing once, when Steven had his first affair, and then I faced the prospect of a life without him. So he slept with someone else. So, for a while, he was unhappy with me. I think back on it now and realize just how inconsequential it was. It's just sex, Elliot. Just trying to find pleasure where you can. He regretted hurting me and I forgave him. Leah, I'm sure, regrets hurting you."

Elliot stiffened. He expected his stomach to spasm,

but it did not. He expected to come up with some indignant reply, but his mind was blank. Joann laughed once more.

"You'll see," she said. "Maybe not now. Maybe not in time to save what you and Leah have. But someday you'll look back, like I'm looking back, and put it all in perspective. We praise the faithful, but I don't know if you and I are any more honorable than Leah and Steven were. They lacked something with us and they found it somewhere else. They hurt us and, at the same time, hurt themselves. Leah's just a woman, Elliot. Not a symbol of anything."

Elliot looked at his mother. Really stared hard at her until he saw exactly what she was. Old and fading, but still showing off a spark in her eye, a coy lilt to her voice. For just an instant, he saw what his father must have seen, a lively woman he couldn't stop himself from returning to again and again. The owner of his soul, too.

"I'm sorry I stayed away so long," Elliot said.

Joann nodded her head and then smiled. "I'm sorry I didn't fight for you to come back. But I'd already done so much fighting for Steven, and I was tired of losing."

They were quiet for a moment and then Joann patted his hand. "You hurt me," she said, "and I forgive you. It's that simple. Stop making everything so difficult, Elliot."

Leah grabbed the paper off the front stoop and ran inside. She had a feeling about today. Last night, around ten, she'd been watching television when suddenly she jerked, as if a gunshot had startled her. She'd often heard of people knowing exactly when a loved one had died. Well, James was not a loved one, but she was more interested in his death than anyone.

She had slept fitfully and, as soon as she heard the newspaper slam against the front door this morning, she ran to get it. Now, she took it to the kitchen table and quickly opened it to the obituaries. She searched each one, but James Arlington was not there.

She looked through the rest of the paper, hoping there would be an article about a prominent Sacramento psychiatrist blowing his brains out, but there was none. Goddammit, she was tired of waiting for him to die.

Leah walked to the kitchen and opened a fresh pack of cigarettes. She loved new packs, loved seeing twenty long Virginia Slims awaiting her. She pulled one out and lit it, then took the smoke deep into her lungs.

Right after she had filled the revolver with bullets, she almost went back and took them out again. She drove around that night until nearly four in the morning, hating what she'd done, loving it, disgusted with herself, and proud. She cried because she'd forfeited her soul, but then she laughed hysterically because she knew she had finally gotten the better of James Arlington.

Now a month had passed and Leah was still holding her breath, waiting for him to die. This should be the easy part. She had worked up the nerve to do it. She had sneaked into his office and loaded the gun. She had gotten out without losing her courage or giving in to her morals. Now, all she had to do was wait, but it was killing her.

She didn't believe she was the only one he'd ever played Russian roulette with. It was part of his whole repertoire and now that he'd found someone new, he'd no doubt introduce her to it.

So why didn't he die? What on earth was taking him so long? After her guilt wore off, she just wanted it to be over. He hadn't called again, but she'd gotten two more manila envelopes addressed with childlike scrawls. She had burned them, unopened. There were times, when she stepped out into her front yard, that she could feel his eyes on her, although when she looked around she saw no one.

After one week, she stopped thinking about going back and taking out the bullets. After two weeks, she stopped feeling guilty entirely and waited eagerly for the news of his demise. After four weeks, she was practically going crazy wondering what had gone wrong, wondering if the woman who spun the cylinder had noticed it was full of bullets, or if James himself had peeked from behind his blindfold. He might have figured out that she had been the one who put the bullets there and he was plotting some great revenge.

Leah walked around the kitchen. The house was too quiet this morning, without the hum of Samantha's television. Samantha was living at Michael's now and working again full-time. Leah had not heard from her for two weeks.

Suddenly, Leah hurried to the phone. She dialed Samantha's work number and her daughter picked up on the second ring.

"It's your mother, Samantha," she said.

There was a silence and Leah wondered what was going on. Why hadn't Samantha called in the last two weeks? She usually called every other day.

"Hi, Mom," she said. "How are you?"

"Pretty good. I was just thinking about you."

"That's nice. I'm kind of busy, though. Can I call you back?"

Leah sucked on her cigarette and squinted when the exhaled smoke sailed past her eyes.

"Will you?" she asked.

Samantha was quiet for a moment. Finally, she said, "A lot has been happening."

"Obviously."

"Michael is pretty serious about us."

Leah stubbed out her cigarette without finishing it. She sat down at the kitchen table.

"How serious?" she asked.

"I think he's going to propose."

Leah could think of nothing to say.

"Please don't tell me I should say no," Samantha went on. "Don't tell me it's not right. Don't tell me I should love him more, or love him the way I loved Dylan. Dylan's not here. I don't know what happened after his parents' funeral. He seems to have fallen off the face of the earth, or at least the face of my earth. Like an idiot, I've called him, but he hasn't called me back. Michael always calls me back. I don't care what you say, that's important."

Leah breathed deeply to try to refill her empty lungs. This was not her daughter. Some imposter had taken Samantha's place, stolen into her soul and turned it to jelly. Goddamn James for what he'd done to her apartment, for stealing her strength away, for making her scared and ready to settle.

"I don't have a right to preach anything about marriage," Leah said.

"You're so stupid," Samantha hissed at her. "You and Dad are so incredibly stupid."

Though Leah knew she should take offense, that comment actually made her smile.

"Yes, we are. We're stupid and proud and stubborn and ignorant and crazy and passionate. We're just like you, Samantha. Just like anyone."

"I've got to go," Samantha said. "How about if I come over tonight for dinner and we can talk."

"Good. But let me say this. Marriage isn't a cure for loneliness and fear. If that's what you're hoping for, you'll be disappointed. You can be standing right beside someone and still be totally alone."

Samantha was quiet for a moment and then said, "Goodbye, Mom. I'll see you tonight."

Leah hung up the phone and stood up. Then she dialed Dylan's number and again got his recording. She too had been calling him, trying to get him to fight for

Samantha, to pry her away from Michael. He had not returned her calls, either. Where the hell was he?

"Dylan, it's Leah. Listen to me. I don't know what game you're playing, but stop playing it. Samantha is going to marry Michael if you don't do something about it. Do something, Dylan."

Leah slammed down the phone and dialed Elliot's number. She got another recording and felt sick to death of answering machines. She left an abrupt message.

"Elliot, it's me," she said. "Give me a call when you get in. It's about Samantha."

Then Leah hung up and walked to the couch. She sat down and listened to the silence. What was happening to all of them? Samantha was engaged to the wrong man, Elliot was living alone in a horrible apartment, Dylan wasn't answering his phone, and James, the bastard, wouldn't die. It was enough to drive a person mad.

That night, Leah made lasagna, Samantha's favorite, and sat on the front porch waiting for her daughter to arrive. Instead, at six-thirty, Elliot drove up.

Leah stood up slowly. She was wearing gray leggings that she was certain Elliot would not approve of and one of Elliot's gray sweatshirts that he had left behind.

Elliot got out of his car. He looked marvelous, better than he had in a long time. The tight lines around his mouth were gone and his face was tanned. He was wearing a denim shirt she didn't recognize and had parted his hair on the right, instead of the left side.

He walked up the path, smiling at her. Leah was astounded that she could feel nervous around her own husband. He was still her husband, after all, if only for a couple more months. She had not thought he was even capable of inspiring goose pimples on her skin.

He reached her and touched her shoulder like an

old friend. Leah looked down at his hand and then he dropped it.

"I got your message," he said. "I wasn't sure when you left it. I've been in Miami this week."

"You what?"

"I went to visit my mother."

Leah leaned back against the house. The night was warm for November, but she shivered as if it were frosty. Elliot opened the front door and they went inside.

"How is she?" Leah asked as they sat down on the couch.

"Good, actually. We went out to dinner every night and she introduced me to her friends. I feel like an idiot, avoiding her for so long."

Leah nodded. If a man could look radiant, Elliot did. His eyes were bright and he could hardly stop smiling. She had gotten after him for years about avoiding his mother, but he had never listened to her. Who was he listening to now?

"I'm happy for you, Elliot."

He smiled. "I told her I'd talk to Meredith, too. See if I can at least get her to take a step toward reconciliation."

Leah was silent and Elliot shifted on the couch.

"You said there was something about Samantha," he said.

Leah nodded. She slid away from him, then stood up and walked aimlessly around the room.

"She's coming to dinner tonight. I hadn't heard from her in two weeks and then, when I called her today, she told me things with Michael were getting pretty heavy. She thinks he's going to propose."

She whirled around in time to see his reaction. As she had expected, he was not shocked or dismayed. The corners of his mouth tilted up wider.

"That's wonderful," he said.

Leah put her hands on her hips. "No, it is not wonderful, Elliot. She doesn't love him. Not like she should love him. She's scared to death after what happened to her apartment and she thinks she can't be alone. She's trying to protect herself, not marry the man she loves."

"Michael's a good man," he said.

"Of course he is. But so what? You're a good man, and look what happened to us. Is that what you want for her?"

Leah knew she shouldn't have said it. She turned away from him and bit her lip. God, she was a mess with him now, as nervous as she'd been when they first met. She felt jittery and awkward and ugly, incapable of saying the right thing.

Suddenly, there were arms around her. Leah jumped a little, and then turned and fell right into him. Elliot's hands were, at first, tentative, but then they slipped into their old positions, one around her waist, one higher, around her shoulders. It was as if there were grooves in her skin and he slid right into them.

She wasn't sure how long they stood like that, holding each other. She was afraid to look at her watch, to make any move that would break the spell. She didn't even move her hands on his back, did not explore him the way she wanted to, for fear that he would pull away. He felt so good, so solid. She remembered James's thin body, the tautness she had found so exciting. Funny that this should excite her now, the roundness of Elliot's belly, the thicker heat of him.

"Do you love him?" he asked. "James, I mean."

Leah stepped back, out of his embrace. Funny that their minds had taken the same steps, from Samantha to Michael to adultery to Leah to James. If Elliot only knew how ludicrous his question was. She hated James, abhorred him. She was trying to kill him.

She could feel the sudden tautness in Elliot's body and suddenly, more profoundly than when they had been together, she regretted every moment she had ever spent with James. She regretted turning to him when she could have turned to Elliot. She had missed so many opportunities to tell Elliot what she felt, to make him understand her. She had never given him a chance to get to know her, the real Leah, all sides. She had hidden her wildness, her passion, just as she hid her cigarettes, afraid that he would hate her if he saw.

She stepped up beside him again, close enough that their shoulders touched.

"No, Elliot," she said. "I never did. I realize it's a little late for explanations, but I thought I needed James once. It seemed essential at the time that somebody look at me as a woman instead of as a wife."

He pulled away and she knew she had said too much. He didn't want explanations. He only wanted the wrong made right. And she couldn't do that, not with this. She couldn't erase what she'd done.

"I've been walking," Elliot said. "Trying to get myself lost."

"Samantha told me. I didn't really believe it."

"It's true. It feels good, to see things I've never seen before. To try something new, after all this time. I even mastered Miami."

He blushed like a child reporting his first success. God, he could still move her. It wasn't fair. She wanted to be done with him, to simply scoop out the portions of her heart that belonged to him and start rebuilding. But the Elliot part of her was too essential; she would collapse without it.

"Listen," he said, "about Samantha. Give her some credit. This thing with her apartment threw her, but she'll come out all right. She always does."

Leah nodded and Elliot walked to the door.

"Tell her to call me tonight," he said. "Trust me on this. It will all work out."

Then he left and Leah ran to the window. She

watched him walk to his car and thought, for the first time in a long time, *There goes a handsome man.*

Samantha came to dinner and repeated all she'd said before, that Michael comforted her, loved her, that he was on the verge of proposing and she was on the verge of saying yes. Leah bit her lip, wished her luck, and ate two helpings of lasagna to keep herself from saying what she really felt.

Two days later, Leah was back to fixing frozen dinners for one. When the phone rang, she was certain it was Samantha, to tell her that Michael had popped the question. Instead, it was a voice that sent a chill through her.

"Leah," James said. "I've been missing you."

Leah leaned against the kitchen counter. She forced herself to breathe, to not reveal her profound disappointment that he was still alive enough to talk to her.

"What do you want, James?" she said.

He laughed and she knew this was the end. Everyone had a certain amount of torment they could stand, but if given an ounce too much, they lost control. She had thought she'd reached her limit when she filled the gun with bullets, but now she realized she could go one step further. She could make him use that gun, watch him die herself.

"I've found someone new," he said, "but honestly it's not the same. She doesn't understand. She doesn't play the games like you did. And since Samantha is living with her new man, you've got to be lonely, too."

Leah didn't move. He was still stalking her, still following Samantha, still prying into their lives. He did it cleanly, infrequently, but she knew that it would go on and on unless she stopped it.

"You're right, James," she said, standing up straight and picking up a cigarette off the counter. "I have missed you. It's been lonely here without Samantha or a man around."

He hesitated and for a moment she thought she hadn't pulled it off, that he was too smart for her. But then he sighed in relief and she knew she had him.

"I told you so, Leah. You know you really are no good without a man."

Leah lit her cigarette. She sucked in deeply, then blew the smoke directly into the phone.

"I'd like to see you," she said. "I've missed . . . our games."

"You don't know how glad I am to hear that. No one plays them like you. Women are so headstrong these days. They want the upper hand. But not you. You like the submissive role. It suits you."

Not anymore. I'm going to watch you blow your brains out, you bastard.

She smiled then and all the nervousness was gone. Just like that.

"When do we meet?" she asked and didn't shiver when he laughed.

"You're eager, aren't you?" he said.

"Yes," she said. "Very."

"How about on Tuesday, then? It will be like old times."

Leah told him she would be there and hung up. She walked to the bathroom and looked in the mirror. What did a woman capable of murder look like? She shivered because she looked just like anyone. Behind every face was a secret, within every body the capability to do anything. As long as there were guns and human passions, no one was safe.

21

Dylan signed all the paperwork, looked at the inventory Daniel Schwartz had made out that itemized all he now owned, and felt a little queasy. When he walked out of the lawyer's office for the second time, as a rich man, he was certain everyone could read it in his face.

He drove around Hartford, looking in all the shop windows, knowing he could buy nearly anything he wanted. At first, the thought infuriated him. Why were some people given so much and others nothing? No matter how hard he tried, though, he couldn't sustain that anger. As he circled one particular block that housed a travel agency, sporting goods store, and pet shop, he started feeling almost giddy. He could walk into that travel agency and buy a ticket to Bermuda. Or to Africa. He could go wherever he damn well pleased.

Dylan made a quick turn into a parking space in front of the agency and jumped out. He walked to the door, put his hand on the knob, and then stopped. What the hell was he doing? Had his father invaded his body?

It had taken only a matter of seconds for wealth to change him. He'd been willing to go his whole life without furniture and up-to-date clothes, even food. Now that he could have whatever he wanted, he suddenly wanted everything.

Dylan backed away and leaned against the wall. He felt as if he were balancing on a tightrope. He'd hate himself if he became his father, showing off his money, spending his nights dreaming about it. But he'd be an idiot not to take advantage of what he'd been given. He could have whatever he wanted. He could buy this whole street, if he felt like it.

He started back for his car. He had nearly reached it when something brown flashed in the corner of his eye. He looked at the pet store window and saw a mangy-looking mutt eyeing him longingly. It was a cross between a chocolate Labrador and collie. It was the sorriest-looking dog he'd ever seen.

Dylan walked to the window and stared down at the mutt. The dog pushed himself up on all fours and stuck his nose up to the glass. He was thin and his hair was long and scraggly. He reminded Dylan of himself. He laughed and walked into the store.

"I'll take that one," he said, pointing to the dog.

The store owner looked at him. "Are you sure? We've got some lovely purebred poodles and—"

"That one," Dylan said and laughed again when the mutt's tail began wagging, as if he understood everything.

Dylan named the mutt Alan, which gave him a good laugh whenever he said it. A hotel was no place for a dog, so the two of them moved into Dylan's parents' house—he would never call it his house—and began planting trees across the lawn.

Alan raced across the acres of grass, thrilled at his new freedom, and, as if he knew exactly what Dylan wanted him to do, ripped up nearly every perfect blade. He took a liking to Sophia's Chippendale chairs and began gnawing on the legs. He peed twice on her priceless Persian rugs. Dylan thought he was perfect.

For a few days, Dylan held out and didn't buy anything but the trees and food for him and Alan. But then, he couldn't help himself. He put Alan on the leash and they walked toward downtown.

The first time he saw something he had to buy, he blamed it on the dog. It was a silver Light Speed titanium mountain bike for five thousand dollars. Dylan convinced himself he bought it only because Alan stopped in front of the bike-shop window and raised his right front paw.

After that, Alan led him toward a clothes store where Dylan bought a leather jacket, several pairs of jeans, denim shirts, and two pairs of running shoes. Every time they went out, Alan showed him something he'd never noticed before, and he found he had to have it.

So Dylan bought things, and planted trees, and stayed in Connecticut. He called EarthAlert, told them what had happened, and that he wasn't sure when he'd be coming back. He didn't add that he wasn't even sure *if* he'd be coming back, that life was a hell of a lot easier in Connecticut, with Alan and money to burn, than it had ever been in his rotten apartment with battles to fight every day.

He hired Daniel Schwartz to sit in his parents' old seats on whatever boards they'd been on. He kept up his father's same investments because, obviously, the man had known what he was doing. He picked a guest room in his parents' house that he'd never slept in and turned that into his bedroom. He ate on the floor in the living room and blared the stereo. He fired the maids and gardeners and cook and let the dirt and dishes pile up. Time passed but he wasn't aware of it passing. It seemed, with enough money, that you could live in the same day forever.

He did all this until he thought to call his old apartment and get his messages. Then the four weeks he'd been away came crashing back to him.

When he made the call, he was sitting at the table in his parents' kitchen, drinking a glass of very old wine from the wine cellar that, to him, didn't taste any different than the boxed stuff. He poured a little in Alan's dish and the dog lapped it up.

He pressed the code to get his messages and then sat back and listened.

"Dylan, it's me. Sam."

Dylan sat forward abruptly, spilling his wine. He had felt so good the last week or two, ripping up the lawn, buying whatever he wanted. He hadn't thought of his old self at all, the poor self, the part of him that had been in love with Samantha.

"I'm . . . I'm moving in with Michael," she said and he leapt to his feet. When had this happened? He'd been gone for a month and this was the first message. She must have done this right after he left for the funeral, as if she couldn't turn to Michael fast enough.

"I . . . " Her voice cracked and Dylan hung his head. He'd thought he could outrun her. He'd thought, somehow, that she didn't even exist here; she didn't have anything to do with this Dylan, the one with the dog and the cash. He'd thought that if he made himself into someone entirely different, she'd no longer mean anything to him.

But now her voice on his answering machine cracked, and it was as if nothing had changed. He had said goodbye, but only with his mouth.

"I wanted you to know, I guess," Samantha said.

"I wish you'd call me. This is hard to say, Dylan, but I need you. I'm scared."

She hung up and Dylan leaned back against the kitchen wall with his eyes closed.

"Dylan, it's Leah," the next message said. "Listen, you don't have much time. Samantha's gone to Michael's. She doesn't love him. That's obvious. But this thing with her apartment has got her so frightened and Michael is, well, you know what Michael is. Invincible. Protective. For the first time in her life she wants someone to protect her. It's hard to believe. Call her, Dylan."

Then: "It's Sam again. I'm sorry. I shouldn't be calling. It's just that I'm at Michael's now. You wouldn't believe how strange it is." She laughed and Dylan's stomach turned. "It's safe here, though. He's even got a security system. I realize now you're not going to call, but I just wanted you to know that I'm all right. Really. I'll be fine."

After that, there were two more messages from Leah, begging him to do something, a message from the EarthAlert office, and another from a carpet cleaner. Dylan hung up the phone and looked down at Alan.

"So, that's it, then," he said. The dog cocked his head and Dylan sat down again. Alan rested his head on Dylan's knee and Dylan scratched behind his ears.

He listened to the silence of his parents' house and wondered what the hell he was doing here, what the hell he'd been doing for the past four weeks. It was as if he'd gone into some kind of trance, believing he could exist without really living a life, without working or loving or talking to anyone but store clerks. What would he do now? Would he buy a mansion, and then hypocritically complain about too much opulence and lumber gone to waste? Would he fight for the rain forests and then realize he'd bought a teak desk without thinking about it? Would he scorn Samantha for falling for Michael's steadiness and wealth, when he too had become a sort of Michael, with a couple of Mercedeses in the garage that he didn't have the heart to get rid of?

Dylan reached into his pocket and took out a wad of cash. He'd withdrawn two hundred dollars in ones from the bank today, just to see what a stack that size looked like. He threw the bills up into the air and watched them float down, like big chunks of green rain.

Samantha walked into the dining room, where Michael had set the table beautifully with bone white china and long ivory tapers. He did the same thing every night, made his dining room look like a fancy restaurant. He lit the candles.

"You'd make someone a fine wife," Samantha said.

"And you'd make a darn fine husband."

They both laughed and Samantha sat down. Michael brought out a bottle of Chardonnay and two spinach salads. He served each of them and then sat down beside her.

They didn't speak at first, and Samantha was, once again, amazed by the absolute silence of Michael's house. There was no one tromping in an apartment above her; no one bellowing next door. No cars pulled into the parking lot; no sirens jarred her awake at night. Michael lived in a prestigious neighborhood nestled safely behind an armed security gate. His house was wired with an infrared motion-detecting security system. It was the safest place in the world and, for that reason, Samantha loved it.

"Like the salad?" Michael asked.

"Very much."

He smiled and she reached out and touched his hand. They had been living together for a month now and Samantha knew that it was because of Michael that she was finally healing. It was Michael who had made her feel safe and protected again. He was the only one who hadn't ridiculed that need, or ignored it, or tried to pacify her. He did something. He took her in and bolted the door. He lay beside her, took her in his arms until she stopped shivering, stayed up with her at night when she woke up screaming, turned on all the lights so she could see that no one else was in the room.

Once he satisfied her need for security, he chipped away at her need to talk. They stayed up late every night, while Samantha re-created the destruction of her apartment. She went over every detail—the shredded couch, the torn books, the sadistic pictures—trying to exorcise them from her mind. She told him what it had felt like when she walked into the apartment—her skin had prickled as if some organism had burrowed underneath the lining and hatched a thousand babies. She told him everything and Michael gripped her hand and took her pain inside himself. Somehow he carried it for her.

And then, when she was tired of talking, he satisfied, finally, her need for love, for sex, for commitment. He was there every night she went to sleep, and he was there every morning. He returned every call, came home when he said he would. Samantha still marveled at the goodness of him, at what a luxury it was to have someone who could be counted on.

"You look happy this evening," Michael said.

Samantha released his hand and sipped her wine. "Yes. Because I have you."

Michael smiled widely and then, abruptly, turned serious. Samantha's stomach immediately began to churn. She knew what he would say now.

"You know how I feel," he said.

Samantha shook her head. "Tell me."

He took both of her hands in his. "I love you, Samantha. I always have. I keep expecting to come home and find that it's all a dream, that you're not really here."

"I'm here," she said.

"We're right together. You've got your career and I've got mine. If you want children, that would be wonderful. But if not, I'm okay with that, too."

"You're too good to be true," Samantha said.

"No I'm not. I'm a mess, really. I'm so in love with you I can hardly see straight."

He looked away, blushing, and Samantha knew that he felt for her what she felt for Dylan. A blinding, obsessive kind of love that knocked him senseless. The scales were never even. One always had to love more and struggle not to lose himself. The other had to be loved, to try not to drown in the constant attention and undeserved glory.

"I love you, too, Michael," she said, and meant it. If he looked at her, really looked at her, he would see that it wasn't the same love as his. It was stable and grounded and manageable. It was the kind you didn't think about when you walked out of the room, the kind that got you into trouble when temptation came along. But Michael didn't look at her. Just as she had avoided looking at Dylan. Who would want to see something like that?

"Marry me, Samantha," Michael said, pulling his chair close to hers. "It can always be like this between us. Quiet dinners and a safe house and the two of us, together."

Samantha stood up and tried to breathe. Oh, he was wrong. So wrong. Her parents had thought it would always be good between them, but it hadn't been. It was exactly when you started to think that, when you expected happiness instead of fighting for it, that you lost it.

"Things always change," she said.

Michael stood up and moved beside her. He touched her shoulder and she fell against him.

"Then we'll change with them," he said. "This will work, Sam. If I have anything to say about it, this will work."

Samantha pulled back to look at him. He was her childhood friend. What better, more trustworthy person was there to marry? Wasn't it wiser to marry someone more in love with you than you were with him? That way you saw yourself through his distorted vision and were prettier, sexier, smarter than you'd first thought. That way you were guaranteed power and security and faithfulness, and you nearly always got things your way.

"I will," she said, and Michael laughed, and swung her around in his arms.

Dylan walked into his apartment, took a deep breath of its musty odor, and smiled. He hadn't thought he'd ever be happy to come home to this dive, but today he was. Today, the concrete-and-plywood table and the ripped sofa bed looked like heaven. Alan raced through, knocked over the plywood tabletop, and Dylan laughed.

He walked straight to the phone and called EarthAlert. Karen, the secretary, answered.

"I'm back," Dylan said. "I'll be in tomorrow."

"Dylan, are you sure? We didn't know if—"

"I know. I didn't know, either. But then, a week ago, I took one of the Mercedeses up to New York and left it unlocked in Harlem. It lasted eighteen seconds. I timed it."

He laughed and felt amazingly good. He felt crazy again, poor again, even though he hadn't been fool enough to give away everything. He'd sat down on his last night at his parents' house, looked at the portrait of them on the wall, and said, "I'm sorry I never knew you. Never took the time to understand. Maybe I do now. Just a little." Then he called the real estate agent and put the place up for sale. He packed Alan into the remaining Mercedes, which he'd decided to keep, and started driving cross-country.

"You're not serious," Karen said now.

"Damn right I am. This old man saw me do it and touched my shoulder. He said, 'You got the right idea, giving it away. Those kids just have the wrong idea, taking what you give.' "

"So you're poor again?" Karen asked.

"God, no. Rich as all hell. I'm thinking of investing in Future Homes. Have them build me a place made totally of recycled materials. Tire walls, plastic counters, solar heat, xeriscaping, the works. I'd live in it and also open it for tours, to get people thinking."

They spoke for ten more minutes about the things Dylan planned to do and then he hung up. He fed Alan and then sat down on his sofa. The lumpy indentations felt marvelous after over a month on his mother's hard-as-a-rock settees. Before he left Connecticut, he called a real estate agent in Florida and put the West Palm Beach house up for sale. He put his mother's jewelry, furs, and furniture up for auction and told Daniel Schwartz to distribute his shares in the shipping and steel companies to the employees. He got rid of everything except his parents' cold, hard cash, which he intended to both have a little fun with and use to help his causes.

It was not such a hard decision. He had needed a few weeks of extravagance; he had to at least sample the life his parents had led. But as those weeks passed, the novelty of being rich wore off. He didn't want anything to do with stocks or property and possessions. But only a fool would turn down cash, especially when he had a cause to pour it into.

Dylan checked out his refrigerator, but it was empty. He searched the cupboards, but could find only a bag of whole grain rice. That was one thing that would change right away. From now on, there would be food in his house. There wasn't anything noble about an empty cupboard.

Dylan walked over to the answering machine. He hadn't checked it right away, because he'd been afraid of what he might hear. The light blinked only once, though, and he figured he could handle one message. He rewound the tape and sat down on the couch. Alan jumped up beside him.

"It's Elliot," the message said. "I'm sure you're surprised to hear from me. I'm surprised I'm calling. But Samantha's my daughter and I'd do anything to make her happy. I got a call from her tonight, a strange one. Michael asked her to marry him."

Dylan had known all along that this would happen. He had camped in the Appalachians and wished Samantha had been there with him to see the sunset. He'd driven across the plains of Kansas and nearly expected to see her beside him, marveling along with him at the flatness of the land. He'd passed the Rockies and had only Alan to tell how beautiful the snow-packed ridges were. And when he'd finally passed the border into California, he would have given anything to turn to Samantha and say, "We're home."

It had taken him a whole country to realize that he saw her in everything, in every sunset and field and river. Just when he realized he couldn't live without her, Samantha had made certain he'd have to.

"I'll tell you, I was happy at first," Elliot went on. "But then I listened to her, and I kept wondering why she wasn't shouting with joy. I'll tell you why. She's hiding. She's afraid to live alone again. If you ask me, she's afraid that you've ruined her, that she'll never love anyone the way she loves you. She loves Michael too in a way. She thinks that's enough. If she'd just look at what happened to Leah and me, she'd realize it's not.

You've got to have more. You've got to have some kind of passion. The kind you and Samantha have. Don't be an idiot and let that go so easily."

The message ended and the tape automatically rewound. Dylan was calm, which surprised him. He reached back and pulled the rubber band out of his hair.

He sat for a long time, staring straight ahead, at nothing. He listened to the sounds of traffic outside his window. The couple from next door came up the steps, arguing.

Dylan dropped his head in his hands. He wanted to cry, wanted to just get it all out in one torrent of emotion and be done with it. But he couldn't. He imagined Samantha and Michael standing at the altar, looking into one another's eyes, happy. She should have happiness. She deserved it.

He'd have to keep silent. Let Michael and Samantha marry in peace. He could not protest, or ask her to reconsider marrying Michael when he offered her nothing in return. He searched himself but still could not find the guts for commitment, no matter how much he cared for her. He was two people, one the man he'd been all his life, the one who was content to be alone, and the other the man who had hardly been able to see the beauty on his drive across the country, because beauty only came to him through Samantha's eyes.

Elliot paced around his small apartment wondering what to do. Now that the tension had eased in the office, he no longer had to put in sixteen-hour days. But what good was time off if he had to come home to this place?

He hated every second of living here, hated even thinking about it when he was not here. He tried to be in the apartment only to sleep and eat. He tried desperately not to think of the comforts of his old home, the easy chair he loved, the king-sized bed instead of the lumpy double he had here. It was no good, though.

He thought of his home every day. He thought of Leah every day.

She was different, stronger, and though this amazed him, those changes excited him. She was like a different woman, like someone he'd never known.

In just about two months, she would no longer be his wife. If they had held out until April, they would have made thirty-eight years. He had thought he would pick out a new diamond wedding band and take her to a small Italian place to propose all over again. She, though, had wanted to go to Europe. They had missed each other by miles, by an entire continent.

He missed her every day. When he went to see her after getting back from Miami, he had been faintly aroused by the smell of tobacco on her. He was more aroused by those clothes she wore, the leggings and his old sweatshirt. He'd thought he would hate her in clothes like that, but really they looked exactly right. When he'd held her, he had to force himself not to make it sexual in any way. And that was funny, because for so long, he hadn't felt anything sexual for her.

Elliot walked past the coffee table, then back between it and the couch. Their lives had all been upended. Samantha was going to marry a man she didn't love while Elliot was divorcing the woman he did. He stopped pacing abruptly. The thought had come out of nowhere and it shocked him.

"I love her," he said aloud. He took another step and then said it again. "I love her."

He had been so certain he was over her, that whatever love had withstood the onslaught of James Arlington had withered in the months since they'd separated. But that was only an illusion. Leah was like a picture he'd been standing too close to. At first, he saw only dots of blue and white, but then, when he was shoved back and the picture was out of reach, he suddenly realized she was a masterpiece of sea and sky, worth millions.

Tonight was Monday, a night when Elliot usually plopped himself in front of the television and sat mesmerized through three hours of football. Leah had liked watching *Murphy Brown* and they had fought over which program to watch the way they always fought, without raising their voices.

Elliot had a feeling Leah did not watch *Murphy Brown* anymore. He wondered if she was even home tonight, or if she was out somewhere, flirting with younger men. He walked to the phone, put his hand on it, then turned and walked away.

What could he say to her now? The divorce would be final in two months and then there would be even less to say. They would see each other on occasion while Samantha planned her wedding. They'd have to dance together at the reception. And then that would be it. Samantha would feel awkward about inviting them both to the same functions. Leah would come for Sunday dinners while Elliot would be brought in only for the big events, for the births and christenings and birthdays.

Elliot stopped pacing and looked around his apartment. He listened to the same silence his mother must have listened to every time Steven left her and he knew he finally understood what she had felt.

Just as his father had owned his mother's soul, Leah owned his. It was not a returnable or exchangeable commodity. One owner per soul, for life, for eternity probably, and Leah had snatched his long ago. Elliot knew, without a doubt, that if he loved again, it would not match what he felt for Leah. It wouldn't consume him, and there would be parts of him left untouched. That was the difference. You could love different people with different parts of yourself, but you could only love one person with all of you.

He imagined himself in this apartment when he

was sixty or seventy, if he lived that long under these conditions. He rarely cleaned, so the dust would have piled up. He never bought anything personal, so the fish picture would still be hanging there. In the morning, he would wake up, look out the window, and still see the parking lot first thing.

His daughter would have married her surgeon and had children, and he would be a minor part of their lives. Leah would have remarried some man who smoked and drank and they'd probably be living in a grass hut in Fiji. They all would have gone on and left him to rot here, in this godforsaken apartment.

He turned and walked back to the phone. He dialed before he could stop himself. He tapped his foot on the floor as he waited for Leah to answer.

She did almost at once, which surprised him. She said hello and he listened for sounds of a party in the background, but he could hear nothing.

"It's me," he said. "Elliot."

He was surprised he could even talk. His mouth was suddenly bone-dry and he took the phone with him into the kitchen and poured a glass of water.

"Is everything all right?" Leah asked.

All at once Elliot knew. Even if they did find a way back together, it would be like starting over, courting someone new, and the thought of that did something funny to him. It made him stand up straight and run his fingers through his hair to straighten it. It made him glance down at his clothes and decide that he'd have to get something new, maybe swap a few of his suits for those Dockers pants Leah had always tried to get him to wear and a few comfortable sweaters. He looked at his gut and made the instant decision to trim down, to start doing one hundred sit-ups every morning.

"Everything is not all right," Elliot said. He stared at the picture of the fish and knew what really bothered him about it. It was the fact that he knew he could do better. He had his art supplies stuffed in the attic at home and he hadn't bothered to bring them out of mothballs for over thirty years. Suddenly, he wanted to run his fingers over the ridges of a canvas. He wanted to put a glop of red oil on his palette and blink at its purity. He wanted to paint again. He would practice and practice until he'd rediscovered his talent and then he would paint a portrait of Leah the likes of which the world had never seen.

"You don't sound like you," Leah said.

Elliot laughed. She had said exactly what he wanted to hear.

"Listen," he said. "Just listen to me and don't say a word until I'm finished."

He waited for her to argue, to tell him to go to hell, but she did not. He smiled wider and gripped the edge of the counter.

"I'm going to go into the office tomorrow and tell my secretary I'm taking a long vacation in April. Two weeks, maybe a month. We've got a new agent who's tireless and the secretary practically runs the place anyway. I've been working nearly nonstop since September and I think I've undone most of Bill's damage."

Elliot walked as far as the cord would let him and then turned around and came back.

"Then I'm going straight to the travel agent," he went on, "and I'll have her book two tickets to England. I'll charge it if I don't have the cash. What the hell do I care?"

He laughed as he heard Leah's intake of breath. He slammed his fist down on the counter.

"If you still want to go," he said, "I want to take you to Europe, Leah. We could be there, standing in front of Buckingham Palace, on the day we got married. Maybe it won't be our thirty-eighth wedding anniversary, but it can be the first of the next thirty-eight."

He stopped then and came back down to earth. His chest was depleted of air, he slumped, he waited for her to hang up on him. He didn't know where his mind had gone, who was speaking through his mouth.

"You're crazy," she said, and he heard the admiration in her voice. His chest expanded again and he was up, up, up on the ceiling.

"I was crazy to let you go," he said. "We could leave in the beginning of April, right before our anniversary. We'll need to get visas, passports, whatever. I need a trench coat. It'll be cold as hell there."

She laughed and it sounded like trickling water. He had not heard that laugh for years.

"You cussed, Mr. Shaperson. I can't believe it."

"Goddamm it to hell, Leah," he said. "I can cuss if I want."

She laughed again, louder, and he held his breath, waiting for her to cut herself off, to remind him that he had once, when he was young and stupid, told her to tone it down. This time, though, she did not, she just laughed, and he laughed with her and thought, *Oh Leah, I love you. I swear I'll make you fall in love with me again.*

"We'd have to plan around Samantha's wedding," she said. "She hasn't set a date yet."

"Fine," he said. "Just say you'll go with me."

He waited what seemed like an eternity for her to answer, although it couldn't have been more than a few seconds.

"What does this mean?" she asked. "In two months, you won't even be my husband anymore."

"If we let the divorce go through," he said. "Isn't that why they make you wait so long? So that fools like us can change our minds."

Again, there was Leah's intake of breath. "Tell me what you're saying," she said.

"I'm saying," he said, "that there's this beautiful

girl I can't get out of my mind and I want to take her to Europe. I want to get to know her. I want her to get to know me. It seemed too late for us and then, all of a sudden, I realized it wasn't. It's really never too late for anything."

"Elliot," she said.

"Does that mean yes?"

"It means you've got two minutes to get here. I've missed you so much."

22

Leah stood by the window as Elliot sped into the driveway. He had made record time racing from his apartment to her house. Her stomach felt queasy and she gripped the curtains to steady herself. She felt awful, but that awfulness felt wonderful. She let him knock for a second and then she opened the door. There was a moment of taking each other in, then he pulled her into his arms.

"Tell me this is real," he said, and she squeezed him and told him it was. She had wanted to ask him the same thing, have him prove she wasn't dreaming. It was almost frightening to suddenly get what she'd been wishing for.

She pulled back and stared at him. She lifted a finger and brushed his salt-and-pepper hair off his forehead. She stared at his eyes, those to-die-for eyes, and smiled.

"I feel strange inside," she said. "Like I don't know you at all."

He smiled, too. "But you like that," he said.

"Yes."

They stepped into the living room and Elliot looked around. She followed his eyes, saw things the way he saw them. He stared first at his chair, lovingly, as if it were a person he had missed. Then the television set, the sofa, then through to the kitchen and dining table. He had missed this place. She hadn't even considered that he would miss his things. There were so many things she hadn't considered at all.

"You haven't changed anything," he said.

"No. Come on."

She led him into the bedroom eagerly, but once they were inside, she felt ridiculous. Elliot was not James. Seductions were for lovers, not husbands. What if he still couldn't perform? What if his touch didn't arouse her? What if it was the same as always, like just another project, and she stared at the clock waiting for it to be done?

They stood there, awkwardly, three feet apart, until Elliot bridged the gap. He stepped right in front of her and lifted a trembling hand. He placed it delicately on her breast and she shivered.

"I've thought of you," he said, his voice hoarse and different.

He ran his fingers slowly around her breast. Her sweatshirt chafed against her and she stepped away to take it off.

She started to take off her bra too, but Elliot stopped her. He walked around behind her and unclasped it. His fingers were hot on her skin and she sighed.

He slid off her bra and then stayed behind her. Slowly, he moved his hands around to her stomach. With James, she had been concerned about the folds in her stomach, the sagging of her breasts, but it had been a long time since she'd worried about these things with

Elliot. Now, she tried to suck in her stomach, but Elliot simply pressed his lips against the back of her ear.

"You're beautiful," he said, and she relaxed against him.

She looked down at his hands. She had forgotten how much she loved the look of them, the thick fingers, the wiry hair below his knuckles. James's hands had been cool and pale and thin. He had touched her stomach once and squeezed the extra flab she had never been able to get rid of after Samantha. He had laughed and called her tubby. She closed her eyes so she wouldn't think of him.

Elliot slid his hands up to her breasts and held her. She could hear his heart racing. Suddenly, she knew it would be all right. He was strange to her now, changed, but he was still Elliot. They would have the best of both worlds, new passion without any fear at all.

She turned around in his arms and kissed him. His mouth felt different, exotic, and yet it tasted just like she knew it would. She pulled him closer and explored him and then tugged at his clothes because they were getting in her way.

Elliot laughed and took them off. Leah slid off her leggings and leapt onto the bed. He followed her, jumping onto his side and quickly pulling her into his arms. They were still laughing when he kissed her again. Then she felt his body on hers, the hardness between his legs, and she pulled him closer, and took him in.

She opened her eyes and watched him as they made love. After a moment, he opened his eyes too and smiled at her. He stopped his movements and took her face in his hands. He kissed her forehead and cheeks and the tears that spilled out over her lashes.

"Samantha was right," he said. "Who knew it could be like this?"

• • •

Afterward, they sat in the kitchen drinking wine. Leah lit a single taper and its light flickered like a jittery ghost across the room.

"Will Samantha be all right with Michael?" Leah asked him, because, after all, despite what had just happened in the bedroom, they were still parents.

"I don't know," Elliot said. "She should be happy, but she's not. She seems almost deadened."

"Yes. That's it exactly."

They were quiet and Leah sipped her wine. She was worried about Samantha. She was terrified and exhilarated by what she planned to do tomorrow night, Tuesday night, to James. Yet, at this moment, she couldn't feel anything but contentedness. Even when she had made love with James, she had not felt this good afterward. There had always been some tension left, perhaps from guilt, or perhaps because he'd always been more concerned with his own satisfaction than hers. Now, though, her body felt loose, sensuous, sated.

Leah took out a cigarette.

"I've been smoking for years, you know," she said.

"I know."

"You do not," she said, lighting her cigarette.

"I do. You'd go out somewhere, have a few, and then stop at the gym and try to wash the scent away. But it stuck to your clothes, Leah. And I found empty cigarette packs in the garbage."

Leah laughed and reached out for his hand. He smiled at her, contented too, and she wondered if it always had to be like this, if God had cut a deal with the devil to make you have to lose something before you could see its worth.

"I'm thinking of painting again," Elliot said.

Leah sat forward. "Really?"

"Yes. There's that godawful picture of a fish in my apartment and it's driving me crazy. I'd like to replace it."

Leah pulled away abruptly and stood up. She walked into the living room, far enough away from the candlelight that Elliot could not see her face.

"So you plan to stay there," she said.

Elliot laughed and came to her. He took her in his arms and she thought, *It's like falling in love all over again.* She could feel the floor give way beneath her and her head spin from the rush. She had longed for this, but she hadn't remembered that falling in love was as frightening as it was mesmerizing. No promises had been made yet, no commitments secured. The truth was, as intoxicating as it was, she felt she needed to hold her breath the whole way through.

"More than anything in this world," Elliot said, "I want to come back here and live with you. Married or not. Whether you love me or not. I just don't want to push."

Leah breathed again, literally opened her mouth wide and sucked in the air.

"Push me," she said finally.

He stared at her and kissed her hard.

In the morning, Leah lay beside her husband, watching him sleep. It was Tuesday, the day she was to meet James. After tonight, things might never be the same. Elliot might never forgive her.

She leaned over and kissed Elliot's cheek. He opened his eyes slowly and then smiled at her.

"I was afraid it was all a dream," he said.

She kissed his lips softly, slowly, licking off the salt, exploring the crevices. She pulled away and looked at him.

"I love you, Elliot," she said.

He slipped his hand around her neck and brought her down to him. Sometime, much later, he told her he loved her, too.

• • •

Leah cooked linguini with clam sauce for dinner that night and tried not to look at the clock. She was supposed to meet James at his office at seven o'clock and by the time they were done with dinner, it was a quarter till.

"I haven't eaten like that for months," Elliot said.

Leah smiled and glanced at the clock again. Elliot's gaze followed hers, but he said nothing. She knew he knew this was the night she had always gone to James. At about this time every Tuesday and Thursday, she had told him she was meeting friends and then stolen away to her lover.

How could she explain this? *Elliot, I need to go out again. Not to have an affair, but to kill my lover.* The thought was so ridiculous that Leah smiled.

"Will you let me in?" Elliot asked, without looking at her.

She took out a cigarette and debated. The problem with her and Elliot was that she had never confided in him. If she was going to start now, the least she could do was tell him something small, not shock him with murder right off the bat. Maybe she could admit she sneaked gin into her orange juice. Or tell him the fantasies she had about teenage box boys. There was no way on earth she could start with this. *Elliot, the thing is, I'm plotting this murder.*

Suddenly, Leah laughed aloud. She didn't know why she did it, except that the whole thing seemed hilarious, like something out of a bad movie. She, Leah Shaperson, a good girl born and raised in suburban Sacramento, had gone into her ex-lover's office and filled his gun with bullets, in an attempt to kill him. And now that that hadn't worked, she needed to go in and finish the job herself.

She laughed harder. It was hilarious, outrageous, and yet she was completely serious. She kept laughing until she noticed that Elliot was not laughing with her, that he was staring at her. She calmed down, took a couple of drags from her cigarette, and then said, "What the hell."

She stood up and paced around the kitchen.

"James was a bastard," she said. "He was molested by his father, given a raw deal right out of the gate, but he was still a bastard. He liked games. Toys. Bondage. Russian roulette. He hurt me a few times, but I figured that was all part of the package."

She glanced back at Elliot, but he was staring straight ahead, motionless.

"After you left that message on his machine telling him he could have me," Leah went on, "he came by the house. When I tried to break up with him, he beat me pretty badly."

Elliot still said nothing, but a muscle twitched in his cheek.

"I thought it was over then, but it wasn't," she continued. "He drives by in the mornings. He calls. He sent some horrid pictures, sadomasochistic stuff. He was the one who went on that rampage in Samantha's apartment."

Leah watched Elliot closely. His face went pale, but his only other response was to clench his hands into fists. She finished her cigarette and ran it under the water. She dropped the butt into the sink.

"I won't stand it anymore," she said. "James will keep on doing this forever, unless I do something. Believe me, I don't mean this as an excuse for him, but I don't think he can stop. In his mind, the only thing that will save him is me. He probably doesn't even think the things he does are wrong. He's just got these demons in his soul and, when he beats up on me, he knocks a few of them down."

She walked around the kitchen, running her hands

along the counter, touching appliances. "I'm not powerless," she said. "He's wrong about that. I was once, when I first started seeing him. I felt helpless and willing to take anything just to get some kind of response. But his biggest mistake is in thinking that people don't ever change or grow up. He believes that certain people—people like me—aren't capable of retaliation. But we're all capable of it, if provoked enough."

She stared at him and then reached for another cigarette. She lit it with shaking hands.

"When he broke into Samantha's apartment," she went on, "I made up my mind that I'd have to stop him myself. I couldn't let him near my daughter again. I went to that arms store over in the minimall and bought bullets. I sneaked into his office and loaded his revolver, the one he uses for Russian roulette. He always keeps only one bullet in the gun, but now there are six. He insists on going first, you see, and he makes his partner spin the cylinder after he's blindfolded. He wants his partner to take the higher risk, to have one less chance of hitting an empty chamber. And he wants to be there to see the other one die. That's exactly the kind of man he is."

Elliot stood up very slowly. Leah gripped the edge of the counter, waiting for him to walk out. She was disgusting, even to herself. But what else could she do? James had backed her into a corner and she either had to give up or claw her way out. She could not reason with him, and pleas for sympathy just egged him on. The only alternative left was to stoop to violence, to lower herself to his level. Sometimes that was all you could do.

Elliot hesitated for a moment and then walked over to her. He turned her chin up with his fingertips.

"Tonight?" he said. "You kept staring at the clock."

Leah shrugged. "It wasn't working. He's still alive. Maybe he only played Russian roulette with me, I don't know. So I thought I'd go there one more time and get him to play that damn game."

Elliot closed his eyes and then pulled her into his arms. She turned her face into the crook of his neck, drank up his scent. She didn't see how he could love her now that he knew what she was capable of.

"You can't go," Elliot said. "What if he decides you should go first? Or sees how many bullets are in the cylinder? Then you're all alone with a madman and a loaded gun."

Leah shook her head. "I have to go. It's my battle."

"It's not, Leah. It's *our* battle. Let me help you."

Leah pulled away. She walked into the darkness of the living room, then back into the kitchen. An ash from her cigarette fell onto her hand and burned her, and she quickly stubbed the rest out.

"There's no other way to do it," she said. "I can't prove anything to the police. I can't make James some other kind of man. If I could reason with him, I would, but he's miles past that. He's obsessed, Elliot. And it will go on and on unless I do something. I'm telling you, it's come down to us or him."

"I believe you," Elliot said softly. "All I'm saying is there has to be some other way. You're talking murder, Leah. I know it seems as if you have no alternative, but there has to be something else we can do. Give me some time."

Leah looked at him. She didn't want to give in. She'd been so keyed up the past couple of days, she'd heard bullets firing in her sleep. But Elliot was right. Maybe James already knew about the loaded gun. Or he might decide to spin the cylinder himself. She knew she wouldn't be able to hide her guilt when he found the five extra bullets.

Elliot led her into the living room. They sat down on the sofa.

"I'll think of something," Elliot said. "I sure as hell won't let him keep stalking you and Samantha."

Leah stared at him and saw another layer of this husband she'd never really known. She had never thought him especially strong or brave. Bravery wasn't called for all that often in the insurance business. But it was there, inside him, just like violence was there, inside her. All it took was circumstance to release it.

"Something has to be done," Leah said. "I mean it, Elliot. I've been living with this too long. I feel like I'm going to explode."

Elliot nodded. "He's never going to hurt you again. But you're not going tonight. I won't let you."

"I really want to kill him," Leah said. "I know that says something awful about me, but—"

"You'd do whatever it takes to protect Samantha. And I'd do whatever it takes to protect you."

"You must think I'm crazy," she said.

Elliot reached out and slipped a hand behind her neck.

"Crazy, courageous, wild. And I love you."

Leah closed her eyes.

"James will call," she said. "He'll wonder where I am."

"I'll answer it," Elliot said.

Leah was surprised by his confidence, the hard set to his jaw. She leaned against him. Her breathing was returning to normal; she hadn't even noticed it was accelerated until she started to calm down. She must have been breathing hard for days, waiting to kill James.

At seven-thirty that evening, James called. Both Leah and Elliot knew it was him as soon as the phone rang. Elliot pointed at Leah to stay put while he walked to the phone in the kitchen.

"Arlington," he said instead of hello. Leah watched

his face, saw him grimace, and hated James to the very core of her.

After a moment, Elliot said, "It's amazing you ever got to where you are with language like that. Listen to me. I'm back. It's over. Leah's not coming to you anymore. Next time you call, there will be a tape recorder taping every word. Next time you drive by, a video camera will catch you in the act. Next time you do anything, I'll have you exactly where I want you."

He slammed down the phone and Leah jumped to her feet.

"What did he say?" she asked.

"Nothing worth repeating."

"You were wonderful, Elliot," she said. Elliot shook out his arms, as if he were shaking James off, then turned to Leah and smiled.

"That's only the beginning," he said.

Samantha sat on the flagstone patio, a blanket wrapped around her. The air smelled of rain; the storm heading in from the west was already thrashing the tops of the trees. Beneath the blanket, she wore her robe, even though it was four o'clock in the afternoon.

It was Saturday and she was tired. The elections had come and gone and the Democrats had fared well in the northern half of the state, poorly in the south. Their hope for a Democratic congressman in Orange County had fallen through. They'd had a nice surprise with an upset in Humboldt County, while the rest had gone about as expected. A few wins and a few losses, and they had started all over again for next year.

Michael had left for the hospital at nine this morning and would be home within the next hour. Samantha had lain in bed this morning, listening to him sing in the shower. She had been living with him for nearly a month and a half now and knew that, every morning, he was thrilled to face the day. He'd been blessed with two passions: medicine and her. He couldn't wait to open his eyes and revel in them.

How could she resist that and everything else Michael had to offer? He had money and he doted on her. He cooked marvelously and liked to do the grocery shopping. A maid came in once a week to clean, so Samantha did not even have to pick up after herself.

Michael worked six days a week, was on call every night, but always made time for her. After they married, she could join the group of doctors' wives, or not. She could continue with her career, or not. She could have children, or not. It was all up to her. Michael was easy.

He was so damn easy that she didn't know what to do. She didn't have to fight him for anything. He loved her exactly the way he should. He said all the right things, made all the right moves. He was perfect really, and that perfection was driving her crazy. He was like a room in *House Beautiful,* flawless in every detail. But you couldn't imagine yourself living in a place like that. You'd be too afraid of tracking dirt on the floor, leaving a hair on the sofa.

She heard the sliding glass door open behind her. She turned and was surprised to see her mother step out, followed by her father. They were holding hands, looking sheepish.

Samantha sat very still, sure she was misinterpreting. But then she looked at their faces, their radiant faces, and it was as if the ship she was sailing on became seaworthy again, as if all it took to make the worst wrongs right were parents who loved each other.

"No," she said.

"Yes," Leah replied, laughing. She leaned over and kissed her. When she pulled back, her face was so joyous, so full of love, that Samantha sucked in her breath. Her father peeked around, kissed her, and he too seemed like a teenager, seeking out and finding Leah's hand, moving his fingers constantly, exploring her.

"When did this happen?" Samantha asked.

"Monday night," Leah said, sitting down in the lounge chair opposite her. Elliot tried to sit down beside her, and then the chair started to tip and they both stood up, laughing. They righted the chair, squashed themselves into the center to correct the balance, and smiled at her.

"How?" Samantha asked.

"She came running to me," Elliot said.

Leah laughed, slapped him playfully, and Samantha had no clue who she was watching. These were not her parents. Her parents did not giggle or play with each other.

"Not true," Leah said. "Your dad just called me. He told me he wanted to take me to Europe."

"Europe?" Samantha asked.

"Yes," Elliot said. "In April, unless that conflicts with your wedding. We'll go for two weeks, maybe even a month. Your mother has always wanted to go, but I've been such a tightwad. Then I thought, what the hell."

His laughter boomed out and Samantha leaned back. She felt awkward, as if the two of them had changed scripts and had forgotten to tell her who she would be playing. Her father did not laugh like that. Before, Elliot and Leah had done their hand-holding in private; certainly they kissed in private. But now they were all over each other right in front of her and, frankly, she just didn't think that was right.

This was more like passion than love, more like what she wanted most for herself, but could not have without Dylan. Their laughter was like a spear through her heart and she lifted her hand up to her chest, as if she could protect herself from it.

"So what now?" Samantha asked, trying to smile.

"Now, we live together," Leah said, and then giggled. "We've never done that, you know. It wasn't allowed in our time."

"But you're still married, at least for another month," Samantha said.

"This is the really crazy part," Leah said. "We're not going to stop the divorce yet. We're going to live right on the verge of it, just to see what it feels like. Maybe we'll even let it go through and start dating again."

They both laughed and Samantha closed her eyes. She should be happy, but she was not. Nothing she felt made any sense anymore.

Michael had asked her to marry him, she was set for life with a good man, and she was miserable. She had taught herself to ignore her Dylan dreams, the momentary lapses when she wanted to call him, the moments now and then when the loss of him turned her whole world sour. She pretended he didn't even exist, that he wasn't out there in the world, and sometimes it seemed as if he really was nonexistent, that if she couldn't have him, he couldn't even be.

Her headaches had stopped, her nightmares were fading, she was busy at work, she'd made time again for her friends, but she still felt empty. Her parents were back together, happier than she'd ever seen them, and their love hurt, as if there were only so much to go around and they were stealing her portion.

When Samantha opened her eyes, Elliot was gone. Only Leah still sat on the lounge chair and she was staring at her.

"Has Dylan called you?" Leah asked.

Samantha stiffened.

"No," she said quietly.

"I'm sorry, Sam."

"Why should you be? It's not your fault. He doesn't

love me, he never did, and I accept that. I love Michael now."

"I'm sure you do," Leah said. "You love him just like I loved Elliot for a while. Without even a tenth of your heart in it. Without any fire or fear."

"Who wants fear in love?"

Leah laughed. "I do. I want to always know that Elliot could leave. I want to know that every time he gets into a car or even walks out on the street, he could get killed. Because knowing that makes me treasure every second I've got with him. It makes me cling to him and revel in the smallest things he does."

"I think that's a horrid way to live."

Leah shrugged. "Maybe. But that's the way you lived with Dylan. You were terrified of losing him."

"Yes. And I did lose him. He couldn't give me what I needed so he walked out. He cut the ties completely. Easily."

Samantha pulled the blanket tighter around her. It was getting colder and the wind was picking up.

"You could fight for him," Leah said.

"No. I called him and told him what was happening with me and Michael. He never responded. That told me everything I needed to know. I was wrong to think I was anything special, that I could change him."

Leah stood up. "Yes, that's wrong. Nobody changes anybody. But people can change themselves. Maybe you could talk to him . . . "

Samantha pulled her knees up to her chest and rested her chin on them.

"No, Mom. I'm going to marry Michael. We set the date for February fifth."

"Oh," Leah said. "Well, congratulations, then."

"It's right to marry Michael. He's the best I'll ever get."

Leah walked over and stood behind her. She put

her hands on Samantha's shoulders and rested her chin on her head.

"Sometimes the best isn't what's right. I know you think it's crazy to love Dylan. He's wild and inconsiderate and he may never love you back the same way. But that's what your heart feels, Samantha. You can't run away from it. You can't hide from it behind Michael's back."

On the day after Leah came clean about what she had planned to do to James, Elliot went to the bookstore and bought out the espionage section. He got copies of every Clancy and Ludlum novel he could find. He let a teenage clerk introduce him to a few new authors and he went home with twenty-five books.

Of course, it didn't mean anything.

He had a different plan in mind for James. For the last two weeks, he had been gathering evidence against him. It was torture, sitting still while Leah told him all the things James Arlington had done to her, but there was no other choice. Leah listed every incident, every gadget James kept in his desk, exactly when and how he'd taken advantage of his role as her analyst and seduced her. When he had gathered all the evidence, Elliot planned to notify the American Psychiatric Association that James Arlington had slept with at least one of his patients. He'd have the man's medical license revoked.

But first, Elliot was going to have it out with James.

And so he read. Mysteries, thrillers, tales of ruthless assassins. First he read only during his lunch hour, but then he found himself glancing longingly at his stack of novels in the evenings, trying to guess who the real killer was, how the hero would solve the puzzle. At first, Leah laughed when he poked his head back into his book rather than watch television the way he used to. But then she began to enjoy the quiet evenings, the way they sat in bed at night, she reading a romance and he a thriller, holding hands but in two different worlds.

He read about car bombs and spy networks and paid killers. He read about men who ran through parades of bullets to save the women they loved. About men who got a thrill out of punching ignorant fools in the jaw.

It wasn't the plot he was after, it was the personalities of the characters. These fictional men kicked and fought and killed so easily, and Elliot wanted to know what that was like. They didn't squirm away from confrontation the way he had all his life; they sought it out.

In every novel, there were justifications for every fight and murder. On a purely theoretical level, Elliot had never believed in violence or brutality. But in the real world, he had to admit, sometimes violence was justified. Sometimes people ignored every hint of logic and reason and you just had to punch them in the face. Elliot especially liked Clancy's and Ludlum's novels because when one of their characters killed, he always explained why, he made you glad he'd done it. Elliot liked that. It put order to the world.

Still, Elliot did not rush his confrontation with James. He drew it out, savored the sensation of being a cat on the prowl, a hawk eyeing its prey from the clouds, a hunter. He got an inexpensive tape recorder for the phone, but James had not called again. He had looked into video cameras, but had not yet bought one, certain that the threat of being caught on tape was enough to keep James away. He took his time reading, planning his call to the APA, getting his evidence against James together. Leah watched him and said nothing; she had reached the point of no return and she gave him time to reach it as well.

He went through seven of the twenty-five books in two weeks. Then, as he put the eighth book under his arm and walked out the front door on a cold morning in mid-December, he felt eyes on him. He checked the parked cars for passengers, but they were all empty. He looked down the block, scanning hedges, looking for eyes peeking through, but he couldn't make anything out. Still, he knew James was there, watching, willing to risk the threat of being caught on camera.

Elliot's skin prickled and he had the strangest sense of violation, as if, without his consent, he were being critiqued and analyzed. He wanted to run, but he forced himself to walk slowly to his car. He opened the door and got in, but still felt the tingling in his scalp, James's eyes locked right on him.

He looked in the rearview mirror, but again the street was empty, nothing moved in his neighbors' shrubs. He imagined doing this every morning, scanning streets and alleys, always looking over his shoulder, as if he were a fugitive on the run, a hunted man. He shook his head and started the car.

He drove straight to the office and, for a few hours, tried to concentrate on paperwork. He wanted to call Leah and hear her say everything was fine. He wanted to call Samantha in Washington, D.C., where she was on a business trip. But he did neither because doing so was tantamount to admitting that James was getting the upper hand. By noon, he was sweating so badly he had to change his shirt. By three, he stopped the pretense of work and took out the file on James Arlington he'd started back when Leah began her affair. It held the investigator's report, pictures, Elliot's own sightings, the comings and goings of James Arlington.

He knew James's hours, knew that tonight his receptionist left at six and his last patient left at ten till seven. He knew that James rarely had a lover on Wednesday nights, that it was the one night a week he spent with his wife.

He knew that it was time. He could not suffer through another day of being peeped at by Arlington. He'd go to James's office tonight and have it out with him.

He would tell James his plan, mention the fifteen-page testimony by Leah detailing everything he had done to her. He'd tell him that her testimony was backed up by a private investigator's report. Then he'd let him know that he planned to contact two of James's other lovers, former patients as well, and then go straight to the APA.

Elliot rubbed his hands in anticipation. He was angry enough. When Leah had told him what James had done to her, he'd nearly run for the door right then and taken the law into his own hands. Had James come after *him*, he could have taken it. But he had abused Leah, stalked Samantha. That set off something primal in Elliot, something dangerously close to savagery. It knocked a whole set of rules out the window, when a man touched his family.

Elliot worked until six o'clock, then called Leah.

"I've had a rush of new policies today," he said, squeezing his eyes shut as he lied. "I'll have to stay late."

"Oh damn," Leah said. "I was making steaks."

Elliot smiled. She used to cook exotic dishes that took hours of preparation. Now she made steaks and spaghetti sauce right out of the jar and he loved it. He didn't have to wait an hour when he came home just to say hello to her. She didn't push him out of the kitchen so he wouldn't see what she was making.

"Go ahead and eat, then," he said.

"No. I want to wait. How late will you be?"

Elliot calculated as best he could. He felt giddy, trying to figure it all out. "Eight, I think. Are you sure you'll wait?"

"Of course. I love you, Elliot," she said.

Elliot stopped sweating for a moment and smiled. Having one chance with Leah had been a gift, but having two had been a miracle.

"I love you, too."

He hung up and sat back in his chair. He would wait until six-thirty, and then he would drive over to James's office.

At five till seven, Elliot took the elevator to the thirteenth floor of James's building. James's last patient should have left five minutes ago and now James would be organizing his notes, getting ready to leave.

As Elliot stepped out onto the thirteenth floor, he noticed that he'd stopped sweating. The shivering had ceased while he drove over here and he was as calm as he'd ever been. He had planned things down to the final detail, even set it all down on paper this afternoon and then burnt it. He smiled, checked that there was no one else in the hallway, then walked the corridor he had walked once before, to James Arlington's office.

He opened the door and stepped into the dark waiting area. The light spilled out from the open door to James's office and Elliot took a deep breath and walked inside.

James was sitting behind his desk, bent over his papers. Elliot stared at him and was surprisingly disappointed. James's pictures had been falsely flattering; Elliot had expected a much more handsome man. The various bones and skin altered by plastic surgery sat awkwardly on his face. His chin seemed slightly askew. The skin was pulled so tightly, it nearly showed the cartilage beneath it. The blond hair was dyed a shade too light to look real. The whole man seemed haphazardly put together, with more focus on the parts than the whole.

Elliot took a step into the room and James looked up. He was startled for a moment, but then he recovered and smiled.

"Well, well," James said. "I've been expecting this meeting for some time. Mr. Shaperson, I presume."

Elliot pulled himself up straight. The muscles in his stomach twitched a little, but he held back a grimace.

"You realize you just gave yourself away." He sounded exactly as he wanted to, cool, unflappable, nearly bored. "You should have no idea what I look like unless you drove past my house this morning and saw me."

James looked down, scratched something on his notepad, and Elliot knew he did it only to give himself time to think of a reply. He had him!

"Look, Mr. Shaperson," James said, looking up again. "I'm busy. I've got patient files to work on and then I'd like to go home. Unless you have something to say . . . "

"I do," Elliot said and walked over to the desk. He stared down at the man until James finally stood up to be even with him. He was slightly taller than Elliot, but very thin. Elliot noticed his hands first; they were bony and white, nearly skeletal.

"Well, what is it?" James asked.

"First," he said, "you leave my wife and daughter alone. You contact either of them one more time, drive by one more time, send one more thing through the mail, and I'll kill you. You got that?"

James did not nod or reply, but his face paled. Elliot had gloves on and James stared at these. They were black leather; Elliot had bought them yesterday.

Elliot stood up straighter. He felt light on his feet for the first time in years. He felt insane. He'd probably been insane since Leah told him about the bullets, since he began dreaming of them going off, one by one, into James's skull. Since he'd realized that he wasn't moral at all. He would sacrifice his entire soul for just a little bit of revenge.

All the doubts were gone now. He didn't know if this new fearless man he'd become had always been a part of him, and he'd simply been afraid to let him out. He only knew that suddenly it was easy to be tough, where before it had always been difficult. It was easy to fight for Leah and Samantha, and he wondered why he hadn't fought all along, over the little things, over everything.

"Let me tell you my plans," Elliot went on. "I've got a speech drafted to give to the American Psychiatric Association. It lists every one of the improprieties you took against my wife. It lists how you seduced her on her second visit, had sex with her in your office, coerced her into bondage and sadomasochistic games. It lists every one of your calls to my house, every day you drove by, every package of explicit photos you sent. It tells of the horror you inflicted on my daughter's apartment and suggests they check out the police report on the vandalism."

"You have no proof," James said. "No one will ever believe you."

"Perhaps. But they'll certainly suspend your license while they check it out. I will also give the APA a copy of the report given to me by the private investigator I hired when you first started up with my wife. He gave me the names of two other patients of yours whom you took as lovers. I intend to contact them. If you treated them at all the way you treated Leah, I'm certain they'll be willing to add their ammunition to the fire."

James was quiet. He turned slightly to the side and Elliot could see the tuck lines behind his ears.

"You'll be ruined professionally, Arlington," Elliot said. "But more than that, you'll be ruined personally. Your wife will leave you, your friends, if you've got any, will walk away. You'll be an embarrassment to your colleagues."

"You're wrong," James said, and there was a catch in his voice. "I'm a good psychiatrist. I've always been good at that."

Elliot faltered; there was nothing sympathetic about the bad guys in the novels. He looked at James's hands, imagined them drawing those horrid pictures on Samantha's bedroom walls, and felt tough again.

"A good psychiatrist does not sleep with his patients," he said. "A good psychiatrist would see the sickness in himself. He wouldn't manipulate a client's trust and force her into playing horrendous sexual games for his own satisfaction."

"You have no idea what you're talking about," James said. "You really don't understand me at all."

Elliot hesitated a second, but he was far past the point of backing off. He spread out his fingers and pressed them down on the desk. He liked the look of that, ten black leather arrows, all pointing at James.

"Before I have the pleasure of ruining you," he said, "there's something else for us to work out. You abused my wife. You devastated my daughter with your sick attack on her home. Now I'm afraid I need some kind of retribution."

James pulled himself up straight and, for a moment, Elliot felt a stab of doubt. Then it was gone. He thought of James hitting Leah, stalking Samantha. He thought of himself, during the three years James and Leah were together, skulking in the shadows, hoping for miracles, hoping someone would do something to make things right again. He had prayed to be some other kind of man, a man who took action, met violence with violence, and now he was that man.

"I won't demean myself with a fistfight," James said.

"What then?" Elliot said, biting his tongue to keep from blurting out the answer. He had not planned for this, had not allowed himself to think of it, but all along, he had known where this meeting would end. That was the real reason he'd read those books. Not to prime himself for confrontation, not to learn about assassins or spies, but to comfort himself that he wasn't alone in thinking that sometimes, in the name of justice, awful things had to be done.

"I have an idea," James said. "That is, if you're man enough."

Elliot's arm twitched when James opened the top drawer of his desk and took out his revolver. He laid it in his hand, ran his finger over the barrel.

"Russian roulette," James said. "Ever played?"

Elliot's arm twitched again and he knew that James saw it, that he mistook it for fear. James smiled.

"No," Elliot said, amazed that his voice was calm, that he hadn't yet broken this off. "But I'm up for it."

"I happen to have a blindfold," James said. "I'll put it on and you can check the cylinder. There's one bullet inside. Spin the cylinder and give it back to me. I always go first."

"Why?" Elliot asked.

"Because I'm a gentleman," he said and laughed.

"You play this often, then."

James got out the blindfold and slid it between his fingers.

"Not for a long time," he said, staring straight at him. "Actually, not since Leah."

James put on the blindfold and Elliot grabbed the gun. He waited until James had the blindfold in place and then he opened the cylinder. Just as Leah had told him, there were six bullets inside, one in every chamber. Elliot's hand shook only slightly as he spun the cylinder and then snapped it shut. He handed the revolver back to James.

"I never lose," James said. "Leah never lost, either. But someday someone will. I certainly hope it won't be you."

He lifted the barrel up to his temple. Elliot could hardly believe he was standing there. At the last second, he knew he would jump in and fling the gun away. After he saved James, he would show him the six bullets, tell him he'd come inches from dying, and then he'd punch him straight in his reworked nose.

Elliot watched James breathe deeply in and out three times. James cocked the gun, wound his finger around the trigger. Elliot stood in silence, stared down at his feet, waiting for them to move. James's hand tightened, Elliot opened his mouth to say something, but then closed it again. He took a step back, to avoid the blood, and watched James pull the trigger.

Elliot got up from bed when he heard the newspaper slam against the house. By the time Leah got up two hours later, he had calmed himself and had the paper open to the People section.

"Good morning," Leah said, smiling. She poured herself a cup of coffee and then sat down beside him at the table. Elliot tried to summon the guilt and remorse, but really all he felt was an edge of excitement.

"You'll want to read this," he said.

He handed her the paper. She took a moment to sip her coffee and then glanced at it. At first, she didn't move at all, but then her hand began to shake and the coffee spilled over and burnt her fingers. Elliot handed her a towel, but she merely held it over the burn and went on reading.

SACRAMENTO PSYCHIATRIST COMMITS SUICIDE

Last night, James Arlington, a noted Sacramento psychiatrist, died from a gunshot wound to the head. The incident occurred in his downtown office and authorities believe it to be suicide despite the absence of a note. According to Detective Augler, in charge of the case, there were no signs of foul play.

Arlington's wife, Elaine, was too distraught to comment. Authorities say that Arlington blindfolded himself before he pulled the trigger. Estimated time of death was seven-thirty. After a thorough search of the scene, authorities found a desk filled with ropes, handcuffs, and other sex paraphernalia.

The plot thickened when two women who saw the report of the suicide on the news last night came forward to tell their stories. They admitted to being patients of Arlington's, as well as reluctant sexual partners.

Mary Granger, a twenty-two-year-old, said, "James and I became lovers after only one session. He was difficult to refuse. He made it seem like part of my therapy. He liked games, bondage, even tried to get me to play Russian roulette, although I never would. He showed me that he only kept one bullet in the chamber and said that the odds were in my favor, but I couldn't do it."

Authorities verified that when Arlington shot himself, the revolver was fully loaded.

Granger also stated that Arlington seemed erratic of late, had canceled a number of appointments, and, in her opinion, was fully capable of suicide.

"I didn't know what to make of him, actually," Granger said. "He's always been moody, but in the last few weeks those moods swings were terrifying. He'd be laughing one minute, crying the next. I couldn't stand to be around him. It doesn't surprise me that he did this."

An autopsy will be performed today and the funeral will take place on Saturday. Arlington was fifty-two years old.

Leah pushed the paper away. She walked to the sink and ran her hand beneath the water.

"You were late last night," she said.

Elliot was hardly breathing. "Yes."

Leah turned the water off and kept her back to him.

"Were you there?" she asked, very softly.

Elliot thought of lying, but, insane as he was, he wanted to take the blame, and credit, for this. He was the man who had brought James down.

"Yes."

Leah breathed deeply a couple of times, then walked back to the table and sat down. She took his hand in hers.

"How was it?"

He shivered a little and she squeezed his hand.

"Not bad enough," he said. "That's the problem, isn't it? With everything we see on the news and in the movies, a little blood just seems normal. The really scary part is that it just wasn't that bad."

Leah stood up from her chair and wrapped her arms around him.

"You say that," she said, "but you're shivering and pale as a sheet."

"I had it all planned out," Elliot said. "I was going to go to the APA, turn him in. But then, when he held that gun to his temple, I couldn't do anything. I was going to stop him from pulling the trigger. I really was. But then . . . I don't know. I crossed over. I wanted him to die."

Leah fell back into her seat, but still held his hand.

"I don't feel like me anymore," Elliot went on. "Not since I walked out on you. All my life I had it figured out. I controlled everything: my emotions, my thoughts, every action. Now I can't even predict what I'll do next. First I'm walking around in strange neighborhoods, then flying over here to win you back, then last night I stood there and watched a man blow his brains out."

They sat in silence for a long time. Elliot had not slept last night. He had lain beside Leah, stiff, his neck aching, his right arm still twitching. He had compared himself to the killers in Ludlum's and Clancy's books and knew he had a lot to learn. They could walk away, have a drink, toast a job well done. He had just felt dead inside, as if a portion of that bullet had ricocheted and grazed his heart.

"Who's to say," Leah said, "that if James had only had one bullet in there, it wouldn't have killed him? He was bound to lose sometime. At the worst, we just sped up the timetable."

Elliot shook his head. He started crying, silently, and Leah pulled him into her arms.

"He was a bad man, Elliot," she said.

He nodded, he agreed, but still he cried and she rocked him.

"He never would have let up on us," Leah went on. "He would have hurt Samantha again. He would have pushed the line further and further, eventually turned that gun on us."

"What will Samantha think when she finds out?" Elliot asked.

"We just won't tell her," Leah said. "She's in Washington, thank God, and won't see the local paper. Besides, she never brings up James anymore. She lives in that house with Michael and erases everything bad from her mind."

She rocked him until he quieted, but still the image came to him again and again. In espionage books, they explained about the trajectory of bullets, the time it took to die, even the amount of blood that came from different parts of the body. But they didn't really tell you what a man looked like when a bullet blasted into his brain, what it felt like to watch that, to know you'd had it in your power to stop his death, but didn't. Just as the bullet hit him, James's mouth had fallen open in a kind of "O." Elliot's stomach had risen up, made him breathless, and then fallen quickly down again as James slumped to the floor, the gun still wedged tightly in his hand. The bullet had cleared his skull and planted itself in the far wall, followed by a splatter of brain tissue. The blood had soaked into the floor around James's face, black as night.

They didn't always tell you, in espionage novels, that men sometimes twitched before they died, like a snake with its head cut off. Elliot had stood there, watching James's body convulse for close to a minute. And the worst part—the thing that proved to Elliot that man hadn't evolved at all, that he, at least, was just as barbaric as a caveman on a hunt, a Roman watching gladiators die for sport—was that instead of saying a prayer for James's soul, he had turned away, walked to the door, and said "Good."

24

Dylan began dating Karen Arnold, the secretary at EarthAlert, on Christmas Eve. He had no family to share the holiday with, nor did she, and so they spent it together getting drunk in a bar and complaining about the commercialism of the season.

Dylan liked her for two reasons. One, because she had just broken up with a ferociously possessive boyfriend and was sincere in not wanting to get tied down, and two, because she was small, blond, and unopinionated, as completely unlike Samantha as possible.

The problem, though, was that when Karen did things unlike Samantha, Dylan nearly shouted at her that she was doing things wrong. Samantha had kissed his ear while they made love; Karen hardly liked to kiss at all. Samantha had always wanted to cuddle after; Karen smoked a cigarette and read the paper. There was nothing wrong with the things Karen did, except that she didn't give him what he wanted most: a reminder of Samantha.

On a cold mid-January morning, Dylan walked into the EarthAlert office and saw Karen sitting at the front desk. He smiled at her. She really was pretty.

"Hi, gorgeous," he said, and she laughed. She was so easy. She didn't love him and she didn't expect him to love her, and he wondered why that kind of relationship seemed so dissatisfying now, when before he would have thought it was perfect.

"There's someone waiting to see you in your office," she said. "An older woman."

Dylan raised his eyebrows. "I'm a sucker for older women," he said and went to find out who it was.

Leah was sitting on his desk, studying his papers. Dylan stopped in the doorway. He knew why she was here, to break the news in person that Samantha had married Michael. He gripped the door, felt his body start to falter. He could almost feel himself falling apart, his hands separating from his arms, his heart from his veins; soon all the pieces would lie scattered on the floor.

"Hello," he said.

Leah turned to him and smiled; he felt a rush of hope at the brightness in her eyes. She did not look like the bearer of bad news.

"Hi," she said. "I've missed you."

Dylan walked forward and hugged her. He had missed her, too. He had even missed Elliot. He had missed everything that had anything to do with Samantha.

"I'm sorry about your folks," Leah said.

Dylan pulled away. "Thanks. What can I do for you?" He had a sharp desire to tell her about the money, the investments he was thinking about making in recycled products and environmental causes, his search for a new apartment to live in until his project with Future Homes was finalized. But before he could say anything, Leah spoke.

"Well, for starters," she said, "you can give me a job."

Dylan stared at her for a moment and then laughed.

"You're not serious."

"I am. I'm back with Elliot, you know. This time I'm going to do it right. I want something to say when he comes home and asks me how my day was. I'm tired of telling him who was on Oprah."

Dylan walked around his desk and sat down. Leah took the chair opposite him.

"We don't have any paid positions open, Leah," he said.

"Fine. Let me be a volunteer. You told me before that you needed a statistician, someone to help you work up all those gloom-and-doom predictions. I can still do that. Or I can answer the phones or stuff envelopes or, at least, stand in front of trees with you. The health of the environment means something to me too, Dylan. I never knew it did, before I met you. Frankly, I never even thought about it before I met you. I wasn't raised to think that way. In my generation, we never dreamed it would be a problem. The earth was so mysterious, it would just go on and on."

Dylan watched her and couldn't help smiling. Her intensity reminded him so much of his own. It always had.

"How many hours a week are we talking?" he asked.

"I thought twenty, to begin with," Leah said, standing up and looking around the office. "Oh Dylan, you won't regret it. Once I get my teeth into something—"

"We could use a statistician," Dylan broke in. "We receive so many reports every day, figures, predictions. You'll have to put them all together and come up with some easy-to-comprehend fact sheets that we all can read and give out to the press. There's no money for a job like that right now—"

Leah clapped her hands like a child. "I'll take it," she said.

Dylan shook his head, wondering exactly how big a fool he was. Every day now, there would be the temptation to ask her about Samantha. He'd have to hear about Samantha's honeymoon, pregnancies, children, career moves. Yet wasn't that exactly the reason he had hired Leah, because no matter how much it hurt, he wanted to know everything? That's what love did. It made you savor the pain, when the pain was all that was left.

"So you're with Elliot again," he said, a moment later.

Leah turned a radiant smile on him and Dylan sucked in his breath. He didn't want to see that love could do that; it could turn your life around.

"For over a month now," she said. "It's not anything like before. No, that's not true. It's like before, but it's also different. We know what it's like without each other now. I think you need to know that."

Dylan stood up and walked to the door. He wanted to get out without asking it. But he stopped at the portal and turned around.

"Has she married him yet?" he asked.

Leah shook her head. "No, not yet. They set the date for February fifth."

Dylan turned away again, so she couldn't see his face. If he could just make it to that date, he'd be fine. Then Samantha would be lost to him, irrevocably, and he'd have to stop dreaming about her, wouldn't he?

"Well, come on," he said, "let's find you some numbers to crunch."

Samantha stood at the window in her office, looking out at the rain that fell in sheets and had, in the last ten minutes, begun to flood the streets. Today was Friday, January 28, the day of her parents' supposed divorce.

Last night on the phone, Leah had said, "Tomorrow's the divorce day. I really don't know what's going to happen. Maybe we'll stop it, maybe we won't. It would be a kick to see the look on our friends' faces when we tell them we're living in sin." Then she had laughed, fully and wonderfully, and Samantha had clutched her stomach and curled down farther in Michael's bed, wishing she could make her parents go away.

Samantha was the one who was supposed to feel the way they felt. *She* was the one getting married in a week. *She* was the one who had a tea-length wedding gown hanging in the closet. The church was booked, the reception would be at Michael's parents' house, and the caterer had confirmed the menu.

She was moving toward marriage, and her parents were heading away from it, and it made no sense at all that they were the happy ones.

The phone rang and Samantha stepped back to her desk.

"Samantha Shaperson," she said.

"It's Michael."

Samantha closed her eyes and tried not to be annoyed. He called her three times a day, sometimes four or five. When she went on that week-long trip to Washington, D.C., he called every other hour.

"I'm kind of busy right now," she said, although she wasn't.

"Just wanted to see what you want me to pick up for dinner," he said pleasantly.

Samantha clenched her jaw. Every day he asked her the same thing, and every night on his way home from the hospital, he went to the market and bought the ingredients for dinner. Then he came home and set the table with china and candles and fresh-cut flowers. He cooked exquisitely every evening, made love to her every night.

Samantha was finding it harder and harder to tolerate him. She adored him, thought he was a wonderful man, but she felt like a hypocrite accepting such devotion when she was unable to give even a quarter of it back. Everyone told her she was lucky, but really Michael was the lucky one. He was lucky to find someone he could pour his heart into. He was lucky to love even when he wasn't loved back, because it was through passion like that that you lived. Being loved was pleasant, it was comforting and safe. But it made you lazy and often mean.

Still, the wedding was on. It was on because Samantha was not as different as she had pretended to be. This might be the nineties, but marriage was still what a girl wanted. She grew up and found a man and stayed thin until he put a ring on her finger. Then, finally, she could relax, put on a few pounds, stop wearing makeup. She could enjoy her friends again, her house, her career, because at least she'd accomplished this one thing. She'd proven she'd been desirable once.

Samantha shivered. She could not believe she was thinking these things.

"You decide," she said.

"No, you," Michael said.

"For God's sake, Michael, pick up hot dogs for all I care. I've got to get back to work."

She hung up and immediately regretted her harshness. He was so good and she wasn't worthy of even a slice of him.

She paced around her office for a minute and then grabbed her purse. She walked down the hall and into her boss's office.

"I've got to leave early today," she said.

Amy Tarkington looked up from her paperwork. "Something serious?" she asked.

"No, not really. Things are slow and, frankly, I need to get out and ride again. I haven't done that for so long."

Amy stared at her for a moment and then nodded. "Fine. See you Monday."

Samantha turned to walk out.

"Oh, Sam," Amy said. "I almost forgot to tell you. I saw your friend the other day."

"Who?"

"You know, the long-haired guy. The one you were seeing for a while."

Samantha stood very still. She reached out for the door and laid her palm against it.

"Dylan," she said quietly.

"That's it. I was at Ikins's office and Dylan came crashing in, as usual. He wants something done about the plans to cart radioactive waste up from San Onofre to Washington for dumping. He's afraid of what could happen along the way."

"What did Ikins tell him?" Samantha asked. Oh, she was cool. Not even a quiver in her voice.

"The usual," Amy said. "That his hands were tied. The waste has to go somewhere and California has run out of places to dump it. Washington wants to take it in."

Samantha nodded. She would be all right. That's what all the pop psychologists said, that eventually time healed all wounds; over months or years, love nearly always loosened its tentacles. But no one told her how to survive now, day to day, how to not hate herself for foolishly loving such a heartless man. Michael's kindness was a daily reminder of how stupid she was, how she couldn't force her heart to go in the right direction.

"He asked about you," Amy said. Samantha took a deep breath. She could feel hope rising in her against her will.

"He wanted to know how you were doing," Amy went on. "How business was. He told me your mother had gone to work for him."

The hope instantly turned cold and Samantha stared at her boss. She was certain she had heard her wrong.

"I beg your pardon?" she said.

Amy laughed. "That's what I said. But he said Leah marched in a couple of weeks ago and told him she needed to work. She's a volunteer now. He's got her analyzing all the data they receive. Supposedly she loves it."

There was only so much a person could stand and Samantha reached her limit right then. She had spoken to her mother twice in the last two weeks and Leah had not said one word about working for Dylan. Her mother still treated her like a child, but she did not feel like anyone's child anymore.

"Sam, are you all right?" Amy asked.

"No. Not really."

"I take it you knew nothing about this."

"No. I'm going to be thirty-six years old this year and my mother and father still treat me like I'm five. I'm sure my mother didn't tell me because she thinks the sound of Dylan's name hurts me."

"Does it?"

"It doesn't matter if it does or not. She can't hide things from me anymore. I'm not her baby. I get so sick of her and my dad gloating over my accomplishments as if they'd done them themselves, or worrying about me as if they're inside my skin. It's *my* life. Mine. I'm totally separate. I think and act all on my own."

Samantha smiled a little when she realized she'd been shouting.

"I'm sorry," she said.

"Don't be," Amy said. "Go home. Ride your bike and let off some steam."

Samantha walked out of the office and drove home. She changed into her cycling pants and a sweatshirt, pulled her hair into a ponytail and then tucked that beneath her helmet. She was going to ride until her mind had cleared, until she had pedaled her disappointment in Dylan and her anger at her parents right out of her body. And then, when she was calmer, she was going over to her mother's to let her have it.

That night, the rain let up and became a light mist. Leah set three place settings on the table, opened the wine to let it breathe, then sat on the couch to wait. Her hands fluttered a little out of nervousness, so she poured herself a glass of wine and drank it steadily.

Elliot came home ten minutes later and took her in his arms. He always did this now, swept her up, kissed her hard, ran his hands down her back. She thought, with regret, of all those years when he had pecked her cheek or just said hello. How many kisses like this had they missed? Thousands? Tens of thousands?

"How was work?" he asked.

Leah laughed. She thought it would take months, maybe years, for those words to lose their luster. All these years, Samantha had been trying desperately to stir up Leah's ambition, to get her out into the world, to make her *do* something. But Leah hadn't listened. She hadn't understood that daughters could teach their mothers, too.

"Good," Leah said. "Karen stepped out for a while and I had to man the phones. I talked to this reporter over at *The Examiner*. He wanted to know what we planned to do about the massive logging project planned for Northern Idaho."

"What did you tell him?"

"I said, 'What do you think we plan to do? We'll chain ourselves to the trees if we have to, barricade the roads, spike the trunks, sabotage the equipment, but that project will not go through. You can tell the precious paper company that!' "

Elliot stared at her and then laughed. "My wife, the radical," he said.

"You better believe it."

Elliot finally pulled away and looked at the table. "Samantha?" he asked.

Leah shook her head and reached for her wine. "No. Dylan."

Elliot took a step back and dropped his briefcase on the floor.

"Would you mind telling me why?"

Leah pulled herself up straight and looked at him. He had not looked the same to her for over a month now, not since the morning he showed her the newspaper and told her what he'd done to James. There were parts of him she knew, mannerisms she recognized, but when she looked into those eyes she loved, she realized that she had never really known him, and probably never would. If someone had asked her if Elliot was capable of watching a man die when he had the power to save him, she would have said definitely not. She would have been so certain of her words, even arrogant in her supposed knowledge of him.

Leah looked at this man, this husband, this lover, and realized that when he looked at her, he saw the same thing, a woman he could not predict with one hundred or even eighty-percent accuracy, even after knowing her for thirty-eight years. She was glad about that. Who would want to be known completely, even by a lover? What were secrets for, except to make you feel more than human, somewhat godlike, the holder of knowledge no one else had access to?

"I invited him," Leah said finally. "He is my boss now, and my friend. And, frankly, I invited him because our daughter is getting married next week to a man she doesn't love. And I think Dylan needs to know that."

Elliot shook his head. He poured himself a full glass of wine. Then he took Leah's hand and led her over to the couch. They sat down, close together, and Leah snuggled against his warmth.

"Why do women always love the bad men?" he asked.

Leah tossed her head back and laughed.

"I love you. You're not bad."

"I'm not so sure about that. I'm not your husband anymore."

They had let the divorce go through. Leah could not explain it to anyone; she hardly understood it herself. She only knew that, late at night, she and Elliot giggled about living in sin, starting over, dating, and it seemed such a shame to waste this opportunity. She looked down at her wedding ring, the one she hadn't taken off even when Elliot moved out. She twisted it around her finger. She could not bring herself to take it off now. He was her husband, certificate or not.

"It's strange," Leah said.

"Are you sorry?"

Leah looked up immediately and smiled. "No. I've always been married to you, Elliot. Even before the wedding, even after you left. Even now."

"Samantha won't understand," Elliot said, looking away.

"There are a lot of things Samantha will never understand about us. That's just the way it is."

"I still feel married," Elliot said. "But I feel a bit wild, too."

Leah laughed.

"So answer my question," Elliot went on. "Why do good women always fall for the men in leather jackets? You all say you want someone stable, someone who can make a good living, be a good father, but then, if you have a choice between someone like that and someone like Dylan, you'll choose Dylan every time."

Leah stood up and walked around the living room. She thought about those three years when she ran from Elliot's bed to James's, when James's games and cruelty appealed to her in some sensual way because she knew they were wrong. How could she explain herself? It wasn't even possible to explain; it was just what she had felt, what she needed to do.

"I can't speak for all women, Elliot," she said.

"No. But what is it about? Do they take you somewhere good men don't know about?"

Leah turned to him. "I can remember it most clearly in high school," she said. "One morning, as I was walking through the front gate, this boy I hadn't even noticed jumped in front of me. He had slicked-back blond hair, a cigarette in the corner of his mouth, faded blue jeans. He smiled and, very gently, lifted my hair up off my shoulder. All I could think was 'Oh God. Oh God.' My heart was pounding. I smiled back and he opened the gate for me. He said 'Get to class, little girl' in this deep, wonderfully gritty voice. My legs buckled, literally. If he'd asked me to run away with him right then, I might have done it."

When Leah was through, she turned and stared at her husband.

"The good guys," Elliot said, "don't make your heart pound."

"Oh, they do. But it takes more effort. I can't explain it, Elliot. I think women *want* to fall in love with the right men. But then we catch a glimpse of the men our mothers warned us about and, I don't know, we lose our minds."

They stared at each other a long time, until the doorbell rang.

"That will be Dylan," Leah said. "Please, Elliot, be nice."

Elliot shrugged. "I'm one of the good guys, remember?" he said. "I'm almost always nice."

They sat around the table, polishing off two bottles of wine and very little of Leah's chicken-rice casserole which, Dylan suspected, she had botched in her nervousness. Still, things were going well. Elliot was talking, even smiling now and then. He was not as hostile as he had been at the cabin. But then, so much had changed since then.

"We plan to go to London first," Leah was saying. They had talked about some of the EarthAlert projects, Leah had told the story of her and Elliot getting back together, and now they were on to vacations. They had carefully avoided the subject of Samantha. The wedding was in one week and Dylan was, despite himself, desperate for information.

He had finally gotten himself out of his ratty apartment and found a new place on the outskirts of town. He had been bringing Karen there more often than he really wanted to, as if he could brand the place with her scent the way Samantha's had branded his old apartment.

"I want to go to Germany," Elliot said. "I want to stay in some castle in the woods."

"I don't know, Elliot," Leah said. "I was thinking we'd confine ourselves to England and Scotland this time."

"This time?" Elliot said and laughed. "Did you hear that, Dylan? This time, she says."

Dylan smiled, marveling at the changes in these people. How had they found their way back to each other? He would really like to know. How could you be like this, laughing, touching, drinking wine together, after thirty-eight years?

They all fell silent then and Dylan poked at his casserole. He tried to take another bite, but Leah had not cooked the rice enough and it was crunchy. Dylan brought his napkin up to his mouth and spit out the piece. He'd seen Elliot do the same thing five minutes earlier.

"Oh, for God's sake," Leah said, standing up and walking into the kitchen. She opened the refrigerator and took out the mayonnaise and mustard, packages of sliced lunch meats and Swiss cheese, and extra-long French rolls. She brought everything to the table and set it down in a heap.

"Do you really think you'll hurt my feelings by telling me I didn't cook the rice long enough?" she said. "You're both sweet men, but honestly, you can tell me when my cooking is a piece of shit."

Dylan looked up, smiled, but it was Elliot who burst out laughing.

"It was a piece of shit, Leah," Elliot said.

Leah punched him playfully. The three of them dug into the food, fixing heaping sandwiches of turkey and Swiss.

They were just finishing dinner when the front door burst open. Samantha came flying in dressed in her cycling shorts and soaked sweatshirt. She yanked off her helmet and her red hair came spilling out. Dylan gripped the edge of the table.

For a moment, he was sure Samantha didn't see him. She walked straight to her mother.

"I'm going to have this out with you right now," she said. "Today I was talking to my boss and I heard about your job with Dylan. Thank you so very much for telling me."

Leah stepped back and tilted her head toward Dylan. Samantha turned his way and jerked only once.

Then she fixed him with a stare that chilled him, that told him that even if he changed his mind about coming back to her, she would not take him now. He felt his breath rush out, as if she were air to him and he hadn't known, until she was gone, that he had needed her to survive.

He stood up, took a step toward her, but she parried by taking a step back.

"Isn't this cozy?" she said.

"Samantha, please," Leah said. "Just sit down and relax."

"I'm not going to sit down and relax," Samantha said.

Dylan had forgotten how striking she was, how unlike anyone. In his dreams, he had re-created her smaller, less defined, less dramatic. How could he have forgotten that she was this tall, her nose and cheeks that pronounced, her hair that vivid shade of auburn? She moved without fear, without an ounce of trepidation, as if she were exactly certain of where she was headed.

She walked up to Elliot and said, "Did you know about this job of Mom's?"

"Of course," Elliot said.

"Why the hell didn't any of you tell me?"

They were all quiet and though Dylan's heart was beating rapidly, though his mind was not completely on the subject because he was thinking, *She's so beautiful. God, I'd forgotten how beautiful she is*, he plunged into the conversation.

"I'm sure your mom was just concerned about what you'd think," he said. "Last time—"

Samantha marched over to him. Even though he could nearly see the sparks flying from her eyes, he was thankful for her anger because it moved her closer to him; it pushed into that space ex-lovers were supposed to keep between them.

"Last time," Samantha said bitterly, standing right in front of him and pointing her finger at his face. She hesitated and in that hesitation Dylan saw what he'd been praying to see, a reflection of himself, a longing.

He reached up and grabbed her finger. She tried to pull away but he held on tightly. He was amazed at how hot her skin was, how good it felt to touch this small part of her. He could make love to Karen, have her whole body open to him, but it was not nearly as erotic as this one little piece of Samantha.

"Last time," Dylan said softly, staring straight into her eyes, "you saw your mother and me in the midst of a friendship both of us were too stupid to tell you about. This time, Leah wanted a job, wanted to do something important, and she knew I could help her. You are marrying another man, Samantha. Whether your mother and I work together should be of no consequence to you. If you love him."

Samantha yanked her finger away and stepped back. She was breathing hard and he realized he was, too. He ran his fingers through his hair.

"It is of consequence to me," Samantha said. She marched over to Leah and stared her in the eye. "Not because of Dylan but because you're still treating me like a child. Just because I'm your daughter doesn't mean I'm incapable of understanding what you do. Stop protecting me. You thought I'd be hurt by this, that the mention of Dylan's name would send me to my room in tears. Well, look at me. I'm marrying Michael next week. I love *Michael*. You can work with Dylan, play with Dylan, do whatever the hell you want with Dylan. For God's sake, just tell me."

Dylan steadied his breathing. I love *Michael*. I love *Michael*. He fell back into the chair, as if her words were fingers, jabbing at him.

"You can stop shouting," Leah said, turning away from her and taking the dishes to the sink. "I hear you very well. You think that being someone's child is a temporary state, ages one to eighteen only. You think you've outgrown it."

"I have outgrown it."

Leah dropped the dishes loudly in the sink. She grabbed her cigarettes off the counter and lit one.

"You never outgrow it, Samantha," she said. "I never outgrew it; I am still Cathy and Wayne McDermott's daughter. Your father never outgrew it. He's still his mother's child."

"Maybe that's true for the two of you," Samantha said, "but now we're talking about me. This is my life. You act as if we'll always have this cord between us, as if I owe you some piece of my life in payment for what you've done for me, but I don't owe you anything. I love you and I love Dad and I always want you in my life, but you need to back off. You need to give me my life, let me lead it, treat me like an autonomous adult."

Leah stared at her. "Fine, then," she said. "You want to know all there is to know? You think you can take it all?"

Samantha lifted her chin. "Of course."

Elliot stepped forward. "Leah, no."

Leah held up her hand. She and Elliot stared at each other and communicated silently. It was eerie, watching them, two people speaking only with their eyes. After a moment, Elliot nodded. Leah took another drag of her cigarette and Dylan searched for and found the last of the wine. He poured it and then gulped it down. Samantha was standing rigid against the wall.

"You don't know about James Arlington," Leah said.

Dylan noticed that Samantha pressed the backs of her legs against the wall, as if that pressure helped her to stand.

"Of course I know. I know what he did to my apartment, what he was trying to do to you. I can handle that."

"Can you handle," Leah said, "the fact that something had to be done about him?"

Elliot stepped forward. "After your mother and I got back together," he said, "she told me what James was doing. How he had sent pictures, called her, driven by the house, done . . . done what he did to your apartment. She was on the verge of doing something drastic and I knew I had to act."

Dylan lifted his glass again, but the wine was gone. He should have known Leah was lying when she said James had an alibi for the night of the break-in. He should have known, only he hadn't been paying attention, he'd been too caught up in the fact that he was losing Samantha.

He knew what was coming. He remembered the articles in the paper a month ago about James's suicide. He had thought it strange, out of character, and he had wanted to ask Leah about it after she came to work for him. There had never seemed the right time to bring it up, though.

Dylan met Elliot's eyes. He had thought Elliot timid and weak, but now he realized that Samantha's father was stronger than he would ever be. He had plucked courage out of nothing, out of an ordinary life.

"I planned to turn Arlington in to the medical board," Elliot said. "Let them take away his license. But while you were out of town, I met him in his office and he suggested, as I knew he would, Russian roulette. I thought I would stop him. I planned to all along until he pulled the trigger. Then I just couldn't."

Samantha started sliding down the wall. Dylan jumped out of his chair and got to her just as she reached the floor. He sat beside her, tried to put his arm around her, but she pushed him off.

"That's not all," Leah said. Her voice was hard,

determined, but Dylan could see the tears in her eyes. She stepped up next to Elliot and slipped her hand into his. "James thought there was only one bullet in the revolver, but I had sneaked into his office weeks earlier and filled it with six. I had planned to go and play that damn game with him myself. As soon as James played again, he'd lose."

Samantha looked at Dylan, as if he were the only sane person in the room.

"I don't believe any of this," she said. Leah walked back to the table and stubbed out her cigarette.

"Believe it," she said. "Your father watched James pull the trigger. He let him kill himself and then he got out of the office before anyone saw him. You wanted to know the truth and now you know it. You wanted to be treated like an adult, told all the facts, and now you'll have to deal with them like an adult, like nobody's child at all."

For a moment, Samantha leaned against Dylan's body. He put his arm around her and held her tightly, drank in the scent of her, the sweat that still clung to her. He knew then that he was lost. He'd probably known it all along but it was while he sat there, on the floor of her parents' dining room, that he knew she held him in the palm of her hand.

"Sam," he said, but just then she pulled away and stumbled to her feet. She walked over to her father.

"You watched this man kill himself when you could have stopped him?" she said.

Elliot stood up straight. "Yes."

Samantha shook her head. "My God," she whispered. She looked at Elliot, then Leah, then down at her hands, as if she had to make sure she was still who she was, when everyone else seemed to have become someone new. Dylan stood up, but before he could reach her, she ran toward the door.

He started after her, but suddenly Elliot was there, holding him back with a strength Dylan never would have guessed he had.

"Let her go," Elliot said.

Dylan tried to shake him off. "But she'll go to Michael."

He finally broke free of Elliot's grip, but by the time he reached the front door, Samantha's bike was long gone. He turned back to Elliot and Leah, even though he knew he gave away everything in his face. He had probably always given away everything, fooling only himself with his declarations of independence.

"She'll go to Michael," he said again, softer this time. Elliot came back to him and put his hand on his shoulder.

"Michael adores her," he said. "He'll take good care of her."

Dylan hunched forward. His skin felt dried up, his bones brittle. He stumbled toward the door.

"Dylan," Leah said, but he ignored her. He walked out into the rain.

Elliot sat in the neighborhood park two blocks from his house. He had spent the better part of an hour setting up his old easel, positioning the crisp white canvas on it, unfolding his old painter's table and putting it at just the right angle to his chair. On the palette he'd had since his days at the literary magazine, he had laid out a few dabs of various oils, black, brown, gray, green, blue, yellow. He had done all of the preliminaries and now he stared at the canvas, sure he was the biggest fool who'd ever lived.

Last night, after Samantha ran out, Elliot had pulled down the ladder to the attic and gone up after his past. It was a night for coming clean and, as he stared at his dusty art supplies, he admitted he hadn't painted for over thirty years simply because insurance salesmen didn't paint. They came home from the office, ate a couple slices of pot roast, watched reruns on TV, and went to bed. He'd kept a set of guidelines in his mind that determined who he should be, rather than just being who he was.

He had taken the art supplies downstairs and this morning, when he got to the park, he had figured, stupidly, that it would all just come back to him. The art had seemed so much a part of him before, genetic, and he assumed it would take only a spark to reignite his creativity. He would start with something easy. A tree perhaps. Or a park bench. But now he sat here, staring at the easy lines of a stone bench and not having a clue how to go about painting it. Had he started with an outline or a focal point? Exactly how had he held his brushes? What color was that? Gray? Brown? Chestnut? Thirty years, and he could no longer trust his instincts. Thirty years, and he had lost all his talent and guts.

He heard footsteps crunching through the frosty grass behind him and then Leah was by his side. She stared at the canvas and then crouched down next to him.

"Trouble getting started?" she asked, as if he hadn't taken three decades off, as if he painted every day and every day he felt exactly like this, terrified by the idea of creating something out of nothing.

"Yes."

Leah stood up again and wrapped his brown cardigan sweater around her. She had taken to wearing his clothes, particularly his shirts and sweaters over her leggings. She looked tiny in them, waiflike.

She walked around in front of him and stared at the empty park. Despite the frosty mornings, the winters in this part of California weren't harsh enough to pull all the leaves from the trees. Those still hanging were brown now, and crisp as apples.

Leah turned around abruptly and stared at him.

"Do you think I was wrong?" she asked.

Before the impulse passed, Elliot made a sudden dash into the brown paint. He began to outline the sweater Leah was wearing. The sleeves draped well below her hands, as if she were a child in her father's shirt.

"No," Elliot said, starting hesitantly. His lines used to be bold, drawn with arrogant precision, but now his hand trembled a little. Still, he formed a fair outline of her body in that sweater.

"We were wrong before," he went on, going back over the lines he'd just drawn, softening the squiggles he'd painted out of nervousness. He blended them into the shadows he would form around her image. "We tried to keep Samantha in childhood forever. We still acted like her parents even when she hated being our child. She deserved to know what happened to James."

Leah tilted her head up to the sky.

"She should be with Dylan, not Michael," she said.

"Yes. Probably. But we can't fix this, the way we fixed her skinned knees and broken dollhouse."

"She won't be happy."

"Then she won't be happy. We keep thinking we're responsible for her happiness, but we're not. Not anymore. She doesn't want us to be."

Leah walked quickly back to his side and stared at the beginnings of the painting.

"The headless, legless woman," she said and laughed.

"It's not easy anymore," he said, gesturing at the canvas.

"No," Leah said, resting her chin on his head. "The best things never are."

Samantha lay beside Michael in bed. His naked leg was twisted around hers. She ran her toes up over his knee and he laughed.

"You're tickling me," he said.

She laid her cheek on his shoulder and smelled him. He wore an expensive cologne, but somehow he still always managed to smell of antiseptic. Whenever he lifted his hands to her face, she could smell the lingering scent of his surgical gloves.

She had come straight home from her parents' house last night and pulled Michael into the bedroom. He had been hesitant, maybe even put off by her aggressiveness, but she hadn't cared.

Last night was the best it had ever been. Last night, she took what she wanted. She demanded his passion, and he responded with an intensity she hadn't known he was capable of.

All through their lovemaking, there was something else between them, a few unspoken words. Last night, Samantha had not paused long enough to consider what they were, but now, in the clear light of morning, it was obvious.

There had been goodbyes in their touch.

He had stroked her breast and his fingers said, *I'll never do this again.* She had kissed his chest and her lips, without moving, murmured, *I'll miss this, the blond hairs here and there.*

There had been no words and yet it was all utterly clear. Their wedding was six days away, but it would not take place. They loved each other, but not in the right way. Last night, Samantha had learned things from her parents that shocked her, upended her whole world, but she could not confide in Michael. He would be horrified. He would quickly and adamantly condemn her parents. He was a doctor and believed that life was sacred, no matter how despicable the body that life was encased in. He saw things as black or white, the way Samantha had once seen things, before she met Dylan.

Now, they lay together, intertwined, and Samantha pulled him tighter. He had laughed just a moment ago when she tickled him, but now she felt his tears sinking into her skin.

"Michael," she said. She lifted her head and kissed

away his tears. She had not said anything, nor had he. But it was as if they'd spent the last twelve hours talking, hashing it all out, telling each other all the reasons why it would never work between them.

"You've always loved Dylan," he said.

She nodded. "Yes. I love you, too."

"But not the right kind of love for marriage."

"No. Not the right kind."

They lay in silence. Samantha had decided to visit her old apartment tonight. The walls would be clean now, the stains from the carpet steamed away. But in her mind, the viciousness that James Arlington had brought to her life would still be vivid, and finally, finally, she would exorcise it.

She did not tell Michael this because he would only worry. That was the difference between him and Dylan. Michael worried while Dylan forced her right back into the fray. If Dylan had been here . . . She gasped a little at how much those few words still hurt her. She had been shocked to see him last night, angry, hurt, and also, stupidly, grateful. What a pathetic reaction. After everything that had happened, she was simply glad to see him again, to touch what she loved, to read in his eyes that he still felt something for her.

"I'm not leaving you to go back to him," Samantha said. "It's over between Dylan and me. But you know it's not right between us. You know—"

"Be quiet," Michael said, bringing his fingers to her lips. "Just be quiet and hold me and let me say goodbye."

Samantha held on tightly. Michael ran his hands down her back, over her hip, around to her stomach. He traced the bones in her arm, her elbow, her shoulder, her neck. He reached up and touched her chin, her cheeks, her brows. He leaned over and stared at her for a long time, without blinking, with an intensity she had never seen before and which, she knew, he would hide away from her as soon as this moment was over. Then he kissed her cheek, slid out of bed, and walked into the bathroom.

Samantha got dressed. She packed her suitcase lightly, knowing Michael would pack the rest of her things for her. She took the suitcase to the front door and then looked back at the house that had never been a home to her, yet was the place where she had found her courage again, her way back to herself, her career, her friends. Michael saved lives every day, and he had saved hers too, without any instruments, with just his touch.

"Goodbye, Michael," she said, knowing he was listening behind the bathroom door. Then she turned and left.

Samantha drove to her old apartment complex and knocked on the manager's door. The woman was startled to see her and wary about letting her in.

"I finally rented the place," the manager said. "It took forever for the talk about what happened in there to die down. The tenants move in next week."

Samantha nodded and pressed forward. She was sweating, but she would go through with this.

"Please, just let me in. I need to see it."

The woman stared at her a moment longer and then nodded. She found her keys and Samantha followed her up to the second floor. The woman put the key in the lock and then stepped back.

"No hysterics?" she said. "I've got enough troubles around here."

"No hysterics," Samantha promised. The woman walked off and Samantha took a deep breath, then walked inside.

She flipped on the light and stared at the empty living room. The walls had been coated with half a dozen layers of bright white paint and the carpet had been steam-cleaned. Samantha looked for signs of the vicious mess that had been here, but none remained.

She stepped farther into the room. She went over the memories, saw the books torn apart, the sofa cushions ripped to shreds, the red wine spilled on the floor. She saw it all and then she squeezed her eyes shut. When she opened them again, the memory was gone, defeated, and she smiled.

She walked slowly into the bedroom. She started shaking when she came to the door, but she opened it. She took a step inside.

Though it had all been cleaned away, she immediately saw the graffiti on the walls, the words "Watch your back, Samantha," beside the bed. And then, like a magic trick, she was in another bedroom, inside her mother's body as James tied her up and hit her. It was not so alien now, a woman letting a man abuse her. She could feel her mother's horror, and her fear, but also the strange edge of excitement and the subdued acceptance, as if this were all Leah had thought she deserved.

Samantha shook her head and then was with her father in James's office, watching James put the revolver to his head. She was certain James had been sure of a positive outcome, had even been on the border of euphoria, and then, a split second later, he was taken totally by surprise. She felt her father's shudder, acknowledged the burden of guilt that landed on his shoulders alone when James slumped to the floor. She had never thought of Elliot as a hero until that moment.

When Samantha looked back at the walls again, they were clean. She walked around the empty room, touching the white plaster just to be sure; all the while her shaking was diminishing and she was smiling. She had been horrified last night when her father had told her what had happened. Yet now she could only feel gratitude and relief.

She turned and walked out of the apartment. She locked the door and went down to the manager's office. The woman took a good look at her and then smiled.

"No hysterics," she said.

"No. Can I use your phone?"

The woman nodded and Samantha dialed her parents' number. Her mother answered.

"Mom, it's me," she said.

Leah hesitated a second. "How are you?"

"Good. I've just been in my old apartment. I've left Michael."

Leah let out her breath. "That's a lot in one day, isn't it?"

Samantha laughed. "I suppose. Mom, I love you."

Leah was quiet for a moment and then she sighed. "I love you, too."

"Can I talk to Dad?"

"He's down at the park, painting."

Samantha smiled. She was not surprised. A month ago, even a week ago, she would have been, but not now.

"Will you tell him something for me?" Samantha asked.

"Of course."

"Tell him . . . Tell him that I'm safe now."

Leah said nothing, but Samantha could tell she was smiling.

On the morning of February fifth, the bride dressed. The groom got ready in a back room of the church and was as nervous as a schoolboy. There were only a few guests in the aisles, close friends and relatives who were able to come on such short notice.

It had all started the Monday before. Leah and Elliot had been reading in their chairs by the fire when Michael stopped by. He stood stiffly, leaning against the mantel as if he might break into a thousand pieces at any moment.

"I suppose you know about me and Samantha," he had said immediately. Leah put her book aside and stared up at him.

"Yes," she said.

"She's staying with her friend Tracy until she can find her own place."

Leah and Elliot nodded. Michael looked around the room, took in every detail and then, as if he couldn't bear to see any more, closed his eyes. Leah stood up and put her hand on his shoulder.

"I came here to talk to you about the wedding," Michael said at last, opening his eyes.

Leah dropped her hand and looked back at Elliot.

"We thought—" Leah began, but Michael cut her off.

"Samantha and I did call it off," he said. "And so I'm offering the day to you. I know you let your divorce go through. I also know that you two adore each other, that if anybody should be married, it's you. Everything is paid for. The church, the caterer, the band. It seems a shame to let it all go to waste."

Leah stood perfectly still, shocked, and yet her body was suddenly warm. She felt Elliot's eyes on her and she turned slowly. He had stood up too and was smiling at her.

"What do you say, Leah?"

It was as if Michael were not even there, as if Leah were seventeen years old again, sitting in that tiny Italian restaurant, feeling her heart burst with excitement. She could not predict what would happen. Perhaps it was marriage itself that had ruined them, lulled them into silence, into monotony, into the belief that you could find passion only with strangers. But when Leah looked at Elliot, she knew she'd risk it, just as she'd risked it thirty-seven years ago. People thought marriage was about commitment and fidelity, but Leah believed it was about risk, about throwing your life up and seeing where it landed.

She took Elliot's hand and held it against her chest. "Will you marry me, Elliot?" she asked.

His eyes looked serious for a moment and then he bent forward and kissed her. From somewhere far away, she heard Michael take a deep breath.

"I assume you won't want your reception at my parents' house," Michael said when they pulled apart.

Leah shook her head. "I think that might be a little awkward. We'll have it here. With just a few friends and family. You'll come, won't you, Michael?"

Michael shook his head. "No," he said. "I don't think so. I think it's probably best if I keep my distance for a while."

He smiled at them so forlornly that Leah wrapped her arms around him.

"If love had any logic," she said, "Samantha would love you."

He nodded and slipped away.

Now, five days later, Leah stood in the middle of the dressing room, staring at herself in the mirror. She was wearing Samantha's tea-length wedding gown, which, with only minor alterations, fit her very well. The amazing thing was, she looked like a bride, happy, glowing, excited to the point of tears. It was a ridiculous notion, a bride at fifty-five, but what the hell. She had the one ingredient a bride should have. Faith. She was probably a fool, but she believed everything would work out all right. She twirled around in her dress.

Samantha walked into the dressing room and caught her in the act.

"You're gorgeous, Mom," Samantha said.

"I can't believe we're doing this." Leah giggled and fell into the chair. She stared at Samantha, saw the ashen face, the clenched hands. She stood up again and put her arm around her.

"This isn't fair to you," she said. "This was supposed to be your day."

"Oh Mom, of course it's fair. I'm thrilled that you and Dad are getting married again. Now, tell me about your honeymoon."

Leah laughed and walked to the window. A few guests were arriving and she waved to an old friend who spotted her through the glass.

"Your father has outdone himself," she said. "He finessed the travel agent into moving all our reservations up from April to this week. We leave for New York tonight and will stay overnight there. Then tomorrow we're off to London. Two days from now, we'll be standing in front of the Tower of London, having a real second honeymoon."

Someone knocked on the door and Samantha opened it. The wedding coordinator smiled at them.

"Most of the guests have arrived," the woman said. "I think we should start."

"Just a minute," Leah said. The coordinator nodded and left and Leah took her daughter in her arms.

"You'll be happy," she said fiercely, more for her own benefit than for Samantha's. Elliot had told her she was no longer responsible for Samantha's happiness, but that wasn't true. She would always be responsible. The burden had fallen to her the instant Samantha was born. All of a sudden there was a baby in Leah's arms and though she'd been nervous for nine months about what to do, how to act, it came to her spontaneously. Her shoulders turned inward to shield Samantha from the harsh light. Her fingers stroked Samantha's skin, she cradled her in the crook of her arm and thought, *You're mine.* Though Samantha would take offense, Leah still thought, *You're mine, Samantha.*

"I am happy, Mom," Samantha said. "Really. Now go get married."

They walked out the door together. Samantha headed down the aisle first, as the maid of honor, and Leah took a moment to listen to the murmur of the guests. Over the top of everyone's heads, she saw Elliot standing at the altar, smiling. It was as if time hadn't moved at all, as if thirty-eight years was just an instant and if you blinked, you'd miss it all.

The ceremony was lovely, Samantha thought. She stood at the right of her mother, while Meredith, Elliot's sister, stood to the left of him. Elliot had forsaken a best man and decided instead to go with family. He had flown his mother in for the occasion. She sat in the first row, still sprightly at seventy-nine. Samantha had seen her and Meredith in the back corner of the church earlier, at first talking heatedly and then, like families nearly always do, finding that they loved as well as they hated. There was only so much shouting you could do before you broke down and held each other.

Whenever Samantha thought *This could have been my wedding,* she shook her head and stopped herself. As lovely as weddings were, they lasted only one day. It was the marriage that mattered, and a marriage with Michael would have been disastrous for her.

She did not allow herself to think of Dylan at all. Not when the minister talked about love, not when her parents exchanged rings for the second time, not when Elliot leaned forward and kissed Leah as passionately as a schoolboy trying to claim what was his.

After the ceremony, the guests came back to Elliot and Leah's house, where the caterers had set up. The band was out on the patio, braving the clear, but cold February day. The music was already blaring when Samantha walked in. It reverberated through the back door and into the house.

People ate and talked and lustily congratulated Elliot and Leah, as if falling in love with the same person twice was a rare and amazing accomplishment. And perhaps, Samantha thought as she watched her parents from the door to her old bedroom, it was. It was easy to fall in love with strangers, people to whom you attached glamorous and flawless traits they didn't merit. But how did you fall in love with someone you knew well, a man whose faults you could pick apart and categorize, a woman you'd seen in curlers and fuzzy slippers?

The band leader walked into the house and whispered something in Elliot's ear. Elliot nodded and, as soon as the band struck up the next song, he and Leah started dancing through the living room. Samantha and a few of the guests quickly pushed the sofas and tables to the walls, and Leah and Elliot waltzed through, oblivious to all of them.

Samantha watched them with moist eyes. Their love that had bloomed and withered and been reborn gave her hope even as it tore her heart. It was more profound than she'd ever imagined, and she realized that the love between her and Dylan, the love she had thought was so grand and intense, had not even come close to matching it.

The front door opened and another person walked in. At first, Samantha didn't notice who it was, but then, as if her body sensed it was someone familiar, she turned and looked.

Dylan stood in the entry, watching Elliot and Leah dance close together. He had tied his hair back neatly and was wearing his best shirt and jeans. He looked around the room, quickly passed by three beautiful women he would have smiled at before, and finally spotted her.

There was no smile, no amusement in his eyes, no flirtation. Leah and Elliot shielded him for a moment, and then danced away, giving her a full view of him.

Samantha gripped the door as he walked toward her. He didn't take his eyes from her face as he approached. When he reached her, he showed an uncharacteristic hesitation, then gestured toward the front door.

"Can we go outside for a moment?" he asked.

She nodded and followed him out of the house. They started down the street she'd walked so often as a child. Back then, she had jumped over every crack, run on springy legs to friends' houses, or hopped her bike off the curb. Now, she walked slowly, sedately, like the adult she had never really wanted to be, careful not to touch the man beside her.

"Your mother told me what happened," Dylan said. "Between you and Michael. I'm sorry."

Samantha nodded. The sun was low in the sky and remote, heating the other side of the world with summer. Here, the edges of the lawns were frosty, the remaining leaves on the trees brown and red. Samantha almost explained about Michael, about why it hadn't worked, but then she merely kept quiet. Michael was hers, a secret all to herself. She would never share him.

Dylan undid his ponytail and ran his fingers through his hair. They reached the end of the block and he gripped the lamppost and whirled to face her.

"I've been waiting to stop dreaming about you," he said.

He stared at her, waiting for her to help him, but she said nothing. She shivered against the cold.

"But now I dream even when I'm awake," he went on. "I don't know what to do."

Samantha stared at his face. For once, it didn't radiate bravado. There was only fear and uncertainty, the two emotions that had raged the strongest within her the whole time she had been with him.

"There's a couple in there," she said, gesturing back toward her parents' house, "who have a love so strong it hurts me to look at them. I thought you and I had something like that, but we didn't. We had passion, but not intimacy."

"Samantha—"

"What they have didn't come overnight," she said. "I think it has very little to do with sex and passion and even commitment. It has to do with time spent together. It has to do with faith, really. The unshakable belief that someone else is in this with you."

They stared at each other a long time. Then Dylan tilted his head.

"There's so much I want to tell you," he said. "About my parents, about the funeral and what happened after. I've got a dog now, Alan."

Though Samantha tried to stop herself from smiling, she couldn't.

"Alan," she said. "Your father's name."

"Ugliest thing you've ever seen, and the best dog I could have asked for."

They looked at each other again and then Samantha turned away. The wind flipped her hair over her eyes and she tucked it behind her ear.

"So much has happened," she said.

"Yes, and now we're back at the beginning, where your parents must have been when they started out. Everyone needs a starting point, Samantha. Maybe we forgot about that last time. We could start as friends and see what comes of it. I could introduce you to Alan."

He smiled a little bashfully, and Samantha didn't even try to fight his effect on her. It was a battle she couldn't win anyway. He held out his hand nervously, wonderfully, beautifully, and she grasped it. She remembered when her mother had told her about the day she met Elliot, how it had seemed as if her heart and body had soared up, up, up into the clouds the moment she realized he wanted her. It was true about the soaring. It was true that, with a little faith, anything could happen.

• • •

Elliot sat on a plane bound for England, staring at his sleeping wife. He had done the same thing thirty-eight years ago, on their honeymoon in Reno; he'd turned the bedside light on and watched his new bride sleep. He still felt like that boy, in awe of a woman, trembling as he lifted a finger to her cheek, marveling at the rise and fall of her chest, as if she performed a miracle every time she breathed.

But back then he'd been cocky. He'd felt no need to rush or worry; the rest of their lives had seemed like forever. Tonight, though, Elliot could feel every second passing, as if time were a rope being tugged out of his hands. Tonight, he knew what fear was, he knew what life was like without Leah. He had loved her at the beginning, but not like this, not with his soul and spirit so that, when he turned around quickly on a sunny day, he caught his shadow caressing her.

Every little bump in the plane made him think about it going down. The thought of letting Leah out of his sight for a second terrified him. All those years, he had hardly thought twice about her driving dangerous mountain roads, or going to the grocery store at night. He had hardly considered the possibility of losing her. Now, because he loved her so much, too much, it was hard to think of anything else.

When he turned back to Leah, her eyes were open. She smiled at him and reached over and took his hand.

"Are we there yet?" she asked.

And as she spoke his fears quieted. The touch of her hand gave him courage and hope. They would have as much time as they had, just like everybody else. But in that limited time, Elliot would pack their lives with as many trips to England, as many kisses, as much love-making as humanly possible.

"Go back to sleep, sweetheart," he said, leaning over to kiss her. "We've still got a ways to go."

About the Author

CHRISTY COHEN, the author of *Twice in a Lifetime* and *Private Scandals*, was born and raised in Southern California. She now lives in Boise, Idaho, with her husband, Robert, and best friend, Cleo the wonder dog.